Praise
Aldebaria

"Intense, addictive and brilliant... iewer

"The Lasaran has everything I lov :
snappy dialogue, action, humor, s ut now
I can add space travel. Booyah!" —I m a ... Reader

"Full of adventures, sizzling passion, romance and yes kick-ass fighting. This book is simply captivating." —Book Dragon

"Dianne Duvall has hit another one out of the park, or should I say, out of the atmosphere... All the humor, honor, love and exciting fight scenes have moved from Earth to space. Can't wait for the next one." —Mrs. Reads-A-Lot

"I can't express enough how gripping this story was. This could be a movie!" —Obsessive Reading Disorder

"An action-packed, hair-raising and heart-rending journey... One moment I'd be on the edge of my seat barely breathing, then swooning, then laughing." —Reading Between the Wines Book Club

Praise for Dianne's Immortal Guardians Books

"Crackles with energy, originality, and a memorable take-no-prisoners heroine." —Publishers Weekly

"Fans of terrific paranormal romance have hit the jackpot with Duvall and her electrifying series." —RT Book Reviews

"This series is earth-shattering awesome and Dianne has quickly become one of my favorite authors. Each of these stories... has been heart-stopping, intense, humorous and powerfully romantic." —Reading Between the Wines Book Club

"Full of fascinating characters, a unique and wonderfully imaginative premise, and scorching hot relationships." —The Romance Reviews

"Fans of paranormal romance who haven't discovered this series yet are really missing out on something extraordinary." —Long and Short Reviews

"This series boasts numerous characters, a deep back story, and extensive worldbuilding... [Ethan] boasts the glowing charms of Twilight's *Edward Cullen and the vicious durability of the* X-Men's *Wolverine."* —Kirkus Reviews

"Paranormal romance fans who enjoy series like J.R. Ward's Black Dagger Brotherhood *will definitely want to invest time in the Immortal Guardians series."* —All Things Urban Fantasy

"Ms. Duvall brings together a rich world and a wonderful group of characters… This is a great series." —Night Owl Reviews

"It was non-stop get-up-and-go from the very first page, and instantly you just adore these characters… This was paranormal at its finest."
—Book Reader Chronicles

"Dianne Duvall's Immortal Guardians is my favorite series hands down. Every character is beloved. Every story is intense, funny, romantic and exciting. If you haven't read the Immortal Guardians, you are truly missing out!"
—eBookObsessed

"Full of awesome characters, snappy dialogue, exciting action, steamy sex, sneaky shudder-worthy villains and delightful humor." —I'm a Voracious Reader

Praise for Dianne's The Gifted Ones Books

"The Gifted Ones series is nothing short of perfection itself. I can't wait to see where she takes us next!" —Scandalicious Book Reviews

"I enjoyed this world and can't wait to see more crossover as the series continues… You will smile, swoon and have a lot of fun with this." —Books and Things

"Full of danger, intrigue and passion. Dianne Duvall brought the characters to life and delivered an addicting and exciting new series. I'm hooked!"
—Reading in Pajamas

"The Gifted Ones by Dianne Duvall combine paranormal romance with historical medieval keeps, magic, and time travel. Addictive, funny and wrapped in swoons, you won't be able to set these audios down." —Caffeinated Book Reviewer

"Ms. Duvall excels in creating a community feel to her stories and this is no different… A Sorceress of His Own *has a wonderful dynamic, an amazing promise of future adventures and a well-told romance that is sure to please."*
—Long and Short Reviews

"I loved this book! It had pretty much all of my favorite things – medieval times, a kick-ass heroine, a protective hero, magic, and a dash of mayhem."
—The Romance Reviews

"Dianne Duvall has delivered a gripping storyline with characters that stuck with me throughout the day and continue to do so long after I turned that last page. A must read!" —Reading Between the Wines Book Club

"A great beginning to a new and different series." —eBookObsessed

Titles by Dianne Duvall

Aldebarian Alliance

THE LASARAN

THE SEGONIAN

The Gifted Ones

A SORCERESS OF HIS OWN

RENDEZVOUS WITH YESTERDAY

Immortal Guardians

DARKNESS DAWNS

NIGHT REIGNS

PHANTOM SHADOWS

IN STILL DARKNESS

DARKNESS RISES

NIGHT UNBOUND

PHANTOM EMBRACE

SHADOWS STRIKE

BLADE OF DARKNESS

AWAKEN THE DARKNESS

DEATH OF DARKNESS

BROKEN DAWN

ALDEBARIAN ALLIANCE

NEW YORK TIMES BESTSELLING AUTHOR

DIANNE DUVALL

THE SEGONIAN

Published by Dianne Duvall, 2021
www.DianneDuvall.com
Editor: Anne Victory

E-book ISBN: 978-1-7345556-4-6
Print ISBN: 978-1-7345556-5-3

For my family

ACKNOWLEDGEMENTS

As always, I want to thank Crystal. You're amazing. And I'm so glad I contacted you back when my first book was about to release because I don't know what I'd do without you. I also want to send love and hugs and a huge thank you to my fabulous Street Team. You all are awesome!! Your continued support means the world to me and I dearly appreciate it. Another big thank you goes to the members of my Dianne Duvall Books Group on Facebook. I have so much fun with you. You never fail to spark a smile or a laugh.

Thank you, Kirsten Potter, for giving my characters unique and entertaining voices that always delight listeners. More thanks go to Anne Victory, who is such a joy to work with, as well as the cover designer, proofreader, formatter, and other behind-the-scenes individuals who helped me bring you ***The Segonian***.

And, of course, I want to thank all of the wonderful readers who have picked up copies of my books. You've made living my dream possible. I wish you all the best.

PROLOGUE

ELIANA SMILED AS she strode down a long corridor on the *Kandovar*. She had been aboard Prince Taelon's spaceship for four months now and still found it hard to believe some days. Five months ago, she had been doing the same old same old back on Earth, spending her nights hunting and slaying psychotic vampires with no thoughts of aliens beyond the occasional sci-fi flick. Then Seth, the immensely powerful leader of the Immortal Guardians, called a meeting and put her in a room with four other female Immortal Guardians and ten female *gifted ones*. After his adopted daughter Ami joined the meeting, he proceeded to shock the hell out of them.

Eliana didn't know Ami well. She'd heard the rumors—that Seth and his second-in-command and closest friend, David, had rescued the shy, petite redhead from a secret, government-funded research installation in which Ami had been tortured three or four years ago. Those rumors had mushroomed when Seth made it clear he loved Ami like a daughter and would rain fire and brimstone on anyone who tried to harm her. Then Ami herself had become legendary when she began to serve as Marcus Grayden's Second, or guard, and helped him defeat thirty-four vampires in a battle those in the Immortal Guardians world still whispered about.

Two against *thirty-four?* No mortal had ever faced those numbers with the immortal he or she served.

Naturally, Eliana had been curious, so she'd had her

sometimes hunting partner Rafe teleport her to North Carolina to meet Ami. Yet not once in any of her interactions with the soft-spoken woman had Eliana guessed the truth of who and what Ami was.

Ami was from another planet. She was an honest-to-goodness extraterrestrial!

A Lasaran princess who also served as ambassador, Amiriska had come to Earth, seeking an alliance and to warn Earth's leaders that Gathendiens—the alien beings who had tried to exterminate her people—were on their way to Earth to exterminate theirs. Instead of doing what Eliana thought would be the logical response—saying *Hell yes, we'd love to form an alliance with Lasara and will gladly accept any aid you care to offer*—the idiots in charge had instead captured Ami, incarcerated her, and tortured her for six months until Seth and David found her.

"Dumbasses," she muttered.

Ganix, the male Lasaran striding along beside her, cast her a curious glance. "Who?"

"Earth's leaders."

"Ah. I concur."

She grinned. It had worked out well though. Not for Earth. The Gathendien threat still loomed, thanks to the dumbasses. But Ami had fallen in love with Marcus and married the eight-hundred-year-old Immortal Guardian. Her brother Taelon had come looking for her and—after a rough and harrowing introduction to Earthlings—had fallen in love with a *gifted one* named Lisa. Then, at Ami's urging, Seth had taken the first steps toward forming an alliance with the Lasaran people. An alliance that had landed Eliana, four of her immortal brethren, and ten *gifted ones* on the Lasaran battleship *Kandovar* four months ago.

Now they hurtled across the galaxy to find new homes on Ami's homeworld.

Life could surprise the hell out of you sometimes.

"Hey," Eliana said suddenly, "do you think one of the pilots on board would give me flying lessons?"

Ganix looked at her as if she'd lost her mind. "No."

"Why not? Women are as capable of piloting aircraft as men. And I want to learn how to fly one of those sleek black fighter craft." Back on Earth she'd learned how to fly both a helicopter and small airplanes just to stave off boredom. Doing the same damned thing every night for hundreds of years tended to get old.

He shook his head. "You aren't a member of the Lasaran military."

"Is there such a thing as an honorary member?"

"No."

"Do you think they'd make an exception?"

"No."

Lasarans were *very* big on rules. The foot of space Ganix kept between them at all times was proof of that. On Lasara, men and women of childbearing age were not allowed to touch unless they were married, or *bonded* as the Lasarans called it. Eliana had thought it more of a general guideline rather than a hard-and-fast rule until she'd boarded the ship.

She supposed it shouldn't bother her. She'd been raised in one of the earliest American colonies by a mother who had vehemently adhered to the stricter social canons of England. A mother who would've fit in quite well on Lasara, she thought with some amusement. But Eliana had grown accustomed to the lax rules of modern times. Before she'd left Earth, she had often hunted with fellow Immortal Guardian Nick Belanger. And since Nick had freely admitted that he only had eyes for his next-door neighbor, Eliana had felt free to hug him and express friendly affection without him misinterpreting it as a come-on.

She missed that.

Inwardly she shrugged. Oh well. She was moving to a planet where the people wouldn't hate her, fear her, or seek to harm her simply because she was different. She thought the sacrifice worth it.

When she and Ganix swung around a corner, Eliana smiled.

Lisa strode toward her, five-month-old little Abby dangling from her front in a sling.

If Eliana thought it weird to be on an alien ship, how bizarre must it feel to be married to an alien prince and the mother of a *gifted one/*alien hybrid?

"Hi, Lisa!" she called, tossing her friend a jaunty wave.

Lisa grinned and waved back.

As Eliana and Ganix drew near, Ganix stopped and bowed. "Your Highness."

Amusement trickled through Eliana, nearly sparking a laugh as she watched Lisa's expression flicker. Clearly, she still wasn't comfortable with either the title or the genuflection.

Lisa smiled. "Hi, Ganix. Eliana."

Abby kicked her feet.

Ganix's curious teal eyes fastened on her.

Thanks to a bioweapon the Gathendiens had unleashed on Lasara decades ago, the Lasaran birth rate had dropped so low that most of the men and women on board had never seen a baby in person. The awe and hope and curiosity the little one always sparked was truly heartbreaking to behold.

Ganix's gaze remained on the prince's heir.

Lisa stopped. "Would you like to say hi to Abby?"

He nodded. "Hello, Princess Abby." He even offered her a bow.

Abby chortled and kicked her legs harder, then flung a hand out toward him and gripped a fistful of his hair.

"Oops!" Lisa sent him an apologetic look and hastily disengaged her daughter's grip. "Sorry about that."

He straightened with a smile. "Prince Taelon is right. She is strong."

"Very much so," she agreed. "Would you like to hold her?"

Ganix kept his hands at his sides. "Touching an unbonded female is forbidden."

Eliana had heard the same thing every time she had inadvertently brushed against or bumped elbows with a male since boarding the ship.

Lisa sent him a gentle smile. "Surely that only applies to females who are of childbearing age. Not children."

He looked uncertain but steadfastly kept his distance.

Poor guy. The longing in his eyes was undeniable. Children were so rare on his world. She knew he'd never held a baby before and obviously wanted to but worried over propriety.

"Oh no," she exclaimed with false dismay, deciding to help him out. "The crazy Earth woman doesn't know the rules." Taking Ganix's hand, she moved it close to Abby.

Abby instantly wrapped a fist around his index finger.

Ganix's eyes widened.

Eliana released him. "Oh no," she said again. "Princess Abby has grabbed the innocent Ganix's finger and won't let go. Surely he dare not offend her and spark a royal tantrum by prying her little fingers loose."

Ganix's face flushed, but he didn't let go.

Lisa laughed and met her gaze. "You're so bad."

She grinned. "I know."

Ganix smoothed his thumb across Abby's little hand. "She's so soft!" he said reverently.

Abby tugged his finger hard.

He grinned. "She *is* strong."

Abby bounced and kicked and waved her fists, jerking his hand around.

He laughed, his joy unmistakable, then glanced beyond Lisa.

Eliana followed his gaze.

Taelon—one of four Lasaran princes, commander of the *Kandovar*, and Lisa's utterly devoted husband—strode toward them.

Dismay flickered across Ganix's features as he gently tried to extricate his finger.

Abby would have none of it and merely held on tighter.

Lisa glanced over her shoulder, then sent Ganix a reassuring smile. "It's okay. He won't be angry."

Eliana didn't think he would be either. Taelon's attention was firmly fixed on his wife's bottom. Desire flared to life in his emerald eyes. He probably hadn't even noticed what was transpiring in front of her.

Unable to free his finger, Ganix orchestrated an awkward bow as Taelon joined them. "Prince Taelon."

Taelon tore his gaze away from his wife and smiled. "Ganix. Eliana." His glance fell to his daughter. "I see she's gained another conquest."

As soon as she heard her daddy's voice, Abby squealed. Releasing Ganix's finger, she turned her head and held out her arms.

"There's my girl." Affection lit his handsome features and filled his voice as he addressed his daughter.

Too cute.

Taelon caught one of his daughter's flailing hands and brought it to his lips. "Are you tormenting Chief Engineer Ganix?" he asked sweetly. "Hmm? I saw you trying to tug his finger off."

She bounced in the sling and babbled baby talk.

Eliana bit back a laugh when color flooded Ganix's face once more.

Taelon smiled as he straightened. "At ease. She isn't of childbearing age. As long as you obtain permission first, you may play with her."

Ganix bowed. "Thank you, Prince Taelon."

Eliana nudged him with her shoulder. "I told you it would be fine. I saw Ari'k holding her earlier."

Ganix jumped at the brief contact and stepped away, glancing swiftly at Taelon to see if he would decry the casual touch.

Taelon ignored it.

Eliana laughed as she addressed the prince and Lisa. "That was freaking hilarious, by the way. Ari'k did *not* know what to do with a squirming baby."

There were two species of aliens aboard the *Kandovar*—Lasaran and Yona. Ari'k was the highest-ranking Yona soldier on the ship. Those tall, stoic warriors fascinated Eliana. Boasting big muscled bodies and tan skin with a distinct grayish hue, their sole purpose was to protect the royal prince and his ship. The Yona never expressed emotion. At all. And they had no idea what to do with a baby when handed one.

Taelon rested a hand on Lisa's back. When she looked up at him, he bent his head and stole a kiss. "Hello, *dashura,*" he murmured.

"Hi."

Damn, Eliana envied those two. They fairly radiated the love they shared.

The closest Eliana had come to experiencing that was an infatuation she'd felt for a handsome neighbor decades ago.

Clearly her neighbor hadn't felt the same, because he had married another woman.

Taelon offered her a smile. "Eliana, how are the other Earth women doing?"

"They're doing well. I would've thought they would be getting cabin fever by now, but there are so many fascinating things on this ship to distract them that they never grow bored."

Ganix cast them all a look of alarm. "Cabin fever? Should I alert the medics?"

Lisa shook her head. "It isn't an illness. It's just a saying we have to indicate someone is starting to go a little crazy from being cooped up in one place for too long."

"Ah." He nodded. "Quite a few of us Lasarans experienced that while awaiting word from Prince Taelon."

Evidently the crew of the *Kandovar* had been stuck up here for three years while they waited for either the return of their prince or confirmation of his death at the hands of Earthlings.

Abby waved a hand and made a little grunting sound. A call for attention, perhaps?

Eliana bent forward and made a series of funny faces at her. The beautiful five-month-old giggled and kicked her legs. "Prince Taelon," she asked as she straightened, "are there any rules that would prevent a Yona soldier from sparring with me?"

His eyebrows rose. "Technically speaking, you aren't Lasaran, so there are no rules governing interactions with you specifically. Has a Yona offended you in some way?"

"Only when he didn't laugh at my jokes," she quipped.

Lisa grinned. "They don't feel emotion."

Eliana sent her a wry smile. "I know. That's what everyone keeps telling me. But I could've sworn I saw a teeny-tiny spark of mirth in Ari'k's eyes the last time I tried to make him laugh. I was kinda hoping I could get him to spar with me so I can see if that evokes any emotion."

Taelon shrugged. "It won't. But you're welcome to engage him if he is willing."

Triumph filling her, she thrust a fist in the air. "Yes! *Woo-hoo!* That big-ass warrior is going down, baby! If I can't make him laugh, I can sure as hell piss him off."

Taelon and Lisa burst into laughter.

Eliana grinned, happy to have a new challenge. Since learning to pilot one of those sleek black fighter craft appeared to be off the table, she would have fun sparring with Ari'k instead and see if the Yona warrior was really as emotionless as everyone claimed.

Still smiling, she rounded on a wide-eyed Ganix. "And *you*, my friend, are going to talk him into sparring with me."

Ganix stared at her in stunned disbelief. "What?"

"I've spent enough time around you to know you can talk anyone into doing just about anything. Come on. Let's go find him." This was going to be so much fun! Taking Ganix's arm, she hurried back down the hallway. "See ya later!" she called over her shoulder.

"You aren't supposed to touch me," Ganix whispered.

Yep. She'd forgotten. *Again*. She was just so used to expressing affection through touch.

When no objections arose behind them, she opted not to release him. "Didn't you hear Prince Taelon? The rules don't apply to me. I can do whatever I want."

Her preternaturally enhanced senses allowed her to hear Taelon murmur, "That wasn't precisely what I meant."

Lisa chuckled. "I know. But she's been really great, watching over all the women, so I say we let her have some fun."

Grinning, Eliana guided Ganix around a corner.

"But the rules *do* apply to me," the Lasaran engineer reminded her, his brow furrowed.

She noticed though that his attempts to extricate his arm were half-hearted at best. Perhaps he was as curious about the casual touch of a female as he was about what it would feel like to hold an infant.

"The rule is that you aren't allowed to touch an unbonded female Lasaran, right?" she asked.

"Correct."

"Well, I'm not an unbonded Lasaran. I'm from Earth. So as Prince Taelon said, technically there are no rules governing interaction with me."

A look of surprise crossed his face. The corners of his lips tipped up in a slight smile as he relaxed in her grasp. "I suppose you're right."

Eliana smiled.

Alarms began to blare.

Both jerked to a halt.

"What's that?" she blurted.

"All crew members to battle stations," a male voice called over the ship-wide speakers. "Repeat—all crew members to battle stations. We are under attack."

Her eyes widened as she looked at Ganix.

The ship rocked beneath their feet as a muffled explosion carried to their ears.

Both stumbled and threw their arms out for balance.

Ganix took off running.

Eliana quickly caught up. "What's happening? Who's attacking us?"

He shook his head. "I don't know." Another explosion rocked the ship, then another and another. "You should get your people to the escape pods."

Alarm shot through her. "Really? Is it that bad?" This ship was freaking huge! What could possibly defeat it?

"We're still in the *qhov'rum*." He dodged to the side as several soldiers raced past.

Eliana still wasn't sure exactly what a *qhov'rum* was, but like a wormhole, it allowed them to cover vast distances of space in a relatively short amount of time. "Is that a bad thing?"

"Yes!" he shouted over the boom of more explosions. "It leaves us less room to maneuver. We're well-armed, but..." The ship shook with more booms. "Get your people into the pods just in case!"

The pause after that *but* was long enough to send a trickle of fear through her. "Where are *you* going?"

"Engine Room 1!"

"Stay safe!" she called after him as she turned down a different hallway. If Ganix thought she should get her people into pods, she would damn well get them into pods.

More soldiers raced past, going the opposite direction. Crew members did, too, both male and female. Putting on a burst of preternatural speed, she raced to the quarters that had been allotted to the Earth women. All the *gifted ones* stood in the open doorways of their quarters, fear painting their faces as alarms continued to blare and the ship rocked with more explosions.

"What's happening?" Ava asked.

Eliana shook her head. "Grab your go bags. Quickly."

Panic flared in every face as the women ducked into their quarters and returned with backpacks.

"The ship is under attack. I'm going to get you all to the escape pods as a precaution." Without further warning, Eliana bent, tossed Ava and Natalie over her shoulders, and raced with preternatural speed to the closest escape pods.

"Get inside," she ordered as soon as she set them on their feet.

The two shared terrified looks.

Eliana returned to the Earth women's quarters, settled Mia and Michelle over her shoulders without a word, and headed back.

A blur swept past as she set the women on their feet, then zipped back toward her.

Fellow immortal Simone appeared beside them. She took in the four mortal Earth women. "Where are the rest of the *gifted ones*?" she asked with a French accent.

"Their quarters," Eliana said. "I'll go get them. Help these get settled in the pods." Eliana raced away, retrieved Sam and Emily, and brought them to the pods.

On her way back for two more *gifted ones*, she swept past Ari'k and three other hulking Yona warriors running in the same direction. As soon as it registered that Prince Taelon, Lisa, and little Abby were in their midst, Eliana backtracked and skidded to a halt in front of them.

"Are you okay?" she called over the noise, turning to jog alongside them as they hurried down the corridor.

"Yes," Lisa called back, her face pale.

Eliana looked at Taelon, who cradled the wailing baby Abby in his arms. "Are you going to one of the escape pods? I can get you there faster."

He shook his head. "Royal transport. The Yona will get us there safely. See to the other Earth women."

She nodded. "I've already gotten six of them into pods. I'll go get the others, then help your people. Yell if you need me." She zipped away in another blur of motion.

Dani and Rachel, two of her fellow immortals, arrived at the Earth women's quarters at the same time Eliana did.

All staggered as another barrage of explosions rocked the ship.

"Ava, Natalie, Mia, Michelle, Sam, and Emily are at the pods," Eliana called over the noise. "Simone is helping them."

Dani nodded. "I'll take Allison and Charlie."

Rachel motioned to the last two *gifted ones*. "I'll take Liz and Madeline."

"Shield integrity compromised," the ship's computer announced in a pleasant female voice. "Shields at seventy-nine percent."

Booms rocked the ship.

The scent of smoke reached Eliana. She exchanged a wide-eyed look with Rachel and Dani. "Go. I'll help the Lasarans get to the pods."

Dani and Rachel took off, racing down the corridors so quickly the men and women they passed would just feel a breeze and barely notice a blur of motion.

The last Immortal Guardian, Michaela, abruptly slid to a stop beside Eliana. "I saw the others at the pods and helped Simone get them settled inside. Is that everyone?"

Eliana nodded. "All accounted for. I'm going to evacuate the Lasarans." She also wanted to check on Ganix. From the sounds of things, the battle wasn't going well.

Michaela nodded. "I will, too."

They sped away in opposite directions.

More booms thundered through the ship.

Eliana jerked to a halt before two Lasarans—a man and a woman—who wore maintenance uniforms. "Are you headed for the escape pods?"

Both nodded, eyes wide.

Eliana threw them over her shoulders and got them to the pods within seconds.

"Thank you!" they called after her in shaky voices as she sped away to help the next Lasaran.

"Shields at fifty-four percent," the computer announced in the same pleasant female voice.

Eliana dashed through the corridors, helping every man and woman she came across get to a pod. As she did, she noted crew members hustling to put out a fire.

This can't be happening.

She passed some of her fellow immortals as they, too, worked their asses off to get as many people as they could into pods. As the number of Lasarans she came across began to dwindle, Eliana detoured toward Engine Room 1.

Everyone she encountered, she helped reach a pod. She tried to help the Yona, but they refused, intent on defending the ship.

"What the *drek* are you doing?" someone shouted behind her.

"Shields at thirty-two percent," the calm computer voice announced.

Eliana turned to find Ganix running toward her. "All my people are in the pods!" she yelled over the noise.

Boom. Boom. Boom.

"Why aren't you with them?" he shouted.

"They're safe! I want to help! What can I do?"

"Shields at twenty percent," the calm female voice announced.

"Nothing!" Ganix shouted. "Get to a pod!"

"I can help!" she insisted. "Just tell me what to do!" Whatever they needed, she could do it a hell of a lot faster than they could.

Boom. Boom. Boom. Boom.

"Shields at thirteen percent."

Ganix grabbed her arm, apparently saying to hell with the rules, and urged her back the way she had come. "You have to go! *Now!*"

"At least let me get more people into pods!"

"There's no time!"

They were almost to another line of escape pods when the wall beside them exploded. The percussive blast lifted Eliana off her feet and hurled her backward as flames seared her. Her head and body slammed into something hard. Bones broke. Pain engulfed her.

She slumped to the floor.

Darkness.

CHAPTER 1

SOMEWHERE IN THE distance a voice spoke, dragging Eliana toward consciousness. She moaned as pain inundated her. The left side of her face and body burned as though flames seared it. Every time she drew in a breath, sharp spikes seemed to drive themselves into her rib cage.

Clenching her teeth, she kept her eyelids squeezed shut and hoped the agony would pass.

The voice spoke again. Male. His words incomprehensible.

"What?" she whispered, trying to make sense of his speech.

He addressed her once more, but she had no more luck deciphering his words.

"What?" she muttered again. "I don't..." Her thoughts remained muddled. "I don't understand. Do you speak English? I can't understand you."

Silence.

Then another male spoke, his voice deep and resonant. "This is Commander Dagon of the *Ranasura*. Our allies the Lasarans lost contact with the *Kandovar* and have enlisted our aid in searching for it. Are you from Earth?"

"From Earth?" she repeated. "Earth as opposed to where?" Her mind and body finally adjusted to the pain enough for her to open her eyes. When she did, her heart slammed against her broken ribs and sheer terror swept through her. "Oh shit."

Endless dark space stretched before her, stars twinkling in the distance. She glanced down.

"Oh shit!" And she was free-floating through it in nothing but a baggy spacesuit and helmet. No ship. No escape pod. Just a freaking suit!

Her breath quickened.

"Where…?" She frantically looked around as much as she could and saw only a few jagged pieces of metal. "What the hell? What happened?"

"You are one of the Earthlings who was on board the *Kandovar*? You are from Earth?"

"Yes. I'm from Earth. What happened? Where the hell is the ship?"

Memory slowly returned. She remembered being on the Lasaran ship. She had been serving as one of the guards for the *gifted ones* who were traveling to Lasara. The journey was supposed to take thirteen months or thereabouts. She'd spent the first four immersing herself in Lasaran culture. It had been amazing. Then alarms had suddenly blared and the ship had begun to shake.

"Can you tell me where you are?" the man asked.

"No. Where's the ship? What happened? Are you Lasaran or Yona?"

"I am Segonian. We are allies of the Lasarans and received a distress call indicating one of their ships had been attacked while passing through a *qhov'rum*."

A *qhov'rum*. Right. That was the wormhole-like tunnel that had been propelling them toward Lasara.

"Where are they? Are they okay?" And how the hell had she gotten separated from everyone else?

"The Lasaran sovereign fears the ship was destroyed. The last data it transmitted indicated that escape pods were being deployed. But none have yet been recovered because they were flung out of the *qhov'rum* at different intervals, scattering them across vast sectors of space. All allies of the Lasarans are currently searching for survivors."

Eliana stared through her clear visor. No escape pods surrounded her. "I don't see anything."

"We can lock onto your location if you activate the beacon in your escape pod."

"*What* escape pod?" she cried. "There *is* no escape pod. It's just me, floating here in a suit!" She didn't care for the strident note that entered her voice but couldn't help it. Panic was riding her hard.

A heavy pause ensued.

"You aren't in an escape pod?" he asked, his voice grim.

"No."

Rapid speech erupted, multiple males, conversing in another language.

The Lasarans had given each of the *gifted ones* and Immortal Guardians from Earth a universal translator implant that would enable them to decipher most alien languages. But Eliana's body had rejected it, so she'd had to wear one in her ear like an earbud. She must have lost it in the chaos of the attack, because she couldn't understand a word these men were saying.

"Hello?" she called, interrupting them.

The commander cleared his throat. "I wished to check the accuracy of my language translator. You are not in a pod? You are only protected by a suit?"

"Yes."

"And neither the ship nor any pods are within your view?"

"Right. There's nothing." Although her helmet did limit her view. "Hold on. Let me see if I can twist around and get a better—" As soon as she swiveled her hips in an attempt to turn around, agony shot through her right side, all the way up into her chest. "Ah! Shit!"

Resting a hand on her side, she held her breath and clenched her teeth.

"Earthling?" he said sharply. "Are you all right?"

"Yes." Maybe the pain would ease if she remained still.

"You are injured?"

"I'm fine," she gritted. But she could feel warm moisture creeping down her right arm, down her side, down her hip, and recognized the signs of bleeding.

"Earthling—"

"Eliana," she corrected. "My name is Eliana." Even in her current, terrifying circumstances, being called *Earthling* was just too weird.

"Are you injured, Eliana?"

"Yes."

"How badly?"

She glanced down. "I don't know. I can't exactly open my suit and take a look, but—judging by the feel of it—I've had worse." Hunting and slaying psychotic vampires on a nightly basis sometimes resulted in injuries that would prove fatal to ordinary humans. As an Immortal Guardian, however, she usually recovered in anywhere from minutes to a few hours... *if* she had a goodly supply of blood on hand.

He spoke softly to someone in that foreign language.

"What's happening? I can't understand you," she said.

"Because you have no beacon, we will have to determine your location by tracing your comm signal. Once we do that, we can come to you, but it will take time."

"Okay."

"How much oxygen do you have left?"

"I don't know. How do I find out?"

"On the left forearm of your suit, there is a flap you can pull back. Can you open it?"

Though the rest of the suit was baggy, the gloves that covered her hands were made of a stretchy material that reminded her of spandex and weren't too huge on her. She found a little tab on her left sleeve and pulled. It drew back as though stuck with Velcro, revealing an electronic screen about the size of a cell phone, bracketed by multicolored buttons. "Okay. Now what?"

"Press the blue button."

As soon as she did, a female voice spoke in Lasaran.

More muted conversation erupted.

"What did she say?" Eliana asked.

Conversation ceased.

"Hello?"

"You have the equivalent of twenty-six Earth hours of oxygen left."

That didn't sound so bad. She had worried she only had minutes left. "How far away are you?"

"We have not yet determined that," he said. "We are still tracing the signal."

"Oh. Okay." She had a sinking feeling that it wouldn't take this long for them to trace the signal if she were only a day away from them.

Crap.

The men returned to their soft conversation. She was glad the commander left the line of communication open. She was trying very hard not to freak out, and hearing their calm voices helped.

She tried once more to remember the events that had landed her out here in the middle of nowhere. "We were attacked," she murmured.

"What?" the commander asked.

"We were attacked, like you said. I was with Ganix. I was trying to get him to help me talk one of the Yona soldiers into sparring with me."

"Sparring with you?" he asked, his voice hesitant, as though he wasn't sure he understood the word.

"Yes. Sparring means… fighting or engaging in battle."

"This Yona offended you?"

She laughed, then grunted when pain shot through her chest. "No. I meant fight with me as if we were training, not as if we were enemies. I had never met a Yona soldier until I boarded the *Kandovar*, and they really intrigue me. They're always so stoic, you know? I mean, they never exhibit *any* emotion. I'd never met anyone like that before and was curious to see if that changed when they fought. Do they get angry? Do they get frustrated? Do they get excited, thrilled by the rush of battle? I was trying to get Ganix to help me talk one into sparring with me so I could find out when alarms started blaring. A voice came over the speaker, saying we were under attack. The ship began to take fire, and the situation degenerated quickly. Ganix told me I should get my people into escape pods in case the worst should happen. Apparently fighting while racing through a *qhov'rum* isn't easy. So I hauled ass to get my charges into escape pods—"

"Hauled ass?"

"Moved quickly."

"What are charges?"

"There were other women from Earth on the ship. I was one of their guards, tasked with keeping them safe. So once Ganix told me to get them to the escape pods, I hauled ass to get all my charges into the pods."

"Were you able to do so?"

"Yes. Then I helped the Lasarans."

"You did not enter a pod with your friends?"

"No. I guess I should have. They were my top priority. But the ship's shields began to fail, and Lasarans were being injured. So I helped as many as I could reach the pods—"

"Even though the Lasarans were not your people?"

She blinked. "Of course. It doesn't matter that they weren't my people. They were kind to me. *And* my friends. So I helped as many as I could." She frowned at the memory. "I would've helped more, but Ganix caught up with me and kept ordering me to get to a pod myself. Then there was an explosion, and... some guy talking gibberish in my ear woke me up." She glanced down. "I wasn't wearing this suit when the attack happened. Ganix must have stuffed me into it while I was unconscious." He had probably tried like hell to get her to an escape pod too. "I hope he's all right."

A moment of silence followed.

"I hope they all are, Eliana."

She liked the way he said her name.

"You're very brave."

A wry smile twisted her lips as she stared through the helmet's visor. "I don't *feel* very brave at the moment." She was actually scared shitless.

One of the other men spoke softly.

Though she couldn't understand what Dagon bit out next, the way he delivered it sounded suspiciously like a curse word.

"What's wrong?" she asked.

He cleared his throat. "We are having difficulty calculating how far away you are."

He sounded grim as hell. And she was going to go out on a limb and guess he didn't lie very often, because she had no difficulty determining he was doing so now.

"Bullshit. You've already calculated it. I can hear it in your voice. How long will it take you to reach me?"

"We will reach you as quickly as we can."

"What's your name again?" she asked.

"Commander Dagon."

"How long will it take you to reach me, Dagon?" Her heart pounded with dread as she awaited his response.

"You are farther away than we anticipated."

Don't panic, damn it. "How much farther? I can stretch the oxygen and make it last."

"No, you can't," he replied, his voice soft with sorrow.

"I can," she insisted. "I can slow my heart rate, slow my metabolism, and slow my breathing so I consume less oxygen. I can do it." Ordinary humans could not. But Immortal Guardians could, thanks to the symbiotic virus that infected them. She could actually slow her breathing and heart rate to such an extent that doctors would declare her dead.

"Lasarans sent us detailed information on Earthling anatomy so we would be able to render medical aid to any we found," he countered. "That information did not indicate that Earthlings are capable of such."

She swore silently. "I know. But not all Earthlings are alike. I'm different. I'm stronger. And I need you to trust me on this, okay? How long does the oxygen have to last for you to make it here?" She could do this. She *would* do this.

A sigh carried across the line. "It will take us one of your Earth months to reach you."

All breath left her lungs.

"A month?" she repeated, head spinning with sudden dizziness.

His voice was full of regret when he answered. "Yes."

Tears burned the backs of her eyes, but she stubbornly blinked them back. "Well… damn. That's a long time." *Too* long. Even *she* couldn't make twenty-six hours of oxygen last thirty days.

Could she?

"We are contacting other members of the Alliance to see if any of their ships are closer to you."

She swallowed past the lump in her throat. "Thank you. I appreciate that." Her mind worked furiously. "In the meantime, would you maybe head my way and see if any of my friends or the Lasarans are somewhere between us? If I survived the attack in a suit, then some of those escape pods had to have made it, too, and they might be closer to you."

"We are already on our way to you and are traveling at top speed."

"Thank you." Even at top speed, they were still a month away. "How long can they survive in one of those pods?"

"The pods have enough oxygen and rations to sustain life for…" He muttered something in his language. "For two of your Earth months."

Relief rushed through her. "Good."

"They were designed in such a way to provide those inside with adequate time to either reach their chosen destination or locate a habitable planet on which they can seek shelter."

"My friends can't do that. They don't know how to pilot those things." The Lasarans had only schooled them on how to activate the distress call beacon, how to calculate the rations they should consume each day, and how to use the weird space toilet inside it.

"As soon as we lock onto their beacon, one of my men can remote pilot the pods for them. The Lasarans have given us the override codes."

"Good." At least they would have a fighting chance.

Dagon fell silent once more. Every once in a while, she could hear him speaking softly to the men on what she assumed was the bridge of his ship.

Fear kept trying to creep in and choke her. Eliana steadfastly pushed it back and turned her mind toward finding her friends.

A thought occurred to her. "Will talking to me keep you from receiving incoming communications from someone else or detecting distress beacons?" Though she had spent four months aboard the Lasaran ship, she still knew little about how one operated.

"No. My communications officer can continue to search for the others while we speak."

"Who is your comms officer?" she asked curiously.

"Janek."

"Can the other people on your bridge hear us talking?"

"Yes."

"Hey, Janek?" she called.

All background conversation ceased.

"Yes, Earthling?"

Despite the gravity of her situation, she laughed… then wished she hadn't when the pain in her side multiplied. "Being called Earthling is just too weird. Call me Eliana."

A pause ensued. "Yes, Eliana?"

"Were you the one who spoke to me before Dagon did?"

"Yes."

"Thank you for waking me."

Another pause. "You are welcome, Eliana."

"No matter what happens to me, please keep searching for my friends, okay? You all seem like good guys. So if I can't save them, I want you to."

"I am searching for them now," he assured her.

"Thank you."

Eliana stared at the stars. She had twenty-six hours of oxygen, and Dagon's ship was a month away.

Correction. She had a little less than twenty-six hours of oxygen since she had been speaking to them for several minutes. "Dagon?"

"Yes?" he responded instantly.

"I'm going to try to slow my heart rate and sleep for a bit. Would you please keep the comm link open so I can hear you?" She was more afraid than she was letting on and didn't want to lose the connection to them even for a second, terrified she might not get it back. "You don't have to speak English or anything. I just…" Tears threatened once more, but she kept them from altering her voice. "It's never quiet where I'm from." Especially since she had preternaturally sharp hearing. "And I'm guessing deep space is completely silent." The last thing she needed was for that silence to close in and make her feel more alone.

"We will keep communications open."

He had a nice voice. A very *telling* voice. She didn't have to see him to know that his inability to save her upset him.

"Thank you."

Closing her eyes, she tried to clear her mind and block out the pain. The latter was pretty damn difficult. The peculiar symbiotic virus that infected her was healing what damage it could. The bleeding lessened. One broken rib slowly shifted back into position in torturously small increments.

Eliana listened to the activity on Dagon's ship.

Her breathing slowed.

Her heart rate decreased.

And consciousness gradually slipped away.

Dagon stood in the center of a circular room. The only furniture in it was a padded bench that hugged the wall all the way around. Breath slow, he waited… and tried once more to turn his mind away from the Earth woman he had failed to save.

A flicker of movement drew his eyes to one side. The wall to his right seemed to shimmer faintly. Spinning, Dagon struck out with his sword and hit metal where there appeared to be none.

A curse filled the air, not his own.

He swung his weapon again and again, each time striking his invisible target. He straightened his free arm. The armor protecting it elongated into a chain that slipped down through his fingers and formed a heavy metal ball on the end. In battle, the ball would be covered in spikes. But now it was smooth.

He swung his sword, then spun and let the ball fly in an arc.

His target grunted when the ball hit.

Barus flickered into view as his camouflage failed. Bending forward, he breathed heavily through his mouth. "I'm glad you didn't hit me any lower with that."

Dagon tried but could find no smile. The ball and chain retracted, merging back into the armor on his forearm. Crossing to the low bench that circled the room, he picked up the scabbard and slid his sword home.

"It wasn't your fault," Barus said behind him.

His words did little to ease Dagon's troubled spirit. "I am aware."

"The Earth woman was too far away."

And she had died alone.

Three days had passed since he had spoken to her. Her oxygen supply had long since run out. But she had not made a single sound. She had wept no tears. She had not begged them to come faster. She had not gasped or struggled to find her last breath. She had simply… slipped away.

Every man on the bridge had grown tenser as that twenty-sixth hour had approached. Though the comms that linked them remained open, they had heard nothing from her since she had told him she was going to sleep for a bit.

No other ships had been closer.

None could have saved her.

"Take comfort," his friend and second-in-command said gently, "in knowing she must have died of her wounds in her sleep. It was the most merciful death she could have found in her situation."

Dagon nodded, knowing it was true. He also took comfort in knowing that if she had died in her sleep, she had died unafraid. "She was not what I expected of an Earthling."

Barus nodded. "The Sectas described them as a primitive, warring society full of people quick to hate anyone who was different. The fact that they captured and tortured the Lasaran princess confirmed that."

"And yet Eliana risked her life to save countless Lasaran men and women." Dagon had spoken with Tiran, commander of the Lasaran ship *Tarakona*. The two of them had become friends after being brought together in the biannual war games conducted to train Lasarans, Yona, Segonians, and additional Alliance forces to fight together in battle against the Gathendiens and other enemies. According to Tiran, some Lasaran escape pods had been recovered. And many of the Lasarans inside them had credited Eliana with getting them there swiftly and saving their lives. "She was very brave."

"And did not deserve the fate dealt her."

Barus had not been present on the bridge when they made contact with Eliana, so Dagon had replayed their conversation for him.

A click sounded in Dagon's earpiece.

"Commander Dagon," Janek said, voice tense, "your presence is requested on the bridge."

Dagon tapped the earpiece. "What is it?"

"I believe I've picked up something on comms."

He glanced at Barus. "You've located one of the pods?"

"No, sir. I think..."

Dagon waited. Janek was not usually one to mince words. "Janek?"

"I think it's the Earth woman. I think Eliana may still be alive."

His heart jumping in his chest, Dagon swiftly turned and strode out of the training room.

Eliana? Still alive? Impossible.

And yet his pace steadily increased until he was jogging toward the lift, Barus right on his heels.

Moments later, he strode onto the bridge and speared Janek with a look. "Explain."

Janek glanced up from his station. He cast the other crewmen on the bridge a quick look.

All were silent, their faces solemn.

Janek's lips tightened. "I wanted to believe her," he admitted. "When she said she could slow her heart rate and make the oxygen last longer, I wanted to believe her. So I left the comm line with her open and…"

"And what?" Dagon prodded impatiently.

Janek hesitated, as though fearing all would doubt him. "I think I heard a moan."

Barus shook his head. "That's not possible."

Janek ignored him and shot Dagon a look. "I know I heard something."

Dagon strode toward his seat. "Let me hear it."

Everyone remained silent as they all listened carefully.

Dagon strained to detect even the slightest rustle of her suit, the sound of a soft breath, *anything*… but heard nothing. "Eliana," he called.

No response came.

Janek shook his head. "I know I heard something."

Dagon trusted him. "Eliana," he said louder.

A sigh carried across the line.

"Max?" Eliana mumbled.

His breath caught.

"I was having the worst dream," she complained groggily.

Murmurings erupted among his crew.

Dagon's heart began to slam against his ribs. How was this possible? "Eliana?"

She emitted a sharp grunt of pain, then—sounding much more alert—said, "Ah hell, it wasn't a dream. That sucks!"

He shared an astonished look with Barus.

"Dagon?" she said. "Are you there?"

"Yes."

"Thank you for leaving the line open. How long was I out?"

"Three days."

"Damn. I had hoped I'd sleep longer than that."

"My apologies. I woke you. We hadn't heard from you in a long time."

"And you thought I was dead?"

"Yes," he admitted.

When next she spoke, her tone conveyed a smile. "I told you I could make the oxygen last longer. How much do I have left?"

"Press the blue button on your sleeve again."

A female voice speaking Lasaran announced, "Fifteen hours and forty-two minutes of oxygen remaining."

Barus shook his head. "How did she make ten hours of oxygen last three days?" he asked in Segonian.

Dagon shook his head.

"What did she say?" Eliana asked.

"You have fifteen hours and forty-two minutes of oxygen left."

"Damn. So I've already used up almost half of what I had?"

"Yes."

"I don't suppose you found any allies who were close enough to swing by and pick me up, did you?"

"No. All were farther away than we are."

"Are you still headed my way?"

"Yes."

"Have you found any other survivors?"

"No. But the Lasarans have recovered several escape pods."

"Were any of my people rescued?" she asked, hope brightening her voice.

"Not yet."

"Oh."

"But we are all still searching."

"Thank you." She had a nice voice, deep for a woman and a little husky from sleep. He didn't like hearing the disappointment that darkened it now. "What about the Yona? Has anyone found any of them yet? I know those guys look and act as though nothing ruffles their feathers, but I'm sure they don't want to die out here either."

"No Yona soldiers have been rescued yet." He opted not to tell her that the bodies of several had been drifting in space near some wreckage found by his fellow Segonians. The soldiers had done what they were trained to do—they had remained on the ship, fighting until the last minute, and died when the ship was blasted apart.

"That sucks."

He frowned. "I don't think my translator is accurately defining the word *suck*."

She laughed, a happy sound that made his lips twitch until she grunted in pain again. "I was wondering how you were speaking English to me. You have a translator?"

"A translator chip," he elaborated. "All starship commanders and crew members have one. The Lasarans sent us an upgrade that included ten Earth languages so we would be able to communicate with you when we found you."

"Cool. I'm guessing your chip is telling you that *suck* means to close your lips around something and create a vacuum?"

"Yes."

"That's actually correct. But the phrase *that sucks* is slang used to express... well, either annoyance or sympathy, depending on how it's used. Like if someone said, *My boss just fired me*, you might respond with *Wow, that sucks*."

He nodded. "I shall commit that to memory."

"So you've spoken with the Lasarans?"

"Yes."

"Do they know who attacked the ship?"

"Gathendiens are responsible."

"Are you fucking kidding me?" she practically shouted, fury entering her voice. "The Gathendiens did this?"

Eyebrows flew up all around the bridge as crew members exchanged looks of surprise.

"Yes."

"The same Gathendiens who used a bioengineered virus to try to exterminate the Lasarans?"

"Yes."

"Okay, seriously, Dagon, you have *got* to find a way to reach me before I die so I can hunt those bastards down and kick their collective asses."

Barus grinned. "I like this woman."

"Who was that?" she immediately asked. "I don't recognize his voice."

"He's my second-in-command, Barus."

"Nice to meet you, Barus," she said, her voice still full of pique. "I take it you don't like the Gathendiens either?"

"I loathe the Gathendiens," Barus replied.

"Good. Then do me a favor and help Dagon find a way to reach me faster so I can help you kick those fuckers' asses."

Grins broke out among the crew.

She didn't ask them to find her so she would live. She asked them to find her so she could exact vengeance. Every man here understood that.

She cleared her throat. "Sorry about that," she said, the words more calm and carrying a little chagrin. "I hope I didn't offend you. I tend to have a foul mouth when I'm upset, and I know nothing about your culture. Do you guys, by any chance, curse or use foul language when you're angry?"

Dagon grinned. "Yes, we do."

The hesitance left her voice, replaced by a smile. "Good. Now if you *really* want to put my mind at ease, you'll all answer *Hell yes, we do* the next time I ask you that." She cleared her throat. "Okay. Here we go. Do you guys, by any chance, curse or use foul language when you're upset?"

"Hell yes, we do," every male on the bridge chorused.

She laughed in delight, then grunted in pain once more. "Thanks, guys. I needed that, even though it hurt."

Dagon frowned. "How are you? How are your injuries?"

"Still there, still annoying, but I've had worse," she said, a shrug in her voice. "Do the Lasarans know I'm out here?"

"Yes."

Heavy silence ensued.

He frowned. "Did you not want me to tell them?"

"No. It isn't that. It's…" She sighed. And for the first time since waking, she sounded hesitant and unsure. "Did they by any chance mention Seth? Does he know I'm out here?"

"They did not mention anyone by that name. Was he on the ship with you?"

"No. He's back on Earth."

"Is he your male?" For some reason, the notion unsettled him.

"My male?"

"Are you bound to him?" He sought the correct English word. "Are you married?"

"To Seth?" Amusement entered her voice. "No. I'm not married. Seth is… my commanding officer, I guess you'd say. But he's also a father figure to me."

"Ah."

"I lost my own father a long time ago. When Seth found me, I was in a really bad place. And he… saved me. I owe him everything. He took me in, gave me a family, gave me a purpose." Her voice thickened. "I can't believe I've failed him like this."

She had behaved with bravery and honor. "You haven't failed him."

"Yes, I have. He trusted me to keep my people safe. He trusted me to protect them. And I failed to do that."

"You got them to the escape pods. That's all you could've done."

"What's worse is I'm probably going to die before you reach me, so I'm even going to fail to bring the assholes who did this to justice."

Dagon took his seat. He didn't want to lie to her. Even with her astonishing ability to conserve oxygen, she would still likely be dead within a few days. "Should that happen, I will seek vengeance for you."

"Thank you."

Quiet fell.

"The next time you talk with the Lasarans, would you please ask them not to say anything to Seth about me?"

"You do not wish him to know you survived?" He and Barus shared a frown. "Surely he will not blame you if you are the only survivor from Earth. You did everything you could to save your friends."

"That's the thing," she said, voice solemn. "He *won't* blame me. He'll blame himself. That's just how he is. He's going to blame himself for putting us at risk, for putting us in this position, for agreeing to let us leave Earth. And if he thinks I died out here alone, in pain, while floating in space for days or weeks, waiting to be rescued… it will tear him up inside. He'll never forgive himself. And I don't want that. So I'd rather the Lasarans just tell him you're all still searching for survivors. That way if I don't make it until you reach me, you can just say I died in the initial attack. A quick death. No suffering."

Dagon could find no response.

"You still there?" she asked.

"Yes."

"You seem like a real stand-up guy."

"I don't know what that means."

"Honorable. You seem like an honorable man. I mean, you wouldn't still be heading my way otherwise. And I doubt lying comes easily to you. I'm sorry if this is a lot to ask, but please think about it, okay? If I die, I die. Seth doesn't need to torture himself imagining a long, drawn-out death. So please ask the Lasarans not to mention me beyond saying you're still searching for me. He doesn't need to know the rest."

Her words made Dagon's chest ache. "I will do as you ask."

"Thank you." Her words soughed out like a sigh of relief. "If I ever get to meet you in person, I'm going to give you a big hug."

He smiled. "I'll look forward to that."

She chuckled again, the sound ending abruptly in a grunt of pain.

Barus's frown deepened. "How bad are her injuries?" he asked softly in Segonian.

Dagon shook his head. "I don't know. She won't tell me."

"What's wrong?" Eliana asked. "Are hugs and public displays of affection forbidden in your culture? I know the Lasarans are pretty strict about that sort of thing."

"No," Dagon assured her. "Even if they were, I would still look forward to receiving yours."

"Good. One hug, coming right up."

CHAPTER 2

ELIANA SMILED AND tried to ignore the throbbing in her side. Her wounds were not healing the way they would if she had a nice infusion of blood. The bleeding had stopped, but pain was a constant companion.

She swallowed. Her mouth was dry, her temperature running hot. She didn't know if that resulted from fever or dehydration.

She glanced around. At least she hadn't peed her pants. Or worse. The virus had done that much for her, shutting down every system it could to prolong her life... which she supposed would actually have the opposite effect on a human.

Lucky me.

Oh well.

"Hey, would it be rude to ask what you guys look like? Because I haven't met that many aliens." She loved Dagon's voice, so deep she could practically feel it rumbling through her damaged chest.

"It would not be rude," he replied. "We are similar in appearance to Lasarans."

"Elaborate, please."

"We are bipedal."

Two legs. That was good. Were his muscular? Because he sounded hot.

"How many arms?" She couldn't resist asking. Sci-fi movies had presented viewers with some freaky variations on the humanoid form.

"Two." Amusement laced his voice this time, as though he fought the impulse to laugh.

"And one head?"

He chuckled, losing the battle. "Yes."

"So you look like humans on Earth."

"In many ways, yes. I believe we may be taller than most Earthlings though."

"I'm okay with that. Most of my brethren are tall." The males were anyway. She didn't think she had ever met an Immortal Guardian male who stood less than six feet. Seth was six foot eight. Eliana barely came up to his armpit.

"We differ in other ways though, like the Lasarans," he admitted.

In her crash course on Ami's people, Eliana had learned that they were very long-lived and had special abilities not unlike those of *gifted ones*.

She wondered what Dagon's were, if he had any. "Are you married? Or bound to anyone?" she asked, trying to remember the correct term.

"No."

The women on his planet must not be too bright, because he seemed like a nice guy. "Just thought I would ask. Wouldn't want to upset anyone by giving you that hug."

Again he chuckled. "What of you?" he asked, surprising her. "Who is Max?"

Surprise flitted through her. "How do you know about Max?"

"You thought I was Max when I called your name."

"Oh. He's just a friend." Max was actually her Second, or human guard, who handled business for her and watched over her while she slept during the day.

"Are you bound to another? Or married?" he pressed.

She laughed, then clenched her teeth and fought the urge to curse when pain shot through her chest again. "No. I'm not married."

"Why?"

Eliana couldn't help but laugh again despite the agony it spawned. "Boy, I love how you say that. You sound baffled."

"I am. You seem to be an honorable woman. Quite a likable one, too, if I may be honest."

"Well, aren't you a charmer?" she teased. "Maybe I'm just too ornery and butt-ugly to attract a man."

Multiple masculine laughs met her ears, Dagon's among them, reminding her that everyone on the bridge was listening to their conversation.

Enough flirting.

Wait. Had she been flirting?

Maybe.

Oh well. She'd needed the diversion.

"I guess I'd better go back to sleep," she announced reluctantly. "Slow my heart rate, try to conserve oxygen."

"Of course." Was that disappointment she detected in his deep voice?

"You still planning to head my way?"

"We are speeding toward you even as we speak."

"Thank you, Dagon." She closed her eyes, slowed her breathing. "Don't forget about me."

"There is little chance of that," he murmured just before darkness claimed her.

"Commander Dagon."

Dagon jerked awake. "Yes?"

"Your presence is requested on the bridge," Barus stated, his voice grim.

Rolling out of bed, he headed for the small connecting lav. "I'm on my way."

A few minutes later, he strode onto the bridge. "Report."

Barus vacated Dagon's chair. "I believe we're approaching some of the wreckage of the *Kandovar*."

Dagon took his seat and stared through the clear crystal window. Dark space stretched before him, a sight he usually found calming. Today, however, large chunks of metal and other debris floated in the distance. "Reduce speed."

"Reducing speed," Galen, his navigations officer, confirmed.

Dagon scrutinized the flotsam. "Are any of the missing escape pods present?" An alarming number were still unaccounted for.

"I haven't seen any yet," Barus replied.

"None have appeared on radar," Galen added.

Janek turned and met Dagon's gaze. "And I'm not picking up anything on comms."

"Any sign of the Gathendiens?"

"No, Commander."

The fact that none of the Aldebarian Alliance members currently searching for survivors had come across the Gathendien ship that committed the vile attack troubled Dagon. The Yona stationed on Lasaran search vessels, soldiers to their core, had warned all allies to keep both their shields and their guard up, suggesting the Gathendiens might be lying in wait to attack any who came to the Lasarans' aid, or worse, might be searching for survivors themselves and picking them off one by one.

Imagining a Gathendien warship coming upon Eliana before he could reach her had kept Dagon from finding much sleep since they had last spoken. He had insisted Janek keep the comm line to her open, though four days had passed since they had heard anything from her.

She had surprised them once. He held out hope she would do so again.

"Galen," he ordered, "guide us through, nice and slow."

"Yes, Commander."

Dagon and the others carefully scrutinized every scrap of debris. They passed two large pieces of the ship's hull that bore scorch marks. Pieces of furniture and personal items indicated this had been part of the living quarters. Living quarters Eliana had helped evacuate, according to Lasaran survivor accounts.

Barus pointed. "There."

Dagon clenched his teeth. Three bodies floated amid the rubble. Two wore protective suits. One didn't. None moved. He glanced at his tactical officer. "Rahmik, are you detecting the presence of any concealed ships?"

"No, Commander."

He turned to Barus. "Send a crew out to bring the bodies aboard. We will return them to Lasara for burial."

Barus touched his earpiece and began issuing orders.

"Remain vigilant," Dagon warned both the bridge and the team readying for their space walk.

Somber silence fell as they watched the squad approach the bodies, aided by small propulsion jets strategically placed on their protective suits.

"All are male," one stated grimly. He didn't have to say they were dead. Their oxygen would have long since run out. The fact that Eliana had survived as long as she had continued to perplex them.

Janek caught Dagon's eye. "Do you think any were from Earth?"

He shook his head. "Eliana said the Earthlings were all female."

None, as yet, had been found.

The women should still have a goodly supply of rations. But Eliana believed they didn't know how to pilot the pods and thus could not seek refuge on any moderately inhabitable planet they might locate. Nor could they prevent the pods from being caught up in the orbit of any *un*inhabitable planet they floated past and—should their orbit decay—crash to the planet's surface. The pods were designed to provide optimal protection in a worst-case scenario, but even they could not withstand being subjected to the surface temperatures of some worlds.

As soon as his men were on board again, Dagon turned to Galen. "Return to full speed and resume course to Eliana."

"Yes, Commander."

Dagon left the bridge. It only took him a couple of minutes to reach the infirmary. Three corpses lay side by side on treatment beds. Two still wore their suits. The third bore only the ravages of his painful death in space.

Chief Medical Officer Adaos stood beside one of those in a suit.

Adaos glanced over at him. "Commander."

Dagon motioned to the casualties. "Can you identify them?"

He nodded. "I just need a drop of their blood. Once I run a scan, I can match each man with a name on the crew list the Lasarans sent me."

Moving to stand on the opposite side of the body from Adaos, Dagon crossed his arms and watched the healer cut the man's suit open. The familiar scents of death arose.

Dagon ground his teeth together. Would he be standing here in three weeks, watching Adaos cut open Eliana's suit? Would he see her face through her helmet's shield, frozen in death?

"You are thinking of the Earthling," Adaos murmured as he took the blood sample.

Dagon didn't deny it. "She has the same amount of oxygen these men had. How is it she has managed to survive when they did not?"

Adaos shook his head. "I still don't believe it's possible. The information the Sectas have gathered indicates that Earthlings are deceptive beings. They even deceived the Lasaran princess into trusting them, then captured and ruthlessly tortured her. The Earth woman must be lying."

"What lie would explain it?"

The healer shrugged. "Could she be working with the Gathendiens?"

"No. She loathes them as much as we do."

"So she says."

"I believe her words to be sincere."

"Then perhaps she is inside an escape pod. Such would easily explain how she has survived so long."

"Why would she lie about being in a pod?"

"Perhaps she hoped it would drive you to find her faster."

Dagon shook his head. "She isn't in a pod." Her panic upon realizing as much had sounded genuine.

"Then I am as puzzled as you are, my friend."

Nodding, Dagon turned to leave. "Send me the men's identities as soon as you've confirmed them."

"Yes, Commander."

Dagon headed for his private office. Once he sank into the chair behind his desk, he tapped his earpiece. "Janek, get me Lasaran Commander Tiran of the *Tarakona*."

"Yes, Commander."

The clear screen that hovered above Dagon's desk lit up, and Adaos's face appeared. "I have confirmed the Lasarans' identities and will send them to you now."

"Thank you."

Adaos disappeared, and three files floated onto the screen. Each boasted a picture of a Lasaran male, a list of identifying information, and a brief description of his life and position.

The screen went blank. Then Tiran's face and shoulders filled it. Like Dagon, he appeared to be sitting at a desk in his private office.

"I have Commander Tiran for you," Janek announced.

"Thank you, Janek."

Dagon gave the comms officer a moment to remove himself from the conversation, then leaned forward. "Tiran."

"Good to see you, Dagon."

"I wish I had a better reason for contacting you."

Tiran's lips tightened. "What did you find?"

"Three of your men, floating in a debris field. Two wore suits. One didn't. All are dead. I'm sending you their identities now." He tapped the screen and sent the files to the Lasaran.

Tiran scanned the files, then spat out an obscenity. "Napelo's lifemate just found out she's breeding."

Dagon swore as well. Pregnancies on Lasara were exceedingly rare thanks to the insidious virus the Gathendiens had released upon them. "I'm sorry I couldn't reach them sooner."

Tiran shook his head. "We've managed to retrieve more escape pods containing survivors."

"Any Earthlings?"

"No. All Lasaran. What about *your* Earthling?"

"I haven't heard from her in four days, but I believe she may still live."

Tiran shook his head, his features dark with regret. "If Lasarans—with their greater regenerative capabilities—cannot survive this long, how could an Earth woman?"

"She said she could slow her heart rate and her breathing to conserve oxygen."

"Sectas believe that is impossible."

Dagon shrugged. "The Sectas are wrong. I heard her oxygen monitor myself. The first time I spoke with her, she had twenty-six hours left. Three days later, she had fifteen."

Tiran frowned, his look turning thoughtful. "Perhaps that explains it."

"Explains what?"

"The peculiar briefing I—and the other Lasaran commanders—received. Our sovereign has been in contact with Eliana's commanding officer."

"Seth?"

Tiran nodded. "I was not able to convey your message regarding the Earthling's wishes before King Dasheon and Queen Adiransia spoke with him."

Dagon frowned. "Eliana didn't want him to know her situation."

"I'm afraid that was unavoidable. Our sovereigns are outraged by the Gathendiens' attack and are even more disturbed by our inability to keep the Earthlings safe." Tiran leaned toward the screen and lowered his voice. "King Dasheon is trying to form an alliance with this Seth that he said would greatly benefit us and fears that will no longer be possible if we do not recover all of the Earth women alive."

Dagon's curiosity rose. "Do you know why only women were in their party?"

"No. He hasn't mentioned that." Tiran's voice lowered further. "But there is something else. Something above my clearance level."

"What do you think it is?"

He shook his head. "I believe those in power think the Gathendiens attacked the *Kandovar* because the Earthlings were aboard."

Unease filtered through Dagon. "What interest would they have in Earth women?"

"I don't know. Nor do I know if the Gathendiens wanted to kill or capture them."

Again, the thought of a Gathendien warship creeping up on Eliana while she was utterly defenseless in her suit drove shards of ice through his veins.

"Our sovereign wanted complete honesty between them," Tiran continued, "so he disclosed all we know to her commanding officer—that at least ten of the women were safely ensconced in escape pods when the ship began to break apart, and we have reason to believe four others were as well."

"What reason?"

"They were last seen helping Lasarans into escape pods and should have been in close enough proximity to duck into pods themselves."

Dagon wasn't as confident of that as Tiran's people. Eliana had been helping Lasarans, and *she* had ended up being launched into space in only a suit.

"Since we've managed to successfully retrieve escape pods carrying Lasarans, we have hope that the Earthlings will also be recovered soon."

"And Eliana?"

"When her situation was imparted, this Seth became enraged. He refused to accept the reality of her imminent demise and kept insisting you race toward her with every ounce of speed your ship can muster, that you not deviate from your course. And no matter how long it takes you to reach her, he demanded you bring her body on board and run whatever scans you must to determine whether she is actually dead."

Dagon frowned. If she was dead when he reached her—and just the idea of it twisted his stomach into knots—they would not need scans to confirm it. What he had seen of the deceased Lasaran men had verified that.

"Eliana said he's like a father to her," he offered as a possible explanation for the Earth commander's behavior.

"Ah." Sadness and understanding darkened his friend's features. "The common belief among Lasarans has been that Seth must be in denial and therefore needs the confirmation before he can let himself fully acknowledge her loss and grieve. It is said that his eyes even glowed with madness when he addressed our sovereign, but the fool who carried that tale surely exaggerated. Earthlings' eyes don't glow."

"No." After talking to Eliana, he had scoured the Sectas' Earthling anatomy database and had found no reports of glowing eyes.

"My king asks that you comply with Seth's wishes and make haste to her location. Once you recover her body, have your healer run the scans requested to confirm her death. Then prepare her body for cryo storage so the Lasarans may provide a ceremonial burial and honor her for her bravery."

Prepare her body. "Tell King Dasheon I will do as requested." The Lasarans had aided the Segonians several times in the past, so Dagon's sovereign wanted to do whatever they could to help.

Tiran nodded but didn't end the transmission. He tilted his head to one side. "You spoke with the Earth woman twice."

"Yes." Dagon released a long sigh. "And she deserves to be honored for her bravery. She is not what the Sectas have led us to believe all Earthlings are."

"Then we will mourn for her as though she were one of our own."

"As will I," Dagon admitted.

He didn't want to mourn for her though. He wanted to save her.

Ending the communication, he headed back to the bridge.

"Commander on the bridge," Barus announced, again vacating Dagon's chair.

Dagon nodded to him, then turned to his tactical officer. "Rahmik, how much speed would we gain if we diverted power from shields?"

Rahmik's eyes widened for a moment before he consulted his screen. "Enough to shave three or four days off our journey."

Barus frowned. "The Yona believe the Gathendiens may be lying in wait, ready to attack rescue ships."

"And the Lasarans believe the Gathendiens attacked their vessel in an attempt to get to the Earth women."

"To kill or to capture them?"

Dagon shook his head. "They don't know. But if the Earth women were their true targets, the Gathendiens will search for them. And Eliana is alone and unprotected."

"You don't know that she even still lives," Barus protested.

"And you don't know that she's dead," Dagon snapped, anger rising. "What if she's still alive when the Gathendiens find her? The Lasarans are our closest allies. Their sovereign has asked us to make reaching her as swiftly as we can our top priority."

"No matter how fast we travel, she'll die before we reach her. She's probably already dead!"

"You can't be sure of that! You—"

"What's wrong?" a female voice murmured.

Dagon and Barus ceased arguing.

Quiet fell as Dagon looked at Janek.

Janek nodded, eyes wide. "It's Eliana."

"Dagon?" she called. "What's wrong?" Her words came slowly, as though she were still trying to awaken from a deep sleep. "You sound pissed."

His heart began to pound as relief flooded him. "What does *pissed* mean?"

"Angry."

"It's nothing," he said, unwilling to tell her that some of his crew questioned the logic of diverting power from shields and reducing their own safety so they could reach a dead woman faster. "Just a minor disagreement."

A rusty chuckle carried over the line. "Sure it is." She started to yawn but cut it off with a now-familiar grunt of pain.

"How are you?" he asked.

"Honestly?" She sighed. "I've been better."

"Your wounds?"

"The same, I think. My temperature seems to be running a little hot. I'm not sure if it's from fever or dehydration though. I'm really thirsty."

She must be starving, too.

"How long was I out this time?"

"Four days."

"How much oxygen do I have left?"

A female voice announced in Lasaran, "Two hours and thirty-seven minutes of oxygen remaining."

"Two hours and thirty-seven minutes," he repeated in English.

"Well," Eliana said, "I used a little less oxygen this time, but... Crap. That still isn't going to cut it. You're—what—three weeks away?"

"Yes. I believe if we divert power from the ship's shields, we may be able to reduce that by three or four days."

"So... two and a half weeks," she murmured.

"Yes."

"Have you come upon any survivors yet?"

"No."

"Any casualties?"

He fought the urge to swear. He hadn't planned to mention that.

"I'll take that as a yes. Were they human?"

"No. All three were Lasaran."

"Were they in escape pods?"

"No."

A pause followed. "Do you know if Ganix was one of them?"

Dagon couldn't remember. "One moment." He tapped his earpiece. "Adaos?"

"Yes, Commander."

"Did any of the Lasaran casualties you identified bear the name Ganix?"

"No."

He tapped his earpiece again. "No, Eliana. Ganix was not among those we retrieved."

"Okay."

Barus frowned. "Who is Ganix?"

Eliana answered before Dagon could. "I'm pretty sure he's the one who saved my life by stuffing me into this suit. I'm really hoping he makes it. What about the others who are out searching for survivors? Have they found any?"

Dagon crossed to his seat and sank down. "They've found both survivors and casualties. Those in the pods have survived. Those who didn't make it into pods lost their lives."

"I'm guessing you would've told me by now if they'd found any of my friends from Earth."

"There has been no sign of them yet."

"Damn."

Dagon debated whether to tell her more and decided she deserved to know all of it. "Eliana…"

"Uh-oh."

He frowned. "What?"

"You're about to give me bad news."

His eyebrows rose. "How did you know?"

"I can hear it in your voice. Did they… Did your superiors tell you to call off the search? Did they tell you not to come for me?"

The dread in her voice pierced his chest. "No. They confirmed that finding you is our top priority."

"Ah hell. They told Seth, didn't they?"

"Yes."

"Damn. I really wish they hadn't done that."

There was nothing he could do about it. "The Lasarans have asked the entire Aldebarian Alliance to make retrieving Earthlings a primary directive."

"Why? Did Seth threaten to rain fire and brimstone on them if they didn't?"

"No." Dagon actually only understood part of that. "They

believe your presence on the *Kandovar* was the reason the Gathendiens attacked it."

"Mother*fuckers*! What the hell?" she blurted, fury lending her voice strength.

Eyes widened around the bridge. A few lips twitched.

Women in their culture were counseled not to use harsh language. Men were, too, but tended to get away with it more than their female counterparts.

"The Lasarans are not certain how they learned of your presence aboard their vessel," he told her. "But they fear the Gathendiens may be searching for Earthling survivors."

"To kill or to capture?" she asked, echoing his own words to Tiran.

"They don't know."

Heavy silence fell, fraught with tension.

"Wait," she said suddenly. "If the Gathendiens' goal is to kill travelers from Earth, they may also try to take out any search-and-rescue vessels they encounter, right? In case you have any of us on board?"

"We believe that is a possibility, yes."

"Then don't divert power from your shields. It's too risky."

Barus shot him a quick, surprised glance.

Dagon shook his head. "We can reach you faster if we—"

"I don't care. I don't want you to risk your lives to save mine. If I didn't hope some of my friends might be floating around out here somewhere, I'd tell you not to come for me at all. How are you on firepower? Can you take out a Gathendien vessel if one attacks?"

"Yes. We have defeated many in the past."

"Good. If you do come upon one, shout a few Earth curses for me while you kick their asses."

He smiled. "I will."

Quiet fell.

"Three weeks," she muttered. "How the hell can I make two and a half hours of oxygen last three weeks?"

Dagon had no answer for her.

"I wish Seth didn't know."

"I believe the Lasarans wished to give him hope."

"I guess so," she murmured, voice somber. Her words slowed,

turned tentative. "Could you by any chance record a message from me to send Seth if I don't make it?"

"Yes." He didn't mention that Janek had been recording every communication with her. Dagon had made a copy of their first two conversations and played them back more times than he cared to admit.

"I mean, I'm still going to try to make it until you get here," she added, "but just in case I don't…"

"Of course."

"Thank you. Let me know when you're ready."

He let a few seconds pass. "We can begin recording now."

"Okay. Let me think a sec."

Almost a full minute went by.

"Okay. Here we go," she said. "Hi, Seth." Her voice cracked. "Damn it. Let me try that again." She cleared her throat. Twice. "Hi, Seth." Her voice broke again, and she sounded close to tears. "Nope."

If Seth was like a father to her, Dagon could understand why the prospect of saying goodbye to him might compel her to weep.

"Damn it, Eliana," she whispered. "Just suck it up and get it done. This isn't for *you*. It's for *him*."

Dagon exchanged a somber look with Barus.

She cleared her throat. "Okay. One more time." When next she spoke, her voice was strong and bright, lending no clue whatsoever of the pain that afflicted her or the grimness of her situation. "Hi, Seth," she said cheerfully. "If you're listening to this, I guess I didn't make it. Hopefully, I went out kicking a *lot* of Gathendien ass. Because those are the assholes responsible for this. The Gathendiens. We made it through the first *qhov'rum* wormhole thing just fine and had just entered the second when those bastards attacked. I got as many people as I could into escape pods. So I hope everyone you placed in my keeping survived. If they didn't… I'm sorry. I did my best to protect them and keep them safe. But doing that out here in space is a lot harder than it is on Earth."

She drew in a deep breath, managing not to grunt in pain this time. "I know you, Seth. I know you're going to blame yourself because I didn't make it. And you're going to regret sending us out here, thinking that this wouldn't have happened if you hadn't agreed to this and that you never should have let us go, but that's bullshit. I don't regret it. At all. Not one minute of it." Joy and awe entered her voice. "Thanks to you, I got to board an honest-to-goodness spaceship, leave Earth, and tour our solar system. How many people aside from Ami can say that? Then I *left* our solar system and flew through deep space. I got to spend four months getting to know people from not one but *two* alien races. I've lived a long time, Seth, and this has been the biggest, most amazing adventure of my life. I'm so glad I had the chance to do this."

The crew exchanged somber glances.

"Look, I know the Lasarans have told you about my situation. I don't want you to torture yourself, imagining me floating out here by myself, afraid and in pain. Because that's bullshit, too. I wish you could see what I can see. I have the most amazing view of the stars. We don't get to see them much at home in the cities because of the pollution and all the lights. But here the stars stretch as far as I can see in all directions. And I'm *not* alone. I met a third group of aliens—the Segonians—who are just as amazing as the Lasarans and the Yona." She chuckled. "They're actually a lot more entertaining than the Yona and not as diplomatically correct as the Lasarans. So they've been really good company. They haven't complained once about me driving them crazy with my chatter, and I'm even teaching them to curse like an Earthling. Am I teaching you guys to curse like an Earthling?" she called.

"Hell yes, you are," all but Barus responded.

She laughed, again managing to do so without revealing the pain Dagon knew it caused her. "You see? These guys are great." Her voice softened, still carrying a smile. "So don't torture yourself imagining the worst. I know you're going to mourn for me, but don't blame yourself and let it tear you up inside." Her words strengthened once more. "Leah, I know you're there because there's no way you'd let Seth listen to this alone. If you even *think* he looks like he's blaming himself, give him a swift kick in the ass for me. You're the only one gutsy enough to do it. Then distract him with a storm or two." She chuckled. "I'm going to miss teasing you two about that."

Dagon could not imagine what she meant.

Her voice softened further, filling with tenderness and affection.

"Thank you, Seth, for sending me on the adventure of a lifetime. I'm so glad you did." She took a deep breath. "I love you. Goodbye."

Her breath hiccupped with a sob on the last word.

Heavy silence engulfed them all.

CHAPTER 3

ELIANA STRUGGLED TO hold back the sobs that threatened.

"Eliana?" Dagon asked softly. And the sympathy in his deep voice only made the struggle more difficult.

"Damn, that was hard," she whispered brokenly. "Do you think maybe you could cut off the goodbye? I don't want him to know I cried."

"Of course."

Every jagged breath sent pain spearing through her chest. She thought she'd held it together pretty well since she'd found herself alone in the middle of nowhere but now wanted to bawl her eyes out. "I don't think I've ever been so dehydrated before that I couldn't produce tears," she muttered. "It feels really weird." And she hated that she had broken down in front of those she now thought of as *the Guys*. She cleared her throat. "Was the rest of it okay? Do you think it will help him?"

"You did very well," Dagon assured her. He was such a nice guy.

"Good. Because I really don't think I have it in me to try again." Staring through her helmet's visor, Eliana took in the vast array of stars. "It really is beautiful up here," she murmured. Seth usually stationed her in big cities where the twenty-four-hour lights and a haze of pollution obscured her view.

"Yes," Dagon agreed.

She had two hours of oxygen left, and Dagon and his crew wouldn't reach her for three more weeks. How could she possibly make so little oxygen last that long?

Only one possibility came to mind.

Dread filled her at just the thought of it, solidifying in her stomach like a block of ice. "Dagon?"

"Yes."

"How familiar are you with these Lasaran spacesuits?"

"I've worn them many times during inter-Alliance training exercises."

"How sturdy are they? Do they puncture easily?"

"No. They're very difficult to perforate or tear." Alarm entered his voice. "Why? Do you think yours is damaged?"

"No. I'm just… thinking out loud."

She had been stationed in New York with a Russian immortal by the name of Stanislav for decades until a few years ago. When a mercenary group had gotten their hands on the vampiric virus and caused major upheaval in North Carolina, Seth had transferred Stanislav there to help. A big battle had ensued when the Immortal Guardians blitzed the mercenary compound, and all had believed Stanislav was killed in an explosion. Much to their astonishment and elation, however, a woman had found him two years later, buried in her basement.

And Stanislav had still been alive.

Because of their advanced DNA, Immortal Guardians didn't die of extreme blood loss the way vampires did. Instead, they slipped into a state of hibernation not unlike a water bear until another blood source came along. The peculiar symbiotic virus had slowed Stanislav's breathing and heartbeat to such an extent that he had survived on whatever tiny pocket of air had been allotted him beneath the soil for two years. His body had not decayed. His organs had not failed. He had been pretty emaciated when Susan had found him, but he had survived.

Eliana had never slipped into stasis before. The mere prospect of it terrified her. Stanislav was actually the only immortal she had ever met who had done so. One of the reasons Seth assigned Immortal Guardians mortal Seconds to watch over them and keep tabs on them was to prevent such from happening.

But what choice did she have? Just over two hours of oxygen had to last three weeks. Even a deep sleep had only stretched what amounted to a day's worth of oxygen a full week.

She really wanted to live. But if she did this, if she forced her body to slip into stasis and the Segonians failed to find her…

"Dagon?"

"Yes," he answered swiftly.

"Is this a secure line?"

"What do you mean?"

"Is there any chance the Gathendiens could be listening in?"

"No. Such would enable them to locate you, so we have taken measures to ensure they cannot intercept or listen to our communications with you."

"Good." Her heart began to pound with anxiety. "There's one more thing I can try that may enable me to survive until you reach me. I haven't done it before now because…" Because it scared the hell out of her. "It will leave me completely vulnerable."

"More vulnerable than you are now?" She could almost see his brow furrowing as he said that.

"Yes. Right now I can wake and respond if you call to me. Or if the Gathendiens show up and bring me on board their ship, I can wake and might actually have a shot at defending myself. But if I do this, I'll lose that ability." She might be able to wake, but she would be too weak to do anything else. And she'd lose this connection with Dagon and would be truly alone. "Will you still come for me if I stop speaking to you?"

"Yes. Finding you and your fellow Earthlings is a top priority of all Alliance nations."

"What if your superior or king or whoever changes his mind and tells you to call off the search?"

"On my honor, I vow I will come for you, Eliana."

She believed him. "Janek?"

"Yes, Earthling?"

She chuckled. "You're just calling me that to aggravate me, aren't you?"

"Yes, Earthling," he responded, a smile in his voice.

"If you cut communication with me for ten minutes, will you be able to reconnect?"

"Yes."

"You have no doubts?"

"None."

"Okay. I need you to do that for me. Cut the connection so we can't hear each other, then reconnect in ten minutes."

Dagon spoke. "What is the purpose of this, Eliana?"

"There's just… something I have to do. That's all. I'll talk to you again in ten minutes."

Low Segonian conversation ensued.

Then Dagon said in English, "Cut the connection."

"Yes, Commander," Janek said. "In three, two, one."

All sound ceased save her breathing. Eliana could no longer hear the murmurings and moving around on Dagon's ship and felt a moment of panic.

"Don't freak out," she told herself. "They'll be back in a few minutes. Just suck it up and get this done."

She tried to steel herself for the pain to come. If her oxygen ran out, she'd die, so she had to slip into stasis fast. And the only way she knew to do that was through severe blood loss.

Holding her breath, she curled her right hand into a fist and drove it into her injured side.

She couldn't help the cry of pain that escaped and was doubly glad Janek had cut communications. Warmth blossomed in her wound.

She repeated the action on her hip. More pain. More warmth. Then the telltale feeling of blood slipping down the outside of her thigh inside the suit.

Eliana gritted her teeth and really dug her knuckles into her side. "Shit!" she gasped. "This sucks!" But the blood flow increased. Her breathing grew labored as she repeated the action with her hip, reopening the wound the virus had sealed. Wave after wave of agony inundated her.

She stopped when she grew light-headed.

It had only taken a few minutes to get the blood flowing. She used the rest to try to get her harsh breathing under control so her voice wouldn't betray her pain.

"This had better work," she wheezed.

"Eliana?"

She damned near wept at the sound of Dagon's concerned voice.

"I'm here." She congratulated herself on sounding almost normal. "Has it been ten minutes already?"

A pause. "Yes."

She laughed, then bit back a groan. "You're a terrible liar."

"It has only been seven minutes," he admitted.

"You were worried."

"Yes."

She found a smile. "You remind me of Ami."

"Who is Ami?"

"You probably know her as Amiriska."

"The Lasaran princess?"

"Yes. How much have you heard about what happened to her?"

"Rumors abound that she went to Earth against her king's wishes and…"

"And?" she prompted.

"She was captured and tortured by Earthlings."

"Yep. Ami came to our planet in peace, seeking an alliance, and the dumbasses in power decided that torturing her would be smarter. Fortunately, Seth and David found her and rescued her. Then Seth pretty much adopted her and loves her like a daughter." She smiled. "Like you, Ami can't lie worth a damn."

Masculine chuckles sounded softly from the bridge.

"In my defense," Dagon said with what sounded like consternation, "you seem to be the only one who can read me so well."

Her smile widened. "Don't worry. Honesty is a good thing. I like that I can trust you." She sighed. The heat that had dogged her seemed to drain out of her alongside her blood, leaving a chill behind.

"Who is Leah?" Dagon asked after a while.

"Seth's wife. They just married a few months ago." Amusement rose. "I'm so glad he found her. She is *exactly* what he needed."

"He needed a woman capable of kicking him in the ass?" he asked, his voice puzzled.

She laughed, then sucked in a sharp breath as pain knifed through her chest.

"Eliana?"

Though she didn't verbally acknowledge it, the concern in his voice soothed her. "She won't really kick him in the ass. That's just an Earth saying." She thought of Seth and Leah and how they behaved when they were together. "She makes him happy. Seth has been taking care of the rest of us for so long and helping us find whatever happiness or contentment we can that I think he forgot to do the same for himself. I don't remember ever seeing him laugh as much as he does with Leah. She's perfect for him."

Cold seeped into her fingers and toes, then crept up her limbs. A shiver shook her.

"Eliana? What is it?" He must have heard something in her breath.

"Nothing." She tried to keep her voice steady. "I'm just a little cold."

"Are the environmental controls in your suit failing?"

"No. They're fine." Her head spun dizzily. "I think it's..." What had she been talking about? "I think it's just the blood loss."

"Your wounds have reopened?"

Crap. Why had she said that? "I'm fine," she lied again and fumbled about for a distraction. "Did I tell you Seth and Leah got married recently?"

"Yes."

She had?

Oh well. "It was a beautiful ceremony." She stared at the stars outside her visor and remembered the lights that had illuminated the wedding guests at the nocturnal ceremony. "Every one of my brethren attended." She smiled. "I never thought I'd see us all come together in one place like that, but somehow Seth managed it. Zach conducted the ceremony. I don't know him that well, but I like him. He's helped me out of a bind and healed my wounds several times. And Leah looked lovely." She chuckled despite the pain it evoked. "The children were adorable." Little Adira and Michael had sparked much laughter when they had raced each other up the aisle while executing their duties as flower girl and ring bearer. "After the ceremony, Seth and Leah danced to one of my favorite songs. It was like something out of a fairy tale." Their eyes had only been on each other as they had waltzed to "At Last." And the love they bore each other had been so clear, so strong, that it had brought tears to Eliana's eyes.

"Is that the song they danced to?" Dagon asked.

Eliana blinked, surprised to realize she had been humming it. "Yes."

"Will you sing it for me?"

She smiled as weariness washed over her. "I'm no Etta James."

"I don't know what that means."

"I can't sing it the way she does."

"Then sing it the way you do when you're alone."

Eliana figured she only had a few minutes before she lost consciousness, so… why not? If going into stasis didn't work, using up an extra three minutes of oxygen would make little difference in the end.

Softly, she began to sing. And as she did, her fear fell away. She really did love the song and now would forever associate it with one of her happiest memories, that of Seth dancing with the woman he loved.

Her eyelids grew heavy.

Her heartbeat slowed.

Then slowed some more.

And more.

The song ended.

"That was beautiful," Dagon said, his voice hushed.

"Thank you."

The world grew quiet. Eliana couldn't even hear her own breathing.

She did still breathe, didn't she? Did her heart still beat?

She closed her eyes, unable to keep them open any longer.

"Dagon?" she murmured.

"Yes, Eliana."

"Don't forget me."

"I won't," he promised.

Darkness enveloped her.

Dagon raced through the corridor. His heart pounded, but he couldn't tell if it was with dread or excitement.

They had heard nothing from Eliana for three weeks, not since she had sung her favorite Earth song in a soft, sultry voice that still haunted him.

Racing around a curve, he nearly plowed into two crewmen who hastily scampered out of his way.

Driven by the need to confirm she still lived, Dagon had called her name a week ago and received no response. She had warned him she wouldn't be able to answer if she tried whatever it was she had tried, but...

What had she done? When she had expressed such unease about the course she intended to take in an attempt to slow her heartbeat even more and live longer, he had deceived her. She had asked Janek to cut communications for ten minutes. Dagon had instead instructed him to mute her end and the bridge's end and only let *him* listen.

A muscle jumped in his jaw.

It had sounded as if she'd hurt herself, something her later reference to blood loss seemed to confirm. But how would worsening her wounds help her live longer?

She had mentioned being hot prior to taking the disturbing action. Had fever driven her into delirium? Had some hallucination tricked her into believing that speeding *toward* death would instead stave it off?

Bypassing the lift, he ducked into a ladder well and swiftly climbed up two floors.

A moment later he burst onto the bridge. "Where is she?"

Galen pointed to the view of the stars that stretched before them.

In the distance, he could barely make out small pieces of debris. "You're sure she's there?"

Janek nodded. "I'm not hearing anything from her, but I have confirmed her comm signal is coming from that area."

Dagon took his seat and struggled for patience. "Reduce speed. Approach with care." Though he wanted nothing more than to hurtle toward Eliana at top speed, he didn't want to accidentally plow into her in his haste. "Barus, assemble the team."

He had discussed the logistics of retrieving her with his second-in-command. Both believed they should heed the Yona's warning and exercise extreme caution.

Barus left the bridge.

The ship crept closer to the debris.

Dagon frowned. There were several large pieces of wreckage—twisted chunks of the Lasaran ship scorched black—that had been nearly invisible from a distance. Eliana had seen no such pieces when they had spoken. Had they blended too well with the dark backdrop of space?

"Dispatch the fighters," he ordered.

Three sleek black fighter craft shot forth from the ship. A gray retrieval vessel moved forward more slowly.

The fighters hovered in a triangular formation, facing outward, ready to defend the retrieval unit from any surprise attack Gathendiens might launch.

Barus returned to the bridge and stood beside Dagon, arms crossed, brow furrowed.

The retrieval vessel stopped amid the wreckage. A portal opened, emitting two men in protective suits. Both used the mini jets on their suits to maneuver around the objects.

"One body spotted," Maarev announced grimly over the comm as he slipped behind a jagged slab of ship. "A male, wearing no suit."

"Any sign of Eliana?" Dagon asked.

The two soldiers tracked back and forth through the debris field.

"No," Maarev said at length.

Dagon sat back in his seat. "Bring the man in for identification."

"Yes, Commander."

He clenched his teeth. If Eliana wasn't there…

"Do you think the Gathendiens reached her first?" Barus asked.

"I don't know." He hoped not but could find no other explanation.

Janek shook his head. "She's here somewhere. I know it."

Though Dagon wanted to believe that, his men would've found her. "The Lasaran suits are bright white. Maarev and Liden wouldn't miss her."

"Then why am I still receiving her comm signal?" Janek countered. "She's here. I'm certain of it. She *has* to be located within three *kells* from us."

Dagon leaned forward, watching Liden maneuver the dead man inside the retrieval vessel. "Efren."

"Yes, Commander."

"Escort Maarev and Liden back, then execute a search of the surrounding area. We're still receiving a comm signal from Eliana and believe she may be nearby."

"Yes, Commander."

As soon as Maarev, Liden, and the deceased male were safely aboard the retrieval vessel, the three fighter ships peeled away and shot off in different directions, disappearing into the darkness.

Long moments ticked past. At least, they seemed long to Dagon. He didn't know why the Earthling... Earth woman, he corrected himself... had come to feel so important to him, but she had.

"I see her!" Efren suddenly shouted. "Or rather, I see someone in a Lasaran spacesuit."

"Coordinates?"

As soon as Efren relayed Eliana's coordinates, both the *Ranasura* and the retrieval vessel raced forward.

Had Dagon not been so worried, he would've smiled. His men were as eager to rescue her as he was.

"There!" Galen pointed.

A tiny white dot guarded by three black fighters grew in front of them.

The figure in white didn't move at their approach, didn't wave or react in any way to the craft around her. Nor did Eliana's voice greet them.

Heavy silence settled upon them all as Maarev left the retrieval vessel and jetted toward the figure.

"It's a woman," Maarev confirmed.

Dagon released the breath he hadn't realized he'd been holding. "Alive or dead?"

"I can't tell. Her eyes are closed and she appears to be injured."

"Bring her aboard," Dagon ordered. Rising, he strode past Barus. "You have the bridge."

Once in the hallway, he ducked into the ladder well and skimmed down to the bottom deck. Less than a minute later, he entered a room separated from Hangar 1 by the same clear, unbreakable crystal that formed the bridge's large window.

Maarev flew inside the bay, a bulky white figure clutched to his chest. The fighters followed, careful not to hit the duo.

The bay doors closed. Maarev's boots lowered to the floor.

As soon as gravity and environment was restored to the hangar, Dagon hit the control that opened the large door. Too impatient to wait for it to rise fully, he ducked under it and strode forward.

Maarev retracted his helmet and adjusted his hold on Eliana. "I did a quick scan and found no signs of life."

Dagon's heart clenched. "Give her to me." He slipped an arm beneath her knees and wrapped the other around her back. Her helmeted head rolled, coming to rest against his chest... and Dagon looked upon her for the first time.

Her face was pale, her features gaunt. The eyelashes that rested against her hollow cheeks were long and dark, the hair he could barely glimpse black.

She weighed so little, even in the bulky suit, and was so small.

Swiveling around, he left the bay. "Adaos."

"Yes, Commander," the chief medical officer answered in his earpiece.

"Meet me in Med Bay."

"I'm already there."

Dagon stepped into the nearest lift. The door slipped closed, leaving him alone with the Earth woman.

"Eliana," he murmured, jostling her a bit. "Eliana? Can you hear me?"

She remained still and quiet in his arms.

As soon as the doors opened, he headed for Med Bay.

Adaos waited inside as promised and motioned to the nearest treatment bed.

Dagon gently placed Eliana on it, absently noting a body covered with a sheet on another bed. Finding the manual latches for the helmet, he flipped them to detach it from her too-big suit, then slipped a hand inside and cupped the back of her head to elevate it enough to ease the protective barrier off.

She had long hair. It poured out of the helmet like water, trailing over his hand and falling off the edges of the bed. Over one ear, the dark tresses were matted with blood. The same side of her face was scraped raw and spattered with crimson streaks and splotches.

Dagon withdrew his touch and stared down at her.

She was not butt-ugly as she had claimed. Even gaunt and wounded, she was pretty, her features delicate.

Adaos ran a small handheld scanner across her chest. Meeting Dagon's gaze, he shook his head. "No heartbeat detected."

"She said she could slow it." Dagon could not yet bring himself to admit defeat.

Adaos held up the device he kept with him at all times. "Enough to confound my scanner?" Sorrow filled his features. "I don't believe so, my friend."

Dagon stared down at her. "We were too late."

Adaos nodded. "We all knew we would be. It was simply difficult for us to admit it when she gave us such hope."

Shortly after his last communication with her, Dagon had caught two of his men wagering over whether the Earthling would be alive or dead when they found her. Infuriated by their callous disregard, he had ordered Janek to replay every communication he had shared with Eliana… except for the seven minutes he had restricted to himself after she requested those odd moments of privacy in which it sounded as though she had hurt herself.

After listening to her conversations with Dagon and the other crewmen on the bridge, every man on the ship had—from that point on—adopted his hope that they would find her in time. Some had even suggested he divert power from shields so they could reach her faster even though they knew they would be placing themselves in danger.

"She isn't what I expected of an Earthling," Dagon murmured as he stared down at her.

Adaos nodded. "The Sectas led us to believe Earthlings bore no strength, no honor."

"Eliana possessed both in abundance." Dagon glanced down her body, which was still encased in the suit. "She's smaller than I anticipated." For some reason, that made his failure to rescue her even harder to accept. "Rid her of the suit, run the scans her commanding officer requested, then clean her up. Let me know when she's ready to be placed in cryo for transport to Lasara."

"Yes, Commander."

Dagon could not stop himself from fingering a lock of her hair.

It was as soft as a *fentorian* feather.

Regret chilled him. He should have known he couldn't save her. He should not have let hope sway him.

Turning on his heel, he left the infirmary and headed back to the bridge.

Adaos watched Dagon leave. Though his friend and commander's face remained stoic, the medic could tell the Earth woman's demise had struck a blow.

Even Adaos felt some despair. He had listened to the woman's conversations with Dagon. The commander had broadcast them throughout the ship after delivering a furious reprimand to two men wagering over her fate. And like Dagon, Adaos had found her rather astonishing. And quite likable.

Until then, he had not understood Dagon's inability to see that she must be deceiving him. As a healer, Adaos had concluded she must be in an escape pod in order to have survived as long as she had. He had studied the detailed descriptions of Earthling anatomy and physiology and known she could not possibly slow her breathing enough to make a day's worth of oxygen last a week.

Yet here she lay… in a suit. No pod had been found anywhere near her.

How had she done it?

Retrieving a scalpel, he began to cut the suit off her, careful not to nick her skin with the laser. He sliced the suit into several pieces that could more easily be removed.

Once he had discarded them all, he stared down at her.

"She's so small," he murmured, parroting Dagon's words. Were she to stand up, she wouldn't even reach his shoulder.

And she was far too thin, confirming that she had indeed survived over a week without food or water before she had died.

The clothing she wore was not typical of Lasarans. A black shirt hugged her from shoulder to wrist and down to her hips, the dark fabric outlining unnaturally conspicuous ribs and a shrunken stomach. Though she was clearly underweight, her breasts were nevertheless fuller than most Segonian women's. Matching black trousers with many pockets loosely covered slender hips and outlined prominent hipbones.

Most of the fabric covering her right side was peppered with holes torn by shrapnel from what he guessed had been an explosion, judging by the scorch marks that marred it. The skin on the right side of her neck bore a raw wound, as did her right cheek and jaw. Her shirt and pants on the right side—as well as any exposed skin along it—were liberally stained with blood on the shoulder, arm, waist, hip, and leg down to her ankle.

The outside of her protective suit had been pristine before he'd cut it. So she must have guessed correctly. Someone had to have stuffed her into the suit while she was unconscious.

He peered at her damaged side and swept his scanner over her. Broken bones. Multiple deep lacerations. A severe head wound. How had she even survived these injuries?

Adaos retrieved a hover tray with a neat array of tools. Leaning over her, he gently nudged back one eyelid and shined a light in her brown eye.

No pupillary reaction.

Again he ran his handheld scanner over her and found no heartbeat.

Silently he reprimanded himself for hoping for another outcome. He was a healer. He knew what was and wasn't possible. He didn't need the extra tests Eliana's commanding officer had ordered to confirm she was dead. He had seen enough bodies while serving in the Segonian military to know. But he would perform them anyway.

Grabbing his med tablet, he tapped the surface several times, activating the full-body diagnostic scanner. A mechanical arm descended from the ceiling and positioned a wand above Eliana's head. Slowly it began to travel down her body, casting a narrow ray of light over her all the way down to her toes. Retracting, it hovered above her chest.

Adaos decided to take a blood sample while he awaited the results. Clearly, there was more to these Earthlings than either the Lasarans or the Sectas knew. He was very interested in—

"Heartbeat detected," the comprehensive scanner announced in the female Segonian voice allotted to all subsections of the ship's computer.

Eyes widening, Adaos spun around. "What?"

"Heartbeat detected."

"Just one?"

"Affirmative."

It couldn't be possible, could it?

He moved closer to the bed. "Any breaths taken?"

"Negative."

"Search for activity on a cellular level."

"Searching."

Adaos studied Eliana's still form but could find no discernable trace of life. Her chest did not rise and fall. No pulse thrummed beneath the skin of her neck. Her eyelids did not twitch.

"Cellular activity present," the comprehensive scanner announced.

It didn't make sense. "Have you detected any other heartbeats?"

"Negative."

"Could you be mistaken?"

"Negative. Cellular anomalies detected."

"What kind of anomalies?"

"Inconclusive."

He frowned. Was the scanner malfunctioning? "Perform a systems analysis."

"Performing systems analysis."

Leaning over Eliana, he again peeled back one eyelid and shined a light in her eye.

No reaction. He ran his handheld scanner over her once more and again found no heartbeat.

The comprehensive scanner must be—

"Systems analysis complete. All systems are performing as intended."

Perhaps he should move the Earth woman to the next bed and use that scanner instead, just to be sure.

He set his tablet on the tray and nudged it out of the way.

"Brain activity detected," the scanner announced.

Spinning around, Adaos stared at the Earth woman.

"Heartbeat detected."

Eyes widening, he approached her.

What the *srul* was happening?

CHAPTER 4

THOUGH LIGHT DRAGGED her—kicking and screaming—toward consciousness, Eliana neither moved nor made a sound. Pain inundated her. Hunger gnawed at her. And thirst…

The light vanished. Darkness returned. But it was no longer complete. Her eyelids merely shielded her from whatever light hovered above her.

Where was she? Why was she so weak? Why did such agony assail her?

Somewhere nearby, a man muttered something in a foreign language.

Alarm cut through her like a knife. She had lived four centuries, give or take a decade, and had learned a lot of languages in that time. Yet she didn't recognize the one he spoke.

She raised her eyelids a tiny bit, just enough to allow her a slit through which she could better ascertain her situation. A cold white room surrounded her. No artistic ornamentation graced the walls, just cabinets, beds, and what appeared to be medical equipment.

A tall man in pale gray clothing stood a few feet away, staring at an electronic tablet of some sort.

Fear struck as she closed her eyes.

This was not the infirmary in the headquarters of the human network that aided Immortal Guardians. Nor was it the infirmary in one of Seth's or David's homes. And the man muttering to himself not far away was definitely not a Second rendering aid or one of the human network's physicians.

When she peeked again, she noticed a still form covered by a sheet on a table not far away.

She closed her eyes. Fury replaced fear.

Gershom, the powerful enemy the Immortal Guardians had recently defeated, had once worked with Russian mercenaries. He had also twisted part of the American military into doing his bidding. Had a new enemy arisen to take his place? Another mercenary group, perhaps, eager to get their hands on an Immortal Guardian so they could use the virus that infected them to create a race of supersoldiers they could hire out to the highest bidder?

It wouldn't be the first time.

But how had they gotten their hands on her? And where was she? Was this a mercenary compound?

Immortal Guardians in North Carolina had destroyed two or three mercenary groups in recent years. But she had not been aware of any such troubles arising in Texas, where she had been stationed for a couple of years now.

She searched her scattered memories for an explanation. Had she been hunting? Though Gershom had been defeated, the vampire population remained unusually high. So high she and most of her brethren hunted in pairs to ensure they could defeat the larger numbers they encountered on a nightly basis.

Had mercenaries engaged in a hunt of their own, hiding until they came upon her after a kill? Was the body on that other bed a vampire? Dread suffused her. Or was it her hunting partner? Had they killed Nick? Or Rafe?

Try though she might, she could find no memory of such nor of being captured.

Logic intruded. It couldn't be one of her brethren or a vampire. The body would've already deteriorated by now if it were. So it must be some other poor victim. Perhaps a human the vampires had been feeding upon when Eliana had attacked?

Cracking her lids once more, she checked to see if the man in gray was facing away from her, then tried to move.

She was so weak!

Her rage increased. Only one substance on the planet could render her this weak and steal her memory: the only tranquilizer that affected both Immortal Guardians and vampires. The one created by humans to torture Ami when she'd been held prisoner in that government-funded research installation. And only enemies of the Immortal Guardians had possessed the tranquilizer in the past. Which meant this bastard *was* a mercenary and was also probably one of several who had been torturing her.

Fortunately, the drug was beginning to wear off.

A female voice emerged from a speaker somewhere above Eliana, but the cadence of her words sounded a little off, as if she were a computer or Siri or the like.

The man mumbled more foreign words, reached for something, and turned to face her. In one hand, he held what appeared to be a syringe with a long needle.

No way in hell was she going to let that bastard tranq her again.

The female voice spoke again.

The man paused, then moved closer. His brows drew down as he leaned over her.

The moment he reached toward her face, Eliana struck.

Pain forced a cry from her lips as she thrust one hand out and knocked the needle from his grasp. She fisted the other hand in his shirt and yanked hard.

Yelping, the man lost his balance and fell half on top of her.

Before he could recover, she raised her head, let her fangs descend, and sank them into his neck.

The man spat out what she suspected was a curse word and struggled for a moment, then relaxed against her. When the virus that infected her had made her immortal, glands had formed above her fangs that released a substance not unlike GHB under the pressure of a bite. That chemical now lulled her torturer into complacency and would rob him of any memory of the attack.

She moaned as her fangs drew his blood directly into parched veins. The beat of her struggling heart strengthened. Soon the virus would go to work, repairing what damage it could until she could find another blood source.

The man grew heavy upon her. His eyelids slowly closed. His knees buckled.

Eliana was so weak she couldn't hold him upright. Retracting her fangs, she cursed as he slid off her and sank to the floor. She lay still for a moment. The peculiar symbiotic virus that had usurped her immune system would first race to repair whatever it deemed most important in terms of securing her survival. Normally that would mean healing her damaged ribs. But apparently this time it heeded her fight-or-flight reflex and began to restore strength and mobility to her legs.

Heart pounding, she struggled to sit up. The effort it took to do so infuriated her. Sending the unconscious man a scathing look, she scooted off the edge of the bed until her feet touched the floor.

Her knees immediately buckled, tumbling her down atop the man in gray.

More pain shot through her.

Eliana ground her teeth and barely succeeded in holding back a cry.

No time to rest. You have to move, she counseled herself. *Now*. She didn't know how much time she might have before one of the other mercenary doctors strode through the door.

When she braced her hands on the man and pushed herself up, her fingers brushed something hard. She glanced down. A weapon was strapped to his thigh.

Eliana hastily unholstered the firearm and held it up. She frowned. It was unlike any handgun she had ever seen. The barrel was larger, making her wonder what the hell caliber bullets it shot. It was also light, boasting no more weight than a pencil.

Was it made of plastic?

It felt like metal, but… Again she marveled at how light it was.

Shaking her head at herself, she reached up and gripped the edge of the bed. The muscles in her left arm and leg shook with effort as she forced her beleaguered body to rise. Breath emerging in pained pants, she started toward the door. Her right leg would not fully support her weight, forcing her to grip every surface she passed to help her remain upright. Each jagged limp sent pain racing up her side. But she had to move. She had to leave. She had to find a way out of this damned compound before the mercenaries realized she was awake.

Though the rest of her body struggled to function, her preternatural senses seemed to work just fine. Both her ears and nose assured her that the hallway outside this room was empty.

Pausing in the doorway, she looked left, then right. White floor. White walls. White ceiling. The hallway curved at each end instead of forming right angles.

Silently she swore. She had really hoped to find a window or two she could simply raise or break and dive out of. Now she'd have to wander around in search of a damned exit.

Hobbling out into the hallway, she performed a mental coin toss, then headed right.

As Dagon stared at the stars that stretched before them, he instead saw Eliana's pale features, frozen in death. The bridge was silent, the mood as somber as though they had just witnessed the death of one of their own. When he had returned, every face had swung toward him with excitement and hope, then had fallen when he announced that they had arrived too late.

His men appeared to be almost as despondent as he was. It said much about Eliana that just a few brief conversations could make so many care for her.

"Janek," he said, "continue searching for other communications. Let us see if we can't locate some of her friends in their escape pods."

"Yes, Commander."

Galen met his gaze. "I will continue to search as well."

Dagon nodded.

Interminable minutes passed in which he couldn't seem to quiet his thoughts.

"Commander Dagon," Maarev abruptly said in his earpiece.

Dagon tapped it. "Yes?"

"I require your assistance in the hallway outside the infirmary." Maarev's voice was tight with tension.

"What—?"

"Stop talking!" a hoarse female voice shouted in the background.

Dagon's breath halted. His heart began to hammer in his chest.

Though women served in the Segonian military, the soldiers were always separated according to gender when sent on assignment: all women on one ship, all men on another.

"Tell whoever you just spoke to that he'd better stay the hell away," the female demanded.

Maarev cleared his throat. "Again, I have a situation that requires your immediate attention."

There was only one female on this ship. And she spoke Earth English.

Eliana.

Jumping up, Dagon offered no explanation when his men started at his abrupt movement and turned to watch him run out of the bridge.

Eliana was alive. She was alive!

His boots pounded the floor as he tore down to Deck 3 and headed for the infirmary. As he swung around a curve, he saw Maarev up ahead, standing stock-still with his hands raised.

Maarev glanced over at him. "Careful," he warned in Segonian.

"Stay back!" Eliana yelled, out of sight.

Dagon halted.

"Whoever you are," she called, her voice a little rougher than when they had last spoken, "move forward slowly with your hands in the air."

Dagon raised his hands as requested and eased forward until he reached Maarev's side.

Farther down the hallway, Eliana leaned against the wall with her left arm fully extended, aiming a tronium blaster at them.

He stared. She no longer wore the bulky, too-big spacesuit. Instead, a black shirt and pants hung loosely on her fragile, far-too-thin frame, blood glistening on most of the right side of it. Her left leg was straight, holding her upright. Her right leg remained bent, only her tiny bare toes touching the floor. She'd braced her right shoulder against the wall... and had left a trail of blood along the white surface as she walked. Her narrow jaw was set, her face creased with pain. And her eyes bore an incandescent amber glow that fascinated him.

"Eliana," he stated, keeping his voice low and gentle. "I am Dagon."

Not even a hint of recognition lit her features. "Stay back or I'll shoot."

He shook his head. "We mean you no harm, Eliana."

A disbelieving huff of laughter escaped her, cut off by a grunt of pain. "Yeah, right. That's why you're armed."

He did indeed bear a holstered weapon. Every soldier on the ship did. It was standard policy so each could defend both himself and the ship if an enemy managed to board without their knowledge.

"Do you not remember me?" he asked.

"No." Her expression darkened. "Were you one of the men who tortured me?"

He frowned. "We did not torture you, Eliana. We rescued you."

She shook her head. "That's bullshit."

He shared a glance with Maarev, who gave his head the slightest shake. Dagon studied Eliana. "Where do you think you are right now?"

She glanced swiftly up and down the corridor. "A mercenary compound would be my guess."

"On Earth?"

She looked at him as if he had lost his mind. "Of course on Earth. Where the hell else would I be?"

According to his translator, mercenaries were soldiers for hire. "We aren't mercenaries. We are—"

"*One* drug exists that can leave me this weak," she snapped. "Just one. A tranquilizer. And the only men who have ever used it against us are our enemies."

"We didn't drug you, Eliana. You are weak because your injuries and lack of food and water have left you so."

She snorted. "Yeah, don't think I missed the fact that you've been starving me, too."

Dagon hesitated, unsure how to respond. She didn't appear to remember having embarked upon a space voyage.

Eliana motioned to Dagon with the blaster. "One at a time, I want you to unholster your weapons and lower them to the floor. Make any sudden movements and I'll shoot you both."

Maarev glanced at Dagon.

Dagon nodded.

Slowly Maarev removed his blaster from its holster and crouched to lower it to the floor. As soon as his friend straightened,

Dagon did the same.

"Now kick them over to me," Eliana commanded. "And make damn sure they reach me."

Dagon nudged both blasters with his foot, sending them sliding across the floor to bump against her bare toes. "Please don't fire your weapon."

"Don't give me reason to," she countered.

"If you fire your weapon and miss us—"

"I won't miss." Both her face and voice remained cold and determined.

"If you *do* miss," he continued, trying to be patient, "you will risk breaching the hull." The walls here were thick enough that she would have to fire several times to do so, but she *could* do so. And though the shields would keep the ship's atmosphere intact, repairing the hole would take time and materials he would rather not spare.

"Breach the hull?" she repeated with patent disbelief. "If you're trying to convince me we're on a ship, don't bother. All you're doing is proving I can't trust you."

"You *are* on a ship."

She sliced the blaster through the air like a knife before aiming it at them once more. "If I were on a ship, I'd know it. Even if the ship were moored, I would feel the movement of the ocean beneath us. We aren't on a ship."

She really did believe she was still on Earth.

Her gaze flickered down to the weapons at her feet, then returned to his. "Make any sudden movements and you're dead."

He nodded. "Understood."

She clamped her full pink lips together and seemed to brace herself. In slow, painful increments, she began to lower herself down to one knee. Moisture beaded on her forehead. The muscles in her cheeks twitched as she ground her teeth together. Her breathing grew ragged, air emerging in harsh puffs.

He could almost feel the agony every movement spawned from where he stood. "Eliana, please let me help you. You can trust me."

She shook her head. "Stay where you are." Keeping the weapon in her left hand aimed at them, she reached down with her right, grabbed Dagon's blaster, and clumsily tucked it in the front waist of her pants. She tried to tuck Maarev's blaster in the back waist of her pants but couldn't seem to bend her damaged arm back far enough.

With a weapon in each hand, she drew in a deep breath. Exhaled slowly. Drew in another deep breath. Exhaled slowly. Then she lunged to her feet in one swift movement. A cry escaped her, muffled by the lips she pressed together.

Drek, watching her suffer was killing him. "What can I do to earn your trust?"

"You can show me to the nearest exit without alerting your fellow mercenaries to my escape."

Dagon could neither show her to the nearest exit nor bring himself to lie to her. "I will take you where you need to go."

Nodding, she motioned to Maarev with one of her weapons. "Knock him out first."

Dagon's eyebrows flew up. "You wish me to hit him?"

"Yes."

Maarev swore foully in Segonian. "Couldn't he just tie me up?" he asked in English.

"And leave you conscious so you can babble about my escape to anyone who happens by? I don't think so."

"*Drek,*" he grumbled. "Dagon's fists are as hard as the gems on Promeii 7."

A twinkle of amusement entered Eliana's eyes. "Too bad."

Maarev turned toward Dagon with a resigned scowl. "I don't suppose you would consider faking it," he muttered in Segonian.

Dagon shook his head. "Such would not win her trust."

"Fine. Just do it."

Dagon drew his fist back and slammed it into Maarev's temple.

Maarev's head snapped back. He stumbled drunkenly. Wavered. Then his eyes rolled around in their sockets, his eyelids closed, and his knees buckled.

Dagon caught him by the shoulders and eased him down to the floor. Straightening, he looked over at Eliana.

Her lips twitched. "That's some punch you have there."

He shrugged.

Her expression hardened. "Don't try it on me."

"I would never hit you," he declared with a frown.

"Because you leave the torturing to your doctors and scientists?" Before he could respond, she motioned with the blaster. "Come closer."

He took several steps toward her and halted.

"Closer," she ordered. "And don't do anything stupid. I tend to be trigger-happy when I'm tense and would hate to damage that pretty face of yours."

She thought him attractive?

With a mental shake of his head, Dagon closed the distance between them and stopped a single stride away from her. Once again, he marveled over her diminutive size. The top of her head barely reached his armpit. And she wasn't even half his weight.

She sent him a warning glare, appearing not at all intimidated by his towering height. "Don't try anything funny."

Though the translator indicated *funny* meant *amusing*, the context of her warning suggested otherwise.

"I won't."

With an awkward hop forward, she closed the distance between them and pressed the barrel of the blaster in her left hand against his ribs. He heard the other blaster clatter to the floor behind him. Then her right hand fisted in the back of his shirt and she leaned into his side.

A little tingle scuttled through him at the feel of her slight body pressed against his. Did she remember him now?

"Get me to the nearest exit," she gritted.

No. She simply couldn't walk without assistance.

Dagon curled his left arm around shoulders so thin he could easily feel the bones beneath the flesh.

"If your hand drifts near either gun, I'll shoot you."

"Understood." He began to walk up the hallway.

Eliana limped along beside him, clinging desperately to the back of his shirt. Her breathing swiftly grew labored.

"Let me carry you," he requested.

She shook her head. "I can make it. I'm stronger than I look."

A great deal stronger, he thought with admiration. Raising his right shoulder, he tilted his head and tapped his earpiece twice. "Attention all personnel," he said in Segonian. "This is Commander Dagon. Clear all forward hallways on Decks 3 and 4 immediately and keep them clear until further notice." Again he tapped the earpiece twice.

Speakers broadcast an echo of his command all over the ship.

Eliana shoved the blaster harder into his ribs. "What did you do?"

"I cleared our path by diverting the crew elsewhere."

She shook her head. "If you're laying a trap or an ambush, you should know something."

"What?"

Those captivating amber eyes rose and met his. "If I die, I'm taking you with me."

He smiled down at her. "*Drek*, you're appealing."

Her brow furrowed. "*Drek?*"

"I believe you would call it a curse word."

"Oh. Well, you're pretty *drekking* appealing yourself, but that doesn't mean I won't shoot you."

His smile broadened into a grin.

When they reached a lift, Dagon stopped.

"What's this?" she asked, eyeing the interior suspiciously. "An elevator?"

He nodded. "We need to ascend to Deck 4."

Eyes narrowing, she let him guide her inside. As soon as the door slid closed, she moved away from him and drew the second weapon. "Get in front of me."

Dagon repositioned himself to shield her from the nonexistent ambush she expected.

The door slid open, revealing an empty hallway.

Eliana peered around him.

"See?" he said calmly. "No ambush."

Brow furrowed, she returned the second weapon to the waist of her pants and gripped the back of his shirt once more.

Dagon slowly settled his arm around her shoulders as she leaned into him again.

It took longer than usual to cover the distance to the bridge, but he didn't mind. He knew every movement caused Eliana pain and didn't want to worsen that by urging her to hasten her steps. He wished she would just let him carry her but could understand her distrust.

He pressed his palm to the reader outside the bridge, then typed in a code. As soon as the door slid open, he guided Eliana inside.

Barus glanced over at him. "Commander on the..." He gaped.

The rest of the crew turned toward the door curiously. Their eyes widened. Their jaws dropped.

Beside him, Eliana stiffened. "Shit!"

Glaring at the men present, she removed the blaster from Dagon's ribs and shoved the barrel under his chin with enough force to tilt his head up and to one side.

"Stay where you are!" she shouted. "If anyone moves, I'll kill him."

Every gaze shifted to Dagon. "Do as she says," he ordered in English so she wouldn't distrust him further.

Barus scowled. "What the *drek* is she doing?" he asked in Segonian.

"Speak English," Dagon told him, using her language, "so she won't think we're plotting her demise. She doesn't remember what happened."

Barus studied Eliana's tense, pallid features. "How much of it has she forgotten?"

"All of it. She thinks she has been captured by soldiers for hire on Earth."

"On Earth?" she repeated. "This again? Where the hell else would I be?"

Dagon motioned to the stars beyond the window. "In what you refer to as deep space."

She stopped scrutinizing every movement of his men long enough to follow his gaze. "What's that?"

"It's a window. Four months ago, you and some of your fellow Earthlings boarded a ship bound for Princess Amiriska's homeworld of Lasara."

She sent him a look that seemed to question his sanity. "Amiriska? You mean Ami? Seth's adopted daughter?"

"Yes. The ship was attacked before you could reach Lasara, and you were stranded in space. We have been racing to reach you ever since we achieved communication with you."

She shook her head. "I don't know what drug you've all been smoking, but—"

"When last we spoke, you had just over two hours of oxygen remaining in your suit and knew it would take us three weeks to reach you." He looked at his communications officer. "Janek, replay our last communication with her from the moment she asked if we could record a message for her until the end of the message she dictated for Seth."

As soon as he mentioned Seth's name, her gaze shot to his. A moment later, her bright amber eyes widened when she heard her own voice ask over the speakers, "Could you by any chance record a message from me to send Seth if I don't make it?"

Shock and confusion darkened her pallid features. Her frown deepened as her gaze darted around the bridge.

Every man present remained silent and still.

As the message she dictated for Seth began to play, she focused on the large window. Gradually she withdrew her weapon. Her fist tightened on Dagon's shirt, then fell away. Limping forward, she stared—transfixed—at the stars beyond the clear crystal. Her right hand gripped each station she passed, leaving small bloody handprints in her wake. Her left hand, still clutching the blaster, dropped to her side.

Several of his men sent worried looks his way, but Dagon only saw them on the periphery of his vision. His eyes never left Eliana.

When she stood only a few strides from the window, she stopped.

Her message to Seth ended.

The ensuing silence stretched until he could bear it no more. "Eliana?"

Without turning around, she murmured, "Do you guys, by any chance, curse or use foul language when you're upset or angry?"

"Hell yes, we do," they all chorused.

A choked sound left her. A laugh? A sob perhaps?

The blaster fell from her fingers, hitting the floor with a clatter.

Slowly she turned to face them, her movements awkward as she kept her weight off her right leg. Moisture glistened in the luminescent amber eyes that met his. "Dagon?"

"Yes, Eliana."

A smile lit her pale features. "You found me."

"I vowed I would."

A single tear trailed down her cheek. Curling both hands into fists, she thrust them up into the air, tilted her head back, and yelled, "*Woo-hoo! Ouch!*" Bending forward, she lowered her arms and gripped her bloody side. "I should *not* have done that," she said on a laugh even as she grimaced.

Dagon took a hesitant step toward her, concerned about the severity of her wounds.

Still smiling, she motioned him forward. "It's okay. I remember you now. I won't shoot you. Sorry about that."

He closed the distance between them in a few strong strides.

"And," she continued as he stopped before her, "I owe you a hug." Sliding both arms around his waist, she pressed her face to his chest and gave him a surprisingly strong squeeze.

Stunned, he tentatively wrapped his arms around her and tried to hug her back without causing her more pain. She was so much shorter than he that Dagon had to duck down a bit to rest his chin atop her head.

"You found me," she murmured, squeezing him even tighter.

"I said I would."

"I can't believe I made it."

"I can't either." And he worried she might still perish of her wounds if they did not swiftly render medical aid. He patted her back. "We should return you to the infirmary and see to your wounds."

"Oh crap," she muttered, all levity leaving her voice. Drawing away a step, she gripped the front of his shirt to help maintain her balance. "Is the infirmary the room I woke up in?"

"Yes. I don't know why Adaos released you, but…"

Unease flitted across her features. "Adaos is the man who was standing over me when I woke up?"

"Yes. He's our chief medical officer."

Biting her lip, she released him and backed away another step, then another. She cast the men around her a quick, anxious look before staring up at Dagon once more.

He frowned. "What is it?"

"When I woke up, I didn't know where I was. I forgot that memory loss could be a side effect of slipping into stasis. So I thought I was back on Earth and that mercenaries had nabbed me and were torturing me."

"Yes. That's what you said when you aimed your blaster at me."

She winced. "Yeah. Sorry about that. The thing is... I... um... might have hurt Adaos."

Dagon stared at her. She could barely stand up and was as weak as a newborn *braemon*. How much damage could she have inflicted?

He touched his earpiece. "Adaos?"

Eliana sent the crew another apprehensive glance when no response came.

"Adaos?" he called again.

She sent him a penitent look. "He isn't going to answer. I'm really sorry. I thought he was a mercenary and—"

Alarm rose. "Did you shoot him with the blaster?" Without his armor—

"No!" she blurted. "I didn't shoot him. I just... rendered him unconscious."

"How?"

She hesitated. "Did the Lasarans, in any of your communications with them, maybe mention that I'm different from most Earth women?"

"No. Different in what way?"

"That's... kind of a long story. Could I tell you later, after we—"

"Commander Dagon." Maarev's voice emerged from the bridge's speakers.

"Yes, Maarev?" He was glad his friend had regained consciousness so quickly.

"I found Adaos on the floor of the infirmary. He's alive but unresponsive."

Eliana winced and whispered, "*So,* so sorry."

Dagon shook his head, torn between concern and amusement. How the *drek* had she managed to knock a man Adaos's size out when she was so weak?

One of the crew members—Galen, he suspected—stifled a laugh.

Dagon kept his gaze on Eliana. "Can you revive him?"

"No," Maarev said.

"Yes," Eliana responded. "Or rather, I can tell *you* how to revive him. And he might be a little loopy for a while after he comes to."

"Loopy?"

"Out of it. As though he's drunk." Her brow furrowed. "Do you have that word? Drunk? Inebriated? Or maybe high?"

His lips twitched. What had she done to the medic? "Yes, we do."

Her expression cleared. "Oh. Good. Again, I'm really sorry. I thought he was my enemy."

Dagon smiled. "Let's go see to you both." Bending, he scooped her into his arms.

She cried out.

He froze. "Apologies. I didn't mean to cause you pain."

Nodding, she pressed her lips together until the worst of it passed. "It's okay. It would've hurt just as much if I'd tried to make it back to the infirmary on my own two feet. Thanks for carrying me. I appreciate it."

Dagon didn't know how she had managed to stand as long as she had. She was alarmingly light. No burden at all to carry. And he could feel the press of every rib against the arm supporting her back.

He looked over at Barus, who studied them with the same concern coupled with astonishment as the rest of the crew. "You have the bridge."

"Yes, Commander."

Jostling Eliana as little as possible, Dagon headed for the med bay.

CHAPTER 5

ELIANA TRIED NOT to cry out again when Dagon gently lowered her to sit on the edge of a bed in the ship's high-tech infirmary.

Adaos was stretched out on the bed beside hers, eyes closed, face pale. The man she had told Dagon to punch hovered beside him, one temple discolored.

When he met her gaze, she extended a hand to him. "Hi, I'm Eliana." She glanced at her hand, realized it was covered in blood, and hastily offered the left instead. "I'm sorry I made Dagon hit you. I didn't remember who you all were."

The man glanced at Dagon, then leaned across Adaos. Instead of clasping her hand, he clasped her forearm just above her wrist. "I'm Maarev. It's an honor to meet you, Eliana."

Her eyebrows flew up. An honor?

She glanced at Dagon as Maarev released her.

Dagon shrugged. "We admire strength and courage. You've demonstrated a great deal of both." He glanced around. "Where are the other medics?"

"Joral has been testing another new weapon."

Dagon grimaced. "How many were injured?"

"Only three this time."

Grunting, he picked up an electronic tablet about the size of an iPad.

A metal wand descended from the ceiling and hovered above Adaos's head. Slowly it moved down toward his feet, casting a bluish band of light over his body.

It reminded her a bit of Max's document scanner back home. "What's that?"

Dagon stared at the screen as the wand retracted. "A comprehensive diagnostic scanner. It will determine what's wrong with Adaos."

"He needs blood," Eliana told him.

Dagon looked up. "What?"

"He needs a blood transfusion."

The calm, female computer voice she had heard upon waking said something in Segonian.

Dagon frowned.

"What did she say?" Eliana asked.

"CC, render results into Earth's English language."

"Blood volume low," the computer said in English. "A transfusion is required."

Dagon looked at Adaos's body.

Maarev frowned. "I see no wounds beyond some odd markings on his neck."

"Are they bleeding?" Dagon asked.

"No."

Eliana bit her lip.

Stepping back, Dagon studied the floor. "Then why is his blood volume low? Where did it go?"

Crap.

Both men turned to Eliana.

She really didn't want to get into the whole *I need blood to survive* thing. That had never gone over well on Earth, so she had little hope that it would here. The Lasarans had been okay with it, or had at least pretended they were okay with it, but that was because Immortal Guardians like Eliana had rescued their princess and kept her safe.

Damn it. These guys had saved her life and been so great about everything. She really didn't want them to start looking at her like she was a freak.

Nibbling her lower lip, she studied Dagon. "Any chance we could speak privately?"

He turned to Maarev and jerked his head toward the doorway.

Maarev issued a half bow, then left.

The door slid closed behind him.

Dagon set the tablet aside. "CC, proceed with blood transfusion."

Eliana gawked a little as another mechanical arm lowered from the ceiling, bearing a needle connected to a tube. A clear liquid sprayed from a hole beneath the needle. Light formed a grid pattern on the bend of Adaos's arm. Then the needle unerringly found his vein and began to transfuse him. "That is so cool."

Dagon returned his attention to her. "Tell me what happened."

Dread coiled in her empty stomach. She had wondered what the Segonian commander would look like, if his face would be as appealing as his voice. Now she knew he was freaking gorgeous. Almost as tall as Seth—who stood six feet eight—he had broad shoulders and a muscled chest outlined by a sleeveless black shirt. The rest of his body was just as fit and packed with muscle. But his face…

She loved his face. Not too soft or pretty-boyish. Not too hard or fierce either. Just perfect, with a chiseled jaw, hazel eyes, and short raven hair.

Those handsome features reflected no hatred, anger, or distrust. She hoped that wouldn't change.

"Eliana?" he prompted.

She sighed. "I took it."

Confusion flitted across his face. "His blood?"

"Yes. I needed a transfusion."

Alarm entered his gaze. "You transfused yourself with his blood?"

"Yes. I'm sorry. But when I woke up—"

"You don't know if our blood is compatible with yours. Lie back." He reached for the tablet again.

"What?"

Moving to stand beside her, he rested a hand on her left shoulder and tried to ease her down. "Lie back. If our blood isn't compatible with yours, you could—"

She held up a hand and steadfastly remained upright. "It is."

He shook his head. "You don't know that."

"Yes, I do," she insisted. "The Lasarans gave me several transfusions while I was aboard their ship and told me both Yona and Segonian blood is compatible. Apparently they had some on hand from the last war games… battle… group-practice thingy the Aldebarian Alliance did."

He released her with a frown. "You required multiple transfusions?"

"Yes. The only blood that I have to steer clear of—as far as I know—is Lasaran. If I'm ever injured badly enough to be rendered unconscious, don't *ever* transfuse me with Lasaran blood. Okay?" The Lasaran medics had seemed quite confident that such would kill her.

"Okay."

Good. Hopefully that would be the end of it.

"Why did you require so many transfusions?" he asked. "Were you injured?"

"No." She worried her lower lip. "I'd prefer to keep what I'm about to tell you between you and me if possible. Some tend to not react well to it."

"All right."

She drew in a deep breath, or as deep a breath as her damaged rib cage would permit. "There are two species of mankind on Earth."

He held up a hand. "Will this be a long explanation?"

"Yes."

"Then lie back and let CC scan you while you tell it."

"Is CC a computer?"

"A computer program."

"Why do you call her CC?"

"Those are the initials of the engineer who installed the program. Lie back, please."

Eliana started to swing her legs up on the bed but stopped when pain shot up her side.

Dagon moved forward and gently eased her legs up for her, then helped her recline.

"Thank you."

He nodded, his face full of concern, and tapped the tablet. Another wand descended from the ceiling and began to sweep over her.

"All I need is another transfusion," Eliana told him. "If you give me that, I'll be fine."

Dagon looked at her as if she had just announced she was a shape-shifting unicorn that farted pixie dust. "You need a great deal more than that, Eliana."

CC spoke in her calm voice. "Skull fracture detected. Concussion detected."

"That explains the headache," Eliana muttered.

"Multiple burns and lacerations detected on face, neck, shoulder, arm. Oblique nondisplaced fracture detected in right ulna. Metal fragments embedded in musculature of same arm. Deltoid. Biceps brachii. Triceps brachii. Brachialis."

Eliana clamped her lips together as the computer continued to list what sounded like every muscle in her arm.

"Oblique nondisplaced fractures detected in seventh, eighth, ninth, and tenth ribs."

Damn it.

"Internal bruising detected. Malnutrition detected. Dehydration detected. Transverse fracture detected in right femur. Transverse fracture detected in right fibula."

Well, crap. The computer or scanner or whatever then went on to list every muscle in her leg that contained shrapnel, making it sound a *lot* worse than it was… for an Immortal Guardian anyway.

Dagon's countenance grew more grim with each pronouncement.

"Severely depleted blood volume detected. Cellular anomalies detected."

Aaaaaand there it was.

"Virus detected. Warning. Possible contagion."

Dagon stared at her.

Eliana couldn't tell if he was alarmed, appalled, or furious. "It isn't contagious," she assured him. "The virus poses *no* threat to you or your crew. The Lasarans would've never let me board the *Kandovar* if it did."

A long moment passed before he spoke. "You are certain our blood is compatible with yours and won't harm you?"

"Yes."

"*All* of our blood, not just one type?"

"Yes."

"CC, begin transfusion."

Eliana warily eyed the robotic arm that descended toward her. She would much rather just sink her fangs into a bag of blood as she had on the Lasaran ship but feared such would repulse Dagon.

A spritz of cool liquid coated the bend of her left arm before a grid pattern lit up her flesh. Eliana tensed as the needle drew closer.

A large hand gripped hers, offering comfort.

Surprised, she glanced up.

Though Dagon's expression remained hard, his touch was gentle.

"Thank you," she murmured. "I've always hated needles." Silly that something so small would bother her when psychotic vampires had been trying to cut her up and decapitate her for centuries. She felt a prick on her skin. Then blood rushed into her parched veins.

"Resume your explanation," Dagon ordered softly.

She nodded. "There are two species of mankind on Earth: humans and *gifted ones*. Most humans are unaware that *gifted ones* even exist. And those who discover it usually either try to kill us because we're different or use us for nefarious purposes."

"You are a *gifted one*?"

"Yes. That's why the computer detected cellular anomalies. It was expecting a human and got me instead. *Gifted ones* are men and women who were born with more advanced DNA."

"What is deoxyribonucleic acid?"

His translator must have only told him what DNA stood for, not its definition. "It's… the carrier of our genetic makeup, I guess you'd say."

He nodded.

"Those of us with more advanced DNA tend to have special abilities. We also tend to react differently when infected with the virus your computer detected."

"What is the nature of this virus?"

She shook her head. "It's unlike any other virus on our planet. Our doctors and scientists"—those who worked for the Immortal Guardians—"are still trying to understand it. We didn't even know where it originated until Ami's brother showed up." Anger filtered in through the pain. "Apparently the damn Gathendiens tried to do to us what they attempted to do to the Lasarans. They manufactured a virus and released it on Earth, expecting it to kill us all off so they could sweep in and take our planet's resources."

Dagon's lips tightened. "It's what they do. Gathendiens do not wage war when they find a planet they wish to claim for their own. They use bioweapons instead to exterminate any beings upon it who would oppose them."

"Well, evidently they didn't realize *gifted ones* existed, because their plan failed."

"What does this virus do to Earthlings? Is it the same one they unleashed upon the Lasarans?"

The Gathendiens had released a bioengineered virus on Lasara that had rendered almost all the females infertile. Those who were able to become pregnant had incredible difficulty carrying their babies to term. Which was why all the Earthlings who had been traveling on the *Kandovar* were female. Lisa was proof that Earth *gifted ones* and Lasarans were biologically compatible and could procreate together. And when Seth had explained the situation to ten *gifted ones*, every one of them had volunteered to journey to Lasara, eager to make a new beginning on a planet where they would no longer have to hide their differences and could fall in love and help Ami's people repopulate.

Eliana and the other female immortals had accompanied them as their guards.

"No," she told Dagon. "The virus the Gathendiens released on Earth behaves almost like a symbiotic organism instead of a virus. It conquers the body's immune system, then takes its place, performing any and all repairs needed. But it takes it a step further than that. Those infected with it heal at a vastly accelerated rate and are much stronger and faster than ordinary humans. They also don't age."

His frown deepened. "How would that be a disadvantage?"

"Well, those are actually the perks. There *are* some downsides, one of which is extreme photosensitivity."

"That word is not translating."

"Sunlight harms us. If we're exposed to it directly, our skin will almost instantly begin to redden, then will blister and worse. If we don't find shelter, it will kill us."

"Then it's fortunate you weren't floating near a sun while we searched for you."

"Yeah. That would've definitely killed me. The virus also causes progressive brain damage in humans, swiftly eroding their impulse control and driving them insane. And the more the virus works to heal us and prevent us from aging, the more blood we need. So humans infected with it—we call them vampires on Earth—hunt and kill other humans for their blood."

"When was this virus unleashed on your planet?"

"Thousands of years ago."

"How have Earthlings continued to survive?"

"The advanced DNA *gifted ones* are born with protects us from the progressive brain damage. We get the strength, the longevity, the ability to heal swiftly, and the unfortunate photosensitivity. But we keep our sanity. So under Seth's direction, we've taken it upon ourselves to hunt and slay the vampires who prey upon humans."

"You're a warrior?"

"Yes. We call ourselves Immortal Guardians. Seth, the oldest and most powerful among us, is our self-appointed leader. And so far we've managed to foil the Gathendiens' plan and keep humanity from dying out."

Dagon was silent for a moment. "How is this virus transmitted?"

"If I wanted to infect a member of your crew—which I *don't*—I would have to drain almost all of his blood, then transfuse him with my own, infecting him on a massive level."

He slid Adaos a look as the robotic arm hovering over the healer withdrew the needle from his arm and retracted. "Did you do that to Adaos?"

"No. I just took some of his blood. I'm sorry, Dagon. I was so weak I couldn't even stand up when I did it, and all I kept thinking was that I had to find enough strength to get out of here before the rest of the mercenaries realized I was awake."

He met her gaze. "How did you take his blood?"

She tightened her hold on his hand, not wanting to tell him, not wanting to see revulsion or disgust wash across his features.

"Eliana?"

She sighed. "When I transformed, the virus provided me with a means to infuse myself with someone else's blood whenever the need arises."

"What means?"

Forcing herself to meet his gaze, she drew her lips back, exposed her upper teeth, and let her fangs descend.

Dagon's face lost all expression.

She waited for him to yank his hand away from hers.

"You drink the blood?" he asked. And she heard the revulsion he tried to keep from registering on his face.

"No. The goal isn't to funnel the blood into my digestive tract. It's to get it into my circulatory system. My fangs behave like this needle." She glanced at the one in her arm. "They draw the blood directly into my veins."

He slid Adaos another look. "The marks on his neck?"

"I bit him." Eliana looked down at their clasped hands, dreading his response.

He gave her hand a squeeze and slid his thumb across her knuckles in a soft caress.

Hope rising, she looked up at him.

"I see now why you were so furious to learn the Gathendiens were responsible for the attack."

"Yeah. What *is* it with those assholes?"

He smiled. "I like this term you use to describe them."

She laughed, then winced at the sharp jab of pain it sparked. "I did warn you that I tend to have a foul mouth when I'm angry."

"Then you will fit in well on my ship."

She studied him, almost afraid to believe it. "Really?"

He nodded. "You seem surprised."

"I am. Most humans—or Earthlings—react badly to what I've just told you. Some tried to kill me when they guessed I was different."

"The Sectas warned us that Earthlings tend to hate those who are different from themselves and often react with violence."

"Sadly, it's true. But not all humans do. There are some who work with the Immortal Guardians and help us."

"As they should. You have saved your planet and prevented them from becoming extinct."

Unfortunately, most humans didn't know that. "What about your crew?" she asked uneasily. "Are you going to tell them?"

"No. I will keep your secret, Eliana. No one else needs to know."

She relaxed. "Thank you."

"Except Adaos."

Wincing, she glanced at the sleeping male. "Because I bit him?"

"Because he's our chief medical officer. I don't know how long you will be traveling with us, but—if I'm understanding correctly—you're going to need regular transfusions."

"Oh. Right." She nibbled her lip. "Do you think he's going to freak out?"

He paused as though deciphering her meaning. "I think he will be fascinated. He will keep your secret though if you ask him to."

Relief filled her. "Good."

"Would you let one of our secondary medics see to your wounds when they return?"

She shook her head. "The transfusion is all I need. I really do heal quickly. If you ran another scan, the computer would tell you my fractured ribs are already mending."

"Affirmative," CC stated. "All fractured ribs are now seventy percent healed."

Eliana stared at Dagon, then whispered, "Was she listening to everything I just said?"

Leaning closer, amusement glinting in his hazel eyes, he whispered back, "Yes."

She laughed, then winced again.

"Easy," he enjoined.

"When I'm finished with the transfusion, could I maybe shower and borrow a change of clothes? I'm going to need to sleep deeply for a bit to fully recover and would rather not do it all bloody and gross."

He smiled. "As you wish."

Eliana's transfusion took far longer than Adaos's had. It took so long, in fact, that Adaos woke halfway through it. And just as Eliana had warned, he spoke and behaved as though he were *drunk*.

Dagon was stunned, having never seen the healer inebriated before.

But it amused Eliana. "Awww. He's a happy drunk. That's so cute."

Seeing her spirits lift raised his own. She had a very expressive face. And despite his assurances, she seemed to expect rejection or disgust or the like from him. Clearly, she had been treated badly in the past.

Once Adaos *sobered up*, as Eliana put it, Dagon left her in the medic's care and returned to the bridge. His crew searched assiduously for more survivors of the attack, a task that continued to prove difficult. They were far from home in a sector of space that saw little traffic or exploration. They couldn't use the *qhov'rum* or their warp drive to cover distance more swiftly for fear they would miss something or someone.

While they searched, the crew expressed their curiosity about Eliana. All were amazed she still lived. All were equally astonished that a woman so tiny and sorely injured could take down Adaos, and they would probably tease him about it for months.

"Commander Dagon?" Adaos spoke in his earpiece.

"Yes."

"Eliana is resting."

"Did you allow her to use the cleansing unit?" She had called it a shower.

"Yes. I also provided her with healing garments."

Dagon was a little surprised they had any of those on board. Healing garments were simple shirts and pants that opened easily to provide healers with access to wounds. Usually injured warriors just rested naked under a cover, their years of training having long since robbed them of any modesty.

"Good."

"The amount of blood she required astonished me," the healer admitted. "Even a warrior thrice her weight who has lost most of his own would not require so much. I can't wait to learn more about this virus she harbors and her advanced DNA. If I could—"

"You will not turn her into an experiment or a creature to study, Adaos," he ordered sternly. "And you will say or do nothing to make her feel like an aberration. If you do, you'll answer to me."

Eliana had demonstrated admirable strength and courage, but that didn't mean she lacked vulnerabilities. Dagon didn't want Adaos to pounce with questions and requests for tests, making her feel like the oddity the humans on Earth had labeled her.

Only hearing his end of the communication, the crewmen on the bridge cast him uncertain looks.

"Of course," Adaos agreed. "Perhaps I could just take a sample of her blood while she sleeps?"

"You will do nothing without her permission."

"Yes, Commander," the medic agreed, resignation replacing the excitement that had colored his words.

"Is there anything else?"

Adaos sighed. "She asked about the body we found near her."

"You told her about that?"

"I didn't have to. It was in Med Bay when she awoke and thought herself back on Earth. After you left, she drew the obvious conclusion and asked to see it. I thought it inadvisable, but she persisted."

"And?"

"It was the Lasaran engineer Ganix, the man she believes saved her life by putting her in the suit."

Dagon swore. "Was she distraught?"

"Yes, but she made a valiant attempt to hide it and merely asked if she could sleep for a time."

She would've learned the truth eventually. Dagon just wished he could've spared her that. "Notify me when she awakens."

"Yes, Commander."

Rising, he nodded at Barus. "You have the bridge." Might as well get some rest while Eliana slept.

"Yes, Commander."

Dagon headed for his quarters. When he entered, some of the tension drained from his shoulders. Always tidy, the room felt quite large. "Lower bed."

One wall shifted, and his big bed folded down. Ducking into the adjoining lav, he used the facilities and the cleansing unit. He smiled. Or the *shower* as Eliana referred to it.

He couldn't stop thinking about her. She was such a curious combination of strength and fragility, of fortitude and vulnerability.

Once soldiers completed their training and were assigned to ships, male and female Segonians in the military had little opportunity to interact with each other outside of war games. Consequently, he usually only encountered civilian Segonian women when home on leave. During the years in which he had worked so hard to climb the ranks, most of those women had avoided him. Soldiers often spent long periods in space and generally weren't considered the best candidates for lifemates. So Dagon's fellow soldiers were more apt to seek companionship on pleasure stations than they were to court a potential wife.

There had always been women on Segonia who found danger enticing and offered themselves to rough-around-the-edges soldiers. The fiercer the soldier's reputation, the more he lured such women. And Dagon's reputation was fierce. But none of those who had coaxed him to their bed had appealed to him enough to want to see them again afterward.

He wondered idly if women in the Segonian military experienced the same difficulties. In the rare instances he *did* interact with female soldiers, they tended to behave more like competitors than someone searching for a potential mate.

Eliana treated Dagon like no other woman had in the past. She treated him like a friend.

Would that change after she recovered from her injuries?

"Dim the lights. Night mode."

The bright lights overhead weakened, leaving him just enough illumination to make out a path to his bed. Sprawling naked on it, he tried and failed to clear his racing thoughts long enough to seek sleep.

"Play 'Eliana.'"

Eliana's sultry voice arose, singing her favorite song, "At Last."

Dagon sighed as peace and contentment suffused him. She might not know it, but Eliana had sung him to sleep every night since she had first crooned that tune.

He smiled as fatigue crept up on him.

Perhaps he could coax her into singing it to him in person.

"Commander Dagon."

He jerked awake. Blinking gritty eyes, he stared up at the dark ceiling. Silence had replaced Eliana's voice, indicating he had unknowingly drifted off. He grabbed the earpiece he'd left on the shelf above the bed. "What?"

"Commander Tiran is hailing us."

How long had he slept?

Dagon peered groggily at the time display across the room and groaned. Not long enough. "Give me a few minutes."

"Yes, sir."

After using the lav and donning his uniform, he headed for his private office and sank into the chair behind his desk.

"Put him through," he commanded Janek.

"Yes, Commander."

Tiran's face appeared. "Dagon."

"Tiran. I'm glad you contacted me. I have good news."

The Lasaran's grim countenance didn't change. "We could use some."

That didn't bode well. "We retrieved Eliana. She is alive and recovering from her injuries."

Tiran's eyes widened. "She survived until you reached her?"

"Yes."

"Was she in an escape pod?"

"No. She was in a suit as she said. She suffered grievous wounds and was a little confused when she awoke. But my chief medical officer has assured me she is healing swiftly."

"Amazing. I'm sure her commanding officer will be relieved to hear it."

Dagon nodded. "What troubles you?"

"A Soturi ship found more wreckage of the *Kandovar*. They've recovered the bodies of multiple Yona warriors and some Lasaran engineers who must have remained on the ship until the end."

No doubt the engineers had hoped to restore power to the shields and give the Lasaran and Yona soldiers more time to fight. Cobus and his engineering crew here on the *Ranasura* would've done the same.

Which reminded Dagon of Ganix. "I'm afraid we recovered the body of one of your engineers as well. Chief Engineer Ganix. He's the one Eliana credits with getting her into a suit before the ship broke apart."

Nodding, Tiran drew a hand down over his grim face. "Send me confirmation once your medic acquires it."

"I will."

Tiran shook his head. "There's more. The Soturi also found the remains of several fighter craft."

"No survivors?"

"None."

"Were there no pods nearby?"

"One. But it was empty. The Soturi commander said it looked as though the hatch had been forced open from the outside."

Dagon frowned. "Any signs that it was occupied?"

"Yes. The Soturis' chief medical officer ran scans and identified the former occupant as one of the men found floating near the wreckage. It appears someone pried him out of the pod."

"*Drek*. Do you think the Gathendiens did it?"

"That is our assumption."

"Then they *are* searching for the Earth women." And had apparently jettisoned the Lasaran male for not being who they wanted.

"Such was our conclusion as well."

Dagon tapped the small screen embedded in the surface of his desk. "Janek."

"Yes, Commander?"

"Apply the heaviest encryption we have to my communication with Commander Tiran, then check for any possible unauthorized data transfers."

"I've already applied the encryption, Commander, and will monitor it for signs of outside attempts to access it."

"Thank you."

Tiran frowned. "What are you thinking?"

Dagon shook his head. "I'm thinking the Gathendiens might have breached your security."

"Impossible."

"It's the only explanation, Tiran. If the Gathendiens wanted an Earthling, they could have abducted any of the billions who currently inhabit the planet without fearing detection or retaliation. Instead, they targeted these particular Earthlings—the ones aboard a heavily armed Lasaran battleship."

"Why would they do that? Why are these Earthlings so

important to them? Why would the Gathendiens risk angering the entire Aldebarian Alliance like this?"

Because they knew the Earthlings on board were different, like Eliana. Because the Gathendiens knew they needed to get their hands on *gifted one* Earthlings so they could find a virus that would kill them, too. Wipe out the *gifted ones* and Immortal Guardians and there would be no one left to keep the first virus from driving every Earthling insane and prevent them from swiftly killing each other and precipitating their own extinction.

The planet would then be the Gathendiens' for the taking.

But Dagon couldn't tell Tiran that without betraying Eliana's confidence. "Scour your communications and look for any possible intrusions. Advise the other Lasaran commanders to do the same as well as the communications officers on your homeworld. The Gathendiens had to have known the Earthlings were on board the *Kandovar*." Even more alarming, they had to have known these were no ordinary Earthlings.

Tiran nodded. "We will search all systems for a security breach."

The screen went blank. Dagon leaned back in his chair to ponder the issue a moment, then left his office and made his way down to the infirmary.

Adaos looked up when he entered.

Eliana lay curled on her side, covered by a sheet. Though dark wavy tresses hid much of her face, she appeared to be sleeping deeply.

"She still rests," Adaos murmured.

"Her injuries?"

"All damage to her skeletal system has healed completely. Some of the damage to her musculature and skin has as well. The damage to her organs is still repairing."

"Did you give her a *silna* to accelerate her healing?" Even with the serum, it would take Segonian warriors longer to recuperate from such wounds.

Adaos shook his head. "A *silna* wasn't necessary. Her ability to repair and regenerate rivals that of the Sectas with their nanodocs."

"Amazing." Dagon crouched next to the bed. Reaching out, he gently drew the hair back from Eliana's face and tucked it behind her ear. "She's too thin," he whispered, noting the prominent cheekbones. Though the burns had healed, some of the cuts and bruising remained. "Did you provide her with sustenance before she fell asleep?"

"Yes. I also fed her fluids and nutrition intravenously."

"She doesn't like needles."

"She slept through it."

Eliana's eyelashes fluttered. Her lids rose, revealing deep brown eyes bereft of the amber glow. She studied him a moment, then offered him a sleepy smile. One small hand burrowed out from under the covers and stretched toward him. Soft fingers came to rest on his cheek and stroked the stubble there. "Dagon."

Warmth unfurled in his chest at the tender touch. His pulse picked up its pace. "Eliana."

She sighed. Her eyes closed. Her hand drooped, her fingers sliding down his jaw.

Dagon caught it, marveling over how small her hand was compared to his. He wanted to remain where he was, smoothing his thumb across the pale flesh of her knuckles as he watched her sleep, but was vividly aware of Adaos's curious scrutiny.

Tucking her hand beneath the sheet, he rose. "I want you to remove any and all information you and CC have gathered about her genetic makeup and her healing ability from the ship's records. You may transfer it to a heavily encrypted data tablet, but it must remain unconnected to the primary records."

Adaos frowned. "You don't wish Command to know about her?"

"I don't wish the *Gathendiens* to know about her. I believe they have breached Lasaran communications. Until we know how and when, we must assume they will attempt to do the same with other Alliance members."

His friend's gaze sharpened. "Why is she so important to them, Dagon?"

"Because she and the other Earthlings who traveled with her are the key to Gathendiens discovering why a virus they released on Earth long ago failed. If the Gathendiens get their hands on the Earth women, they can remedy their mistake and render all Earthlings extinct."

Swearing, Adaos turned to the primary medical console. "I will erase all information regarding her from the system."

Dagon turned to leave. "I'll have Janek erase all our verbal communications with her as well." All except the copy Dagon kept on his personal data pad.

The Gathendiens wouldn't take the time to search every individual tablet, because they would first have to *obtain* those tablets.

And Dagon would make damned sure that didn't happen.

CHAPTER 6

DAGON BROODED IN his chair on the bridge, endless stars stretching before him.

Janek had purged all records of their communications with Eliana. He had also carefully examined their comm network and found no indication that the Gathendiens had either listened to or intercepted any communications relating to the Earth women or the *Kandovar*.

Tiran found no security breaches on his end either, something Dagon found worrisome.

How else might the Gathendiens have learned about the special Earthlings?

"Is this it?"

Dagon sat up straighter when Eliana's voice filled the bridge.

"No," Adaos responded.

"What does it do?"

"It opens communications with the bridge."

"I don't want to open communications. I want to open the door. What about this one?"

"No."

"This one?"

"Pressing buttons indiscriminately will not open the door, Eliana."

"Well, you're taking too long, and patience has never been my strong suit. What about this one?"

"You do *not* want to press that one," Adaos intoned darkly.

A long pause ensued.

"Actually, I kinda do," she countered impishly.

Dagon smiled.

Several crewmen chuckled.

"If you would but step aside," Adaos said in long-suffering tones, "I will open the door for you."

"I need to learn how to do it myself."

"Why?"

"So I won't have to drag you up here every time I want to hang out with Dagon and the guys."

"That's *Commander* Dagon. And you need security clearance for that."

"Okay. How do I get that?"

Dagon tapped several commands into the console on the arm of his chair. "Security clearance granted," he announced. "Press your palm to the lock, Eliana."

A second later, the door slid up.

Eliana stood on the other side of it, Adaos looming behind her.

She smiled as she looked up at the slot through which the door had vanished. "That is so cool. The doors on the *Kandovar* did that, too."

Dagon rose, drawing her gaze.

Her brown eyes brightened with pleasure. "Hi."

He started toward her but slowed to a stunned halt. *Drek*. She was beautiful.

During the two days she had slept, her wounds had healed completely, leaving her skin pale and perfect. The weight she had lost had been restored, eradicating the gauntness and prominent bones. A uniform nearly identical to his graced her alluring form. Tight black trousers encased shapely legs and nicely rounded hips. A sleeveless black shirt like his own left slender arms bare and hugged full breasts.

His eyes fastened on her chest. Segonian women rarely had breasts that size. Their hips were not as round either. Both accentuated a waist so narrow he could easily span it with his hands.

Striding forward, Eliana held her arms out to the side and said, "Ta-da! I'm awake!"

He smiled. "So I see." Even her hair was lovely. No longer lank, it flowed down her back to her waist in thick, shining waves. "You are recovered?"

Smiling, she strolled toward him.

His heart hammered in his chest. The way she walked... Strong and confident, yet arousingly sensual. It was all he could do to keep his body from responding in ways his uniform would not conceal.

"I'm recovered," she declared. "And wonderfully clean. You would not *believe* how good that shower felt after being bloody and gross for a whole month."

Don't imagine her naked. Don't imagine her naked.

Adaos entered behind her. "If she had stayed in the cleansing unit any longer, the rest of us would've had to do without."

Dismay widened her big brown eyes. "Oh crap. I forgot you probably have a limited supply of—"

Dagon waved off her concern. "He jests. We have plenty of water."

She narrowed her eyes at Adaos.

Adaos offered her a crooked grin and shrugged.

Chuckling, Eliana returned her attention to Dagon. "So? What do you think?" She motioned to her new clothing. "Adaos showed me the coolest thing. It's this room the size of a phone booth. You step in, lasers shine all over you and take your measurements. Then a few minutes later, it flings folded clothing at you."

He laughed at her description of their uniform generator. "Making new uniforms on demand is more efficient than storing boxes of multiple sizes."

"I bet it is. Adaos kept trying to steer me toward a gray uniform, but I'm more comfortable in black. Is that okay?"

Black was usually reserved for soldiers in the Segonian military, but it complemented her fair skin and dark hair so well that he was willing to overlook it. "Yes. It suits you." And technically speaking, she *was* a soldier... just not in the Segonian military.

"Thank you." She glanced at the rest of the bridge crew and tossed the men a wave. "Hi, guys."

They smiled and returned her greeting.

She turned to his communications officer. "Are you Janek?"

He stood. "I am."

Eliana crossed to him and offered her hand. "Thank you so much for opening communications with me. You saved my life. And listening to you guys when we weren't speaking kept me sane."

He clasped her forearm. "I'm glad we were able to rescue you, Earthling."

Laughing, she released him and glanced over at the navigations officer. "Are you Galen?"

Galen's eyebrows rose. "Yes. How did you know?"

"I recognized your voice when you said hello." Crossing to him, she extended her hand. "Thank you for finding me."

Galen stood and grasped her forearm. "I'm happy I was able to do so."

A disturbing... something... crept through Dagon as he watched her smile up at the other men. He didn't like her touching them. Didn't like them smiling down at her. And definitely did not like the appreciation in the gazes they swept over her form.

She turned to Dagon. "And *you*..." Closing the distance between them, she stopped a breath away. "Thank you for not giving up on me."

"I vowed I wouldn't."

She shook her head. "Most men would've assumed I was dead when I stopped responding."

He *had* thought her dead when she'd stopped responding. "I hoped you would achieve the unachievable."

Smiling, she once more slid her arms around his waist, pressed her face to his chest, and hugged him tight. "Thank you so much, Dagon."

This time he didn't hesitate to close his arms around her. Though her head still didn't even reach his shoulder despite her standing straighter, her form was strong now, fuller, and felt far too good against his own.

"You're welcome." That was the correct response in Earth English, wasn't it?

"Wow," she said in a breathy voice. "You smell really good."

His cursed body instantly responded.

His men stared.

Eliana stiffened. Tilting her head back, she glanced up at him.

Pink blossomed in her cheeks. "I'm sorry. That was incredibly inappropriate. I can't believe I just said that." Lowering her arms, she backed away and cleared her throat. "Blame it on… I don't know. Space sickness. Is that a thing? Space sickness? From spending too much time floating in space?"

"Okay," he said slowly, borrowing her word and allowing her the cover.

His men grinned.

"So." She clasped her hands together with another smile, eager—it would seem—to change the subject. "Now that I'm all better, let's talk weapons."

Willing his body to cool down, Dagon stared at her. "Weapons?"

"Yes." She once more motioned to her shapely form. "Mine are gone, and I feel really naked without them."

Don't imagine her naked.

Drek. He couldn't help it. He imagined her naked.

So did his men, judging by their expressions.

Dagon shot them all a glare.

Most hastily returned their attention to the consoles before them.

Janek and Galen continued to watch Dagon and Eliana, smiles toying with the edges of their lips.

"Do you by any chance have an armorer or weaponsmith on board?" Eliana asked hopefully.

"Yes."

"Excellent."

"He can supply you with blasters and—"

"Actually, I'm more of a blades kind of gal."

He studied her. "A blade will not protect you from a blaster."

"Is there a metal that can repel blasterfire?"

"Yes."

"Then blades can and *will* protect me from a blaster if your armorer fashions them out of that metal," she replied confidently.

Dagon wasn't sure how to respond. An enemy could fire multiple rounds in the time it would take her to swing a single blade in her own defense.

"Trust me," she said. "I know what I'm doing."

He wasn't sure she did. This was, after all, her first foray into space and the company of alien races that possessed technology superior to that found on Earth.

"I've done things you thought I couldn't before, right?" she asked.

"Right."

"Then let's go talk to your armorer."

With a mental shrug, Dagon escorted her from the bridge.

They strode down the corridor and around a curve, where they came upon two crew members heading their way. Both men stopped midstep and stared.

Eliana smiled. When she and Dagon came abreast of the men, she halted and offered her hand. "Hi. I'm Eliana."

Oglin glanced at Dagon, then clasped her forearm. "I'm Oglin." He performed a slight bow. "It's an honor to meet you, Eliana."

She shook her head. "The honor is mine."

Oglin's eyes widened. Maintenance crew members were not as highly valued as others in Segonian society. High-ranking members of the military, medics, educators, and engineers were offered the greatest respect while the contributions of the maintenance crews went largely unremarked.

When Oglin released her, Eliana offered her hand to the other crewman.

The younger man eagerly clasped her forearm. "I'm Brundil. And I, too, am honored to meet you, Eliana."

Smiling, she waved her free hand. "You guys saved *me*, not the other way around. The honor is all mine."

Brundil shook his head. "We didn't save you. We're only members of the maintenance crew."

She propped her hands on her hips and shrugged. "Hey, everyone has a role to play. The maintenance crew keeps the ship in tip-top condition, right?"

Oglin exchanged a glance with Brundil.

Brundil nodded. "Yes."

"Well, Dagon might not have reached me in time if you hadn't. So, again, thank you both for saving me."

Brundil puffed out his chest with pride and smiled. "I'm glad we could be of service."

Dagon and Eliana resumed their journey.

He stared down at her.

A smile still flirting with the corners of her lips, she glanced up at him. "What?"

He shook his head. "Nothing. This way." He led her to the nearest lift.

The door slid open, revealing three more men. One wore the garb of an engineer. The other two were pilots. All stared in fascination at the petite Earth female.

Dagon cleared his throat.

The men hastily moved back to allow them entrance, offering their commander gruff greetings.

As soon as the doors slid closed, Eliana whirled to face them. "Hi. I'm Eliana." She thrust out her hand.

The soldier closest to her blinked, then clasped her forearm. "I'm Nakhob."

"Thank you for saving me, Nakhob."

He shook his head. "Maarev was the one who retrieved you, not I."

Eliana looked up at Dagon.

"Maarev is the soldier who collected you and brought you on board," he explained.

"Oh. Well, Maarev may have brought me on board, but—as far as I'm concerned—everyone on this ship saved me." She offered her hand to the next soldier. "Hi. It's nice to meet you. You are…?"

The soldier clasped her arm. "Tugev. It's an honor to meet you, *ni'má*."

"What does *ni'má* mean?"

Dagon spoke. "It's a title used in place of a name to address a woman. *Ni'má* is used for unbonded women. *Na'má* is used for bonded women. It's the female equivalent of *sir*."

"Oh. Like *miss* or *ma'am*. Okay." She extended her hand to the engineer. "Hi. I'm Eliana."

The engineer smiled, clasped her arm, and introduced himself. And so it went… all the way to the armory. Every time they encountered others, Eliana greeted them with a smile, introduced herself, and thanked them for saving her, leaving many staring after her with surprised, pleased, and in some cases, besotted looks.

Amusement sifted through Dagon, as did admiration. He could find no indication of subterfuge, no hint that she merely spouted empty flattery. Eliana seemed to genuinely care about each and every man she met—no matter their hierarchical status—and was thankful for their contributions to her rescue.

She also appeared to be completely unfazed and unconcerned by the fact that every man she encountered towered over her.

After greeting three more soldiers, she grinned up at Dagon. "They sure grow 'em big out here in space."

He laughed. "You're quite small compared to Segonians."

"Even the women?"

He nodded. "Most female Segonians are close or equal in height to the males."

"I haven't encountered any females yet."

"You won't. Not on this ship. The *Ranasura* has an all-male crew."

She frowned. "Women aren't allowed to serve in your military?" Her tone left no doubt of her disapproval.

"Women *are* allowed to serve and are offered the same respect as their male counterparts. But when outfitting ships, our military separates soldiers according to gender."

"So somewhere there's a ship like this one with an all-female crew?"

"Yes. Several."

"Female commanders? Female soldiers? Female engineers?"

"Yes."

"Do the women get paid as much as the men do?"

Puzzled by the odd query, he answered, "Of course."

"Are they really offered the same respect?"

"Certainly." Why wouldn't they be?

Her frown receded, leaving a thoughtful expression. "The separation by gender thing is weird. But I like the equal-respect, equal-pay thing."

"You don't have that on Earth?"

"No. That's actually pretty rare where I come from."

A statement which confirmed more of the negative things he'd read in the Sectas' Earth research. "Yet you are a soldier."

She nodded. "In a unique army very few people on Earth know

about. And my brethren all respect me and treat me as an equal." She smiled wryly. "Mostly. Some of them *do* tend to be more protective of me than they are of the other guys… kind of like they would be if I were their younger sister."

Dagon could understand that. He felt *very* protective of her. But he sure as *srul* didn't think of her as a sister.

The weaponsmith's workspace was located on the same floor as the armory and the training facilities. The latter included large rooms with high ceilings in which multiple men could train and exercise as well as smaller rooms in which soldiers could train in fewer numbers.

Unless the occupants desired solitude, they left the doors open.

As Dagon escorted Eliana down the long hallway, her steps slowed. Her head swiveled from side to side while she peered at the occupants of the rooms they passed.

Suddenly her steps halted. Her eyes widened. Backtracking, she planted her petite form in the doorway of one of the smaller combat training rooms. Several moments passed as she stared raptly at whatever took place within.

Dagon moved to stand behind her, wondering what had captured her interest.

Maarev stood inside. To anyone unfamiliar with Segonians, it would appear he was alone, swinging a staff in a series of exercises. But Dagon knew better. Maarev battled two soldiers in full camouflage.

Eliana swung around to gape up at him. "You have invisible soldiers?"

Shock tore through him. How had she known?

Segonians were one of the least threatened species and most dreaded foes in the known universe because they could make themselves virtually invisible to anyone not wearing infrared goggles. Even those who had thought themselves clever in the past by using infrared technology to view them while attacking had learned a hard lesson when the Segonians had simply waited until their enemy's guard was down and the infrared technology not handy, then delivered devastating retaliation. Eliana should not have known there was anyone else in the room with Maarev.

A grunt broke the silence, followed by a series of thuds.

They looked toward the men.

Maarev turned to face them, staff in hand.

Two other soldiers—Liden and Efren—flickered into view as they abandoned their camouflage. Liden bent forward and grabbed the ribs Maarev must have struck when Eliana's voice distracted him. Efren picked himself up off the floor with a groan.

As all three men focused on Eliana, their faces lit with surprise.

Dagon shifted to stand beside her so he could read her expression.

A wide grin flashed straight white teeth as excitement bloomed in her pretty features. "That is *so* cool!" She strode forward, reaching Efren first. "How did you do that? How did you just disappear and reappear like that? You never left the room, so I know you didn't teleport."

Efren sent Dagon a questioning look. Generally speaking, Segonians only revealed their abilities to members of the Aldebarian Alliance. Most others didn't know how exactly the Segonians did what they could do and thought it all some sort of deeply classified technology.

"I'm sorry," she said. "That was rude of me. Hi." She thrust out her hand. "I'm Eliana."

Efren clasped her arm and offered her a slight bow. "I'm Efren. It's an honor to meet you."

As she had with all the others, Eliana shook her head and insisted the honor was hers. She moved on to Liden. "Hi. I'm Eliana."

He straightened with a wince and clasped her forearm. "Liden."

With her free hand, she clapped him on the back much as a fellow soldier would. "Sorry about that. He probably wouldn't have nailed you like that if I hadn't interrupted."

Maarev grunted. "I would have nailed him regardless," he intoned, borrowing her term.

She laughed. "You *do* appear to have mad skills. Hi, Maarev."

"Hello, Eliana. It's good to see you have recovered."

"Good to see you've recovered, too. Again, I apologize for making Dagon hit you." Her smiled faltered. "Wait." She glanced at Dagon. "Didn't Nakhob say Maarev was the one who retrieved me and brought me on board?"

He nodded.

She swung back to Maarev. "Oh wow. Thank you so much. I would totally hug you right now, but I think I shocked some people when I hugged Dagon."

Maarev stared. "Is my translator correct in defining a hug as an embrace?"

"Yes."

He slid Dagon a look. "You hugged Commander Dagon?"

"Twice actually."

Efren gaped.

Liden grinned and held out his arms. "*I* helped search for you. *I'll* take a hug."

Dagon scowled. "No, you won't."

Liden lowered his arms and sighed. "No, I won't."

Laughing, Eliana returned to Dagon's side. "Can all your soldiers go invisible like that?"

"Yes." Since she would be traveling with them for an indeterminate length of time, she would find out eventually even if he didn't tell her. And instinct led him to trust her with the information since she had trusted him with secrets of her own.

"Will you tell me how?"

"Perhaps after we visit the armorer."

"Okay." She tossed his soldiers a wave. "Nice meeting you."

Their responses followed the two of them out into the hallway.

Dagon studied her, trying to ignore the unconsciously smooth sway of her hips and focus instead on the myriad of questions that mentally bombarded him.

She glanced up and caught him staring. "What?"

"You aren't at all intimidated by my soldiers, are you?"

"No. Should I be?"

"They are all fierce warriors."

She grinned. "I am, too."

Had she been another, he might have laughed. She seemed so small and delicate. But he knew what she had been through, what she had suffered and survived. He'd read the accounts of the Lasarans who credited her with saving their lives. And she had incapacitated Adaos while so weak she could barely stand.

He thought fierce an apt description for her. "They are also far taller than you and more than twice your weight," he pointed out. "You don't find that disconcerting?"

She snorted. "Hell no. I'm barely nipple high when I stand next to Seth. Same with David and Zach. Pretty much all my male brethren are taller than the average Earthling." Craning her neck, she peered into another training room that hosted five soldiers engaging in battle.

Curiosity bombarded him. "How did you know he wasn't alone?"

"Who?"

"Maarev. How did you know he wasn't alone in the training room?"

She winked up at him. "I'll tell you after I spar with some of your men. I love it when opponents underestimate me."

He smiled. "I imagine *many* underestimate you. Despite the confidence with which you comport yourself, you appear very fragile."

"But I kick a *lot* of ass," she boasted with a grin.

He laughed. "I'm sure you do." And he looked forward to watching her kick it.

I love his laugh, Eliana thought. More of a chuckle, it rumbled through her like thunder. And his smile…

Dagon had a great smile. It made an already handsome face even more so.

It also made her heart flutter in her chest and butterflies tickle her belly. She had already been drawn to him before they met. While she'd been out there floating in space, unable to do a damn thing but hunger and thirst and try to ignore the constant pain that battered her, Dagon's voice was the one she had wanted to hear most. *His* had been the voice that had soothed and distracted her, tempering her fear.

Though she had tried to make light of it, she had been in agony the first time she'd met him face-to-face. Then she'd been anxious while explaining how she differed from ordinary humans. So she'd only absently noted that he was attractive.

Now, however, with his arm occasionally brushing her shoulder as they strode down the corridor, his enticing scent teasing her, and his hazel eyes sparkling with mirth… She found herself as besotted with him as her former hunting partner Nick had been with the single mom who lived next door.

Dagon stood roughly six feet five inches tall and had broad, muscled shoulders clearly defined by the tight black shirt he wore. It reminded her a little of a mock turtleneck T-shirt with an insignia on the neckline that she guessed indicated his rank as commander. She'd seen different insignias on a few other soldiers' shirts, but none had been as fancy as his. Personnel not of the soldier variety instead wore uniforms of various colors that denoted their divisions with their titles embossed on their chest near the right shoulder.

She snuck another surreptitious glance at the imposing man beside her. His hair was black and cropped short. Thick, straight strands shone beneath the overhead lights, sparking fantasies of combing her fingers through his hair to see if it was as soft as it looked. His skin bore a nice tan, as if it were August and he'd spent every day of summer at the beach, but it held a bronzish hue when she looked closer that set him apart from humans. Straight dark brows hovered above greenish-brown eyes that bespoke amusement. He had a strong jaw, straight nose, and the shadow of stubble, all of which tipped him away from pretty boy and more toward ruggedly handsome.

Dagon's shirt clung to a thick chest and left his muscled arms bare. His black trousers resembled the cargo pants Immortal Guardians favored on Earth but had fewer pockets. They also molded to his muscled thighs with every step he took.

Even the way he walked appealed to her—long, strong, powerful strides, his big boots thudding like a drumbeat on the floor. Though he tempered his steps a bit to accommodate her shorter legs, she liked that Dagon didn't slow to a crawl as if she were a child he thought couldn't keep up.

He paused and motioned for her to enter a room near the next curve in the hallway.

Smiling, she stepped through the doorway. Her eyes widened as she slowed to a halt. Much larger than she'd expected, the room appeared to be divided into two sections. On the right, several men sat at tables about the size one might find in an office cubicle on Earth, polishing and servicing weapons. On the left, one man stood alone with his back to them at a U-shaped workspace that boasted a plethora of electronic equipment and tools she couldn't identify.

The wall beyond him displayed dozens of weapons, each different from the previous one. She noted multiple firearms. Some looked like they could take down a damn dinosaur. That or blow up a ship. Others were so small and compact that even Eliana could hide them in her clothes with none the wiser. There were also staffs with a wide variety of lengths and tips. Most were plain. A few, however, swirled with beautifully engraved designs. A variety of maces graced the wall as well, and… She practically salivated when her gaze landed upon the blades—long, short, straight, curved, and everything in between.

She looked up at Dagon, who waited patiently beside her while she looked her fill. "I'll have one of everything, please," she said, her voice full of awe.

He threw his head back and laughed.

All heads turned. Eyes widened. The seated men set down their weapons and rose.

Eliana didn't know if it was because their commander had entered the room, if it was a chivalrous thing for her, or if they were simply shocked to find a woman in their midst.

The solitary man on the left turned with a frown that smoothed out the instant he spotted them. Abandoning whatever he toiled over, he removed a pair of white gloves, tossed them on the table, and headed their way. "Commander Dagon."

Dagon nodded. "Joral."

Joral's curious gaze settled upon Eliana. He was older than Dagon, his short dark hair graying at the temples, and slimmer of build beneath the leathery-looking apron he wore. Nevertheless, his shoulders and arms bore plenty of muscle, leaving her no doubt that he personally tested each weapon he created.

Dagon rested a hand on Eliana's back, setting her pulse to racing. "This is Eliana of Earth. Eliana, this is Joral, our chief weapons designer."

She extended her hand to the man. "Hi. It's so nice to meet you."

Joral's eyebrows rose as he grasped her forearm. "I'm honored to meet you, Eliana."

When he released her arm, she smiled and motioned to the room around them. "I have to tell you… this is my new favorite place."

Dagon chuckled. "Eliana is a warrior on her world and—like all soldiers—holds a deep appreciation for fine weaponry."

Joral's face lit with amusement, little creases appearing at the corners of his eyes. "Then you are very welcome here."

She grinned. "Let's see if you're still saying that after a day or two of bumping into me every time you turn around."

His smile broadened.

Eliana turned to the other men, who watched with avid interest, and offered them a wave. "Hi. I'm Eliana. Thank you all for coming to my rescue."

The men shared startled looks, then offered half bows and murmured responses.

Eliana turned back to Joral. "So, Joral." She hesitated. "May I call you Joral?" She wasn't sure what the social protocol was in Segonian society or their military.

"You may."

"Excellent. So, Joral… I lost my weapons in the battle with the Gathendiens and feel totally naked without them."

Joral's gaze dropped to her chest, then hastily returned to her face. "I would be pleased to outfit you with new weapons, Eliana." He motioned for her to join him as he strolled toward his workspace. "Is there anything in particular you have in mind?"

"Well… what I *really* want is one of those." She pointed to the wall of weapons.

"Which weapon are you pointing to?" he asked, following her gaze.

"All of them. I want a wall just like that in whatever room I end up staying in."

He stopped and cast her a look of stunned disbelief.

Dagon laughed.

Eliana did, too, then shrugged. "What can I say? I love weapons."

Joral chuckled.

"That's what I *want*," she continued, "but not necessarily what I need, so I can narrow it down if you'd like."

"I would appreciate that." Still smiling, Joral bypassed his workspace and guided her to the wall. "Perhaps we could start with a tronium blaster." He reached up and plucked a blaster about the size of a 9mm off the wall. "This T-23 would suit you well."

"Dagon suggested blasters, too, but I'm more of a blades kind of gal."

Joral frowned. "Blades might have sufficed on Earth, but out here blasters are far more efficient."

"If I have to carry a blaster to put everyone's mind at ease, I will. But I'd like the rest of my weapons to be blades."

Joral looked over her shoulder.

Eliana did, too.

Dagon crossed his arms over his chest. "She would like you to fashion her some blades made from *mlathnon* or *alavinin*."

Eliana nodded. "Any metal that can repel blasterfire."

"With handles that will absorb stunners instead of serving as conductors," Dagon added.

Eliana didn't know much about stunners but nodded.

Joral stared at her. "Blades cannot defend you from blasterfire."

"They can if you make them out of whatever metal Dagon just named."

Joral again glanced at his commander.

Dagon shrugged. "We didn't think she could survive until we reached her, yet she did."

Eliana wanted to hug him again because she knew he still thought she could not defeat blasters with blades but was willing to give her the benefit of the doubt.

"As you wish," Joral said, his inflection and expression questioning the wisdom of her request. "Which weapons do you prefer?"

Eliana studied the blades. "Are any of these made from the right metals?"

"No. These are strong enough to puncture armor but would be damaged by blasterfire. If you see a design you like, however, I can make what you need."

"Could you, by any chance, make blades based on a design I provide?"

He stiffened. "None of these are to your liking?"

"Actually, they all are," she told him honestly. "I wasn't kidding when I said I wish I could have one of everything here. But I'd feel more comfortable wielding weapons that are identical to the ones I've already trained with until I can get a feel for these."

"Ah." He relaxed. "Understandable. Come with me." Herding her into his workspace, he retrieved what appeared to be a large piece of glass about the size of a poster board. Setting it on one of his white tables, he motioned to it. "Show me what you wish your weapons to resemble."

She eyed the clear glass. "How do I do that?"

He picked up an object that resembled an all-black pencil. "You may use this to draw directly on my design tablet."

Several gasps erupted behind her.

She looked around.

Dagon's eyebrows nearly touched his hairline.

Perhaps Joral didn't often allow others to use his tablet?

"Thank you." Eliana took the alien pencil. It was light as a feather and had the feel of a crayon with the paper peeled off. Leaning down, she touched it to the glass. A black line appeared on the surface as she moved it. "What do I do if I want to erase it?"

"Use your finger," Joral instructed.

She drew a finger across the line and watched a swath disappear. "Cool." The pencil worked more like a paintbrush, she soon discovered, the lines thickening if she applied more pressure and thinning when she applied less.

Eliana was quite adept at drawing. She had lived roughly three centuries before radio and television were invented. And she had often filled the long hours in which she had to remain indoors and eschew the sun with sketching and painting and other hobbies. In short order, she provided Joral with detailed drawings of a katana, a shoto sword, a sai, two daggers, and three throwing stars.

By the time she finished, Joral was leaning down beside her, his arm brushing hers while he murmured absently to himself.

Dagon did the same on her other side, commending her on her drawing skills.

Setting the pencil down, she straightened.

The two men stayed where they were, admiring the weapons

displayed on the tablet. She fought a smile. Both were so tall that leaning down and resting their elbows on the table barely lowered them to her height.

Joral motioned to the katana. "What length did you have in mind for this?"

She held her hands apart the proper length, then motioned to one of the swords on the wall. "About the same as that one with the swirl etched into the blade."

Joral tapped one corner of the design tablet. When several icons appeared on the bottom of the screen, he tapped one, selected the katana, then pressed another symbol.

Eliana's eyes widened when her drawing of the katana rose off the tablet and became a three-dimensional hologram standing on its tip. She looked up at Dagon as he straightened. "That is so—"

"Cool?" he suggested, his eyes twinkling with merriment.

She grinned. "Yes."

Joral touched the three-dimensional sword. The image flickered a little as he pinched the tip of the blade and pulled down. The katana lengthened. "Like this?"

"Yes," she told him. "Exactly like that."

"What of the width of the blade? Will this suffice?"

Eliana motioned to the image. "May I?"

"Of course."

More gasps arose behind them.

Eliana touched the edges of the blade. The tips of her fingers tingled a little as she adjusted the width. "Like this."

Joral nodded. More questions followed regarding the pommel, the cord wrap, the guard, the blade collar, the temper line, the ridge, the weight, the scabbard.

"Commander Dagon," Maarev said faintly.

Dagon reached up and tapped his earpiece. "Yes?"

"Unit 3 is ready for evaluation in Training Section 3, Simulation Room 2."

"I'm on my way." He met her gaze. "Apologies," he said, his deep voice carrying a hint of regret. "I've business I must attend to."

Disappointment rose. She had hoped to spend more time with him. "Okay. Is it all right if I stay here?" She sent Joral an inquisitive glance.

The weapons designer nodded. "I require more specifications before I can begin fashioning your weapons."

She looked up at Dagon.

"Stay as long as you like. I'll find you once I've carried out my duties."

And just like that, her good mood was restored.

CHAPTER 7

A FEW HOURS later, Eliana's stomach began to rumble, indicating it had been a few hours since Dagon had left. She and Joral had succeeded in perfecting the design for katanas, shoto swords, sais, daggers, and were finishing up the last throwing star when heavy boots thudded behind them.

She glanced over her shoulder. Her heart began to beat faster. Happiness filled her, and she couldn't hold back a smile.

Dagon.

He made her feel like a teenager again. And that was really saying something since she was so damn old. "Hi."

His handsome features lit with amusement. "Still at work, I see."

"Yes." She winked and confided in a loud whisper, "After you, Joral is my new favorite person."

The weapons designer chuckled. "I believe we have finished, Commander. I will start on the weapons forthwith. Until then…" He crossed to a bare wall and touched it. A crease formed in the surface. Then a section of it slid back to reveal an arsenal of weapons.

Eliana smiled. It reminded her of the armories in David's and Seth's homes.

When Joral returned, he held out a holstered tronium blaster and a sheathed dagger. "Perhaps these will do until yours are ready?"

"Thank you." Eliana wrapped the holster's belt around her waist and fastened it. Made for men far larger than she, it sagged and settled around her hips. The sheathed dagger she strapped to her thigh on the opposite side. Once finished, she straightened. "Ahhhh. Much better."

Joral crossed his arms and shook his head with a smile. "You truly *are* a warrior."

"Yep." Her stomach rumbled again.

Dagon grinned. "And have a warrior's appetite. Would you care to join me for last meal?"

"I'd love to." After thanking Joral once more, she tossed the other men a wave and a goodbye and strode from the room at Dagon's side.

Silence fell upon them as he led her down the corridor and into a lift.

"Apologies," he murmured.

She even liked his voice. So deep and rumbly. She wondered how much deeper it might get when lust consumed him, then mentally reprimanded herself for letting her thoughts stray in that direction. "For what?"

"I didn't intend to be away so long."

"That's okay. I kinda have a thing for weapons, so I had fun." She sent him a teasing glance. "What about you? How was work?" She nudged him with her elbow. "Did you miss me?"

He smiled. "I did."

And damned if the admission didn't speed her pulse. "Good."

The lift deposited them on another deck.

Dagon filled her in on some of the work he'd done during his absence, which included taking a call from a Lasaran commander by the name of Tiran. "I do have news for you regarding the Lasaran prince."

She slowed to a halt, unable to tell from the inflection of his voice if this was going to be good news or bad news. "And?"

"He, his Earthling lifemate, and their baby have been rescued and safely delivered to Lasara."

Relief filled her. Lisa, Taelon, and little Abby were safe. "Anyone else?"

He nodded. "Four Yona warriors were recovered with them."

"Good." That meant Ari'k and the three Yona she'd seen with the royal couple had survived as well. Then she frowned. "I'm guessing whoever found them had to travel quite a distance to get them home. Why didn't the Lasarans tell you sooner?"

"They opted to keep the information classified until the prince and his family were back on Lasaran soil."

"So the Gathendiens wouldn't target whatever ship they were on?"

"Yes."

"Can I talk to Lisa and Taelon?" She would really love to confirm their well-being with her own eyes.

He shook his head, his face betraying regret. "I asked the same thing, assuming you would wish to contact them. But Commander Tiran said direct communication with the Lasaran homeworld is being restricted to their own military forces for a time."

She frowned as they resumed their stroll. "Do the Lasarans believe their communications have been compromised?"

"They have as yet found no breaches in their system, but…"

"If the Gathendiens attacked the *Kandovar* because they knew unique Earth women were on board, then they had to have come across the information somewhere."

"Precisely."

"Has anyone found more of my friends from Earth?"

"Regrettably, no."

The news made Eliana want to weep. A little more than a month and no word? The escape pods only contained two months of supplies. If the Lasarans and the other members of the Aldebarian Alliance didn't find her friends in the next few weeks…

"We're still looking," Dagon said softly.

Swallowing back the dread and the feeling of helplessness that threatened to swamp her, she nodded.

He motioned to a doorway up and to the right, then rested a hand on her lower back.

Warmth seeped into her skin through the shirt she wore, distracting her for a moment as they entered the large room. Then she stopped abruptly.

Eliana had seen a lot of eateries over the years: restaurants, bars, military mess halls, food courts in malls, cafeterias in the headquarters of the human network that aided Immortal Guardians, the cafeteria on the *Kandovar*…

This one was by far the best of the bunch. The floor was shiny white. Instead of long rectangular tables, it boasted round tables capable of seating six to eight people. Most of the modern, comfortable-looking chairs were filled with big male bodies. Crew members formed short lines before a wall that reminded her of an order counter at a take-out restaurant. Even as she watched, a man behind the counter handed a soldier a tray. But she found her gaze drawn away from them and to the far wall.

She stared in fascination. What appeared to be large faux windows adorned the walls, displaying not stars set in deep space but scenery one might find on Earth if one lived in the country. A golden sun sank toward a distant horizon, casting warm amber light on trees with pale beige, almost white trunks and dark green foliage. Mountain peaks stretched up high in the distance, seemingly determined to pierce the sky. White that she assumed was snow topped each imposing bluish-gray peak while lower elevations boasted foliage that ranged from a green so dark it was almost black to a pale greenish-yellow. Above those mountains and the sinking sun, three moons hovered in the darkening blue sky, one a little larger than the other two.

At the base of the mountain, bracketed by stands of trees, lay a tranquil meadow. Tall grasses rippled like ocean waves as a breeze wafted over them, their movements hypnotic and calming. Occasional splashes of color interrupted the sea of green with red, pink, purple, blue, black, white, and yellow.

Wildflowers?

The utter beauty of the scene mesmerized her.

Silence fell over the cafeteria.

She looked up at Dagon. "Is that your homeworld?"

"Yes. That is Segonia."

The faux windows again drew her gaze.

"It's beautiful," she proclaimed reverently. The computer screens or whatever they were even behaved like real windows, spilling golden sunshine into the cafeteria at the same angle the sun would if the scene were real.

"It is," he agreed. "We often spend long periods of time away from it, so we equip all our ships with these to assuage some of our longing for home."

She smiled. "That's beautiful, too. And thoughtful." Then she noticed the lack of motion in the large room and realized that every man present had gone still and was staring at her. "Hi." She offered them a friendly wave. "I'm Eliana. Thank you all for rescuing me. I really appreciate it."

Rugged faces brightened with tentative smiles as masculine murmurs arose, offering multiple greetings that blended together and stretched her smile into a happy grin.

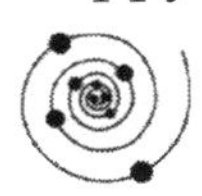

Dagon shook his head. Eliana seemed determined to charm them all. Even the surliest of his men cracked a smile at her greeting and her offer of thanks.

Increasing the pressure on her lower back, he guided her over to the order counter. The men in the line closest to them all stepped back as she and Dagon approached.

She glanced up at him. "Is that for you or for me? Because I don't mind waiting in line."

He smiled. "It's for both of us." As commander of the ship, he was accustomed to being shuttled to the front of the line, particularly since he usually picked up his meal and took it back to his office to absently consume while he performed some of the more tedious work his position required. But Eliana must not be used to such accommodation because she whispered apologies to the men they passed.

Dagon stopped before the counter.

The man who faced them always reminded him of Joral.

Kusgan was older with graying hair cropped short. But he boasted the heavily muscled physique of a younger warrior. A scar that looked as though it had been spawned by fire marred part of the man's neck and jaw, tugging his smile down slightly on that side as he greeted them. "Commander Dagon."

"Kusgan," Dagon said with a nod. "This is Eliana of Earth."

Smiling, she extended her hand. "Hi. It's nice to meet you."

His graying eyebrows rising, Kusgan grasped her forearm. "An honor to meet you, *ni'má*."

"You can call me Eliana."

"Thank you. What may I serve you, Eliana?"

"I have no idea." She glanced up at Dagon. "Any suggestions?"

He frowned. "I'm not familiar with the Earthling palate, so I'm uncertain what will appeal to you." He should've asked Adaos about it.

The cook beside Kusgan handed the soldier beside Eliana a tray.

She studied the food on it and drew in a deep breath. "Ummmm…" Though she carefully kept her expression blank, he got the distinct impression she didn't care for what she saw or smelled. Turning, she peered through the tall men in line behind her. "Hold that thought."

Dagon watched curiously as she strode through those in line and headed for a nearby table. Maarev, Liden, Efren, and five other warriors looked up at her approach.

"Hi, guys," she said with a smile. "Don't mind me. Just pretend I'm not here."

Amused, he watched her slowly circle the table and study their trays, subtly inhaling the scent each bore. She was so diminutive that—even while seated—the men were her height or taller.

She stopped beside Maarev and pointed at his plate. "This." Turning, she met Dagon's gaze. "I'll try whatever Maarev is eating, please."

Maarev glanced over at Dagon, then back at Eliana. "I don't think you would find this to your liking."

Dagon couldn't see the contents of his tray. "What is it?" he called.

"Vestuna."

Oh. No. He didn't want that to be her first taste of Segonian food. "He's right. I don't think you'd care for that."

Eliana frowned. "Are you sure? It smells really good… like lasagna seasoned with habanero peppers."

Maarev shrugged. "You would probably find it too spicy."

She narrowed her eyes as though he had just insulted her. "Oh, would I?" Or maybe issued a challenge. "May I have a taste?"

Maarev again glanced at Dagon.

Shrugging, he motioned for his friend to indulge her.

Maarev speared a selection from the red-and-green dish and held his utensil out to her.

As she leaned forward and closed her lips around it, drawing the tasty offering into her mouth, Dagon suddenly wished he had said no. Every muscle tensed in protest as something he couldn't quite believe was jealousy slunk through him. He did *not* like seeing Eliana eat from another man's utensil. And he sure as *srul* didn't like the way Maarev watched her lips as she chewed.

Fortunately, the expressions flickering across Eliana's lovely features soon distracted him.

Surprise lit her face as she chewed. Pleasure followed. Then her eyes widened. Tears welled in them as flavor and fire exploded on her tongue. *Vestuna* was exceedingly spicy. Though he loved it, Earthlings might have a less robust constitution. He shouldn't have let her try it. Or he should have at least cautioned her to take a smaller bite.

She began to chew faster. And faster.

Maarev's lips twitched. So did the other men's.

As soon as she swallowed the fiery mouthful, Eliana grabbed Maarev's glass and took a hasty drink.

Some of the men chuckled.

At least Maarev was drinking *naga* juice. The sweet berry soothed some of the burn when one consumed spicy foods.

"Ahhhh," she breathed in relief as she set the glass down. Then she pointed at the plate and sent Dagon a smile. "I definitely want that. I *love* spicy food, and that is *delicious*!"

The men all grinned. Some laughed in delight and raised their glasses to her.

She patted Maarev on the shoulder. "Thank you."

Smiling, Dagon shook his head while he watched her stroll toward him. *Drek,* she had an alluring walk. "You are full of surprises, aren't you?" he asked as she joined him.

"Yep," she replied with a grin. "That's me. I'm just a natural-born enigma."

He laughed and turned to Kusgan. "A salad and some *vestuna* for both of us."

"Yes, Commander." Kusgan left and returned with two trays. Dagon's was heaped with warrior-sized portions. Eliana's boasted maybe half as much, which still seemed more than he thought someone her size could consume.

She hesitated, then reluctantly took the tray.

Dagon studied her. "Eliana? Have you changed your mind? Would you like something else?" Perhaps the continued burn in her mouth drove her to question the wisdom of consuming more.

"Nnnnno." She glanced up at him, hesitated as though she wanted to say something, then turned back to Kusgan. "No, it's fine." She smiled. "It's good. Thank you."

When she would've turned away, Dagon caught her elbow. Her skin was so soft, he noted absently. "You may speak freely, Eliana."

Every man waiting in line behind and beside them watched her curiously.

She bit her lip, then looked at Kusgan. "Well..."

Kusgan waited patiently.

"Would it be rude to ask for more?"

Kusgan's face lit up. "No, *ni'má*." Reaching out, he took her tray. "How much would you like?"

She pointed at Dagon's tray. "That much."

Dagon grinned. The men around them all laughed.

Most Segonian women were nearly as tall as the men, but even those in the military did not eat such large portions. He could not imagine someone as small as Eliana finishing off that much food but would enjoy watching her try.

"As you wish." Kusgan left and returned with a tray heaped as high as Dagon's and a pitcher of *naga* juice.

Once Eliana took her tray with a bright smile and a "thank you," Kusgan handed Dagon the pitcher. "To soothe the burn," he said with a grin.

Dagon took it, lips twitching. "Thank you." The men around them parted, allowing them passage as they left the counter.

"Could we sit by a window?" she asked. "The scenery is so beautiful. And I've really missed being outdoors during the months I've been in space."

"Of course." He guided her through the tables.

Every man they passed seemed alternately fascinated by her and amused by the amount of food she carried.

Dagon stopped before an empty table next to a holowindow and set his tray and the pitcher upon it. Then he drew out a chair for Eliana and waited for her to sit before taking a seat across from her.

This table and others near the windows were smaller, seating four or five instead of eight. Dagon instantly liked that it allowed him to sit facing her with less table separating them.

Eliana admired the sunset depicted in the window. The light it spilled across them bore the simulated warmth of the sun. Releasing a little sigh of contentment, she looked at Dagon. "This is nice."

He smiled and filled the glass on her tray with the sweet *naga* juice. "I'm glad you like it."

"If that were a real window, I wouldn't be able to sit here. The sunlight would burn me." Picking up a utensil, she speared some vegetables.

His movements slowed as he filled his own glass, then set the pitcher down. "You cannot withstand any sun exposure at all?" He recalled fondly the afternoons he had spent on the beaches of Segonia or hiking in the mountains while on leave. It saddened him to think she could not enjoy such simple pleasures.

She sent the tables around them an uneasy glance, then lowered her voice so none would overhear. "I can withstand a few minutes. But if I remain in the light long enough to burn, I'll need a blood transfusion." She delivered the vegetables to her mouth and gave them an experimental crunch. "Mmmmm."

He smiled. "Good?"

Nodding, she swallowed. "The maroon leaves taste like spinach. And the orange and green leaves remind me of lettuce. I used to make salads with both back home." She ate another mouthful. "The little yellow slices look like carrots but taste like walnuts. And the things that look like tiny cherry tomatoes remind me of raisins. It's a delicious combination."

"I'm glad it's to your liking." Dagon speared some salad and munched away. "Do you miss Earth?"

She consumed another mouthful. "I miss my brethren. My hunting partners, Nick and Rafe. My Second, Max. Seth, David, and the rest of my makeshift family." She made no mention of the family into which she had been born. Had they, like so many others on Earth, treated her badly for her differences? "I also miss the outdoors," she continued. "Moonlight. A cool breeze." She sent him a wry smile. "I'd say I miss the fresh air, too, but I've spent the past several decades living in cities with a lot of pollution, so fresh air was pretty hard to come by."

He reached over and touched the wall beneath the window. When a line of symbols lit up beneath it, he tapped one. Translucent hologram curtains appeared on either side of the window. He tapped another button, then pressed and dragged a bar.

The curtains billowed out as a breeze wafted over them, carrying with it familiar scents from Segonia.

Grass. Trees. Flowers.

Eliana went still and closed her eyes. Several tendrils of hair swept across her forehead. "It smells like home," she whispered reverently. "The way it was *before* the industrial revolution. Like the forest I used to play in when I was a child."

Dagon stared, arrested by her beauty, by the pleasure her features conveyed.

The breeze waned.

Opening her eyes, she watched the holographic curtains settle back against the window. A moment later, the grasses depicted in the image rippled with waves that raced toward them. The curtains again billowed gently, rewarding them once more with the sweet scents of the outdoors.

She looked at Dagon.

His heart began to thud heavily in his chest.

"That's amazing," she breathed.

He swallowed but said nothing, just continued to study her, utterly enthralled.

She took a big bite of *vestuna*. A few seconds later her eyes began to water. "Man, this is good," she wheezed.

Chuckling, Dagon nudged her glass toward her. "Drink this. It will soothe the burn."

She took a long drink. "Mmm. This is good, too, like tea sweetened with berries."

He smiled as she eagerly dug into the *vestuna*, his favorite dish. He consumed it regularly, so he was at least partially immune to the burn.

Eliana's eyes continued to tear up. She even sniffled a few times. But it didn't stop her from eating every bite on her plate. While she did, she peppered him with questions about Segonia, pointing to the plants outside the faux window and asking what each was called.

As they dined and chatted, the sun depicted in the holowindow dipped lower and the light altered accordingly, the angle changing and bursting with shades of orange. Then the sun disappeared altogether, leaving three moons and a light dusting of clouds in the darkening sky. Bioluminescent insects flickered to life in the distance. Some of the flowers in the grassy meadow began to glow.

"Your world is fascinating," she murmured, taking in the beauty.

"No more so than you," he replied softly. He could not recall the last time he had enjoyed a meal or a woman's company so much. Eliana thoroughly enchanted him.

Her pretty brown eyes met his and clung.

And Dagon found himself wondering what it would be like to sink his fingers into her long midnight tresses, tug her forward, and kiss those soft-as-sin lips.

His gaze dropped to her mouth. And her lips *would* be soft as they met his, her tongue both spicy and sweet from the *vestuna* and the *naga* juice she had consumed.

Desire slithered through him.

He looked up… and lost his train of thought. Eliana was staring at his mouth. The tip of her pink tongue slipped out and glided across her lip as the brown of her eyes gave way to luminescent amber.

"Your eyes are glowing," he murmured.

Her gaze shot to his. Stiffening, she squeezed her eyes shut. "Sorry. I um…" She shook her head. "Sorry about that. I was…" She seemed to search for an explanation, made a sound of aggravation, and shook her head again. Opening her eyes, she sent him a cautious look. "What about now?"

He studied her. "They're back to brown."

"Good." She glanced around the cafeteria.

Dagon's dislike of Earth intensified as he realized she feared someone else might have seen it and would react badly. He followed her gaze, ready to reassure her if she caught anyone staring.

Much to his surprise, the room had mostly emptied while the two of them dined.

Returning his attention to Eliana, he studied her. How might he put her at ease, help her understand that member races of the Aldebarian Alliance were all different in their own ways and would not disdain her for exhibiting distinctions of her own?

Perhaps if he asked about them, he could show her that her unique attributes would spark curiosity rather than hatred. "Why do your eyes glow sometimes?"

Her shoulders relaxed a little when whatever negative reaction she had expected did not manifest. "It's an involuntary response to pain or strong emotion."

He nodded thoughtfully. "That explains why they were glowing when we first met." It also explained why her commanding officer's eyes had reportedly glowed when the Lasarans had apprised him of her situation. Tiran's source had cited madness, but Dagon thought it more likely that concern, fear for her, grief, or a combination thereof had caused it.

"The pain was pretty bad," she admitted.

Dagon deemed that an understatement considering the long list of injuries the comprehensive diagnostic scanner had listed. "Why were they glowing a moment ago?"

She shifted. Uneasiness crept into her pretty features once more as she glanced at the window. "The scents coming in through the window... or the simulated window... remind me of my childhood home."

"Ah." He had hoped she might have been experiencing the same surprising surge of desire that had gripped him, but she had merely been longing for home. He motioned to her tray. "Are you finished?"

"Yes. It was very good." She smiled as he transferred her empty plate and bowl to his tray. "Your company was good, too. Thank you for dinner, Dagon."

"It was my pleasure, Eliana." And it truly *had* been a pleasure. Most evenings he absently consumed his dinner while working in his office. This had been a nice change. And Eliana's company had left him loath to see the evening end.

After stacking his tray atop hers, he rose with them and grabbed the pitcher.

Eliana followed him over to a window that was adjacent to the order counter.

Kusgan appeared in it as they approached. When he took the empty trays from Dagon, he smiled at Eliana. Mischief sparkled in his eyes. "How much of your *vestuna* did Commander Dagon consume?"

"None."

His features betraying his surprise, he glanced at Dagon.

Dagon smiled. "I ate none of her portion. She finished the meal herself."

When Kusgan gaped at Eliana, she burst out laughing. "What can I say? I have a warrior's appetite."

Kusgan's craggy face lit with delight. "Indeed you do. I look forward to serving you again tomorrow, Eliana."

"Me, too. Have a nice night."

Eliana heard Kusgan wish her well or issue some other polite farewell but didn't process it. Her thoughts scattered, then started jumping around like children in a bouncy house when Dagon once more rested a hand on her lower back and guided her out of the mess hall. The heat of his big hand filtered through the soft fabric of her shirt. Her skin tingled. Her heart beat a little faster.

How could such a simple touch stir her so?

"I guess I should ask," she said, hoping he wouldn't see the mad flutter of her pulse in her neck as they strolled down the hallway.

Two maintenance workers headed toward them. Eliana paused, introduced herself, and thanked them for coming to her rescue.

Once the smiling men continued on, Dagon glanced down at her. "Ask what?"

"Was it rude of me to eat so much? I don't really know anything about your culture, so it belatedly occurred to me that women in your society might be expected to eat smaller portions." When Eliana had been mortal, her mother had always counseled her to eat dainty little servings. But Eliana had spent the many years since surrounded by powerful immortal males who ate as much as Dagon and who couldn't care less about the quantity she consumed. And she tended to consume copious amounts. Doing anything with preternatural speed or strength burned a *lot* of calories.

He shook his head. "Segonian women are expected to eat whatever amount they require to achieve optimal health, just as the men are."

"But what about on a ship? Are there specific, rationed amounts each person on board should stick to?"

His eyes glinted with amusement as his lips twitched. "Are you worried you'll eat your way through our stores if I impose no limits?"

She grinned. "Maybe."

He laughed. "We have plenty of food and drink on board. You've no worries there, so eat as much as you wish."

"Okay, but you may come to regret that when you see how much I can put away."

He shook his head. "I believe I saw that tonight, so I doubt you'll surprise me."

She nudged him with her elbow. "Don't forget your own words, Dagon. I am *full* of surprises."

"You are indeed," he said with another smile.

She grinned. The way he said it made it sound as if he really liked that about her.

They took the lift to Deck 3, where Dagon led her down a long corridor with a lot of closed doors adorned with what she guessed were Segonian numerals. Stopping before one, he placed his palm on the reader. The door slid up. "These will be your quarters while you're with us."

"Wow." She stepped inside and turned in a slow circle. "This is bigger than I expected." Bigger than the cabin she'd had on the *Kandovar*, for sure. This room looked like something one of the higher-ups might use. She bit her lip. "I'm not putting anyone out, am I?"

His brow furrowed. "I'm not certain what that means."

"You didn't kick Barus or some other higher-ranking officer out of this room so I could have it, did you?"

"No."

"Because I don't want anyone to get his shorts in a bunch over it. I am totally fine with taking a smaller room or even sleeping in Med Bay." The last thing she wanted to do was piss someone off by swiping his cabin.

"You'll sleep here," he responded. When she opened her mouth to issue another objection, he held up a hand. "This room is usually empty. We reserve it for commanding officers and other important and honored visitors. Prince Taelon has used this room in the past, as has one of his brothers."

Prince Taelon? Really? She wrinkled her nose. "I'm not royalty, Dagon."

He arched a brow. "Perhaps not. But as the sole member of your kind on board, you may consider yourself the *Ranasura*'s unofficial ambassador to Earth."

Surprise flitted through her. "Ambassador, huh? Ooh la la. I sound so important."

He grinned. "You are. Come over here for a moment." Once she returned to his side, he motioned to the electronic panel by the door. "This is what you'll use to open and seal your door." He placed his hand on the pad, then typed a series of commands into the interface. "Place your palm here."

She splayed her fingers and pressed her palm to the pad. It didn't cover nearly as much of the surface as his had.

He nodded. "Thank you."

As soon as she withdrew her hand, he again pressed his palm to the smooth surface.

A tranquil female voice spoke. "Access granted to Eliana." It was the same voice she'd heard in the infirmary.

Eliana smiled. "She spoke English."

"Yes. And CC will accept any commands you issue in English as well." He pressed his index finger to one corner of the panel and held it. "I need you to answer a few questions for me now."

"Okay."

"Eliana, where are you from?"

"I'm from Earth."

"Eliana, how did you come to be here?"

She stared at him a moment. "I was traveling to Lasara on the *Kandovar*. Some jerkwad Gathendiens attacked us. There was an explosion. I woke up, floating in space by myself in only a space suit. And a month later you showed up and rescued me."

"Eliana, would you please count slowly from one to twenty for me."

"Ooooookay." This was weird. She slowly counted to twenty while he watched her, his face alight with amusement.

"Eliana, please count from one to twenty as quickly as you can."

She recited the numbers so quickly her words nearly blended together into one sound.

"Thank you." He removed his finger from the panel. "CC, extrapolate Eliana."

"Extrapolating Eliana," CC responded. "Extrapolation complete."

Eliana stared at him. "I have no idea what's happening right now."

He chuckled. "I was helping CC learn your voice so she will accept your commands."

"Oh." She smiled. "Good. For a minute there I thought you'd gone a little wacky in the wicky woo. You know what I mean?"

"No, I don't," he answered honestly.

She laughed. "Don't worry about it."

He again motioned to the panel. "You have to use your palm print to enter or leave, but the rest of the commands may be given verbally. Try dimming the lights."

"Okay." She cleared her throat and looked up at the ceiling. "Hi, CC. Eliana here. Would you please dim the lights for me?"

The lights dimmed.

Again he chuckled. "You don't have to greet CC."

Wrinkling her nose, she lowered her voice. "I know. It just seems rude not to."

Smiling, he shook his head. "You won't hurt CC's feelings if you don't greet her first."

"Affirmative," CC confirmed. "I am not a sentient life form. I am a software program incapable of feeling emotion."

Eliana turned her gaze up to the ceiling. "Thank you for clarifying that, CC. Would you please brighten the lighting for me?" The lights returned to their previous luminescence. "Thank you." When she glanced back at Dagon, she took one look at the humor reflected in his handsome features and issued a self-deprecating laugh. "I know. I can't help it. This is going to take some getting used to."

"Didn't you use voice commands in your quarters on the *Kandovar*?"

"No. Prince Taelon had them retrofit our rooms with manual controls so it would feel more like home."

"Ah." He motioned to the cabin around them. "Do you have any questions?"

She looked around. There was a comfy-looking chair in one corner, perfect for reading, a small table with two utilitarian chairs, an entertainment vid screen, a couple of panels she thought might cover recessed closets, a nook with one of the alien snack-and-beverage dispensers she had never been able to figure out on the *Kandovar*, and a doorway bracketing the entrance to a dark room. "I don't think so. I assume that room over there is the lav?"

"Yes."

"What about…?" She turned in a circle again. "Is there a bed?"

"Yes." He pointed. "It's in that wall. To activate it, just say *lower bed*."

"Lower bed," she parroted.

A bed that was as wide as a king-sized bed back home, but longer, folded out of the wall. Thin mechanical arms that held the covers and pillows in place retracted as soon as the bed was horizontal.

Eliana studied the massive piece of furniture, then arched a brow at Dagon. "Do you think it's big enough?"

"For someone my size? Yes."

Some imp inside made her wink. "I'm going to tuck that tidbit away for future reference." Oh crap. She did not just say that!

Before he could respond, she took three steps and leaped toward the bed. Spinning in midair, she landed on her back, arms and legs splayed.

"Ahhhh," she breathed. "It's as comfortable as it looks." Not too hard. Not too soft. Just perfect. Linking her fingers, she tucked them behind her head and crossed her ankles.

Amusement once more stretched Dagon's lips in a smile that resurrected the warm tingly feelings his touch always inspired. And she couldn't help but notice that the bed beneath her was *definitely* big enough for two.

A mental image formed of him prowling toward her, climbing onto the bed and caging her between his arms as he lowered his large, muscled body atop hers.

Desire slithered through her, but she resolutely tamped it down. What the hell was wrong with her?

Dagon smiled. "I'm glad it's to your liking."

What was: the bed or his body?

"I'll leave now so you can rest."

Swiveling, he pressed his palm to the panel and opened the door.

"Hey, Dagon?" she called softly.

He glanced over his shoulder.

Sitting up, she sent him a smile. "Thank you." When he turned back to face her, she gave in to impulse, scooted off the bed, closed the distance between them, and wrapped him in another hug. "For everything."

He slid his arms around her and held her close.

Damn, it felt good.

A long moment passed. Then she forced herself to release him and backed away with a smile. "Good night."

He smiled. "Good night, Eliana."

CHAPTER 8

THE NEXT DAY, Dagon stood beside Galen's console as the navigations officer pulled up the map he'd requested.

"We found Eliana here." Galen pointed to the hologram. "The Soturi found the empty pod here. And these are the coordinates of the other pods Alliance members have recovered."

Multiple green dots flared to life on the diagram, all astoundingly far apart.

Dagon shook his head. "That's a *srul* of a large field to search."

Galen nodded. "And the pods will run out of life support in approximately thirty Segonian days."

"No stations or satellites have picked up stray signals?"

"A few, but not from any of the pods that contain Earth women. Every member of the Alliance is scanning for signals."

Dagon looked at Janek.

His comms officer nodded. "I've heard nothing yet but will continue searching."

Galen proceeded to display the location of every Alliance member's ship.

"What's this one?" Dagon pointed to a gray dot.

"The Akseli pirate, Janwar."

Janek frowned. "Why is *he* heading out here?"

"To search like the rest of us," Galen said with a shrug.

Dagon stared at the dot. Tiran had told him the notorious Akseli pirate was the one who had rescued Prince Taelon and his lifemate, which had come as something of a shock. Janwar wasn't a member of the Aldebarian Alliance. He was, in fact, scorned by most members. Because he was a pirate. One who frequently operated outside the law. "Janwar is the one who found Prince Taelon and his Earthling lifemate," he murmured. "But he just delivered them to Lasara. How did he travel so far from there in such a short time?" Particularly with one of the *qhov'rums* still damaged.

Rahmik joined them. "Rumor has it he has a new ship with technology so advanced that its speed cannot be matched."

"How did he manage that?"

Janek grunted. "He's a pirate."

Rahmik shrugged. "Even so, Prince Taelon now considers him an ally."

"And he has apparently joined the search-and-rescue effort," Dagon commented.

"Yes." Rahmik nodded at the map. "Maybe he thinks the Lasaran sovereigns will reward him well if he rescues more survivors."

"Or perhaps he intends to ransom them," Janek muttered.

Dagon shook his head. "Not if he wishes to remain in Prince Taelon's good graces." The Lasaran royal family held a lot of sway even among nations like the Akseli, who were *not* members of the Alliance, something that could prove useful to the rebel-turned-pirate.

The Akseli government had placed an impressively large bounty on Janwar's head, but thus far no one had attempted to claim it. Tales of the Akseli pirate's cruelty to those who crossed him abounded. But Dagon had always believed one should judge a man not according to rumor or hearsay but according to his actions. And the man's actions had all been aboveboard when the two of them crossed paths.

"I met him once."

Galen looked at him in surprise. "You did?"

Dagon nodded. "The Earth women will fare far better in his hands than they would in the hands of the Gathendiens, so I hope his search will prove fruitful." And wished he could get his hands on whatever technology Janwar had acquired that bestowed upon his ship such astonishing speed.

"As you were," Dagon murmured. Returning to his chair, he

sank down in it and reached for his data pad. He was just beginning to read through each division's night shift reports when the bridge access door rose to reveal Eliana.

Staring up at the slot into which the door had vanished, she grinned. "Ha! Take *that*, Adaos."

Several crewmen chuckled.

Eliana tossed them all a wave. "Hi, guys."

All returned her abbreviated greeting.

Smiling, she strolled toward Dagon, her swaying hips once more drawing his gaze. "I shouldn't tease Adaos. He's been really nice to me, considering."

Galen snorted a laugh. "Considering you knocked him on his ass while you were a hair away from death?"

More laughter erupted.

"Hey," she said, "don't be so quick to laugh. I can knock every man here on his ass and would be happy to demonstrate it once I'm ready to spar with you."

The amusement that lit the men's expressions clearly expressed their disbelief, but Eliana seemed to take no offense.

Dagon rose as she approached him.

Still smiling, she stopped and tilted her head back to smile up at him. "Hi there."

"Hello. How did you sleep?"

"Very well, thank you." She motioned to the tablet he held. "Am I interrupting anything?"

He shook his head. "Just catching up on the night shift's reports."

"Any updates on the search for survivors?"

He nodded. "More Lasarans have been rescued."

"Any Yona?"

Regret filled him. "No, though several bodies have been recovered."

"Damn." Her brow furrowed. "I really like those guys. I hate to think they might have died in the battle, all of them except the royal guard, I mean."

"The possibility that some survived remains. There were many escape pods on the *Kandovar*, and many fighter craft. If Yona soldiers piloted any of the latter, they could have survived the conflict."

"I hope so." She looked lost in thought for a moment, then visibly shook it off. "May I join you?"

"Of course."

Before he could say more, she set a data pad he hadn't realized she carried on the arm of the commander's seat, then crossed to an empty chair at a weapons station that was usually only manned during battle. Leaning over it, she clutched the arms and moved as though to lift it.

It didn't budge. Eliana frowned at the chair and bent to try again.

Dagon opened his mouth to tell her the chair was strongly magnetized to the deck and would have to be turned off to move, but he lost his thought when the chair groaned and shifted a hand's span. His eyes widened. That should not be possible. Even *he* couldn't move a chair once the magnetic charge had been activated. They were designed that way to prevent them from moving when the ship engaged in battle.

"What the *drek*?" Galen muttered.

Eliana looked up and froze when she noticed everyone staring at her. Straightening, she bit her lip.

The silence stretched.

Fiddling with the tie on the blade sheath strapped to her thigh, she met Dagon's gaze. "Is moving a chair forbidden or something?"

He shook his head. "You should not have been capable of moving it at all. It's magnetized to the deck."

She glanced down at the chair. "Oh. Um..." She darted the others a look. "Maybe it's malfunctioning. How do I turn off the magnets?"

"There's a button under the seat."

Bending down, she felt around. "Ah. There it is." She gave the chair an experimental wiggle, then smiled when it moved easily. "Good."

Much to the further astonishment of the crew, she carried the chair over and plunked it down beside Dagon's. "Should I reactivate the magnet?"

"Such would be wise, yes."

As soon as she did so, she retrieved her tablet and sank into the chair. "This is perfect," she told him with a grin. "I can see everything from here."

His men all gaped… except for Janek. His comms officer looked as though he were choking on laughter he sought to repress.

Eliana could see everything from her position because she was seated beside *him*, the commander. *No one* sat beside Dagon. His was a position of rank and honor, one earned after many years of serving in the military. Even Barus merely *stood* beside him rather than sitting beside him when both occupied the bridge.

Yet Eliana had dragged a chair over and was making herself quite comfortable. She even stretched her alluring, black-clad legs out in front of her, crossed them at the ankles (her small feet barely able to reach the floor), and sank a little lower as though settling in to read.

Dagon retook his seat.

Eliana sat so close that his elbow brushed her arm.

He arched a brow, amusement sifting through him. "Comfortable?"

"Yes, thank you."

Smiling, he shook his head and once more picked up his data pad.

Eliana turned her attention to her own and activated it.

After a long pause, the crew returned to work, but Dagon didn't miss the curious glances they slid his way.

He tried to focus on the messages and updates his tablet conveyed but found Eliana's presence too distracting. She smelled good, like the soap commonly distributed to the cleansing units and the *naga* juice she had consumed at first meal mixed with her own unique scent.

Her dark-as-space hair gleamed beneath the overhead lights. Her brown eyes focused intently on her screen as she swiped her finger from right to left over and over again.

"What are you doing?" he asked. Was she looking for something? The speed at which she swiped seemed to indicate she hadn't found it yet, whatever it was.

"Learning," she murmured absently.

Learning? Learning what? She didn't stay on one page long enough for him to even glimpse the subject, let alone long enough for her to absorb whatever information it conveyed.

Dagon didn't know what to make of it. "Can I help you find something?"

Pausing, she smiled up at him. "No, thank you."

He caught a quick glimpse of what appeared to be an English/Segonian language translation guide before she resumed her swiping.

Did she seek the meaning of a particular word? Perhaps one she had overheard for which the translator she now wore in her ear could find no equivalent?

If so, she wouldn't find it without pausing to examine the pages she flipped through so quickly.

Shrugging it off, he returned to work.

A few hours passed. Normally Dagon grew restless when he sat in one place for too long. But not today. There was something comforting about having Eliana beside him. Even more so when she turned sideways in her chair, draped her legs over the far arm, and leaned back against Dagon's side, resting her head on his forearm.

He stared down at her in surprise.

Tilting her head farther back, she looked up at him. "Am I in your way like this?"

His mouth suddenly dry, he shook his head.

She smiled. "Good." Then she went back to swiping her screen.

Warmth blossomed in his chest and spiraled outward as... something suffused him.

Peace?

Contentment?

Yes, he concluded. It was nice, having her so close and breathing in her scent while he worked.

His men continued to dart looks their way that vacillated between astonishment and amusement, but said nothing.

Dagon enjoyed Eliana's presence so much that he couldn't even find it in him to scowl at them.

He and Eliana shared mid meal together in the mess hall. Once more she surprised and delighted him with the amount of food she consumed as she peppered him with more questions about Segonia, his life, and the Aldebarian Alliance. He lingered longer than he ordinarily would have, then reluctantly left her to return to work.

He was tempted to ask Eliana if she'd care to join him, but knew he would get more done without the distraction. After updating Tiran on Eliana's health, he participated in an Aldebarian Alliance holoconference with the other commanders participating in the search-and-rescue effort. Some were puzzled over the Gathendiens' actions and wondered why the Earth women were so valuable that the Gathendiens would risk launching a war with the entire Alliance in order to obtain them. Others simply assumed the Gathendiens had leaped at an opportunity to study a new race of people they might wish to conquer. *All* wanted to stop the *grunarks* from annihilating another species.

Dagon opted not to tell them that the Gathendiens had already released a bioengineered virus on Earth and wanted the women so they could ascertain why it hadn't worked. The Aldebarian Alliance was unanimously determined to rescue the Earthlings and punish the Gathendiens, so he saw no need to violate Eliana's confidence.

Unfortunately, the Alliance members' determination did not alter the fact that no other Earth women had yet been recovered. Dagon was examining a preliminary map the Sectas had produced of possible projection paths the escape pods might have followed after bursting out of the *qhov'rum* when a voice carried over the comm link in his earpiece.

"Commander Dagon," Joral said.

Dagon tapped it. "Yes?"

"Eliana's weapons are ready."

"Excellent. We'll retrieve them before last meal."

"Yes, sir."

Dagon checked the time. He could use some exercise after the long hours of inactivity he'd spent today. If he left now, he could train with some of his men before locating Eliana and escorting her to the armory. He grinned. Her appreciation of weapons appeared to rival his own, so he would enjoy seeing her face brighten with pleasure when Joral showed her the blades he had fashioned for her.

Dagon headed down to Deck 2, intending to join one of the units training in Section 2. However, his steps slowed to a halt in Section 1. Backtracking, he peered into one of the smaller training rooms. Maarev, Liden, and Efren were again engaged in battle. That wasn't surprising since they did so every day. Everyone aboard the *Ranasura*—even members of the maintenance crew—was required to train frequently to ensure the safety of all on board. But today Eliana lounged on the bench, watching them. Leaning back against the wall, she sat with one leg stretched along the cushions and one leg hanging off, her small booted foot swinging idly as she watched the men fight.

As though sensing his stare, she glanced over at the doorway.

Dagon's heart gave an increasingly familiar flutter at the smile that graced her pretty features when she spied him.

"Hi," she said, her voice full of cheer.

"Hello." He leaned his shoulder against the doorframe. "What are you doing?"

"Learning," she replied, just as she had earlier.

A thud sounded. Someone grunted. Moments later, Liden flickered into view. Bending forward, he clutched his ribs.

Efren laughed.

Eliana grinned and pointed at Dagon. "This time it was *his* fault, not mine."

Liden huffed a laugh and winced as he straightened. "Correct."

Amusement trickled through Dagon as he assessed Eliana. "Have you been distracting my soldiers while they train?"

"Yes, I have," she admitted without shame.

"Intentionally?"

"Yes."

"For what purpose?"

"Learning."

He expected her to say more, but the one-word answer seemed to satisfy her. "Would you care to take a break? I believe Joral has some weapons for you to inspect."

Eyes widening, she sat up straighter. "Weapons? What weapons? *My* weapons?" she asked quickly.

"Yes."

Leaping to her feet, she punched the air above her head. "*Yes! Woo-hoo!* See ya later, boys. Joral has some goodies for me."

Dagon couldn't help but grin at her almost childlike excitement.

The other men smiled and shook their heads, not just because her love of weapons entertained them but because she looked as though she had seen far fewer solar cycles than they had, yet she referred to them as boys.

As soon as she reached Dagon, Eliana grabbed his arm and tugged him out into the hallway. "Did he mention which weapons he finished?" she asked, practically bouncing on her toes as she urged him down the corridor. "Or weapon singular? Is it the katana? I hope it's the katana. Or maybe the shoto swords. Or—"

He grinned, finding her joy contagious. "He didn't say."

"Walk faster!" she commanded brightly. "Come on. Step to it. Your legs are a lot longer than mine, so I know you can do it. Go! Go! Go!"

Dagon laughed. She was so *drekking* adorable. And so full of life and joy despite the month of agony and fear she had suffered. "I don't wish to outpace you."

"You can't. I'm faster than I look. Get moving, handsome."

Handsome? Did she really think so?

Shaking his head at himself, he increased his speed.

Eliana easily matched it.

He lengthened his stride and picked up his pace even more.

Eliana kept up, not appearing to struggle in the least.

Curious to see how fast would be *too* fast for her, he increased his speed even more. By the time they reached the armory, passing multiple soldiers and crew members who stopped to gawk at them with wide eyes, he was walking as swiftly as he could without breaking into a jog. And Eliana remained at his elbow, never faltering.

Considering how much shorter her legs were, Dagon found it baffling. And entertaining as *srul*. It reminded him of the days in his youth when his mother had instructed him and his brother not to run and they had competed to see who could reach their destination the fastest without disobeying her.

Though Dagon had worked hard to become the commander of his own ship, he sometimes found the long stints in which his daily routine didn't change… dare he say boring?

Not with Eliana aboard though.

Smiling, he glanced down at her lovely face. A flush of excitement adorned her pale skin as stray wisps of black hair escaped her long braid and danced on the breeze their rapid pace created.

No. Boredom was the *last* thing he felt now.

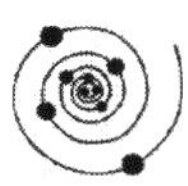

Eliana burst into the armorers' workroom and skidded to a halt.

Heads jerked up. Gazes latched onto them.

Beside her, Dagon chuckled.

Her heart pounded wildly against her rib cage as she looked up at him. And it wasn't a result of their brisk walk. He was so damned handsome… especially while he wore the boyish grin their unofficial race had spawned.

"You appear to love weapons as much as I do," he said, his eyes sparkling with mirth.

She grinned. "If that's true, then you love them a hell of a lot." Turning to the men who were seated at stations, repairing or cleaning weapons, she tossed them a wave. "Hi, guys! How's it going?"

They looked at each other.

"How is what going?" one asked.

She shrugged. "Your day. Your work shift. Life. I don't know. *You* choose."

He nodded. "All is going well, *ni'má*."

"Happy to hear it." She turned to face the design area and—as eager as a child on Christmas morning—skipped over to the chief weapons designer. "*Jor*-al," she sang.

Joral turned.

"Dagon said you have some goodies for me."

He smiled as she approached. "Indeed I do, Eliana." Reaching beneath a counter, he collected what reminded her a little of an area rug that had been rolled up. Placing it atop his design table, he unrolled the fabric.

A dozen throwing stars came into view first, glinting in the overhead light. He revealed two sheathed daggers next, then a pair of shoto swords, a couple of sais with grips that would fit her hands perfectly, and not one but *two* katanas.

"Ooooooh," she breathed reverently, her fingers itching to grab them. She had expected one or two weapons, not *all* of them. How the hell had he finished this many so quickly?

She dragged her gaze away from the gleaming metal and looked up at Joral. "You crafted them all from *mlathnon* or *alavinin*?" Though she had dedicated much of the day to swiftly learning the Segonian language, she was pretty sure she slaughtered the pronunciation of both metals.

"Yes, *ni'má*. Every blade you see here can repel blasterfire." The slightest shake of his head indicated he still thought her batty for believing she could fight off someone with an energy blaster while armed only with blades.

Eliana grinned. "Excellent." She motioned to the pretties. "May I...?"

"Of course."

She reached for a katana first. In the tight confines of a spaceship's hallway, the katana might not be the best tool to use, but it had been her weapon of choice ever since Seth had given her one shortly after her transformation.

Eliana held the weapon in both hands, admiring the workmanship Joral had put into the scabbard, the cord wrapped around the handle, the engravings on the guard, the blade collar... She slid him a look. "You're good."

Crossing his arms over his broad chest, he arched a brow. "I'm *better* than good."

She smiled. "Let's see, shall we?" Curling her fingers around the handle, she slowly drew the blade from its sheath.

When Dagon held out a hand, she passed him the scabbard.

Eliana held the sword horizontal to the floor and rested it upon the index finger of her free hand, shifting it until she found the balance point several inches distant from the guard. She nodded approvingly. "This sword has good cutting power." The farther the balance point from the guard, the stronger the cutting power. And any sword wielded with preternatural strength needed that.

"Every blade I craft has good cutting power," Joral stated with unabashed pride.

"I can believe that." She had wielded many swords over the

centuries and knew quality when she saw and felt it.

Glancing behind her, she backed away until she stood in a large bare area, then tossed the blade into the air. The sword came close to striking the high ceiling before the ship's artificial gravity drew it down again. As soon as the handle was in reach, she gripped it and started swinging. Familiar *whooshing* sounds filled the silent room as she swung the sword as if she battled multiple vampire foes. Though she carefully refrained from using her phenomenal speed, the blade still blurred as she spun and thrust and slashed at imaginary enemies in front of and behind her, twisting and ducking as though they fought back.

By the time she finished with a flourish, she was grinning big. It felt exactly like the katana she had lost in the battle with the Gathendiens, like an old friend with whom Joral had reunited her.

"I love it!" she proclaimed as she looked up from the blade.

Every man in the room stared at her, the workers with wide eyes, Joral with his arms now at his sides and a smile creasing his craggy features, and Dagon with obvious admiration… and something else.

Desire, perhaps?

Or was that merely wishful thinking? Because she sure as hell desired him.

Joral broke the silence. "You're good."

She grinned. "I'm *better* than good."

Barking out a laugh, he shook his head. "I believe you. But even the best swordsman or swordswoman can't repel blasterfire with a blade."

Eliana did not doubt she could, but opted to respond with "We'll see."

"Commander Dagon." Janek's voice emerged from speakers Eliana couldn't spot, his voice taut with tension. "Your presence is required on the bridge."

All levity left Dagon's handsome features as he tapped his earpiece. "I'm on my way, Janek." He handed Eliana the katana's scabbard. "Report."

Eliana didn't hear whatever Janek said because Joral murmured, "I'm glad the sword pleases you," as she sheathed the katana.

Dagon strode toward the doorway. "You're certain?"

Eliana kept her eyes on him even as she thanked Joral.

Stopping, Dagon looked at her over his shoulder. "You may wish to accompany me, Eliana. Janek believes he has located an escape pod."

Her breath caught.

Joral took the katana. "I'll hold this for you. You may retrieve it and inspect the other weapons later."

"Thank you." She hurried to join Dagon. "Has Janek communicated with whoever is in the pod yet? Is it one of my friends?" she asked as they strode down the corridor.

"He has attempted to communicate with the occupant but has received no response."

Anxiety rose. "Could it be empty? Could one of your allies have already rescued whoever was inside it?"

"No. All commanders in the Aldebarian Alliance are notified when a pod, a survivor, or a casualty is found so we can map the trajectories of their expulsion from the *qhov'rum* and use it to estimate where more may be located."

"That's smart."

"Also, whenever Alliance-sanctioned ships retrieve survivors, they collect the pods as well to return to the Lasarans."

She could understand that. It probably cost an arm and a leg to manufacture those things. Leaving them to float in the middle of nowhere would be a waste of both money and resources.

It might also give anyone outside the Aldebarian Alliance access to at least some of the Lasarans' advanced technology. Back on Earth, military outfits sometimes took pretty extreme measures to keep their technology from falling into the hands of enemy nations. The Lasarans would likely want to keep the Gathendiens from acquiring *anything* that might make them a more formidable opponent or help them survive space battles in the future. Based on the little bit of history she'd learned on the *Kandovar,* the Lasarans were likely already planning to attack the Gathendiens in retribution and either destroy them altogether or decimate their armies to such an extent that the Gathendiens would never again be able to wreak destruction upon others.

Though some might view that response as harsh, Eliana didn't. The Gathendiens wanted to kill every man, woman, and child on

Earth. As far as she was concerned, they deserved to meet the same fate they intended to dish out.

Tension thrummed through her as she and Dagon reached the bridge.

Janek glanced at them. "I picked up a distress beacon and traced it to a Lasaran escape pod."

"Show me," Dagon commanded.

Janek glanced at Galen. "Sending you the coordinates."

Galen's fingers moved across his console. A holographic map rose above his station. "Here." A bright red dot appeared amid the stars.

Eliana had no experience at all when it came to reading star charts. But her Second, Max, had an app on his phone that would alert him to nights when a comet, planet, eclipse, meteor shower, or the like might be viewed with the naked eye or through his fancy telescope. So she knew enough to understand that some of the bright specks in the sky that her fellow Earth dwellers mistook for stars were actually planets.

The red dot they now studied was awfully close to a cluster of lights that she was pretty sure weren't all stars.

"What are those?" She pointed to the cluster.

Dagon answered, never taking his eyes off the hologram. "The pod appears to be nearing a solar system similar to yours in which five planets observe elliptical orbits around their sun."

"Is that a good thing or a bad thing?" Images of an escape pod barreling through a solar system, getting caught up in a planet's gravitational pull, and crashing onto one of its moons danced through her head.

"Neither. Janek will seize control of the pod using the override code the Lasarans gave us, then will input a course devised by Galen to guide the pod *toward* us instead of *away* from us. Once that is accomplished, we should reach it more swiftly."

Hope rose. "Can you tell if anyone is inside it?" A lack of response didn't necessarily mean no one occupied it.

"Janek can determine that as soon as he initiates the override."

"Initiating override now." Janek's fingers flew across his console, typing as one might on a keyboard, though she saw no keys. Then he dragged one finger to the left.

A long moment passed. Then another.

Shaking his head, he mumbled something under his breath and repeated the motions.

Minutes ticked past.

Eliana bit her lip, desperately wanting to ask what the holdup was. But maybe there *was* no holdup. Maybe this was just how long it took to zip messages back and forth through space.

"Janek?" Dagon queried.

Or maybe not.

The comms officer released a huff of frustration. "The pod isn't accepting the override code."

"Hail it," Dagon commanded.

Janek worked whatever magic he did at his station. "Occupant of the escape pod, this is Communications Officer Janek of the *Ranasura*. Please respond."

Eliana held her breath.

Silence reigned.

"Occupant of the escape pod, this is Communications Officer Janek of the *Ranasura*, a Segonian vessel in good standing with the Aldebarian Alliance. We have picked up your distress signal and wish to render aid. Please respond."

More silence.

Eliana wondered if that might be because he spoke Segonian. "If one of my friends is in the pod, she may not understand you. Five of us only have—or had—translators you fit in your ear." The Lasarans had tried to surgically implant permanent translators in each of them, but the virus that had usurped the Immortal Guardians' immune system had rejected the implants, quickly and painfully forcing them out. "I lost mine during the attack. Maybe they did, too."

Janek repeated his greeting in Segonian, then English, Lasaran, and a fourth language that didn't sound familiar.

"What language is that?" she asked Dagon softly.

"Alliance Common. On some planets, translation implants and earpieces are quite expensive, so a common language was devised for any who can't afford one but nevertheless wish to be able to communicate with alien races."

"Oh."

Janek still received no response.

"Maybe the person in the pod doesn't know *how* to respond," she suggested. The *gifted ones* from Earth could probably figure it out. They were much more tech savvy than the immortals who'd accompanied them on the voyage. Most Immortal Guardians were a lot older than even the great-grandparents on Earth and were just as likely to be confounded by new technology, something that drove their Seconds to affectionately bestow "old fart" monikers upon them.

Judging by Janek's expression, he might give Eliana and her fellow immortals similar nicknames. "If you wish to respond," he instructed the occupant, "touch your finger to the flashing yellow light on the pod's command console and hold it while speaking."

More silence.

"If you are injured and unable to move, you may activate voice commands by speaking the pod's unique identifier number, then saying *initiate voice command*. The identifier number should be prominently displayed on the ceiling of the pod."

When even that generated nothing, Eliana looked up at Dagon. "Maybe they're afraid to respond. I risked a hell of a lot by trusting you. For all I knew, you could have been Gathendiens *posing* as good guys. Whoever is in that pod may not be willing to take that risk."

His brow furrowed. "What do you suggest?"

"May *I* speak to whoever it is? If it's one of my friends from Earth, hearing my voice will reassure her."

He motioned to Janek's station. "If you believe it will help."

Eliana moved to stand beside Janek. "What do I do?"

"When I press this, speak your message." He touched a finger to his screen, which she could now see illuminated multiple windows that showed a map, some kind of wavy lines that jumped whenever he spoke, and text she recognized as Segonian.

He nodded to her.

"Hi," she said, greeting the escape pod. "This is Eliana. If you were on board the *Kandovar* with me, I want to assure you that it *is* safe to respond. The Segonians are allies of the Lasarans and are one hundred percent trustworthy. They rescued me and now wish to rescue you. So if you're able to, please respond."

She held her breath, hoping to hear Simone or Ava or *any* of her friends express their relief at having been found.

But that hope dissipated as seconds, then minutes, passed in silence.

She looked at Dagon.

"Perhaps the pod is empty," he suggested.

Or perhaps the person in the pod was dead. If the override code on the pod was malfunctioning, other things might be malfunctioning, too. Crucial things, like the life support system.

But Eliana couldn't bring herself to voice the possibility, as though just saying it aloud might make it true. So she nodded. "How long will it take to reach it?"

Dagon looked at Galen.

"It's moving away from us, so it will take longer. My current estimate is six days."

Dagon frowned.

"What?" she asked.

He turned toward Janek. "It's only six days away. Why are we only now picking up the pod's distress signal?"

Janek glanced at Eliana briefly, then shook his head. "I don't know."

"Bullshit," she blurted, stomach sinking. "You *do* know. You just don't want to upset me."

He grimaced, confirming she had guessed correctly. "I can only surmise that whatever malfunction prevented the pod from accepting the override code is also affecting other systems and limiting the reach of the signal."

So she wasn't just being paranoid. The malfunction could have spread to other systems.

Eliana hated the feeling of helplessness that overwhelmed her then, hated knowing there might be nothing she could do to save her friends, that they could die out there, lost and alone.

In the past, there had *always* been something she could do when faced with tough situations. There had *always* been actions she could take to overcome whatever difficulties arose. If vampire populations increased at an alarming rate, leaving Immortal Guardians who hunted alone facing numbers they couldn't conquer single-handedly, she and her brethren could hunt in pairs to alleviate the threat. If she were severely injured and unable to contact her Second, she could do as she had done with Adaos and find an alternate blood source that would give her the strength needed to seek shelter. If some asshole intent on launching Armageddon managed to nab some Immortal Guardians he intended to torture and kill, she, her immortal brethren, and the human network that aided them could descend upon the enemy's base en masse and wreak bloody fucking havoc, delivering death to their enemy and freeing her friends.

And if she found herself alone, floating out in space in nothing but a suit, she could choose to trust the deep voice that spoke to her, offering sanctuary.

Hell, she had even managed to help her hunting partner Nick finally get together with his next-door neighbor just by inviting Kayla to kick back and relax with them one night.

There had *always* been some way Eliana could try to resolve things.

But this?

She shook her head.

This was so far beyond her experience and control she wanted to weep.

All she could do was wait and see what happened when they reached the pod.

Her eyes met Dagon's.

"*You* defied the odds," he reminded her softly. "Whoever is in that pod can, too."

That helped a little. If it were Simone or one of her immortal brethren, perhaps they didn't answer because they had slipped into stasis the way she had.

Lifting her chin, she gave her fears the mental middle finger. "You're right. My friends can defy the odds, too."

Dagon turned to Galen. "Set a course for the pod."

"Yes, Commander."

Six days, Eliana thought. She had six days to prepare.

CHAPTER 9

THE NEXT MORNING began much like the previous one had. Dagon sat in the commander's chair on the bridge. Eliana appeared, then dragged a chair over, plunked it down beside his, and proceeded to swipe through screen after screen on her tablet.

When she leaned closer and rested her head against his biceps, all kinds of warm tingly feelings leaped to life inside him. Dagon even found himself fighting a sudden urge to lean down and press an affectionate kiss to the top of her head. Instead, he occupied himself with trying to guess what she was searching for, but—as she had the previous day—Eliana swiped through the screens without pausing.

"What are you doing now?" he asked, unable to quash his curiosity.

"Learning," she replied once more.

It was a response he heard often in the days that followed, which rapidly fell into a routine. Every morning Eliana sat with him on the bridge and *learned*. Then they shared mid meal, parted for the afternoon, and came together again for last meal.

Dagon's favorite hours of each day were now those he spent with Eliana. Even when they each focused on their own tasks and didn't speak much, he liked being with her. He also enjoyed lingering over *dinner* as she called it, learning more about her as they shared last meal, the two of them smiling and laughing so often they raised eyebrows among the crew.

Almost a week into her stay with them, Dagon once more found himself eagerly anticipating her company after a particularly long afternoon full of holoconferences, problem solving, training evaluations, and other tasks his position as commander required. But he couldn't find her. When he didn't see her in any of the open-doored training rooms, he checked Med Bay, the mess hall, and her quarters. He even checked the armory.

"CC," he commanded finally, "locate Eliana."

"Searching," CC promptly replied. "Eliana is currently located on Deck 2 in Training Section 3, Simulation Room 1."

Dagon turned up the hallway and soon entered Training Section 3. Soldiers snapped to attention as he approached and passed. The light outside Simulation Room 1 glowed white, indicating one could enter without disrupting the simulation.

Dagon slipped inside, the door closing behind him. Bright flashes of light flared, simulating an explosion, then subsided. Abruptly engulfed in near darkness, it took a moment for his eyes to adjust enough to examine the scene. Three of his soldiers—armed with simulation-safe weapons—stood in the center of the large space. The walls, floor, and ceiling replicated a shadowy shuttle bay one might find on an Akseli battle cruiser. Several enemies were down, their armor still smoldering from either the energy blasts that had struck them or the explosion that had temporarily blinded him as he entered.

Since a stunner could render a soldier's camouflage inaccessible, all Segonian soldiers were ordered to train both with and without it. The three before him cautiously approached, then entered a corridor that branched in two farther down the way. Or the soldiers *appeared* to enter the corridor. The floor of the simulator allowed them to make the motion of walking forward without actually moving from their position in the center.

A faint rustling sound arose.

One of the soldiers held up a hand and issued a signal.

The others ceased moving. All lowered to a tense crouch, weapons ready.

A loud crunch sounded.

The three men spun to the left.

Dagon followed their gaze and nearly burst into laughter.

Eliana lounged on a bench, an open bag of *jarumi* nuggets in one hand. The slender fingers of her other hand bore a light coating of pale yellow dust as she crunched the tasty snack. "Nope," she said, her mouth partially full, "that was me again. Sorry."

Sighing in a way that suggested this wasn't the first time she had distracted them, the men straightened. Quoba—the party leader—made another hand motion, and the three resumed their simulated trek forward.

Dagon opened his mouth to speak, then hesitated.

Eliana stopped chewing and glanced at the hallway ahead of them on the right, then at the trio.

The men continued forward.

Again she glanced at the hallway, then at the soldiers.

An Akseli soldier in full-body armor stepped out of the hallway on the right and fired at the soldiers.

The three dodged the blasts and returned fire until the Akseli collapsed to the floor.

Eliana looked at Dagon. "I'd duck if I were you."

All three of his soldiers spun toward him, their bodies in a crouch. Two sighed and straightened, lowering their weapons. One fired.

Simulated blood spewed from Dagon's chest.

The two seasoned soldiers cursed.

The younger soldier stared at Dagon with wide eyes and flushed a deep scarlet as he stuttered an apology.

Dagon sent Eliana a baleful glance. "What are you doing?"

"Learning." A smile lit her features as she rose and motioned to the flustered soldier. "As is he." Popping another *jarumi* nugget into her mouth, she crossed to the young man. "Don't sweat it, Brohko. Just assume that every enemy you face is fighting dirty. I've used that tactic myself to trick an opponent into stabbing one of his own men." She tilted her head, her look turning thoughtful as she wiped her fingers on her pants, leaving yellow dust streaks on the black fabric. "Actually, I've used that one a lot. You'd be surprised how often it works."

"I wouldn't," Quoba muttered.

Brohko flushed again.

Eliana pointed behind the men. "You'd better look out."

None of the men even glanced over their shoulders, determined not to fall for another ruse.

"No, seriously," she said. "The simulation is still running."

Dagon looked past the men.

An Akseli soldier leaned out of the hallway on the left and lobbed an e-grenade.

As the trio whirled around, Eliana jumped up, caught the simulated grenade, and hurled it back with impressive speed.

An explosion lit up the hallway on the left.

The three soldiers gaped at her.

"Yes!" Spinning around, Eliana grinned up at Dagon. "That was *awesome!*" The fingers of her free hand curled as though she held a ball. "It felt like a real grenade! How does it do that?" The other hand still held her bag of *jarumi* nuggets.

Brohko stared at her. "How did *you* do *that*?"

She shrugged. "Just lucky, I guess."

Dagon seriously doubted that. "Pause simulation."

The simulation halted.

Eliana faced him once more, her expression turning earnest. "Now, if this were a real-world situation, would that grenade have exploded on contact or shocked me or anything?"

He shook his head. "E-grenades operate on a timer and are not triggered by contact."

"Is the time allotted always the same?"

"Yes. But sometimes the thrower will hold the e-grenade a moment before hurling it to reduce the time soldiers have to flee."

"Good to know." Before he could respond, her face lit with another smile. Holding up the bag in her hand, she pointed at it. "Have you tried these? They are freaking delicious."

How did she make him smile so easily? "*Jarumi* nuggets? Yes, I've tried them."

"They taste like nacho-cheese-flavored corn chips with a hint of whatever makes *vestuna* so spicy. This is my second bag."

He laughed.

Brohko stared at her. "You eat *vestuna*?"

Nodding, she handed the bag to Dagon. "Would you hold this for a minute please?" Once both hands were free, Eliana motioned to Brohko's weapon. "May I?"

Brohko looked at Quoba. After receiving a nod of permission, he handed over the osdulium rifle.

Eliana nudged her way between the men and stared at the frozen image. "Dagon, would you start it up again please?"

"Resume simulation," he commanded.

Smoke billowed from the hallway on the left. Boots clomped against the floor in the distance.

Eliana looked toward the hallway on the right, raised the O-rifle, and waited.

The footsteps sped up into a run as they grew closer.

Quoba and Tarok raised their weapons.

Then Eliana fired.

A bright ball of energy struck the wall and burned a hole through it.

She fired again. And again.

Cries of pain erupted. Several thuds sounded just before an Akseli soldier stumbled into view and fell to his knees, a scorched hole in the center of his chest.

"Okay," Eliana said with a smile. "I'm done."

"Pause simulation," Dagon ordered.

Staring down at the weapon in her hands, she turned it first to one side, then the other. "Hm." She handed it back to Brohko and reclaimed her snack bag. "Just checking." Delving into the bag, she drew out a dusty yellow nugget and popped it into her mouth. Her eyes closed as she chewed. "Oh man. These are sooooo good." When she opened her eyes, they sparkled with mirth as she looked up at him. "Seriously, you're going to have to hide these from me, or I'll end up eating every bag on the ship."

Shaking his head with a smile, he motioned to the door. "Shall we?"

She nodded and tossed the men a dusty wave. "Thanks for letting me sit in, guys."

All three nodded, the older two watching her with bemusement while Brohko stared at her with poorly disguised adoration.

Dagon shook his head as they left the simulation room. Brohko wasn't the only one to do so. Dagon had seen the same look on other faces.

Srul, he'd had to fight to keep from donning it himself a time or two. Eliana fascinated him.

And amused him.

Astonished him.

And aroused him.

She was just so *drekking* appealing. He had not discovered a single thing about her that he didn't like.

After devouring what must have been the last nugget, she tilted her head back and poured the crumbs at the bottom into her mouth. When she caught him watching, she covered her mouth and laughed. "Sorry about that. I burn a *lot* of calories." Again she wiped her hand on her pants, adding to the yellow dust that already decorated her thigh, then folded the empty bag and tucked it in one of her pants pockets. "So."

He arched a brow. "So?"

She patted the wall beside her, careful to use her clean hand. "What material are these made out of?"

"The walls?"

She nodded. "Most walls on Earth are made of gypsum plastered between two sheets of stiff paper. So they're easily damaged."

He nodded in the direction of the simulation room. "Is that what you were doing? Determining how hard it is to pierce a wall?"

"Yes. Back home, firearms you would probably consider primitive can easily propel projectiles through walls. Even brick walls."

He knew little of what warfare was like on her planet. "To answer your question…" He clasped his hands behind his back so he wouldn't be tempted to rest one on the base of her spine. Or lower. "The walls are made of metal."

"All of them?"

"All of them." He motioned to his left. "The closer to the exterior of the ship you get, the thicker those walls become."

"In case weapons fire should breach the outer surface?"

"Yes. The nearer the center…"

"The thinner the walls."

"Correct."

"Would you—?" She patted her pants pockets, then frowned. "Hang on a sec." Spinning around, she jogged back the way they had come.

Dagon tried but failed to keep his eyes from straying to her bottom.

Sooooo incredibly tempting in her tight pants.

Halting before Simulation Room 1, she poked her head in. "Sorry to interrupt, guys." She slipped inside as Quoba paused the simulation.

"Is this another lesson?" Brohko asked.

"No. I forgot my tablet." A moment later, she stepped back out into the hallway. "See ya later!" Breaking into a jog, she swiftly returned and halted before Dagon. "Would you please bring up a diagram of the ship for me so I'll know where I am with regard to the exterior at all times?" She handed him the data pad.

Dagon complied and handed the tablet back to her.

"Thank you." As she studied the screen, her face grew somber. "I should have done this on the *Kandovar*. But I was so caught up in the whole traveling through outer space for the first time thing. And the Lasarans made it seem as commonplace as taking a bus or something, so I just focused on the areas I liked the most and didn't think to..." Shrugging, she lowered the data pad and stared, unseeing, down the corridor. "I don't know. Maybe if I'd bothered to learn stuff like this on the *Kandovar*, I could've guided Ganix to a safer area and..." She looked down, swallowed hard, and shrugged again. "I don't know. Maybe he would've survived instead of dying while trying to save me."

Dagon rested a hand on her shoulder and gave it a gentle squeeze. "You don't know that's how he died," he said softly.

Tilting her head back, she met his gaze. Hers reflected both certainty and guilt. "It's how he died, Dagon."

So she was spending her days on the *Ranasura* "learning" in the hope that she might prevent such tragedies in the future. Eliana had saved dozens of lives when the *Kandovar* was attacked and yet flayed herself with guilt over one she had not.

Applying pressure to her shoulder, he drew her toward him and wrapped her in a hug. "I'm sorry you lost your friend."

Sighing, she leaned into him and looped her arms around his waist. "What if I lost *all* my friends?" she asked in a small voice.

"Prince Taelon and his lifemate survived," he reminded her, trying not to notice how right her body felt pressed against his.

"We're still searching for the others."

"But time is running out, isn't it?" Straightening, she backed away. "I mean, those escape pods can only support life for two months."

"Occupants can extend that if they ration. And if they find a habitable planet, there's no telling how long they could survive. Perhaps indefinitely if conditions are right."

"That's a lot of *ifs*."

"*Ifs* keep us fighting in untenable situations."

Her somber features softened. "Yes, I guess they do." Drawing in a deep breath, she held it a moment, then released it. Though her face brightened with another smile, he knew her well enough now to glimpse the sorrow she tried to hide behind it. "So, how soon is dinner? Because I'm famished."

Amusement rose despite his concern for her. "You just ate two bags of *jarumi* nuggets."

"I know. But I really wanted four."

He laughed. "As it happens, I came looking for you so that I might ask you if you would again care to join me for last meal. They have already begun serving."

"I would love to. Lead the way."

Once more, Eliana pleased Kusgan by requesting a warrior's portion. Dagon guided her to a table by another holowindow so she might enjoy the scenery and scents of Segonia.

Murmured conversation flowed around them as they dove into their meals.

As soon as he finished, Dagon pushed his tray aside, rested his elbows on the table, and leaned forward so he could lose himself in Eliana.

He didn't think a woman had ever intrigued or entertained him more. No woman had attracted him so intensely either. And Eliana did it without artifice or affectation. She didn't tease him with coy glances or seemingly innocent touches that weren't so innocent as some women had in the past. She just chatted and smiled and laughed in ways that made him feel lighter and kept a perpetual smile on his lips.

"So everyone on board is required to train, even the maintenance crews?" she asked.

"Yes."

"What about the kitchen staff? Do they train?"

"Yes."

"And the guys in engineering?"

"Yes. The *Ranasura* is a battleship. When conflict arises, we are the first sent in to handle it."

"Kinda like the marines back home. First to fight. Last to leave."

He nodded. "An apt description. And as you learned on the *Kandovar*, enemies can strike without warning. The more advanced an enemy's society is, the more likely they are to use subterfuge."

"Or just plain fight dirty like the Gathendiens, attacking in the middle of a damn *qhov'rum*."

Again he nodded. "In one of our earliest conflicts with the Gathendiens, some of their troops managed to board one of our battleships. Many of our soldiers were off-ship in fighter craft. The soldiers still on board were outnumbered and overwhelmed. All were slain. And the civilian crew members who remained lacked the skills necessary to emerge as victors when they attempted to fight back."

Her face sobered.

"It was the first and last time an enemy succeeded in seizing one of our ships."

"What happened? Did you get it back?"

He ground his teeth. "No. More Segonian battleships arrived to take it back. When the Gathendiens realized they were surrounded and would not be able to hold the ship they'd seized, they flew it into another of our ships. Both were destroyed, and many lives were lost."

Her lips tightened. "I hate those bastards."

"As do I. But we learned from our mistakes. We still employ civilians in non-combat-related positions. But every person on this ship is required to complete a designated number of hours of combat training every week."

"That's smart." She sat up straighter. "I'll begin my own training in two days." When he arched his brows, she smiled. "There are still a few things I want to learn first."

"You don't have to train, Eliana. You're—"

"Yes, I do. The more I learn," she stated evenly, "the more likely

I am to save lives the next time shit goes down."

Dagon had no wish to see her dive into battle, at least not until she became more familiar with the kind of battle that took place out here in space. But *vuan,* he respected her. "All right."

Leaning forward, she lowered her voice. "By the way, what's the Segonian equivalent for *shit*? Your language guides don't include curse words."

He laughed. "The most common equivalent you'll hear throughout the Alliance is *bura*."

"Good. Then don't give me any *bura* about being a guest and not needing to train."

He grinned. "I wouldn't dare."

Brohko interrupted them to exchange a few words with Eliana. Then another soldier did the same. And another. And another. It seemed as though half the mess hall's occupants stopped by their table to bid Eliana good night. And she knew almost every man's name.

Srul, even Dagon had trouble remembering a few of them, more familiar with their faces than their names.

He left her a moment to turn their trays in.

Kusgan shook his head in amazement. "Are you sure she didn't scoop some onto your plate when you weren't looking?"

Dagon laughed. "I'm sure."

Eliana kept up a steady stream of conversation while he walked her to her quarters.

Silently, Dagon admired the curve of her full breasts, the unconscious sway of her hips, the enticing bow of her upper lip that nearly drove him to dip his head and steal a kiss. But he didn't know what actions were deemed acceptable on her planet. Yes, Eliana touched him frequently, nudging him with her elbow, resting a small hand on his arm while she laughed over something he'd said just to see her smile, leaning against him when they sat beside each other on the bridge. She had even hugged him. Several times now.

However, the fact that such casual touches were acceptable didn't mean that more intimate contact was, too. Brushing his lips against hers, for example. Slipping his tongue inside to taste and tease hers. Sliding his hands around her waist and drawing her tight against his body so she could feel how hard she made him. Peeling her clothes off layer by layer—

"You're quiet all of a sudden."

Blinking, he glanced down and found her regarding him curiously. "Apologies. I don't mean to be."

She sent him a commiserating smile. "A lot on your mind?"

A lot of *her* on his mind. "Yes."

"Me, too."

They stopped before her cabin. Eliana pressed her hand to the pad on the wall, then watched the door slide up.

She grinned. "I don't think I'll ever get tired of that."

So adorable. "Are your accommodations to your liking?"

"Very much so. This room is definitely swankier than the one I had on the *Kandovar*."

As she turned to face him, Dagon again marveled over her size. The top of her head didn't even reach his shoulder. Everything about her screamed delicate and fragile. But when he'd watched her swing her katana with fascinating strength and expertise…

Well. The dichotomy of it captivated him. Titillated him. And, yes, aroused him. He'd wanted to pull her into his arms and do all manner of things her people might find offensive.

Still did.

She stared up at him.

Did he imagine it, or did the air suddenly feel charged?

A faint glow entered her gaze before she lowered it. To his surprise and pleasure, she leaned in to give him another treasured hug. "Good night, Dagon."

Since he knew hugs were acceptable, he eagerly wrapped his arms around her and held her close. "Good night, Eliana."

Despite her diminutive size, she felt good against him. The desire that had been flirting with him intensified, almost daring him to risk offending her by letting his hands stray. He was a hair away from giving in to the impulse when she released him, turned away without looking at him, and entered her room.

The door slid closed between them.

Well, *drek*.

Eliana hesitated when she reached the door to the bridge. She had come damned close to doing something stupid last night. Or maybe something awesome.

She growled softly. Would it have been stupid or awesome?

Much to her frustration, she couldn't tell.

She had spent centuries treading lightly around Immortal Guardian males on Earth. Most were as lonely as she and wished they could find a woman who would love them enough to spend eternity with them. But none of them had knocked her socks off or heated her blood the way Dagon did. So she had always carefully kept all contact casual.

Once she'd left Earth, she had then spent four months around Lasaran men who looked at her as if she had just flashed her bare breasts if she so much as brushed against them while walking down a hallway. And now that she very much *wanted* to push past casual contact and pursue greater intimacy with a man, she found herself beset with annoying doubts and insecurities.

Add to that the fact that she knew little to nothing about his culture (apparently personal data tablets didn't come with a nice list of clear-cut societal guidelines because the crew already knew them) and didn't want to do anything that might break any rules or offend him or anyone else on this ship and…

Yeah. She didn't know what the hell she was doing.

Or rather, she didn't know what the *srul* she was doing.

Sighing, she placed her palm on the reader. The door slid up. As soon as she entered the bridge, her gaze went straight to Dagon.

Glancing over, he smiled, his handsome face lighting up.

Holy hell, it made her feel good when he did that. Just one smile and warmth filled her, her lips stretched in a grin, and happiness bubbled up inside her.

She was so freaking smitten. "Hi."

He rose. "Hello."

She offered the rest of the crew a wave. "Hi, guys."

"Eliana," they chorused, making her feel like Norm on the sitcom *Cheers*.

Dagon retrieved the chair she had been using and plunked it down beside his. "You missed first meal."

She wrinkled her nose. "I know. I had trouble sleeping last night." Too busy picturing him naked. "So I woke later than usual." When he frowned, she headed off whatever he intended to say by holding up her tablet and a bag of *jarumi* nuggets. "Don't worry. I came prepared."

He laughed.

The two of them settled into their seats. The rest of the crew had grown accustomed to her presence, it would seem, because far fewer curious glances alighted upon her as she allowed herself the luxury of leaning against Dagon's arm while she situated her tablet on her lap and opened her bag of snacks.

What did he make of her leaning against him like this? He never complained. If anything, she thought it amused him, or perhaps the initial astonishment of his crew amused him. Eliana would've worried that he might simply view her as a little sister since she was so much shorter than most Segonian women if she hadn't felt his body respond to hers last night when she hugged him, which was what had led to her picturing him naked and had kept her up half the night.

She fought the urge to roll her eyes at herself. As if she hadn't already been picturing him naked. Dagon had a seriously drool-worthy body. But the fact that he hadn't *acted* on the lust his body had divulged made her doubt even more the wisdom of throwing caution to the wind, kissing the stuffing out of him, and making her own desire known.

Wouldn't he have tried to cop a feel by now if such was acceptable in his society?

Calling herself a wuss for not simply asking him, she devoted her attention—or most of it anyway—to studying one diagram of the ship after another on her tablet while she munched the tasty *jarumi* nuggets. She was determined to learn every inch of this massive ship. Like the Segonians, she would learn from mistakes of the past.

Fortunately, she had an excellent memory. Not as excellent as Ethan's. That fun-loving American Immortal Guardian could remember every second of every minute he had ever lived with crystal clarity. He even remembered the day he was born.

She frowned. Perhaps if her memory were as freakishly sharp as Ethan's, she would remember Ganix helping her before he died. Perhaps she would remember exactly *how* he had died. What if she had roused briefly and just couldn't recall it?

Guilt twisted her stomach into a knot whenever she thought of the *Kandovar*'s chief engineer. Ganix wasn't the first man who had died trying to protect her. One of her Seconds had done the same long ago. She had vowed then that it would never happen again. Yet it had. Because she hadn't understood enough about her new environment. Nor had she known enough about how battles were fought out here in space or how the ships worked. Even knowing what the walls were made of, how thick they were, and which ones provided the best protection might have enabled her to save Ganix's life. Instead, his body lay in cryostasis, awaiting delivery to Lasara for burial.

"Eliana?" Dagon spoke softly.

She glanced up.

"Your eyes are glowing," he murmured.

Swearing, she squeezed her eyes shut and counted to ten before opening them. "What about now?"

"They're brown again."

"Thank you." She glanced around, relieved that none of the crew had noticed the slip.

"What troubles you?" Dagon prompted, keeping his voice low.

She shook her head. "Just… thinking about Ganix again and wishing I could've saved him."

Nodding his understanding, he leaned a little closer, offering silent solace.

Tilting her head until it rested against his biceps, Eliana went back to studying the ship.

Hours passed. She and Dagon shared mid meal. Then the two parted ways as had become their habit. Eliana watched him walk away, admiring every loose stride and the ripple of muscle beneath his uniform. Just before he reached the curve at the end of the hallway, he glanced back.

Smiling, she waved and started walking backward.

He grinned and waved back, then disappeared from view.

Resolution filled her.

Spinning around, Eliana took off down the hallway, picking up speed until she was running.

Moments later, she burst into Med Bay. "Adaos! I need you!"

CHAPTER 10

ACROSS THE ROOM, Chief Medical Officer Adaos jumped and spun around. Something clattered to the floor behind him as he eyed her with alarm.

"What is it? Are you injured?" He gave her a swift once-over. "Is someone else injured?" Bending, he grabbed a medic bag stashed beneath the table and strode toward her. "How many are hurt? Where are they?"

Another man in a medic uniform grabbed a second bag and stepped forward, brow furrowing with concern.

Chagrin swept through her. "No one is injured," she hastened to assure them. "I'm sorry I startled you both." She looked to Adaos. "There's just something I need to discuss with you."

He drew a small scanner out of his pocket and held it out in front of her. "Something of some urgency, too, judging by your biometric readings." Setting the bag down, he stared at her expectantly.

She glanced at the other man, who watched her with unconcealed curiosity. Leaning toward Adaos, she asked in a low voice, "Is there somewhere private we could talk?"

His eyebrows rose. Then he looked at the other man. "Leave us, please."

The man left without hesitation, closing the door behind him.

"CC," Adaos said.

"Yes, Chief Medical Officer Adaos."

"We are not to be disturbed unless someone requires immediate aid."

"Yes, Chief Medical Officer Adaos."

He frowned at Eliana. "Do you require a transfusion?"

"No." She shifted her weight, a little embarrassed now. How exactly should she broach this with him? "Actually, yes. I could use a transfusion." It *had* been a few days. And this would give her a minute to figure out what to say.

He motioned for her to lie on a nearby exam table. "Transfuse Eliana with Segonian blood as prescribed in her file."

"Beginning transfusion," the computer said in her gentle female voice.

Unease momentarily distracted Eliana. She really did hate needles.

A robot arm descended from the ceiling. A grid pattern lit up the bend of her left arm as a cool spray coated her skin. Then the needle pricked her and blood began to flow into her veins.

Adaos studied her. "Do you wish me to hold your hand as Commander Dagon did?" Not an ounce of sarcasm or condescension laced his words, just a desire to ease her discomfort.

He was a good guy.

"No, thank you."

He nodded. "What did you wish to discuss with me? Have you a physical ailment? I admit I expected to see you sooner after I heard you've been eating *vestuna*. I fear it may be too spicy for an Earthling's digestive tract."

She smiled. "I'm used to spicy food. That's not it."

"You have another complaint?" Brow furrowing, he picked up a nearby data tablet. "Lasaran doctors warned us that the Earth women we retrieved might experience psychological issues after suffering the trauma of the Gathendiens' attack."

"The ones like me who need blood transfusions won't. We're using to fighting and battle, blood and death. But the others might," she conceded.

"So you're contending with no psychological effects?"

She started to shrug but remembered in time that a needle was still stuck in her arm. "Just worry for my friends and the anxiety that brings." And guilt, of course. Not just over what happened to Ganix. But because she felt like crap for making herself at home on this ship while her friends could be out there somewhere, alone and afraid in those pods. Or maybe crashing in those pods. Hell, she didn't know if her immortal brethren had even made it *into* pods. The last time she'd seen them, they had been helping the Lasarans like her. They might not have had a Ganix nearby to get their asses into suits or into pods if they waited too long to do it themselves.

Not knowing their fate really ate at her. Sure, they *could* be in pods. Or they could be floating helplessly in space in a suit like her. Or they could be floating in space *without* suits like Ganix had. The peculiar virus that infected them could heal a hell of a lot of damage. It could even allow Immortal Guardians to slip into a state of hibernation as she had if their blood volume dipped too low or they lacked access to food or water for extended periods of time. But could it enable them to survive in the cold vacuum of space with no protection?

She didn't think so.

"Eliana—"

"Nope. I didn't come here to talk about that."

The needle withdrew from her flesh. The mechanical arm retracted. The tiny puncture wound healed as she sat up and swiveled to dangle her legs over the edge of the bed.

Adaos took her arm and studied it. "Amazing. You heal as swiftly as a Lasaran."

She pointed at him. "That's what I want to talk to you about."

His eyebrows rose. "It is?"

"Yes. You want to know more about me, right? You want to run tests, take samples, and study me?"

"Yes," he responded eagerly.

"Can you do it confidentially and ensure that no one else will ever get their hands on the data? Because if the Gathendiens gained access to your research, it would be devastating, not just to my brethren but to my entire planet." Immortal Guardians were the only ones keeping vampires in check. If the Gathendiens found a way to exterminate Immortal Guardians with another virus, humanity would be lost.

"I would take strict measures to ensure that no one other than myself could access the information."

"Then I suggest we engage in a little quid pro quo."

Again he frowned. "Quid pro quo?"

"Yes. You know—if *you* do something for me, then *I'll* do this for you."

His expression turned guarded. "What would you require me to do?"

"Tell me everything there is to know about Segonian social etiquette, especially with regard to courtship and mating rituals. I need to know what's allowed and what isn't."

His brow smoothed out. His light green eyes sparkled with mirth as his lips twitched. "Would this need to learn about Segonian mating rituals pertain to your interactions with anyone in particular?"

"That depends. Do patients on this ship have doctor-patient confidentiality?"

"By that, are you asking if I am compelled as a medic to keep anything you share with me private?"

She nodded.

"Of course… as long as it doesn't endanger the other occupants of this ship."

"Good. Then yes," she admitted, "it *does* pertain to someone in particular. I am totally smitten with Dagon and want to know what I can and can't do about it. Earth's rules are incredibly lax on that. Pretty much anything goes as long as it takes place between consenting adults, bonded or unbonded. But I just spent four months aboard a Lasaran ship with men who went out of their way to avoid touching me. I mean, if I so much as brushed their arms while passing them in the hallway, they looked at me as if I'd just goosed them."

"What does *goosed them* mean?"

"Pinched their bottoms."

He came damn close to guffawing over that. "Lasarans are quite strict when it comes to interactions between unbonded men and women," he said as he brought his mirth under control. "They are an older society with significantly longer life spans, so—until their recent difficulties—they slowed their population growth by enacting stringent social protocols. But we Segonians only live an average of one hundred and fifty years, so our society is more lax with regard to regulating social interactions."

"How lax? Because everyone seemed pretty shocked when I hugged Dagon on the bridge."

He tucked his medic bag back in its place beneath the table. "I heard about that." A small smile tilted his lips as he leaned back against the counter and crossed his arms. Eliana hadn't realized until then that he was quite handsome and—like Joral—was built like a warrior. "The cause of their shock was twofold. Most people are intimidated by Dagon."

"Because of his rank? Or because he looks like he can totally kick ass?"

His teeth flashed in a grin. "Both. And because he is usually somber of nature, which can make him seem rather grim and foreboding."

Really? Dagon was usually somber? She would never have guessed that. He usually smiled and laughed freely when they were together.

"And you're so small and delicate in appearance," Adaos continued, "that the crewmen on the bridge were likely shocked that you didn't fear him."

"The first time they saw me, I shoved a blaster under his jaw and threatened to blow his head off."

"*Drek,* I wish I could've seen that," he said on a laugh.

She wrinkled her nose. "Yeah. Sorry about that. About biting you, I mean."

He waved a hand in dismissal. "You've already apologized, and I don't hold it against you. You're a soldier. Soldiers do what they must to survive."

"Thank you." She pondered what he'd said. "So it wasn't so much the hug that shocked them but my lack of fear?"

"Yes."

"Tell me more about the other reason it shocked them."

He shrugged. "I doubt any of them have ever seen Dagon embrace a woman or freely express affection for one before."

She stared at him. "Why? I know he isn't gay." Kinda hard to miss the fact that her hugs aroused him.

"Gay?"

"Attracted to other men."

"Ah." He shook his head. "No. His interests lie only with

women. But he's a solitary sort. And when we dock in spaceports to pick up supplies or make repairs, he doesn't visit the bars or pleasure houses with the other men. He remains on the ship."

Seemed kinda lonely. "Then hugs are okay?"

"Yes."

"What about kisses?"

His smile broadened. "I'm sure Commander Dagon would like your kisses."

"With tongue?"

"Yes."

"What about touching? Can I hold his hand?"

"Yes."

"Can I… hmmm… How should I put this?" She nibbled her lower lip. "Feel him up?"

He clamped his lips together, leading her to suspect he was once more struggling to hold back laughter. "Do you mean fondle him?"

"Yes. I'll go with that."

"As long as he desires it, you can touch him like a lover."

"What about intercourse? Can we make love?"

"Yes."

"If we do, will we be breaking any laws? Like no sex before marriage? Or…" She thought of some of the sci-fi romance novels she'd read. "If we make love will we be mated for life?"

A look of pure horror crossed his features. "*Drek* no!"

She laughed. "You look pretty appalled by the idea."

"I am." He gave a little shudder. "If I had bonded to the first woman who *drekked* me, I would have been locked into a miserable, loveless existence."

She stared at him. "Wow. If you hated her so much, why did you sleep with her?"

"I didn't hate her. I just didn't know her well. Once I did…" Again he shuddered. "I pity the poor *grunark* who ended up with her."

She wasn't sure what *grunark* meant, but apparently he'd dodged a bullet there.

Eliana slid off the table. "Okay. So… no one will think I'm a total slut if I kiss or hug Dagon in public?"

"My translator isn't defining the word *slut*."

She tried to think of a generic equivalent that would translate easily and might be less offensive than *whore*, which was the term she'd heard the most often in her youth. But all she could come up with was "Someone of loose morals, I guess?"

"Ah." He smiled. "No. No one will think you're a slut if they see you hug or kiss Dagon."

"What if we… become intimate?" She was not exactly comfortable talking about this. She'd been born four centuries ago when women didn't even mention such things.

"None will seek to shame you for that."

She relaxed. "Excellent." She could now act on some of those impulses that plagued her whenever she was around Dagon's sexy ass. Butterflies filled her belly at just the thought of it. "Well, I guess that's all I need to know. Thanks."

"Actually, it isn't," he countered.

The butterflies died at his somber tone. "Okay." She leaned back against the table. "Tell me." *Please don't let it be that Dagon is engaged.* He'd said he wasn't bonded, but that didn't mean he didn't have a lover somewhere that the other guys didn't know about. That would totally suck. And would explain why he hadn't acted on his desire.

"I've been studying the data Sectas have amassed about Earthlings," Adaos began.

Now *he* looked uneasy.

"And?" she prompted when he hesitated to finish his thought.

"And there is a very important difference between our two cultures."

Oh crap.

"Once they enter into a relationship, Segonians are a wholly monogamous people."

She hadn't realized she was holding her breath until it rushed out in a relieved whoosh. "Oh. Good." She had never been a *playing the field* kinda gal and was glad she didn't have to worry about Dagon doing the same. She had no interest in sharing him.

Adaos continued. "You can't pursue more than one man at a time."

She nodded. "Okay. I wouldn't do that anyway."

"I wish to be very clear about this, Eliana." Both his expression and tone were so earnest they bordered on threatening. "If you embark upon a sexual relationship with Dagon, you *canno*t seek the attention of someone else on this ship. Even flirting that you might consider innocent would be viewed harshly unless you first ended your relationship with Dagon."

Irritation slithered through her. "I said I wouldn't do that." And she couldn't help but feel insulted that he thought she would. "On my planet we call flirting with one guy when you're committed to another cheating. And I am *not* okay with that." Crossing her arms over her chest, she scowled at him. "Besides, the only man I want to get naked with is Dagon."

He held up a hand in a placating motion. "All right. I know little of your people beyond what the Sectas have told us. I meant no disrespect."

Apparently the Sectas knew a lot. Cheating and playing the field was pretty common on Earth. "Okay," she mumbled.

"You should also know that when Segonians bond, or *marry* as you Earthlings say, we bond for life. That's why—like Lasarans—we call our spouses our lifemates. There is no divorce on Segonia."

"Oh." She hadn't really thought that far ahead. She was just so attracted to Dagon and enjoyed his company so much that she'd…

Well, she hadn't thought beyond the desire to spend more time with him and eventually get him naked. Now that she *did* though, depression landed on her shoulders like a vulture, digging its talons into her flesh.

Silence encapsulated them, stretching into awkward territory.

Adaos tilted his head to one side and studied her intently. "That disturbs you?"

Uncrossing her arms, she rested a hand on the edge of the exam table behind her and drew patterns on it with her index finger.

"Eliana?"

Closing her eyes, she shook her head and forced herself to ask, "What about children?"

"Children?"

She opened her eyes enough to stare down at the table. "If a woman can't give a Segonian man children… is that a deal breaker?" She dropped her gaze to the floor. "I mean… if pregnancy wasn't an option, would he not want her?"

"You believe you are infertile?" he asked, the kindness in his voice almost sparking tears. "Nothing in your initial exam indicated as much."

"It isn't that. It's the virus." The virus the damn Gathendiens had unleashed upon them. "We don't know what it would do to a baby." She forced herself to meet his gaze. "None of us—no Immortal Guardian females—have ever gotten pregnant. And no Immortal Guardian male has ever impregnated a human woman because..." She shrugged helplessly. "We don't age."

Clinical curiosity entered his sharp gaze. "Are you like the Lasarans? Do you age very slowly? Some of them have been known to live a thousand years."

Wow. That was some seriously slow aging. "No. We don't age *at all*. And we don't know if the virus would keep a baby from aging, too, if the child would mature intellectually and emotionally but be forever trapped in the body of an infant, or how the virus might affect a developing fetus. And none of us wanted to risk it. That's actually one of the reasons Seth wanted all the Immortal Guardians who made this trip to be female. He knows how much some of us wish we could have children and was hoping either the Lasarans or the Sectas could help us find a way to carry and birth a healthy child free of the virus."

Adaos stroked his jaw as he considered her thoughtfully. "There may be a way to prevent transmission of the virus from mother to child in the womb. Or perhaps we could find a cure for it altogether. We are more advanced in our knowledge of medicine than Earthlings."

She glanced around at the high-tech gadgets the infirmary boasted, then at the scanner above her that could pass a wand over her and—within seconds—tell her every single thing that was damaged. "Yes, you are. But the Gathendiens created this virus in a lab. It's unlike anything else our scientists on Earth have seen and behaves more like a symbiotic organism. The first thing it does is destroy our immune system, then take its place, leaving us with a totally jacked-up catch-22: if you eliminate the virus, we'll be left with no viable immune system."

"So you think a cure could kill you."

"A cure *would* kill us."

He shook his head. "Not necessarily. Segonian knowledge and understanding of viruses by far exceeds that of Earthlings. Not just because we are centuries ahead of you technologically but because we have not been limited to only studying viruses and bacteria on our homeworld. Space exploration—and our membership in the Aldebarian Alliance—has given us the opportunity to study viruses and bacteria from many other worlds in many other solar systems. Alien viruses, bacteria, plants, and animals. Worlds that are populated *and* worlds that are not. Worlds that we have not even visited ourselves but that have been visited by fellow members of the Alliance who engage in the sharing of information. Your commanding officer was wise to send you to us."

She tried futilely to tamp down the spark of hope that flared. "So you think there's a way around it, that I may one day be able to get pregnant without infecting the baby with the virus?"

"I believe it's possible, yes. Because the virus was engineered in a lab, I will need to study it extensively before I can say anything with certainty though."

She extended an arm. "Then take whatever samples you need."

Dagon studied the holographic map Galen displayed. Red dots marked places casualties had been found. Green dots marked places escaped pods supporting survivors had been successfully retrieved. Yellow dots marked two places in which empty escape pods had been recovered.

More color appeared on the map every day. Though a few clusters drew his eye, he could find no definitive pattern. Some of the escape pods and survivors were found close to the *qhov'rum* from which they had been ejected. Others had been flung far away from it like Eliana.

"Show me Alliance vessels performing search-and-rescue missions."

Purple dots appeared.

Galen pointed to a gray one. "This is the Akseli pirate Janwar."

Once again Dagon marveled over the speed at which Janwar's ship traveled. "Has he reported finding anyone?"

"No. But we received a report earlier that he did engage a Gathendien scout ship in battle. He wished to take the pilot alive for questioning but was unable to."

That Janwar had run into a Gathendien ship at all seemed to confirm the belief that those *grunarks* were looking for survivors, too.

"Show me all planets in these sectors"—he motioned to three—"that have an atmosphere hospitable to Earthlings and Segonians."

A few blue dots joined the others on the map.

He pointed. "This one isn't far from the pod we seek. If the pod is empty and we don't pick up any other communications, we'll go there next."

Janek joined them. "This one?"

"Yes."

"I'll see what I can pick up on comms."

Dagon looked at his tactical officer. "Rahmik, learn what you can about the planet and report back to me. I want to know if it's home to any sentient life forms who might have retrieved the occupant of the pod."

"Yes, Commander."

Maarev's voice floated out of the bridge speakers. "Commander Dagon."

"Yes?"

"A situation has arisen in Group Training Room 4."

Dagon frowned. "What kind of situation?"

"Is the situation me?" Eliana asked, her words quieted by distance. "Are you talking about me?"

"Yes," Maarev replied.

"You know I can hear you, right? I mean, I'm standing right in front of you."

"Yes."

Dagon fought a smile. "What's the problem, Maarev?" Was Eliana distracting the soldiers again? Considering the lesson Brohko had learned the previous day, that might not be a bad thing.

"What are you doing?" Maarev demanded suddenly, surprise altering his voice.

"Dragging you down to my level," Eliana replied, her voice

louder now. "I don't have one of those communication thingies. If I get up in your face, can Dagon hear me?"

"Commander Dagon," Maarev corrected.

A long-suffering sigh carried through the speakers. "If I get up in your face," Eliana said as though striving for patience, "can Commander Dagon hear me?"

"Yes."

"Okay. So here's the deal, Dagon—"

"Commander Dagon." This time when Maarev corrected her, Dagon could hear his friend's amusement.

"You *want* me to hurt you, don't you?" Eliana nearly growled.

Every man on the bridge laughed.

"Anyway," she continued, "as I was saying, Commander Dagon, I came down here to train with your men, but all of them keep wussing out and refuse to spar with me. They're all too afraid you'll kick their asses if they try to kick mine. But I *really* need to get some practice time in. Would you please tell them it's okay to fight me?"

Shaking his head, Dagon headed for the door. "Tell her I'm on my way, Maarev."

As he left, he heard Galen whisper, "Bring up video of GTR4."

"I'm already on it," Rahmik responded.

When Dagon reached the corridor outside Group Training Room 4, he found it packed with soldiers vying for a position that would allow them to see inside. A single scowl snapped them to attention and sent them scattering to other rooms.

Dagon entered the large training room and closed the door. Seventeen men occupied the benches along the walls, leaving a gap between them and Eliana, who frowned as she watched the melee in the middle.

Maarev once more battled Liden and Efren in the center of the room, but this time none were camouflaged.

Dagon skirted the edge of the training mat and sat beside Eliana. His arm brushed her shoulder. His thigh pressed against hers as he leaned back, knees comfortably splayed, boots planted on the floor. He could've left some room between them but just didn't want to.

She didn't seem to mind as she glanced up at him.

He arched a brow. "Learning again?"

"No." She sent Maarev a dark look. "I've already learned everything I wanted to from observing. To learn the rest, I need to spar, but everyone is too chicken to take me on."

Although Dagon suspected his translator wasn't defining *chicken* accurately, he believed he gleaned her meaning. "You're a great deal smaller than us… *and* smaller than Segonian women… with less musculature. They're afraid they'll hurt you."

Now *she* arched a brow. "And that you'll kick their asses if they do?"

"Yes." It was a valid concern, though he opted not to say as much.

"Then tell them you won't."

He hesitated. He couldn't guarantee he wouldn't react badly if one of his men hurt her. The soldier in him understood her need to train and prepare as best she could for any battles that might lie ahead, but the man—the nonsoldier part of him—was so drawn to her. He cared more for her every day and couldn't bear the thought of her getting injured.

She placed a small hand on his where it rested on his thigh and gave it a squeeze. "We're only a couple of days away from the escape pod. I need to familiarize myself with whatever passes for hand-to-hand combat out here before we find it. I need to be prepared. For *anything*."

Dagon saw again the sorrow in her pretty brown eyes and wanted to spare her more in the future, so he quashed his protective instincts. For now.

"Halt," he commanded.

The soldiers ceased fighting and faced him.

"Maarev, Liden, have a seat," Dagon ordered. "Efren will battle Eliana now."

Every man in the room sat up straighter.

Reaching beneath the bench, Eliana drew out a training sword with a dulled blade.

Dagon stayed her. "Let's start with staffs."

Shrugging, she rose and headed to the center of the room. "Okay."

Brohko jumped up and handed her a wooden staff.

Eliana thanked him and gave the staff a twirl as Maarev and

Liden retreated to the benches. "Maarev and Liden don't have to leave. I can fight all three at once."

A few soldiers laughed in disbelief.

Eliana ignored them.

Recalling the way she had swung her *katana,* Dagon was inclined to believe she spoke the truth. But he would proceed with caution nevertheless. "One will do for now."

Efren took the staff a fellow soldier handed him.

Eliana studied him thoughtfully. "You aren't going to get your shorts in a bunch if I win, are you?"

He blinked. "I don't know what that means."

"You aren't going to be upset, are you? If I win?"

"No. Will you be upset when I defeat you?"

She grinned. "Not gonna happen, my friend."

He chuckled. "We shall see. Let us begin."

The words had no sooner left his lips than Eliana struck.

Surprise lit Efren's face as he blocked her strike. And the one that followed. And the next and the next. She had good form, a sharp gaze that seemed to miss nothing, and was swift on her feet. A true warrior, as Dagon had expected.

She shook her head. "You're just playing defense. Play offense. Come on. Try to hit me."

Dagon silently agreed. Efren was simply reacting to her strikes instead of attempting any of his own.

Until Eliana swept his feet out from under him and landed him on his ass.

"I'm serious," she stated. "Hit me."

Efren glanced at Dagon as he rose.

Dagon ignored the nervous flutter in his stomach. "Do as she says."

Efren altered his fighting technique accordingly, blocking Eliana's swings and attempting a few of his own.

But Eliana fended off every blow and once more landed him on his ass. "I've watched you fight, Efren. I know you're better than this." Frustration painted her features as she shook her head. "Quit *drekking* around. I get that you don't want to hurt me. But Gathendiens *will*. You pussyfooting around isn't going to prepare me for that. Come and get me, damn it."

Imagining Eliana coming up against Gathendien soldiers unprepared must've changed Efren's mind about taking it easy on her, because he began to fight in earnest then.

And what a fight it was.

Dagon leaned forward, propping his elbows on his knees as he watched Efren do his damnedest to take Eliana down. Cheers erupted from the other soldiers, many of them for Eliana. One would think Efren would have the advantage since he was a lot taller and had a much longer reach. But Eliana was fast and skilled and—

Efren caught her across the back and sent her sprawling to the floor.

Every man gasped.

Dagon rose, his heart in his throat.

Efren stared down at her in horror.

It had been a hard blow.

Eliana laughed. Rolling over onto her back, which must hurt like *srul*, she held up a hand.

Efren swiftly clasped it and pulled her to her feet.

As soon as she stood, she smiled and clapped him on the back with her free hand. "I let you get that one in so you—and everyone else here—would see I won't shatter." She sent Dagon a meaningful look.

He sat back down, his heart still pounding in his chest.

She didn't walk stiffly or wince when she bent to retrieve her fallen staff. "Okay." Facing Efren again, she twirled the staff. "Now that *that's* out of the way, give me all you've got."

His eyes alight with admiration, Efren did as ordered and swung. Cheers once more erupted as the two engaged in fierce, single-minded combat. Dagon had fought Efren many times in the past and could tell the soldier held nothing back. Yet time and again Eliana emerged the victor.

She helped Efren up after felling him once more. "Now Maarev and Liden."

Maarev and Liden glanced at each other. Maarev jerked his head toward the center of the room.

Liden rose and approached Eliana.

She shook her head. "Both of you. *And* Efren if he's up to it."

Efren chuckled. "I think I'll just watch this time and catch my breath."

Eliana smiled. "Thanks for sparring with me. It was fun." She sent Maarev an expectant look. "Well?"

Dagon caught Maarev's eye and nodded. After watching her spar with Efren, he had no doubt she could handle herself well.

And she did, landing both seasoned warriors on their asses and doubling them over with swift, unanticipated strikes again and again.

"Now do the invisibility thing," she told them.

They glanced at each other.

"What?" Maarev asked.

"Do that thing you were doing the first time I saw you sparring. Go invisible."

Both men looked at Dagon.

He hesitated. Eliana was an amazing warrior when faced with larger opponents she could see. But with two opponents she *couldn't*?

She turned to face him. "Ask me what I'm doing."

"What are you doing?" he asked.

"Learning." She looked at every man who had laughed when she'd claimed Efren would not emerge the victor, then met Dagon's gaze. "As are they."

Yes, they were. Eliana was reminding every man present that they should never underestimate an opponent.

And yet he hesitated.

Silence fell as everyone awaited his decision.

"Commander Dagon?" she prompted, using his formal title and demanding his respect, demanding he treat her as an equal.

He nodded at Maarev and Liden. "Do it."

The men went into full camouflage, their specially designed uniforms doing the same. The two essentially vanished from sight to anyone who was not Segonian and dropped their staffs.

Eliana held up hers. "Do you want me to forgo mine as well, or should I keep it?"

"Keep it," Liden said.

Tense silence ensued as Maarev used the distraction of Liden speaking to circle around behind Eliana. As a Segonian, Dagon was able to sense the men's locations, though he couldn't see them. But Eliana lacked that ability. And both men moved without making a sound.

Every face along the benches sobered and filled with dread.

No man here wanted to see her felled, Dagon least of all.

"Begin," he ordered.

Liden dove for Eliana, who ducked and swung her staff. Liden flickered into view momentarily, doubled over from a blow to his stomach. Then Eliana spun and swung again. A thud sounded. Maarev flickered into view, clutching his ribs, then vanished once more.

Mouths dropped open.

Had she been using her treasured katanas, both men would've been seriously injured.

Maarev and Liden tried a frontal assault, a side assault, struck from both sides at once, and from in front and behind. Each time, Eliana prevailed.

How the *srul* was she doing that? Even *he* had difficulty spotting the warriors and relied mostly on the unique sense that allowed him to feel when another Segonian was near.

Just as Dagon began to relax, Eliana tossed her staff aside and fought the men with her bare hands.

Her tiny, almost childlike, bare hands.

Which apparently struck like stones, because she *still* emerged the victor.

Until the cheering began.

No longer fearing for her safety, the other warriors present began to shout praise and encouragement, the roar almost deafening.

Eliana's head suddenly snapped back, blood spraying from her nose as her feet left the floor and her small form flew backward.

Gasps cut off all yelling as she landed flat on her back with a thud.

Maarev reappeared, staring down at her with alarm. Liden flickered into view behind him.

Fury rolled through Dagon as he rose.

But Eliana was already sitting up. Her upper lip and chin glistened with blood. "Yep." She dragged a forearm across her face, wiping away some of the crimson liquid and smearing what was left across one cheek. "That's what I thought."

Maarev had struck her in the face?

Dagon took a step forward, his hands forming fists.

Eliana shot him a warning look, then extended a hand to Maarev.

Clasping it, Maarev gently hauled her to her feet. "Forgive me."

"For what?" she asked. "Hitting me?"

"Yes."

"Why? That's what you're supposed to do when you train." She laughed. "And I gotta say, you have one *srul* of a punch there, champ. I haven't been knocked on my ass like that in a long time."

Maarev didn't seem to know what to say to that.

Eliana glanced around, then frowned. "What? Why does everyone look so freaked out? Don't you guys ever train with women?"

"Yes," Maarev answered.

Liden stepped up beside him. "But our women are significantly larger than you."

Maarev nodded. "You're far more delicate."

Eliana stared at him a long moment, then burst out laughing. "Delicate?" she repeated, nearly folding over she was so amused. "As in I'm a *delicate* freaking flower? Dude, I kicked your ass. *And* Liden's. *And* Efren's. A *delicate* woman couldn't have done that."

Maarev's shoulders relaxed. His face even lightened with relief as the corners of his lips twitched.

"And don't forget the condition I was in when you brought me on board. You saw the injuries I suffered and can guess the pain I was in." She pointed to her nose, which had already stopped bleeding. "*This* is nothing." She held up a hand, palm out. "Although I should warn you—in case we find them—that I'm a bit of an aberration when it comes to Earthlings. Most of my friends would not fare well if you hit them. Only five of us are warriors. So keep that in mind if you spar with any."

Maarev nodded. "Of course."

"Good." Smiling, she delivered a light punch to his shoulder. "Then let's get back to it, big guy."

Maarev looked at Dagon.

Dagon studied Eliana, who eyed him intently above her sunny smile. He could almost hear her asking him to trust her and back her on this. Seating himself, he gave the men an abrupt nod. "Proceed."

Maarev and Liden seemed to disappear as they again assumed their camouflage.

The three began to fight again.

Somber silence eclipsed the room, broken only by the grunts Maarev and Liden emitted each time Eliana struck them. Once more she emerged victorious. Over and over again.

"Halt," she called suddenly. Straightening, she turned a look full of exasperation on their audience. "Seriously? Now you're silent?"

The soldiers glanced at each other.

Eliana groaned. "Come on, guys! If you're quiet, I know where they are." She motioned to Maarev and Liden with unerring accuracy despite their camouflage.

How? Dagon wondered. *How* did she know where they were? His men knew how to move soundlessly.

"If you're noisy, I don't," she continued, which indicated that she could nevertheless hear them. "And battle is often noisy. I need to find a way to determine where you guys are when you're camouflaged—which, incidentally, I still want to know how you do it—so I won't accidentally kill one of you if we find ourselves fighting the Gathendiens together."

Dagon thought any battle with the Gathendiens would most likely be fought with fighter craft and battleship cannons but opted not to mention it. Eliana was clearly a warrior through and through and—as such—wisely wanted to be prepared for anything. He admired her greatly for that... even though every hit she took made him want to kill the soldier who delivered it.

"Suck it up and stop worrying about me," she went on. "I need you guys to do what my fellow warriors on Earth would do. Cheer me. Jeer me. Ruthlessly ridicule Maarev and Liden here for being felled so many times by someone half their size. Whatever you want to do. Just make some damn noise. I'm trying to learn."

For a long moment, no one said a word.

Then Brohko thrust a fist into the air and shouted, "Kick their asses, Eliana!"

She grinned big. "*That's* what I'm talking about."

CHAPTER 11

ELIANA SMILED AT the soldiers as they filed out of the training room. It had taken a long while, but she had finally succeeded in taking down both Maarev and Liden while they were camouflaged. Preternaturally sharp hearing allowed her to pinpoint their location and movements easily when all was silent. The men moved quietly. She'd give them that. But not quietly enough to elude an immortal's ears. And she could hear their heartbeats when they *didn't* move, giving her a method of locating them even when they stood still. But once the shouting began, she lost those advantages.

The men had gotten in some good hits, pausing each time to assess her injuries even when she landed on her feet, which was both annoying and endearing. But she kept fighting, searching for some way she would be able to track them in battle. And eventually she began to catch glimpses of the barely noticeable ripple their camouflage sometimes created with movement.

Thank you, extraordinarily sharp vision.

If that did not suffice, she brought scent into play. Her nose was as efficient as that of an arctic fox, enabling her to single out each man's scent and differentiate it from the cheering onlookers. In the past, she had only used her eyes, ears, and nose to *locate* the psychotic vampires she hunted. Once she found them, she relied solely on speed and skill to defeat them in battle. The change in technique would require more practice on her part in order to perfect it.

"Thanks, guys," she called after the men, determined to train with them daily.

Maarev smiled, one eye nearly swollen shut, his nose bloody. "Training with you was an honor, Eliana. You are a true warrior."

"The feeling is mutual, big guy."

His puffy lip split as he grinned and left the room.

Eliana kept a smile plastered on her face while she offered more goodbyes and teasing comments to the rest of the soldiers, never letting on that every breath she took felt like someone was shoving daggers into her chest. She definitely sported at least a couple of broken ribs. She might have suffered a few sprains, too. Maarev's hands were like freaking bowling balls. But she couldn't let them see it or they'd start babying her and refuse to spar with her again.

Dagon stood on the other side of the room, his big arms crossed over his broad, muscled chest. He looked grim as hell. And she couldn't be more enamored of him. He had allowed her to train with his men today, respecting her ability to hold her own in a fight despite her diminutive size. That was an incredible turn-on. Even a few of her fellow Immortal Guardians failed to give her that, treating her like the delicate flower she'd mentioned earlier. It was why she had enjoyed hunting with Stanislav and Yuri so much in New York, then with Nick and Rafe in Texas. Had they been with her now, the most those four immortal males would've done was offer her a handkerchief to wipe the blood from her face. She had always been able to trust them to do what Dagon did—treat her like an equal.

Yet she had never felt for them what she felt for this Segonian male.

Once the last soldier filed out, Dagon closed the door.

Eliana kept her smile in place as he approached her.

"Are you all right?" he asked.

"I'm fine." Or she would be soon.

Stopping before her—so close that his wonderful scent enveloped her—he stared down at her. After a moment, he crooked a finger beneath her chin and tilted her head back so he could examine her features. He brushed his thumb across her lower lip, which was puffy and sore from one of the blows she had failed to duck.

Her breath halted at the sweet caress. Her heart began to pound against her aching ribs. How she wanted to rise onto her toes and kiss him, sore lip and all. She could not recall ever having wanted a man so much and finally felt free to act upon it. But she was all sweaty and bloody and gross.

"You're sure?" he asked, his deep voice soft.

"I'm sure." She curled the fingers of one hand around his wrist and gave it a squeeze. "Thank you. For not interfering and for trusting me to hold my own."

His lips curled in an irresistible smile. "Maarev isn't the only one who packs a *srul* of a punch."

She laughed. "Damn straight." He didn't know the half of it. She had actually held back when she struck the other warriors, knowing a punch delivered with preternatural strength could kill them.

Much to her delight, Dagon drew her into a gentle hug, then left his arm around her as he guided her to the door, his big hand sliding down to rest on her back. It felt so good she didn't even care that he was inadvertently putting pressure on the bruise Efren had left with his staff.

"Maarev and Liden will feel *my* punches when we train together tomorrow," he muttered.

"You've already punched Maarev once on my behalf."

He grunted. "Once was not enough."

She laughed, then wished she hadn't as pain sliced through her. "Just don't beat him so badly that he—or any of the other soldiers—won't wish to train with me anymore."

He halted. "You wish to train with them again?"

"Of course."

Dread crept into his handsome features. "Did you train on the *Kandovar*?"

"Several times a week."

"With whom?"

"My fellow Immortal Guardians. And with a few of the female Lasarans. But I had to hold back quite a bit with the latter. I didn't think the Lasarans would appreciate it if I accidentally landed one of their women in the infirmary." She shrugged. "I don't have to hold back as much with your guys, so I'd like to keep training with them."

His dark brows flew up. "You held back while fighting Maarev and Liden?"

"Yes."

"Efren, too?"

"Yes."

He stared at her with an almost comical look of disbelief.

She grinned, silently cursing when her damn lip split again. "I told you. I'm stronger than I look."

"Yes, you are." There was no mistaking the admiration in his gaze as it traveled down her body like a bold caress.

Eliana reveled in the warmth it generated inside her, happy to let it distract her from the pain.

Turning away, he opened the door. "Perhaps we should have Adaos check your injuries just to be safe."

She waved away his concern. "I'm fine, Dagon. Seriously. I've lived through thousands of battles. This was nothing." It really wasn't. Psychotic vampires armed with blades had done far worse to her in the past, as had humans armed with guns.

He paused in the hallway. "If you're certain."

"I'm certain." She gave his arm a squeeze. "Stop worrying and go back to whatever you were doing when Maarev interrupted your work."

He hesitated. "What are *you* going to do?"

She winked. "Snag another bag of *jarumi* nuggets, then decide what I want to learn next."

He smiled. "Will you at least rest while you do it?"

"I'll think about it," she quipped.

Shaking his head, he gave her lips a last look, then headed down the hallway.

Eliana remained where she was, watching him until he rounded a curve and left her view. Grimacing, she rested a hand on her sore ribs and headed for the lift at the other end of the corridor. A few moments later, she strode into Med Bay.

One of the younger medics looked up and gasped.

Adaos swung around. His pale green eyes widened. "Eliana? You look like you've been brawling with a *palari*."

She laughed, then grunted as pain stabbed her in the chest. "You should see the other guys."

A twinkle of mischief entered his normally somber eyes. "I *have* seen them. Maarev, Liden, and Efren were just here, asking for *silnas* to speed their healing."

The younger medic gaped. "*You* are the one who injured them?"

Adaos frowned and jerked his head toward the back of the bay.

Closing his mouth, the young medic swiftly ducked into the hallway back there and left them alone.

Adaos crossed to stand in front of her and raised his hand scanner. "I'm surprised Dagon didn't insist on accompanying you."

"I told him I was fine."

Censure entered his gaze. "You lied to him?"

"No. I *am* fine. Or I *will* be. All I need is a transfusion."

He grunted. "You've fractured your ribs."

"Yes," she agreed with exaggerated solemnity. "*I* fractured them."

His lips twitched. "Maarev and Liden fractured a few of their own."

She grinned. "Hell yes, they did."

He chuckled. "I thought that would please you. Come. Let us transfuse you so your wounds will heal faster."

"Thank you."

Eliana crossed to the bed he nodded toward and hopped onto it, stifling a groan.

"Recline, please." He adjusted it so she wouldn't have to lie flat.

Again she grimaced. "You don't have to go through all this. Just give me a bag of blood." She'd rather siphon the blood into her veins via her fangs than do the needle thing.

He shook his head. "This way is faster."

She leaned back, grumbling beneath her breath.

Adaos tapped some commands into the data tablet he always seemed to keep handy.

Seconds later, she watched with dread as the mechanical arm descended from the ceiling. A cool spray unerringly found the bend of her arm.

"I knew it!" a deep voice rife with irritation growled.

Her head snapped around.

Dagon marched into the room, a dark scowl creasing his

forehead. "You said you were fine."

"I *am* fine," she insisted. "Or I *will* be as soon as I— *Ouch!*" Jumping, she glared down at the needle that pierced her arm. "Damn it! I wasn't ready."

Dagon's boots thudded as they ate up the floor between them. Stopping beside her, he once more crossed his arms over his massive chest. "You said you were fine," he repeated, the statement an accusation.

A little twinge of guilt struck. "I *am* fine..."

His eyes narrowed.

"...ish," she qualified. "I'm fine-*ish.* All I need is a blood transfusion."

"You should've told me."

"Did Maarev, Liden, and Efren tell you they were heading to Med Bay?"

"No. They didn't need to. I've trained with them on many occasions and knew they would come here for a *silna* if their injuries would otherwise take days to heal. I don't know you as well though, so I rely on your honesty to guide me."

Eliana had been all ready to feel defensive, but that sort of took the wind out of her sails. "I know. I'm sorry. It's just..." She let her head drop back against the bed. "I planned to grab a bag of blood when I got here and didn't want you to watch me sink my fangs into it. I told you. That sort of thing never went over well back on Earth."

"Adaos could have transfused you the way he is now."

"I know." She sent the medic a squinty-eyed look. "This is worse." Wrinkling her nose, she avoided Dagon's gaze. "Do you know how embarrassing it is for someone in my line of work to be squeamish about needles?" It was a weird-ass phobia to have for someone who was stabbed and slashed with knives so often. "Daggers, throwing stars, sais, shoto swords, katanas, broadswords, bowie knives, tactical knives, machetes... none of those even faze me. But show me a tiny damn needle and I get nervous." Her scowl deepened as heat crept into her cheeks. "Like I said, it's embarrassing."

Relaxing, he leaned a hip against the bed and took her hand in his. "I just watched you take down three men who were two heads taller than you and more than twice your weight with just your bare hands and a staff. The fact that you dislike needles doesn't lessen my regard or my respect for you in the least."

She risked peering up at him through her lashes. "Really?"

"Really. Everything I learn about you merely makes me admire you more."

She smiled, feeling all warm and fuzzy inside now. "You're so sweet, Dagon."

Adaos snorted.

Dagon shot him a dirty look, then sat beside her on the bed, one foot still braced on the floor, the other knee drawn up to rest against her hip. "You aren't the only one who is learning here, Eliana."

"I know," she acknowledged softly and squeezed his hand. "There's a saying on Earth: old habits die hard." She sighed, the action easier now that the virus—fueled by the blood transfusion—raced to heal her damaged ribs. "I told you, people who are different in my world aren't treated well. And after years of dealing with that stupid *bura*, it just became second nature for me to hide my differences."

He covered her hand. "You can trust me."

"I know. And I do trust you." She really did. "It's just a habit I need to break, a sort of... unconscious self-defense mechanism." She sent him a wry smile. "Aaaaaand I might have been a little afraid you'd refuse to let me train with your men again if you knew they'd fractured some of my ribs."

Fury darkened his features. "They fractured your ribs?" he nearly roared.

"Just a couple," she hastened to tell him.

Across the room, Adaos looked up from whatever he was doing. "She fractured several of theirs as well."

"Damn right I did," she boasted.

A dark smile touched Dagon's lips as satisfaction lit his gaze. "Good."

She grinned.

Adaos winked at her. "And it may interest you to know, Eliana, that there are currently two soldiers on board who faint at the sight of needles. A third comes close to doing the same at the sight of blood."

Dagon sighed. "Is the latter Brohko?"

"Yes."

Eliana laughed. The young soldier *had* looked a little woozy earlier when she and her sparring partners inadvertently drew blood.

Dagon smoothed his thumb across her hand. He seemed in no hurry to leave and stayed with her while the virus did its thing after the transfusion ended.

The fact that she healed quickly didn't mean Eliana felt no pain. Sometimes healing hurt as much as incurring the initial injury. But she found it much easier to ignore with Dagon's muscled thigh pressing against her hip and his hand holding hers.

"I know you heal swiftly," he said finally, "but would you allow Adaos to give you a *silna* to speed your recovery even more?"

She glanced at the medic. "What exactly does a *silna* do?"

"It boosts the immune system and enhances the body's ability to repair injuries and overcome illnesses, shortening recovery time." Adaos glanced at his commander, then met her gaze. "But because of the manner in which your immune system differs from ours, I don't think it advisable."

Dagon frowned. "Why?"

Eliana smiled when Adaos opted not to reply, liking him even more for adhering to his promise to keep her patient information private. "It's okay." She squeezed Dagon's hand. "The weird virus the Gathendiens created has basically replaced my immune system. So we don't really know what a *silna* would do—if it would aid the virus in making repairs or attack the virus and maybe make things worse. If it eradicated the virus entirely, it would leave me with no viable immune system."

His frown deepened as his fingers tightened around hers.

"But don't worry. I don't need a *silna*. I'm healing fast enough without it and should be fine by the time we finish last meal." Or after a long healing sleep.

"Commander Dagon," a faint male voice said.

He tapped his earpiece. "Yes, Janek?"

"You have an incoming communication from Commander Tiran."

"Direct it to my office. I'll be there in a moment." He gave their clasped hands a pat, then released her and rose. "An incoming communication awaits me."

"Okay." She should probably tell him her ears were sharp enough to allow her to overhear anything broadcast over his earpiece. Dagon had been awesome about accepting the peculiarities she had already demonstrated, so she thought he'd take it well.

"You'll be all right?"

She smiled. "Yes. As soon as I'm done here, I plan to have a shower and maybe lie down for a bit. I always heal faster when I sleep."

Adaos perked up. "You do?"

"Yes."

"Would you sleep in here and allow me to monitor—"

"Adaos," Dagon intoned with a warning scowl.

Eliana wondered if the medic would reveal that she had agreed to let him study her if he would allow her to pump him for information about how to woo Dagon.

When he didn't, she sent him a smile. "Maybe next time."

"Only," Dagon interjected, "if you're comfortable with it."

"Okay."

Turning away, he strode for the door but hesitated when he reached it and looked at her over his shoulder. "Will you join me for last meal?"

Her heart gave a little flutter as she nodded. "Absolutely."

Smiling, he left.

Dagon barked out a laugh. He and Eliana had shared yet another enchanting last meal together while a holowindow bathed them in the light of a setting sun. Now they headed toward her quarters.

As they did, he silently admitted he was loath to see their time together end, so he restricted his pace to a leisurely stroll while she regaled him with comical tales of other opponents who—like Efren, Maarev, and Liden—had dramatically underestimated her ability to defeat them.

Every time she grinned or laughed, warmth suffused him and

stretched his lips in a smile. And every time she bumped his arm with her shoulder or nudged him with her elbow, little tingles raced along his flesh and stole his breath. How would she respond if he suddenly interrupted her and told her she made him feel like a youth experiencing his first infatuation?

That he felt young at all amazed him. His arduous climb up the chain of command had been a long one, peppered with both wins *and* losses that had taken their toll. Some soldiers he'd considered friends had grown bitter and hostile when they were passed over for promotion in favor of him. Many others had simply drifted away when differing missions had parted them for months at a time. Dagon reconnected with the latter whenever they all ended up in the same place. It was one of the reasons he enjoyed the Aldebarian Alliance's biannual war games so much. They enabled him to see old friends again.

But there were others he would *not* see again. Those who had fallen in combat.

Every life lost under his command had cost him and resurfaced periodically to haunt his dreams.

Yet now, as Eliana nudged him again with her elbow and stared up at him with her pretty brown eyes full of amusement, he fought the desire to reach out, twine his fingers through hers, and swing their arms between them in a rare boyish burst of joy.

He might have actually done it, too, if they didn't pass soldiers and other crewmen so frequently.

Eliana seemed as reluctant to end their time together as he, her steps slowing more and more as they approached their destination. Alas, they reached her quarters anyway.

"And what did he say once he regained consciousness?" Dagon asked, fighting another smile as he awaited her response.

She placed her palm on the reader and opened her door. "He said his grandmother was right: dynamite *does* come in small packages."

Amusement once more bubbled up inside him. "Is my translator right? Is dynamite an explosive on Earth?"

"Yes."

He laughed.

She did, too.

Apparently, all Immortal Guardians on Earth were assigned

Seconds, who seemed to be the equivalent of the Lasaran royal family's Yona guard and protected them. The one in question—a hulking man named Kevin who had guarded Eliana years ago—had driven her mad, constantly underestimating her ability to take care of herself. This Kevin, she'd explained, had spent most of his life watching over five younger sisters and just couldn't seem to break the habit, transferring all the concern and overprotectiveness he felt for them onto Eliana's narrow shoulders, insisting he accompany her on all her hunts and hovering so much she had finally broken down and—at Seth's suggestion—shown him just how capable she was of defending herself.

Eliana stepped into her room and turned to face him. "Kevin is now married with four daughters, so I have no doubt that he repeats that mantra often."

He chuckled. "As well he should."

Anticipation usurped amusement's place as he stared down at her, waiting for her nightly hug.

Perhaps tonight he would linger and—

"Greetings, Eliana," CC said in her serene voice.

Blinking, she glanced over her shoulder, then up at the ceiling. "Hi, CC."

Dagon hid his amusement at her tendency to look up whenever she addressed the computer.

"You have one communication awaiting your attention," CC announced.

Eliana looked at Dagon. "Is that like a phone message?"

He considered his translator's definition of *phone*. "Yes."

"Did *you* send it?"

"No."

"Who did?"

A good question. Who on this ship believed they knew Eliana well enough to message her privately? His brows drew down. "I don't know."

"Maybe Anat has reconsidered giving me flight lessons."

He stared at her. After Dagon, Anat was the most experienced and highest-ranked fighter pilot on the ship. Dagon knew that most of the men stationed on the *Ranasura* thought their commander grim and foreboding. But Dagon appeared downright ebullient when compared to Anat.

"You asked Anat to give you flight lessons?" To borrow one of Eliana's Earth terms: that had been ballsy.

"Yes." She wrinkled her nose. "But he said no. The other pilots warned me he'd refuse, but I figured I'd give it a try anyway."

He tried to hold back his next question but failed. "Why didn't you ask me?"

Her brow furrowed. "You mean ask your permission? Was I supposed to do that first?"

"No. Why didn't you ask *me* to give you flight lessons?" He understood her fierce drive to learn everything she possibly could that might aid her in the future but inwardly balked at the image of Eliana and Anat crowded together in a flight simulator.

"Oh. Because you're… you know." She motioned to his uniform. "The commander. You run the ship. You have more important things to do." She nibbled her lower lip. "Aaaaand I didn't want to wear out my welcome."

Confused, he glanced down at the deck.

"Why are you looking at my boots?" she asked.

"According to my translator, *wear out my welcome* means eroding through frequent use the surface of a mat with the word *welcome* printed on it that Earthlings place outside their doors."

She grinned. "Your translator got it wrong. Wear out my welcome means…" She shrugged. "I don't know. Make a nuisance of myself, I guess. I've already insinuated myself into a significant portion of your day, Dagon." Her smile dimmed a bit as uncertainty crept into her features. "I didn't want you to get tired of having me around all the time."

So while he had sought any and every excuse to spend *more* time with her, she had worried he might want *less*? He took a step closer to her. "I believe the likelihood of that is nonexistent."

Her eyes dilated as his shadow fell over her. "Really?" she asked softly.

"Really." He nodded to the reader inside her door. "Do you want to listen to your communication?"

Her gaze fell to his lips. "Sure. How do I do it?"

"May I enter?"

"Absolutely," she said, her voice a tad husky, then flushed as she backed away to give him room.

Dagon joined her in her cabin, and the door slid down, closing them inside and blocking any prying eyes that might notice if he sought more than a hug tonight.

Because he *really* wanted to seek more than a hug tonight.

He glanced at the electronic pad beside the door. "You can activate the reader with your palm, then press this." He demonstrated the steps. "Or you can use verbal commands and tell CC to play the communication."

"Okay." She glanced up at the ceiling. "CC, would you please play the communication?"

So *drekking* cute.

"Playing communication," CC responded.

A male voice floated out of the electronic pad. "Eliana. It's Adaos."

Dagon's smile faltered, replaced by a frown. Why was Adaos contacting her?

"Since I was unable to observe firsthand how sleep accelerates your healing," his friend said, "would you join me in Med Bay before first meal? I'd like to execute another full-body scan to determine how well your bones have healed, see what effect the process had on your blood volume, then take another blood sample to examine your viral count."

Fury suffused Dagon. "I told him to leave you alone," he growled. "I ordered him unequivocally *not* to treat you like an experiment or some bizarre creature here for his scrutiny!"

Her eyes widened. "He isn't."

Unappeased, Dagon motioned angrily to the panel. "He just said he wants to draw more of your blood to study. And he *knows* how much you hate needles!" All thoughts of eliciting more than a hug from Eliana slipped away as he spun toward the door, intent on confronting Adaos and making it *very clear* this time that—

"Dagon, wait!" Eliana grabbed his arm and tugged him around to face her. "It isn't what you think."

"It's exactly what I think! He intends to—"

"I told him he could!" she nearly shouted.

Until then, he hadn't realized he'd raised his voice to a near-shout himself. "What?" he demanded, then winced when he failed to speak more softly.

"I told him he could study me," she said quickly.

He shook his head. "You've a sweet nature, Eliana. If you're trying to protect him—"

"I'm not. It's true. I told him he could study me."

Confusion buffeted him. "Why would you do that?" Her discomfort around needles and the infirmary in general had not been feigned. He was certain of it. And her fellow Earthlings had made her so self-conscious about—if not fearful of—revealing the extent of her differences that he couldn't imagine why she would agree to Adaos treating her like a lab subject.

Releasing his arm, she stuffed her hands into her back pockets and shifted her weight from her left leg to her right, then back again. Her gaze darted around the room, skittering past his without lingering.

"Because he had something I needed," she mumbled.

He clamped his lips together and tried to puzzle it out. Something she needed? "If you're referring to blood..." Surely Adaos had not given her the impression he would withhold the transfusions she required if she didn't let him study her.

If he had, Dagon was certain it had been inadvertent.

"No, of course not," she said, quick to defend the medic. "He's been great about the transfusions. This was just a quid pro quo kind of thing."

"I don't know what that means."

"I told Adaos he could study me and I would share everything I know about the virus and my species with him if *he* would share something with me."

He crossed his arms over his chest. "And what might that be?"

Pink crept up her neck and filled her cheeks as she shuffled her feet, looking sheepish as *srul,* and muttered something he couldn't hear.

"What?"

Emitting a growl of her own, she spoke louder. "Information on Segonian courtship rituals and the societal dos and don'ts that surround them." She peeked up at him through long dark lashes as though trying to gauge his reaction.

Everything within him went still. "Segonian courtship rituals?"

he repeated softly. "Why would you wish to know more about that?"

She sighed. "Because I couldn't find anything about it in your informational databases, and I've been wanting to do *this* for a long time."

Reaching up, she rested her small hands on his stubbled cheeks, then rose onto her toes and drew him down for a kiss.

His heart stuttered to a halt, then began to slam against his ribs. The first gentle brush of her lips hit him like an electrical current. His breath caught. Hers did, too. She drew back a fraction to stare up at him with wide eyes that acquired an amber glow.

Then Dagon slid his arms around her and locked her against him. Dipping his head, he claimed her lips with greater urgency, letting her feel the heat that had been flaying him inside ever since she had walked onto his bridge, fully recovered from her wounds, and drawn him into a hug. He caught her lower lip between his teeth, then drew his tongue across it in a slow caress.

Moaning, she parted her lips.

Dagon slipped his tongue inside to stroke hers, deepening the kiss, teasing and tantalizing until she inched even closer. His hard cock pressed against her stomach. Her full breasts pressed against his upper abdomen.

"You're too damn tall," she murmured, breaking the kiss long enough to draw in a gulp of air.

Dagon trailed his lips across her cheek and nipped her earlobe. "You're too *vuan* small," he countered. He felt a shiver go through her as he nuzzled her neck.

"So *vuan* means *damn*?"

He huffed a laugh. "You want a lesson in Segonian and Alliance Common curse words *now*?"

"You're right." Drawing back a fraction, she smiled up at him, her face flushed with desire. "Let me taste those lips of yours again."

"*Srul* yes."

They came together almost desperately. Dagon loved her taste, the way she clutched him tighter when he teased her with his tongue.

Resting her hands on his shoulders, she jumped up suddenly—her mouth never leaving his—and locked her legs around his waist.

He groaned as she settled her center over the hard cock his uniform pants constrained. Fire licked through him, searing his veins. Sliding a hand down to her lovely ass, he urged her to rock against him.

"Oh yeah," she whispered. "This is *much* better."

He grinned... and couldn't remember ever having done so before while engaged in a passionate moment. But Eliana made everything *else* more fun. It didn't surprise him that she made this more fun, too.

Wrapping her arms around his neck, she tunneled her fingers through his hair. Her short nails raked his scalp, sending shivers of pleasure down his spine. "You smell so good," she moaned, then trailed kisses across his jaw and nuzzled his neck. "I love your scent."

Drek, she made him burn.

She was so light... or perhaps she was simply so strong with those shapely legs of hers flexing around his waist... that he had no difficulty supporting her with one hand. Slipping the other between them, he cupped a plump breast and squeezed. He found the hard peak, stroked it, and delivered a light pinch. Her legs tightened as she ground her core against him. Both moaned.

Then cold air rushed between them as she released him and backed away.

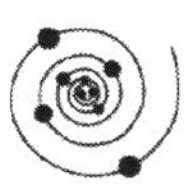

Eliana stared up at Dagon. Need pounded through her, speeding her pulse.

Dagon watched her, his expression fierce as he lowered his hands to his sides and curled them into fists. He looked like he wanted to pounce, to devour her.

And she sure as hell wanted the same.

"We're wearing too many clothes," she blurted.

He blinked. Then relief swept over his features.

Her lips twitched. "What? Did you think I was going to stop and say good night?"

He smiled. "Perhaps. I know less about Earthling mating rituals than you know about ours. But if you *do* wish to stop—"

"*Srul* no."

He laughed. "Then I suggest we remedy the *too many clothes* issue."

She winked. "Want to race?" Her hands twitched. She was tempted to just rip his clothes off, something that would only take her a second. But she didn't want to do any preternatural stuff. Not their first time. She wanted this to be just a man and a woman with burgeoning feelings for each other coming together to explore and bring each other pleasure.

"If it will mean you get naked faster? *Srul* yes." Reaching over his shoulder, he fisted a hand in his uniform shirt and dragged it over his head.

Eliana practically salivated at the way his bronze muscles—as large and well developed as she'd guessed—flexed. His shirt hit the ground.

Carefully restraining herself to the speed of a mortal, she pulled her own shirt over her head and dropped it. The two them exchanged wry smiles then as they took a moment to divest themselves of their weapons and carefully set them aside.

"CC, lower the bed, please," Eliana said.

The heat in Dagon's expression intensified as the large bed lowered behind her. Her pulse picked up its pace, her heart slamming against her ribs.

Dagon removed his earpiece and set it on the shelf beside the bed. He lowered his hands to the waist of his pants. "You're sure?"

She nodded. "I want you." More than she'd ever wanted *anyone*. Or any*thing*. This man stirred her in ways no other had in her long life. She yanked off her boots.

He yanked off his.

She shucked her pants and stood before him, clad only in her lacy black bra and matching bikini panties.

He shucked his pants and underwear and straightened, gloriously naked. "You're beautiful," he uttered, his voice a deep rumble that sent a shiver through her.

"So are you."

He strolled toward her, all grace and sinewy muscle.

Her gaze skimmed down his chest and washboard abs to his groin. Other than the bronze tint to his skin, he looked like a human male, his hard cock jutting toward her. He was also big. Not surprising. He was big all over. But thankfully he wasn't *Holy Hannah, that's gonna hurt* big. No, Dagon was… perfect. Her gaze roved back up his muscled form to his face.

Absolutely perfect.

He stopped so close his cock bumped her stomach. "Will this be your first time?" he asked softly. And the concern in his hazel eyes merely made her adore him more.

"No." Resting a hand on his warm chest, she toyed with the dark hair that dusted it. "Will it be yours?"

"No." He smiled. "But I admit it's been a long time."

She smiled back. "For me, too." Far longer than for him. And even if it *hadn't* been a long time, she was so primed and ready for him he could practically make her come with a kiss. Reaching behind her back, she unfastened her bra and let it fall to the floor. "Good thing we won't have to go slow then."

He stared at her. "*Drek,* you're beautiful." He palmed both breasts, weighed them, squeezed them, drew his thumbs over the taut pink tips.

Sensation shot through her. "Dagon," she whispered. "I need you."

Growling low in his throat, he swept her up in his arms and laid her on the bed.

Eliana's pulse quickened as he knelt at her feet. Leaning forward, he tucked his fingers in the straps of her panties and drew them down her legs. The small scrap landed somewhere on the floor behind him. Then he curled his fingers around her ankles and drew her legs apart.

Her heart slammed against her rib cage and need thrummed through her as he stared at her mound.

His eyes rose and met hers. "I want to taste you."

Pleasure rose at just the thought of it. "I'm good with that."

Amusement lit his handsome features as he settled himself between her legs. Then he slid his arms beneath her thighs, gripped her hips, and lowered his mouth to her center. Eliana sucked in a breath when he found her clit with his tongue, then moaned as he teased and explored it.

"You're sensitive here," he murmured.

"Yes. Very."

She buried her fingers in his soft-as-silk hair as fire darted through her. He growled when she fisted her hands in the short locks and arched up to meet each lick and flick and stroke of his tongue.

"Dagon," she panted.

He slipped a long finger inside her, then another, stroking her as he continued the sensual onslaught with his tongue, feeding her need, driving it higher until ecstasy crashed through her, drawing a cry from her lips as she came hard, bucking against him and riding out the pleasure until every muscle went limp.

Dagon kissed his way up her stomach, drew a sensitive nipple into his mouth, and drew on it hard.

Just like that, she wanted him again, her body undulating against him.

He met her gaze. "So *drekking* beautiful." He settled his big body between her thighs, careful to keep the bulk of his weight off her.

Eliana saw the amber glow of her eyes reflected in his as she cupped his face in her hands and drew him down for a kiss that expressed both the desire he inspired and the affection she felt for him. She could hear his heart slamming against the rib cage in his powerful chest, could feel the tremor in the tense muscles that revealed how desperately he wanted her, could imagine how fantastic it would feel if he unleashed all that need and plunged the hard length prodding her deep.

"Take me, Dagon," she murmured. "I want to feel you inside me."

She didn't have to ask him twice. Dagon claimed her lips in a fiery kiss even as he reached between them and positioned his cock at her slick entrance.

Both gasped as he drove deep. Sensation shot through her.

Dagon stilled, breaking the kiss long enough to study her features. "Still good?"

She wrapped her arms around his waist and slid her hands down to grab his ass. "Sooooo good." Circling her hips, Eliana ground against him.

He groaned. Withdrawing almost to the crown, he drove his hard length home again. "You're so tight."

She wanted to say *You're so big* but lacked the breath as he thrust deep again and again. He palmed one of her breasts again, pinched the stiff peak. Fire shot through her.

"More," she breathed, his scent surrounding her, almost as great an aphrodisiac as his touch. "Harder."

He growled, driving deeper, harder, holding nothing back, altering the angle of his thrusts so he stimulated her clit every time they came together.

"Yes," she panted. "Dagon."

It felt so good. *He* felt so good. His weight pressing down on her, the hard muscles of his back bunching beneath her hands as she explored and urged him on. He lifted his head, met and held her gaze, the intensity in his features stealing what was left of her breath. He was so fucking beautiful, his eyes nearly hypnotizing her as she met him thrust for thrust until another orgasm swept over her. Throwing her head back, she cried out as ecstasy engulfed her. Her inner muscles clamped down around his hard length, squeezing and pulsing again and again.

Dagon stiffened above her and called her name as he came, filling her with his warmth.

Their hearts competed to see whose could beat the fastest as the pleasure slowly faded. Both breathed heavily as their muscles relaxed. When he shifted slightly, Eliana tightened her hold on him, unwilling to relinquish the closeness yet, residual ripples of pleasure still rocking her.

Dagon carefully rested a little more of his weight on her, probably worried he might crush her, she thought with some amusement. Supporting the rest of his mass on an elbow, he drew his other hand up and cupped her face, smoothed his thumb across her cheek in a sweet caress as he stared down at her. Then he dipped his head. And his lips brushed hers in a kiss so tender it brought tears to her eyes.

Wonder filled her. And something more as he rolled them to their sides, their bodies still joined.

Eliana draped a knee over his hip and snuggled her face into his chest.

Dagon cupped the back of her head in one large hand and pressed a kiss to her hair.

Sighing as peace suffused her, she closed her eyes.

CHAPTER 12

ELIANA RELEASED A sigh of disappointment as sleep slipped away. She had been having the most wonderful dream. She really hated to see it end.

As awareness of the big muscled body spooned up behind hers seeped in, her eyes flew open. It *hadn't* been a dream.

She smiled.

Dagon's bare flesh warmed hers. His biceps pillowed her cheek. His breath tickled the back of her neck. The long, hard length of his arousal was trapped between his thighs and her bottom. Just the thought of how it had felt, driving deep inside her, made her flush with heat and renewed arousal. But she nearly forgot that heat when she reached for his hand… only to realize it wasn't there. Nor was his arm. Sort of. She could feel his arm beneath her head, but she couldn't see it.

Her heart began to pound. She hadn't turned the lights off before the two of them drifted into slumber, so the room was dimly lit. Even if it lay in darkness, she would still be able to see. Her eyes were as sharp as a cat's, granting her excellent night vision that allowed her to easily discern shapes, though determining color could be tricky.

But it wasn't dark. She *could* discern color. And whatever pillowed her head did not bear Dagon's bronze skin tone.

In tiny, incremental movements meant not to disturb him, Eliana sat up. Some of the long ebony strands of her mussed hair were trapped beneath his heavy body, making it a bit tricky, but she managed to disentangle them.

A minute later she knelt, naked, on the mattress and gazed down in awe at her Segonian lover.

She would not have known Dagon occupied the bed if she couldn't hear his heartbeat and his soft breaths. The sheets were a serviceable white. The pillows, too. As bedding often does, both bore wrinkles and creases, hills and shadows. And Dagon's skin matched them precisely. Every inch of his exposed flesh had assumed the color and appearance of the sheet and pillow beneath him. Even his hair and eyelashes mimicked it, as did the stubble on his cheeks. The only part of him that *didn't* match it was the shoulder under which her hair had been trapped. That was streaked with black that rapidly shifted to white and assumed the appearance of bedding while she stared in fascination.

His other arm rested atop the covers. Where white sheet met gray blanket, his skin color altered accordingly. Half of his arm was white, the other gray. Both were shadowed in a pattern that replicated the folds of the bedding. Even his long fingers blended in.

Curious, she slipped her hand beneath his.

Those long fingers curled around hers. Some of the gray on the back of his hand and fingers transmogrified, adopting her skin tone until it looked as though she had instead rested her hand *atop* his.

"That is awesome," she whispered.

Dagon sighed and rolled onto his back, his hand slipping from hers. For a moment, he didn't blend in with the sheets and blanket, the pattern of white and gray off a bit. Then the color of his skin shifted, the shadows morphing until they again precisely mimicked the bedding.

It reminded her of an octopus she had once seen in a documentary. The muscles and chromatophores in its skin had enabled it to change both its color and surface texture within seconds to mimic its surroundings.

When she had touched Dagon's hand, his skin had still been soft and smooth, but then so was the bedding it resembled. If he were lying on something spiky or rough, would his skin assume that texture?

She glanced around the room, tempted to find something poky

or bristly to slip beneath his hand just to see.

Dagon sighed again in his sleep. The arm she had used as a pillow moved, the fingers of his hand splaying on the sheet. It slid down several inches, then back up.

His brow furrowed slightly.

Again he moved his hand across the sheet.

She smiled. Did he search for her?

His puckered brow became a disgruntled frown when he didn't find her.

Too cute.

Within seconds, the white and gray that painted his skin morphed into the bronzish tan he usually bore. His eyelids fluttered, then opened. Blinking, he stared up at the ceiling for a moment, then turned his head to frown at the empty space beside him. But as soon as he saw her kneeling down by his hip, the sun chased his stormy expression away and he sent her a sleepy smile.

"There you are."

Her heart turned over at the affection that laced his deep voice. "And there *you* are," she said with a grin.

His eyes narrowed, amusement and suspicion warring in them as he reached for her. "What are you doing?"

Eliana let him draw her down until she lay atop him. "Trying to think of something poky or pointy to put under you."

He blinked, his expression going comically blank. "What?"

"I was going to say bristly, but I don't think I've seen a single hairbrush since I came aboard your ship. You guys all seem to prefer combs."

"You wanted to shove a hairbrush under me?"

"Yes."

A long moment passed. "Is this an... Earthling copulation thing?"

"You mean a sex thing?"

"Yes. Is this an Earthling sex thing?"

She laughed. "No. I wanted to see if your skin texture can change to match your environment or if it's just the color. When I woke up, you looked like the bedding."

"Ah." A look of chagrin crossed his face. "Apologies. I haven't slept with a woman in so long that it didn't occur to me to warn you."

She tilted her head to one side. "By slept with, do you mean you haven't fallen asleep beside a woman or that you haven't had sex in a long time?"

He winced. "Both. I've spent most of the past several years in space. When we dock with space stations or visit allied worlds, we usually aren't there long enough to foster relationships with the women we encounter and are forbidden from sleeping beside any non-Segonian women we might seek out for temporary pleasure."

"Why?"

"Those who aren't from our homeworld but know of our ability to camouflage ourselves so efficiently believe it's a result of classified military technology."

She combed her fingers through his soft hair, which was once more as black as hers. "Is it?"

He shook his head. "It's purely biological. We're born with the ability."

She thought of Taelon and Lisa's daughter Abby. "Wow. I bet that makes parenting a lot harder. I've seen what infants and toddlers can do. How much more mayhem must they create when they can be virtually invisible while doing it?"

He grinned. "The camouflage doesn't manifest itself in children until they reach..." He seemed to search for the right word. "Puberty? Is that the correct Earth term? The time at which boys begin to physically mature into men and girls into women?"

"Yes." She toyed with the hair on his chest. "Does just the color change? Or can you change the texture of your skin, too?"

The soft skin beneath her hand shifted, grooves forming straight lines, the color altering until his chest looked as though it had turned into tree bark. The hair changed color and texture, too, until it resembled a light moss that coated it.

Eyes wide, she sat up and ran her hands over him. "That's amazing. It even feels like tree bark, only warmer."

"In terms of texture, we can only change that on our chest, our back, our upper arms, and our thighs. Our face, too, to some extent." One rough shoulder lifted in a shrug. "Unfortunately, changing the texture takes a lot of concentration, and we often lack the time for that in battle. So we usually rely on simpler color changes to conceal us from enemies."

She nodded. "I have telekinetic abilities, but they require so much focus that I rarely have the opportunity to use them in battle." A thought occurred to her. "Wait. When I bit Adaos and he lost consciousness, why didn't he go all camoflaugey like you?"

His lips twitched. "It tends to not work if we lose consciousness due to injury."

Just like Nick. Her former hunting partner could shape-shift into just about any animal he studied. But once he lost consciousness, he automatically returned to his natural form.

"What about your uniforms?" she asked. "Maarev, Liden, and Efren were fully dressed when I sparred with them, and they completely disappeared—visually speaking."

"That's a fairly recent technological advancement, one we didn't achieve until a couple of centuries ago. Until then, our soldiers had to strip off their clothes if they wanted to confound their adversaries with natural camouflage."

"Yikes."

He grinned. "I wouldn't want to fight naked either."

"Gotta protect your family jewels, right?" When he stared at her blankly, she wiggled atop the lap she straddled.

His sucked in a breath, hardening even more beneath her, and clamped his hands on her hips. Then he laughed. "Family jewels. An apt term."

She grinned.

"Seven or eight generations ago, our scientists discovered a way to infuse the fabric of our uniforms and our armor with nanochromatophores that react to the chemical change that takes place in our skin when we camouflage ourselves."

"So *it* changes whenever *you* change?"

"Yes."

"Wow. I know I probably say this like ten times a day, but that is so cool."

The wood texture on his chest returned to smooth skin.

She let her hands rove his warm muscles, toyed with the hair on his chest. "I feel kinda weird that I didn't ask you this before, but is Dagon your first name or your last name?" It sounded like a first name, but she thought soldiers in the military back home used their last names.

"By last name do you mean my family name?"

"Yes."

"Dagon is my first name. My family name is Strostaav."

She repeated it a time or two in her head. "So in the Segonian military, soldiers and their commanders address each other by their first names?" She hadn't heard anyone call him anything other than Dagon or Commander Dagon since she'd met him.

"Yes."

"Weird."

He smiled. "It wasn't always so. But several centuries ago, a beloved Segonian king was captured and slain by an enemy while en route to an Aldebarian Alliance conference. An investigation into the incident revealed that the surprise attack was not a surprise at all. Our enemy had learned the identity of the commander of the ship that would carry our king, used the commander's full name to locate members of his family, then kidnapped and tortured his wife and youngest children until the commander gave them the information they needed to orchestrate their assassination."

"That's messed up."

"Before the military had even completed its investigation, our enemy used the same tactic to eliminate the king's successor, hoping our planet would descend into chaos."

"Was it the Gathendiens?"

"No. It was an enemy long vanquished now. But we learned from the event and transitioned over to using only first names and unique identifier numbers that are classified."

To keep both their families *and* their ships safe.

"Commander Dagon Strostaav," she murmured, testing the name, then smiled. "I like it. It suits you."

Sliding his hands up her sides, then around to her back, he urged her to lean down until her lips were mere inches from his. "And what is your family name?"

Her pulse picked up when he brushed her nose with his. "Hunt." She had stopped telling her fellow Immortal Guardians and their Seconds her surname years ago because she'd grown tired of them asking if she was serious, then pointing out the irony of someone with the name Hunt basically being forced into the vampire-hunting profession.

"Eliana Hunt," he murmured. "I like it." Those irresistible lips of his turned up in a smile as he closed the distance between them and claimed hers.

Damn, he could kiss. And when she remembered some of the other things he could do with that talented mouth, she clutched him tighter.

A deep, grumbly sound of approval vibrated his chest as he rolled them to their sides. One of his large hands found her breast. Her nipple tightened. She moaned as he delivered a light pinch.

"Commander Dagon," a tinny male voice said.

Dragging her lips from his, she glanced at the earpiece that lay on the shelf by the bed. Dagon used the opportunity to trail hot kisses down her neck while he nudged a thigh between hers. Abandoning her breast, he slid one of his big hands down over her hip and thigh, tucked his fingers behind her knee, and drew it up to rest over his hip.

"Commander Dagon," the voice repeated.

"Dagon?"

"Hmm?" He nibbled his way down to her breast and closed his lips around the sensitive peak.

She bit her lip as heat flooded her. "Galen is calling you on your earpiece thingy."

He drew back. "What?"

"Galen is calling you on your earpiece thingy," she reluctantly repeated, wanting his lips back on her breast. And other places.

His brows lowered in a dark scowl. *"Drek."*

She laughed, amusement taking some of the edge off her desire.

He sent her a wry smile. "Apologies, *milessia*."

Eliana narrowed her eyes playfully. "That had better not be another woman's name."

His teeth flashed in a grin. "It isn't. It's a Segonian endearment. What time is it?"

"I don't know." She glanced up at the ceiling. "CC, what time is it?"

"The time is 10:27."

Dagon's eyes widened. "Did she say *ten* twenty-seven?"

"Affirmative," CC replied.

Eliana bit her lip. "Looks like we overslept." By this time, Dagon had usually already finished first meal and been on the bridge for a couple of hours.

Sighing, he reached for his earpiece. As soon as it was in place, he tapped it. "Report."

"We have a visual on the escape pod," Galen announced.

Dagon met her eyes, his expression sobering. "I'll be there shortly."

Eliana stared through the crystal window into the hangar bay.

The enormous door on the far side rose, revealing darkness incongruent with the morning hour.

Even after spending months in space, she still wasn't used to such. She had never lived in a place where darkness reigned even during the day but—like many of her immortal brethren—had often wished she could. She had always thought being able to work during the day like the majority of humans did would make her feel less like an outsider and more a part of society. The advent of twenty-four-hour stores, gas stations, and the like in the past century had helped lend her life as much normality as possible, she supposed, since those amenities required humans to work the night shift, too. But she'd had to wait a long damn time for that to come around, having been born in what was now the United States in the early seventeenth century.

It was one of the reasons Seth and his second-in-command, David, always opened their homes to immortals and their human Seconds, giving them a place to gather together with others who "worked the same shift" and feel more like a team or a family instead of oddballs who lived in isolation, always on the outskirts of social engagement.

This extraordinary trip into space had eradicated her need to work and move about only at night and had enabled her to be part of the day shift for the first time in centuries. She hadn't felt this *normal* since her days as a mortal. And despite the display of space that filled the bridge as she spent her mornings *learning* beside Dagon, she had grown so accustomed to seeing the rising, peaking, and setting of the sun displayed in the mess hall's simulated windows that she actually forgot sometimes that it was always dark outside the ship.

Clunks sounded as the magnetic clamps attached to three sleek fighter craft retracted, luring her attention back to the hangar. The fighters rose to hover above the floor. Then, one by one with military precision, they shot out of the bay.

Tension thrummed through her, tightening every muscle and making it difficult to stand still. Even with the escape pod close enough for retrieval, the *Ranasura*'s scans had found no signs of life within. Nor could Janek gain access to the pod's systems with the override code despite having consulted the Lasarans.

A beam of light leapt from the hangar and streaked toward the round white orb that floated in the void beyond the ship. As soon as the light struck, it spread until it encompassed the entire escape pod like Spider-Man's web.

"What's that?" she asked, fighting the urge to bite a thumbnail.

"An acquisition beam." Dagon stood beside her, his arms crossed over his chest while he watched the activity that transpired out in space.

"Is that like a tractor beam?" Wasn't that what they called it in sci-fi movies?

He hesitated. "My translator is defining a tractor beam as a heavy, metal bar used in the construction of Earth agricultural vehicles."

She would've laughed if she hadn't been so tense. "No. In sci-fi movies—or what you might call entertainment vids—on Earth, sometimes spaceships have invisible tractor beams that can lock onto ships and pull them inside whether those ships want to come along or not."

He nodded. "Acquisition beams work in a similar fashion. Most of the time, we use them to quickly and easily transfer heavy machinery aboard: ground vehicles, tools and replacement parts for engineering, ammunition cases, dietary provisions, and the like. Sometimes we use them to retrieve damaged fighters or other craft after a battle. But on rarer occasions, we use them as you've described—to seize control of smaller enemy craft, pirate vessels, or that of fugitives and force them aboard."

"Seriously? There are pirates in space?"

"Yes. Many."

She grunted. "I suppose that shouldn't surprise me." There were always people out there who wanted to get something for nothing and—lacking a moral compass—stole to appease that desire.

The three fighters surrounded the escape pod, noses pointing outward to take on any who might challenge them. Eliana wasn't sure how those fighters maneuvered, but they had no difficulty slowly creeping back toward the ship, keeping the distance between them and the escape pod to a minimum.

Guided by the acquisition beam, the pod floated into the bay and descended to the deck with nary a bump nor a scrape.

Eliana moved closer to the window. "How smooth is the exterior supposed to be?" Faint striations—uniform in the direction they followed—coated its surface. The shallow ridges lacked the scorch marks she would expect to see if someone had attacked the pod and blasted it with e-cannon fire. So maybe the grooves were just part of the design?

"It should be smooth," Dagon murmured.

The anxiety clawing her stomach increased another notch. "Wouldn't there be scorch marks or something if it had come under attack?"

"Not necessarily. But the markings *would* be more random. These are uniform, so they may have simply resulted from the pod crashing through the walls of the *qhov'rum*."

That lent her some hope.

Magnetic clamps rose from the hangar floor and locked onto the pod with simultaneous thunks.

The three fighters darted away to perform some kind of scouting maneuvers before returning to the hangar.

When the large door slowly began to close, sealing the silent darkness outside, she glanced up at Dagon. "I need to be in there when they open the hatch."

"Eliana," he said softly, her name carrying a reluctant protest.

"I know," she said when he offered nothing more. "I know what we might find inside it." Every gruesome possibility had played out in her head at least a hundred times in the days it had taken them to reach this point.

They might find a dead Lasaran. Or a dead Yona. A dead *gifted one* whom Eliana had succeeded in getting into the pod but had failed to retrieve before death claimed her. A *gifted one* who had escaped the attack on the *Kandovar* only to die when the escape pod's systems malfunctioned and robbed her of the life support she needed. Or the body of a *gifted one* who had been brutally slain by Gathendiens who had found her first. Or simply the empty clothing of one of Eliana's deceased immortal brethren.

Her throat thickened.

Whenever a vampire or immortal died, the peculiar symbiotic virus that infected them swiftly devoured him or her from the inside out in a desperate bid to continue living, leaving nothing behind but their clothing and weapons. If one of her immortal brethren had died in that pod, likely the only thing that would enable Eliana to identify her would be the scent left behind on a pile of clothing.

If Dagon's men tromped around inside the pod first, she might lose that tenuous connection.

"Please," she murmured. "It's important to me."

After a moment's hesitation, he nodded. Uncrossing his arms, he rested a hand on her back.

Eliana drew comfort from the light touch. She knew he merely wished to spare her if opening the pod revealed the worst. But she tenaciously clung to the hope that she might instead find a healthy *gifted one* who simply hadn't been able to fix whatever had gone wrong with the pod's communication system. Or perhaps an immortal who—like Eliana—had slipped into stasis and whose heartbeat had slowed enough that the *Ranasura*'s scans couldn't detect it.

As soon as the hangar door sealed, Dagon pressed his free hand to the reader beside the entrance, then typed in a code.

She took a step toward the entrance as a door slid up.

"Wait." Catching her arm, he drew her back and nodded to the dozen or so soldiers behind her.

Eliana had been so consumed by her thoughts that she'd forgotten about the security contingent he had ordered to meet them there.

The soldiers strode into the hangar and moved to surround the escape pod. All aimed weapons that reminded her of the network's grenade launchers back home, but these fired white-hot balls of energy.

Only when the men were in place did Dagon escort Eliana inside.

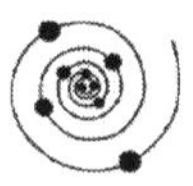

Maarev, Liden, and Efren disembarked from their fighters and joined them as Dagon and Eliana moved to stand in a gap left by the security team.

Dagon heard footsteps behind him and glanced over his shoulder.

Adaos and Secondary Medic Salok positioned themselves some distance away, a hover gurney and a bag full of emergency equipment at the ready.

Dagon gave them a nod, then faced forward and addressed Maarev. "Open it. But make no move to enter."

Maarev approached the pod.

The rest of the soldiers tensed, as did Eliana.

"The grips have all been sheared off," Maarev murmured as he studied the white exterior.

A young engineer by the name of Lanaar jogged over to him, handed him a *kada*, then backed away.

Maarev pulled a corner off the palm-sized device and dropped the larger piece. The falling piece of tech expanded to a hoverboard the length of a man's arm and just wide enough to support his feet.

Maarev stepped up onto it, then thumbed the piece in his hand. Rising smoothly, the board carried him up to the pod's hatch.

"Why is the hatch so high?" Eliana asked softly. For the first time, she evinced no excitement over discovering yet another new *alien gadget* as she put it.

Dagon kept his eyes on Maarev. "To prevent the pod from filling with water when opened after an ocean landing."

"Oh."

Chief Engineer Cobus appeared at Dagon's elbow with a small silver globe in one hand and a small data pad in the other.

A clunk claimed everyone's attention as the hatch shifted

outward a few inches, then began to roll to one side.

Maarev swiftly dropped down to the floor, stepped off the hoverboard, and raised his weapon.

Light spilled forth from the pod.

Silence reigned for several interminable seconds.

Dagon took the *ziyil* and tablet from Cobus. He tossed the *ziyil* up and tapped the tablet's screen. The silver ball halted midfall and hovered in the air. His eyes on the ball, Dagon slid his finger across the screen in a snakelike motion.

The ball zipped up and darted through the pod's entrance, disappearing from sight.

Streaks of light shot out of the hatch, then vanished.

When Dagon again moved his finger on the tablet, the *ziyil* floated out of the pod and lowered to hover a short distance away from them.

Dagon looked down at Eliana. "Are you sure you want to see this?"

A muscle leaped in her jaw. "Yes."

He tapped the screen.

A three-dimensional hologram formed around the silver ball, re-creating every scanned surface of the interior of the escape pod.

The *empty* escape pod.

Though no human, Lasaran, or Yona—live or dead—occupied the space, someone clearly had at one time. Wrappers from nutrition bars littered the floor. What appeared to be discarded clothing formed a shallow pile in one corner.

"Son of a bitch," Eliana snarled and stepped forward.

Dagon caught her arm. "Wait."

Radiating anger, she pointed at the hologram. "That clothing belongs to one of my friends, Dagon."

"You're certain?"

"Yes. But I won't know which one until I get inside. None of us brought much clothing with us because we all decided to defer to Lasaran customs and adopt their mode of dress once we reached Lasara. So whenever my friends got bored with the limited wardrobe they packed, they would mix and match each other's clothes. I've seen at least three of them wear that."

"If the Gathendiens took your friend," he cautioned her, "they could have rigged it with pressure sensitive devices that could—"

Shaking off his hold, she motioned to the ball. "Did that silver-ball thing pick up any signs of explosives?"

He consulted the tablet. "No. But it can only scan surfaces for residue."

"I don't care. I'll risk it." In the next breath, she raced forward three steps, then leaped up, sailing high over Maarev—who jumped up but failed to catch her—and landed on the edge of the hatch, leaving all of them gaping up at her.

Dagon swore as she ducked inside. Tossing the *ziyil* and tablet to Cobus, he jumped on the hoverboard Maarev had abandoned, snatched the controller out of his hand, and flew up to the pod's hatch.

Pocketing the controller, he readied his rifle, quietly stepped off the hoverboard to crouch in the hatch's entrance, and peered inside.

It was a tight space, fairly typical of Lasaran single-occupant escape pods. There was enough headroom to prevent a Lasaran or Segonian male from having to duck once inside. But the only furniture it boasted was a harness-equipped seat that could recline enough for the occupant to use as a narrow bed.

With her back to him, Eliana walked around the seat but didn't have room to do much more than that. A miniscule lav that he knew from experience offered no elbowroom occupied a narrow nook. The rest of the interior was taken up by the artificial gravity and atmospheric generators, nutrition-bar and vitamin-liquid dispensers, and everything else that made the pod perform the functions it did.

Dagon scanned every surface but discerned no threat.

Eliana drew in a long breath and held it.

And he could almost see her cataloging every scent and combing through them to find her friend's. "Eliana."

She jumped. Spinning around, she held up a hand. "Don't come in yet," she said, a request more than an order.

He nodded.

Kneeling, she picked up the colorful discarded shirt, brought the soft fabric to her nose, and again inhaled deeply. Tears filled her eyes as she looked up at him. "Cucumbers," she whispered, her voice hoarse. "It's Ava's."

"Ava is one of your friends from Earth?" he asked softly.

Her throat moved in a hard swallow as she nodded. Clutching the shirt to her chest, she looked around. "Her go bag is missing."

He slipped inside, though his bulk made the tiny pod feel even more cramped. "What's a go bag?"

When a tear spilled down her cheek, Eliana impatiently wiped it away and blinked the rest back. "It's like a bug-out bag or a rucksack full of survival essentials along with some personal items she wouldn't have wanted to leave behind like photos or small keepsakes." She shook her head as a bitter laugh escaped her. "We didn't think the women would actually need them. But we wanted them to be prepared for anything."

She picked up what looked like a lightweight coat that had also been discarded and brought it to her nose. More moisture welled in her eyes. "Ava always wore cucumber-scented deodorant."

Every tear that raced down her cheek tore Dagon up inside. Needing to comfort her, he rested a hand on her shoulder and squeezed. "I see no signs of a struggle, no blood spilled. It's possible she has not been harmed."

"Then where is she? Why hasn't she contacted the Lasarans?" Eliana shook her head. "If anyone who was a friend of the Aldebarian Alliance had found her, we would know it by now."

"Whoever found her may be unknown to the Alliance," he pointed out. "This sector remains largely unexplored, Eliana. Galen located a solar system nearby that has a planet with an atmosphere that is hospitable to Earthlings and Segonians. It's possible that a sentient society similar to ours inhabits it and has rescued her."

"If someone rescued her, why didn't they take the pod with them?"

"If they're new to space travel, it might have simply been too large to fit inside their craft. Or if they are more advanced, a freighter could have found her on its way home and might not have had room for it if its cargo bay was already full of supplies."

"Or maybe the Gathendiens took her, or some of those space pirates you mentioned."

He sighed. "Those are possibilities as well, yes." He wouldn't lie to her to generate false hope. "But past encounters with both lead me to believe that neither of those parties would have left the pod behind. Even if they had to tow it behind them with an acquisition beam, which is not ideal when traveling long distances and can be hazardous when entering a planet's atmosphere, they would have held on to it for study or—in the case of pirates—to sell or salvage for parts and tech."

Rising, she released a despondent sigh. "You're trying to make me feel better, aren't you?"

He curled an arm around her and drew her close. "I'm trying to help you understand that more than one explanation is possible out here, particularly in a sector we know little about. Yes, we believe the Gathendiens are searching for survivors, but they may not be the only ones exploring nearby solar systems."

Leaning into him, she tilted her head back to meet his gaze. "What if there's someone out here who is even worse than the Gathendiens?"

He arched an imperious brow. "Then—to use one of your Earth phrases—we will find them, rescue Ava, and kick their asses."

Her hand clenched in the soft fabric of Ava's shirt as she issued an abrupt nod. "Hell yes, we will."

CHAPTER 13

DAGON WATCHED ELIANA weave her utensil through the *vestuna* heaped on her plate. She had carried very little of it to her mouth, concern for her friend Ava having banished her voracious appetite.

He wished there were something he could say to bring a smile back to her face. Wished he could promise her they would find her friend unharmed. Wished he could guarantee her that they would *find* her friend, whatever her condition, but too many variables denied him that.

Galen had set a swift course for K-54973, the nearest planet with a breathable atmosphere. He had found it on a star map the Sectas had created while constructing the *qhov'rums*, but neither he nor Rahmik could find any other information about it in the Alliance database.

Janek constantly searched and listened for comm signals. The fact that he had come across none seemed only to darken Eliana's mood. But no signal didn't necessarily mean no civilizations. If a sentient species *did* inhabit one of the nearby planets and they had encountered Gathendiens in the past, they might not welcome contact with other alien races.

A single survivor floating, helpless, in an escape pod?

Possibly.

A Segonian battleship?

Doubtful.

Engineering was running diagnostics on the pod and searching its database for clues that might reveal what had happened but had barely gotten started, in part because they had to tread carefully lest they trigger what Eliana called booby traps. Dagon still thought it would be uncharacteristic of the Gathendiens to have left an escape pod behind if they took Ava. But they were dishonorable *grunarks*, their behavior growing increasingly erratic, so he couldn't omit the possibility.

Reaching across the table, he clasped Eliana's free hand.

She gave it a grateful squeeze. "Not much of a dinner companion, am I? I've barely said a thing all evening."

He smoothed his thumb across her soft skin. "Quiet doesn't trouble me when I'm with you, *milessia*."

That managed to lure a faint smile from her. "I don't suppose you'd care to tell me what *milessia* means, would you?"

"Another time perhaps."

Nodding, she released a long sigh and set her utensil down. "I can't eat anything tonight. I'm too…" She shrugged. "Do you think you can down some of this for me? I don't want to hurt Kusgan's feelings."

"Kusgan is a soldier," he reminded her. "He'll understand."

She looked toward the kitchen. "I guess he's probably heard about the empty escape pod, huh?"

"Everyone has," he told her. "I've raised the alert level of the ship while we wait for engineering to finish a more detailed sweep and analysis of the pod. We'll likely remain on alert as we venture into K-54973's solar system."

She nodded, then glanced down at his empty tray. A wry smile momentarily lit her features. "I'm glad my boring company didn't lessen *your* appetite."

He shrugged. "It's a holdover from my earliest years in the military. Like everyone else, I began my career as an infantryman. And as often happens in battle, we didn't always know when we'd have our next meal. So if an opportunity arose, we ate whether we were hungry or not." He gave her hand a last squeeze, then rose, stacking her tray atop of his.

"Could we maybe stop by the bridge and see if anything new has come up?"

He would've been commed if it had, but nodded. "Of course."

They headed toward the kitchen.

"Maybe we could take Janek and Galen something to eat. I think they both missed mid meal, and I didn't see them in here tonight."

Even when consumed by her own worries, she thought of others. "An admirable idea."

Several minutes later, they strode onto the bridge.

Dagon handed his comms officer a closed container.

Janek's eyebrows flew up. "What's this?"

"Last meal."

His jaw dropped. Galen's did, too.

Eliana stepped up beside Dagon, her face at last lighting with a true smile. "You act like you've never been served a meal by your commander before."

"I haven't," Janek said.

Dagon chuckled. "Well, you've Eliana to thank for it. It was her idea."

Janek grinned. "Thank you, Eliana."

Galen's stomach growled.

Eliana chuckled. Taking the second container from Dagon, she turned to the navigations officer. "Don't worry, Galen. We didn't forget you. You get one, too."

He gave her a broad smile. "Thank you, Eliana."

Laughing, she set the container on the edge of the navigation console.

The ship jolted suddenly… hard enough that Dagon had to brace his feet to keep from toppling to the deck. He threw out a hand and grabbed Eliana's arm when she stumbled.

She glanced down at the container she'd set on the console, then looked up at him with wide eyes. "Oh shit. Did I do that? We shouldn't have brought them dinner!"

An alarm began to blare.

Dagon shook his head. "It wasn't you." He addressed the crew. "Were we fired upon?"

Galen and Janek dropped their meal containers to the floor. Every man present consulted his screen, some raising holographic images above their consoles.

"No ships are registering within firing range," Galen announced.

"Shields?" Dagon asked.

"Shields remain at one hundred percent," Rahmik answered.

Dagon stared through the crystal window. "Whoever it is could be cloaked."

Galen shook his head. "Infrared isn't picking up the presence of ships, and I'm not reading any energy signatures."

Janek turned to Dagon. "There's nothing on comms either."

"Then what the *srul* happened?"

"Here." Rahmik pointed to the hologram hovering in front of him. "An explosion damaged Forward Thruster 2. Engineering is battling a fire."

"Open comms," Dagon ordered. "Engineering, report."

Clangs and shouts carried over the speaker as Chief Engineer Cobus spoke. "Forward Thruster 2 has been damaged in an explosion. I don't know yet how badly."

"Any casualties?"

"A few. None life-threatening. I've summoned medics, and we're putting out the fire now."

A distant expletive carried over the speaker.

Dagon's scowl deepened. "Cobus?"

"One moment, sir." A second voice murmured words he couldn't catch. Then Cobus spoke again, his words grim. "Switching to a private channel."

The speaker went silent.

A beep sounded in Dagon's ear. He tapped his earpiece.

"Commander Dagon?" Cobus asked.

"Yes."

"We found what's left of a device that we believe triggered the explosion. It was sabotage."

Eliana's eyes widened. "What?"

Dagon shot her a quick look. Had she heard Cobus? "What can you tell me about it?" he asked the engineer.

A long pause ensued. "There isn't much left of it but… the design is one I've not seen before."

The ship jolted again.

Eliana staggered, but maintained her balance.

Dagon swore. "Cobus?"

"We're okay. That wasn't here."

Rahmik spat an epithet. "Forward Thruster 3 is down. Another explosion took it."

Dagon's lips tightened.

Eliana stared up at him. "I don't believe in coincidences."

"I don't either," he growled. They had retrieved an empty escape pod, and hours later the *Ranasura*'s thrusters started exploding? "Someone must have come aboard with the pod."

Janek shook his head. "Our scans detected no life forms."

Eliana looked back and forth between them. "Has anyone ever fooled your scans?"

"Not in years," Janek answered. "And even the escape pod's system recorded no life forms aboard."

Dagon ground his teeth. "Then whoever it is has found a way to elude the scans. We need to find him before he blows up something else."

Eliana's mind raced. Dagon paced back and forth as he used private channels to quietly order his soldiers to conduct a search of the ship, starting with the hangar bay in which the escape pod rested.

How had someone managed to sneak aboard? How had she and the others missed it? The fighter pilots had spotted no other craft while they were out there in space with it. She, Dagon, and the others had stood just outside the hangar and watched the acquisition beam bring the pod in, and no suspicious characters had clung to its exterior. She had even walked around *inside* the pod and had seen nothing. No one. The only things she had noticed were the clothing and—

"I smelled something," she blurted suddenly.

Dagon turned toward her. "What?"

"In the escape pod," she said. "I smelled Ava, the nutrition bars she ate, the beverages she drank, the sanitizing spray she used… and something else."

The men around them fell silent as Dagon studied her. "What was it?"

"I don't know. It was faint. I've never smelled it before and thought it was the chemicals in the space toilet or vitamin supplements or something else included on the pods that you don't use on your ship."

"Describe it."

She glanced around, searching for an adequate description that wouldn't confound them with references to Earth that they wouldn't understand. "It was sharp. But it had a nonbiologic scent to it, too. Like… the inside of a Lasaran space suit dappled with swamp water?" Or a vinyl shower curtain that had soaked in stagnant water for a couple of weeks.

"Gathendiens," every man spat.

Guilt flooded her. "I'm sorry. I didn't know what it was. I thought it was the toilet or something." If she had mentioned it sooner…

Dagon crossed to Rahmik. "Bring up a schematic of the ship and highlight Hangar 3 and the locations of the explosions."

A three-dimensional hologram of the ship appeared above his station.

Dagon studied it a moment. "He couldn't have left the hangar without the code and a palm print."

A quick check confirmed two men were down in Hangar 3, having been ambushed from behind as they left. Most of their fellow engineers had been in the mess hall until the explosions began and so hadn't found them yet.

"The first bomb was planted here," Dagon murmured, pointing. "The second there." He motioned to the hallways that linked them. "These corridors have too much traffic for anyone to navigate without notice."

Eliana moved to stand beside him and studied the map. "What about ventilation ducts? Can you show us those?"

Rahmik added the ventilation duct layout to the map. "There are enough turns in the ducts that I would think he would've gotten lost in there. *If* he could even fit."

Dagon shook his head. "Gathendiens are cunning *grunarks*. If he familiarized himself with the schematics of all Aldebarian Alliance vessels, then he would have little difficulty navigating the turns. Add electrical, plumbing, and gravitational generation."

Lines—thick and thin—formed a maze in the map, clustering

together in the walls of primary corridors.

Eliana motioned to one such wall. "Can a man fit in this one?"

"Yes."

Rahmik looked doubtful. "I'm still not picking up any unauthorized life forms."

Eliana studied them. "Could it be an android? There weren't any on the *Kandovar*. But Prince Taelon said some cultures in the Alliance have them." She was dying to get a glimpse of one because they were said to be very lifelike.

Dagon shook his head. "That would explain why the life form scanners didn't detect him. But the scent you mentioned indicates it's a Gathendien."

"Then he's either in the walls or in the ventilation ducts," she concluded. "What would his next target be?"

He studied the map, then pointed. "Forward Thruster 5 is closest." Spinning toward the door, he tapped his earpiece. "Maarev, meet me on Deck 1, Corridor 12 with a security team."

"Yes, sir."

Eliana charged after him as Dagon left the bridge, keeping pace even after he broke into a jog. When he offered no protest, she couldn't help but ask, "Aren't you going to tell me I should stay behind?"

"No." He swung around a curve and raced toward the lift at the end. "For some reason, our sensors can't locate him, so I need you to do that for us."

Surprise and pleasure warmed her as they dove into the lift. As the door closed, she glanced up at him and found his piercing gaze focused upon her.

"You have a superior sense of hearing," he stated.

"I do." She smiled. "How did you know?"

He grunted. "You weren't the only one learning yesterday."

Damn, she liked him.

A *lot*.

When the door slid up, they leaped forward. Maarev, Liden, Efren, and several others waited for them around a curve, all packing major weaponry. Eliana had memorized the layout of the ship, so even had there not been a sign marking it, she would've known they stood outside the engineering room that housed

Forward Thruster 3.

Dagon quietly informed his men of the intruder, then ordered them all to remain silent.

Eliana strode along the corridor, heading toward Forward Thruster 5 and following the path that the ventilation ducts and other utilities followed. There were a lot of men on board the *Ranasura*. Crewmen who hurried to help douse the fires and assess the damage. Soldiers who conversed in the rooms around them as they prepared for battle. She was doubly glad now that she had sparred with Maarev and the guys, because that experience had helped her exercise her rather rusty ability to filter out nonessential sounds and hone in on the movements of the enemy they now hunted.

Dagon and his men followed closely on her heels as she navigated the path in search of her prey, silently waving away any crew members they encountered. Eliana began to worry the Gathendien had gotten too great a head start on them and might reach the engineering room that serviced Forward Thruster 5 first. The door was just around the next curve and—

She halted abruptly, backtracked, bumping into Dagon, and stopped.

A barely perceptible scrabbling sound reached her sensitive ears.

She pointed at the wall and mouthed the word "there."

Dagon turned to his men and murmured, "Where's the cutter?"

Before they could answer, a man wearing an engineering uniform jogged around a corner some distance away and headed toward them.

Eliana winced at the thuds his boots produced as he joined them and held up what looked like a small, skinny blowtorch.

"Cobus said you needed me to cut into a wall?"

The scrabbling sounds quickened but remained impressively faint.

Since Dagon and the others didn't react, she assumed they couldn't hear it.

"Too late. He's on the move." She took off down the corridor.

Dagon followed, barking over his shoulder, "Lanaar."

The engineer hastened forward.

But Eliana shook her head. "No time. He's almost there." If she recalled the diagrams correctly, he was only a yard or two away from an intersection in the walls. A quick right turn and a straight shot forward would enable him to reach the thruster housing, whereas she would have to zip down to the door, press her palm to the palm reader, wait for the door to rise, then enter, listen to see if he's already progressed beyond that room and if he had, wait for Dagon or one of the others to catch up, enter the code all engineering rooms required to enter, and…

Hell, just thinking about it wasted too much time.

She performed a quick calculation. Since Dagon intended to cut into the wall, she didn't have to worry about the ship losing atmosphere if she damaged it. She wished she knew more about the metals and how hard they were to penetrate but lacked the time to ask.

There were at least two more walls between this one and the exterior of the ship, so…

Stopping short, she palmed a dagger, drew her arm back, and—utilizing every ounce of her preternatural strength—slammed the blade and her fist into the wall right in front of the Gathendien.

Or so she thought.

Pain shot through her hand and raced up her arm as her fist plowed through metal and…

"Oh gross," she gritted, her voice strained. "I think…" She grimaced in both agony and disgust as something warm and gooey coated her damaged flesh. "I think I just punched a hole in his chest." She hadn't even meant to stab him really. She'd just thought the blade would facilitate her piercing the wall so she could block his forward progress. But her fist was now encased in something that felt like rubbery flesh. "Is that possible? Are Gathendiens so fragile that you can punch a hole in their chest?" She glanced at Dagon and the others.

Every man gaped at her.

Something metal clattered to the floor on the other side of the wall.

"Well, don't just stand there," she urged. "Cut him out before he blows us all up." She thought it a safe guess that he still carried explosives (he wouldn't be heading toward the next thruster if he didn't) and wondered if that was what she'd heard hit the floor.

The engineer leapt forward and started cutting into the wall with a laser torch.

The Gathendien staggered. Thick hands pried at her wrist, trying to force her to release him.

"Ouch. That hurts, damn it," she growled. Tucking the fingers of her free hand into the hole she'd punched, she pulled at the edges but accomplished little more than widening it a bit. It was thick enough that she would not have been able to penetrate it had she not used the awesomely strong dagger Joral had made for her.

When the Gathendien's weight pressed forward as though he were bending at the waist, she tried to bring her telekinesis into play and freeze him in place. But her telekinetic abilities were of little use when she couldn't see her target and—even then—required concentration that pain tended to shatter. So she had to rely on preternatural strength to keep her fist right where it was and hold him upright. If he had indeed dropped the explosive, she didn't want him to be able to pick it up and activate it.

If it weren't already activated.

The alien continued to struggle. Every movement sent shards of pain slicing through her. It felt like she'd broken every bone in her hand. And maybe her wrist as well.

A steady stream of curses spilled from her lips as Dagon joined her.

"Can you withdraw your hand?" he asked.

"No. He dropped something. If I don't hold him in place, he'll be able to bend down and pick it up."

Dagon turned to the engineering guy. "Lanaar, cut here and here. Quickly. And *don't* burn her."

The man nodded. Abandoning the circle he had been cutting, he brought the torch as close to Eliana's arm as he could and began to cut the two lines.

Eliana again felt a rush of affection for Dagon when he used his hands to form a shield of sorts between her flesh and the hot laser beam. As soon as the engineer finished, Eliana patted Dagon's hands to get him to withdraw them, then tucked the fingers of her free hand into the hole and pulled.

A triangle of wall began to curl back under the pressure.

Dagon grasped the edges on either side and pulled with her. As soon as the hole was wide enough, he shoved his arm in and grabbed the alien. "I have him. You can let go."

Relieved, she drew her hand—still fisted around her blade—out of the wall and stared down at it. A thick blue gel with a strong metallic scent coated it. Dropping the blade, she gingerly cupped her damaged fingers and glanced up at Dagon. "This is what Gathendien blood looks like?"

He studied her hand. "No. I don't know *what* the *srul* that is."

Tilting his head, Dagon tapped his earpiece. "Adaos, we need you on Deck 1, Corridor 12 immediately."

"On my way," his friend responded.

Dagon clamped his lips together as he studied Eliana's damaged hand. It was already beginning to swell. And she had clearly broken multiple bones in it.

His fingers tightened around the intruder's neck. The intruder offered no struggle other than to rest more weight on Dagon's hand.

If Eliana had—as she feared—punched a hole in the intruder's chest, Dagon might be the only thing holding the alien upright.

His gaze again lowered to the viscous blue liquid that coated her hand and wrist.

She shifted her weight from one foot to the other. "I'm sorry. I didn't mean to stab him. I just thought the blade would help me pierce the wall easier so I could grab him, but I miscalculated his forward momentum."

He frowned. "What?"

"Do you think Adaos will be able to save him?"

He stared at her. "You think I summoned Adaos for the intruder?"

Her brow furrowed. "Well, yeah. He's not going to be of much use to us if he dies."

Unbelievable. "I summoned him for *you*, Eliana. You've broken every bone in your hand." Punching through a *drekking* wall no one else on this ship could breach without a laser torch or the sustained fire of a tronium blaster or O-rifle.

She forced a smile, though her eyes bore a faint amber glow that betrayed her pain. "Actually, I'm pretty sure I missed a few."

The men clustered around them continued to gape at her, their gazes darting from her to the wall to Dagon and back. Dagon didn't think even a Yona warrior could punch through these walls. He didn't blame his men for being astounded by Eliana's success in doing so.

The laser stopped. Lanaar swiftly stepped back.

Dagon nodded to Maarev.

His friend reached for the segment of wall outlined by the burn marks and pulled hard.

The metal bowed outward with a groan, revealing a blue mass in the shape of a man roughly Dagon's height.

And it did indeed have a hole the size of Eliana's small fist in its chest.

Dagon yanked the being out and forced him to the ground, where he lay on his back, unmoving.

"What the *srul*?" Maarev muttered.

Eliana drew so close to Dagon that her shoulder brushed his arm. "Is that...?" Her face scrunched up in confusion. "Is that his skin?" She studied the alien from his bald head to his toeless feet.

Dagon did the same. The hole in its chest steadily oozed that thick blue liquid. But streaks of maroon infiltrated it. Kneeling down, he touched the edges of the wound. "I've never encountered a bipedal being with skin this blue before."

She crouched down beside him.

"Careful," he warned, distrusting the creature's stillness.

Nodding, she rested her injured hand on her thigh and retrieved her dagger. "You seem surprised. Is this not a Gathendien?"

He shook his head. "Gathendiens don't look like this. They're reptilian, their colors ranging from pale yellow to dark green. And their flesh is much harder to penetrate."

Maarev snorted. "She punched through that wall as if it were cloth. I don't think she'd have any trouble penetrating a Gathendien's scales with her blade."

Eliana flashed him a smile but sobered when she once more regarded the being on the floor. "He has no features."

Dagon examined the blue skin. "I believe this is a suit."

"But how does he breathe in it? Or see? It even covers his eyes."

If he had eyes. Dagon couldn't discern any.

Adaos jogged around a curve with his bag and hurried to join them.

Dagon cupped a hand around Eliana's elbow and rose, drawing her up beside him. "Eliana's hand needs tending."

"Screw that," she said and motioned to the form at their feet with her dagger. "What can you tell us about this?"

Adaos's eyebrows shot up. "What the *srul*?"

"That's what *I* said," Maarev uttered.

Adaos waved his portable scanner over the intruder. "The scanner detects no life save a faint signal where his chest has been punctured."

Eliana frowned. "Is the blue goo his blood?"

Adaos studied the readings on his tablet. "No. The dark red liquid is."

The *blue goo,* as Eliana referred to it, must be what blocked their sensors.

Liden cleared his throat. "Commander?"

When Dagon and the others turned to look at him, he held up a device that looked like a small data tablet with a cylinder attached. "This is the explosive device he dropped. It appears Eliana halted him before he could set the timer."

Dagon silently berated himself for becoming so distracted by Eliana's injuries, her astonishing strength, and the bizarre intruder she'd captured that he'd forgotten the *drekking* explosives.

Efren leaned into the hole and drew out a bag. "There are many more in this."

Enough to cripple the ship and leave it motionless and unable to maneuver if attacked.

Eliana had just saved their asses.

Adaos set his med pack on the floor and withdrew a hover gurney twice the width and length of his data tablet. Holding it waist high, he pressed a corner. The board extended until it was long and wide enough to carry a man Dagon's size, then hovered in the air.

Eliana's eyes widened. A smile lit her pretty face, supplanting the pain and confusion. "Cool!"

Adaos smiled and motioned for her to climb aboard.

She sent him a condemning look. "Oh hell no. I don't need that. Put *him* on it." She motioned to the intruder. "I accidentally stabbed him, so you need to patch him up before he dies. If he came aboard on the pod, then he knows what happened to Ava."

Dagon agreed. "I'll carry Eliana."

She scowled up at him. "What?"

"I'll carry you so Adaos can transport the intruder on the hover gurney."

She rolled her eyes. "My legs are fine, Dagon. My *hand* is injured. If *Maarev* hurt his hand, would you insist on carrying *him*?"

Srul no. But Dagon didn't feel for Maarev what he felt for Eliana. Not that he could tell her that. Yet. Not while surrounded by his overly curious soldiers. That was a conversation best held in private. "No."

Maarev nudged Eliana with his elbow, careful not to jostle her injured hand. "Maybe the next time you kick my ass, I'll let him carry me to Med Bay."

Her frown melted into a smile. "Maybe I'll carry you myself, big guy."

Laughing, Maarev glanced at the hole in the wall and shook his head. "I believe you could."

Glaring at his friend, Dagon wrapped an arm around Eliana's waist and gently drew her back to give his men more room to work. "Get him on the gurney."

They bent over the intruder.

"*Drek*, he's heavy," Liden declared with a grimace as he and Efren hoisted the being onto the hover gurney.

Efren nodded.

As soon as they released him, both men wiped their slimy hands on their uniforms, their faces creased with disgust.

Whatever the *blue goo* was, it continued to ooze from the hole in the man's suit.

When Adaos detached the small corner controller from the hover gurney and aimed it down the hallway, the board carrying the intruder silently floated forward.

Dagon glanced down at Eliana.

Her eyes widened. Then she sent him a big grin and whispered. "I want one!"

Chuckling, he kept his arm around her as they followed Adaos and his patient to Med Bay.

CHAPTER 14

DAGON'S MIND WHIRLED as the past few minutes caught up with him. He had known all along that Eliana possessed an abundance of internal strength. She had exhibited it many times since the *Kandovar* had been destroyed. But the incredible physical strength she had just demonstrated...

He could not remember if she had mentioned having such when she had reluctantly confessed the ways she differed from other Earthlings. He had been too focused on her injuries, the transfusion she'd needed, the fangs she'd displayed, and the vulnerability she'd tried to conceal while she awaited his reaction.

He had never encountered a being her size who could punch through thick metal walls. And he could think of few *larger* beings who were capable of it.

Androids? Yes, depending on their purpose.

Cyborgs? Definitely.

Men or women of any Aldebarian Alliance race who had *not* been mechanically enhanced? No.

Eliana really *had* held back when she'd trained with Maarev and the others.

Upon reaching Med Bay, Dagon let Adaos enter first with the intruder. Then he and Eliana followed. Maarev, Liden, and Efren joined them and positioned themselves within lunging distance of the intruder while the rest of the security contingent guarded the door.

The hover gurney settled upon the nearest empty treatment bed.

Segonian males with burn wounds occupied two others.

Adaos ordered the medics treating them to transfer their patients to the private rooms in back lest they be injured if the intruder awoke and sparked violence. Judging by the sounds of it, some of the rooms down the hallway were already occupied by injured men.

When Eliana would've stopped beside the intruder's bed, Dagon applied pressure to her back and led her past it to the closest private exam room.

Dragging her feet, she craned her neck to look back over her shoulder. "What are you doing?"

"You need a transfusion."

She jerked her attention back to him. "That can wait."

"No, it can't." Her hand continued to swell and was now discolored by more than the blue slime.

"Yes, it can. I want to see what's under the blue goo."

"I do, too." He picked up the med tablet just inside the door. "So let's do this quickly, shall we?" He gestured to the bed.

When she opened her mouth to balk, he arched a brow, daring her to refuse.

Clamping her lips together, she crossed to the bed.

She was so much smaller than the men on his ship that the bed was too high for her to simply slide onto. Dagon didn't want her to have to stop supporting her injured hand, so he set the data tablet aside, gripped her narrow waist, and lifted her up to sit on the edge of the bed.

Her eyes met his, that fascinating amber glow brightening briefly. "Thank you."

Nodding, he withdrew his touch and used the tablet to order a blood transfusion for her.

Eliana scooted a little to one side so she could peer through the open doorway and see what was happening in the main room. She nevertheless stiffened when the mechanical arm bearing the needle descended from the ceiling.

"It will infuse your injured arm," he told her, moving to stand beside her.

Resting her damaged hand on her thigh, she grabbed the edge of the bed with the other as she warily eyed the needle.

Dagon turned to face the doorway, curious to see what Adaos would discover, and unobtrusively reached behind his back to take her free hand in his. Some of the tension in her form eased as she gave his hand a squeeze.

"Thank you," she whispered.

He didn't know if she thanked him for holding her hand or for doing so behind his back where the others wouldn't see it and guess her dislike of needles. Why she believed they would perceive such as a weakness after the strength she had just displayed baffled him.

In the next room, the hover gurney shrank back to its initial size.

Adaos tugged it out from under the intruder and set it aside. Grabbing his med tablet, he activated the full-body scanner.

A long moment passed as all waited to hear what it would reveal.

Eliana's grip tightened slowly on his hand, becoming almost painful.

He glanced at her and found her face paler than usual. Her lips clamped together. A muscle in her cheek twitched. When she caught him staring, she loosened her hold.

"Sorry," she whispered. "The bones are shifting back into position. It hurts like hell. I mean *srul*. It hurts like *srul*."

He stroked his thumb over the back of her hand. "Squeeze as hard as you want to," he murmured so the others wouldn't hear.

Though pain pinched her features, the corners of her lips turned up in a faint smile.

Adaos swore. "The scanner is stymied by the blue liquid. It's reading little more than a heat signature emanating from the puncture wound." Setting his tablet aside, he strode away from the exam table and left Dagon's line of sight. A clattering sound filled the silence.

Adaos returned to the intruder's side a moment later with a glass tube in one hand and a long narrow instrument in the other. Leaning forward, he collected a sample of the odd, viscous blue liquid, adding a dollop of the dark red. Once he was satisfied with the quantity inside the tube, he left Dagon's sight again.

Eliana's grip relaxed. "Much better," she said on a sigh.

He studied her injured hand. Though it was still swollen and discolored, it looked better. "Is it repairing?"

She nodded. "The bones are all aligned properly again, but it will take more time for them to heal completely. I'll be fine by tomorrow."

Amazing. Reluctantly releasing her hand, he reached for the med tablet. "Extend your arm."

As soon as she held it out, he ordered a stabilizer. A mechanical arm descended from the ceiling. Eliana eyed it warily.

"No needles this time," he promised softly.

Before she could respond, the end of the mechanical arm divided into two. One branch slid beneath her forearm. The other moved to hover above it. White foam shot forth from both and coated Eliana's arm and hand. She jumped but kept her arm still. As the foam dissolved, the *blue goo* disappeared, leaving her flesh clean. A clear spray followed, which Dagon knew would disinfect the area. Then a colorless gel coated her skin, beginning halfway up her forearm and continuing down until her wrist and all but the tips of her fingers received a thick layer.

"What's that?" she asked and moved to touch it.

Dagon clasped her free hand again before she could. "Wait."

The mechanical arms emitted a flash of light.

The gel hardened instantly.

She stared. "Is that a cast?"

Dagon released her and sought a response. "I don't think my translator is defining that accurately."

"What is it telling you a cast is?"

"A sculpture made by the shaping of molten metals."

She smiled. "That *is* one definition. But *cast* in this sense refers to a hard plaster doctors on Earth apply to broken arms to hold them steady while the bones heal."

He nodded. "Then it is a cast."

"What do *you* call it?"

"A stabilizer."

"Makes sense." Smiling, she scooted off the bed. "Now let's go see what's happening with the blue guy."

Relieved, Dagon escorted her from the private room and approached the prone blue figure the same time Adaos did.

The chief medical officer now carried a laser scalpel.

"What can you tell us?" Dagon asked.

"The blood is Purveli."

Shock rippled through him. "You're certain?"

"Yes. The blue is an unknown metal that remains in a liquid form unless frozen or heated to four hundred and twenty *gogans*." Frowning, he tucked the laser scalpel in a pocket and gingerly clasped Eliana's stabilizer. She remained still while he inspected it. "I see no traces of the metal on her skin. But I should take a sample of her blood to see how much she absorbed and run tests to ensure it isn't toxic to her species."

Dagon regarded her with alarm.

"I'm fine," she assured them.

Unappeased, Adaos warned, "It could be a slow-acting poison."

She shook her head and motioned to the intruder. "Wouldn't he be dead by now if it was?"

Adaos glanced at the blue figure. "The suit he wears blocks our sensors. He may already be dead."

Her eyebrows flew up. "Then why the *srul* are you standing here talking to *me*?"

Dagon motioned to the room they'd just left. "We should collect a blood sample to ensure—"

"Nope," she insisted. "I'm fine. Trust me, guys. I'm *very* hard to kill. If you want to take a blood sample, you can do it later."

When Adaos hesitated, Dagon nodded toward the intruder. "Proceed."

Adaos drew out the laser scalpel. Positioning it above the center of the intruder's forehead, he made an incision that he extended down the intruder's smooth, featureless face to his torso, then to his groin. Four more incisions traced paths down the intruder's legs and arms. Once finished, Adaos set the scalpel on a nearby tray and pulled the edges of the blue skin-like exterior open.

Viscous blue liquid spilled out to coat the medic's hands. More oozed down to the table and over the sides to drop onto the floor with a splatter.

Eliana frowned at Adaos. "If you think it's poisonous, shouldn't you be wearing gloves or something?"

"I am," he murmured, his focus on the patient.

Dagon supposed that to Eliana it appeared that he wasn't. But

Adaos would have sprayed his hands and arms with a clear liquid that formed a protective barrier before touching the puzzling figure.

More blue plopped down to the floor, its consistency somewhere between a liquid and a solid.

"CC," Adaos commanded, "activate disinfection bots."

Small square cleaning bots zipped out of a lower cabinet across the room and swarmed over the floor around them, suctioning up the liquid and coating the floor with disinfectant.

Dagon glanced down at Eliana to gauge her reaction.

She watched the busy little bots work, then looked up at him with brown eyes that sparkled.

"Let me guess," he murmured. "You want one?"

Her teeth flashed in a grin. "Yes, please."

Tamping down his amusement, he returned his attention to the exam table.

At Adaos's command, a mechanical arm descended from the ceiling and coated the intruder with white foam.

As it had on Eliana's arm, the foam dissolved the blue substance, leaving behind…

"A Purveli male," Dagon uttered, studying him in confusion.

"You seem surprised," Eliana commented.

"I am. Though the Purvelis are not part of the Aldebarian Alliance, they have never exhibited hostility toward Alliance members." The male was more slender than others Dagon had encountered, but he bore distinctive, barely discernible scales and a silvery skin tone, which Dagon knew without examining more closely was paler in front and darker in back. The Purveli's long hair pooled on the table in silver waves that would look black when dry. And though Eliana's fist had penetrated the Purveli's suit, only her blade had pierced his chest.

She studied the male curiously while Adaos took more readings. "So why is this one working with the Gathendiens?"

"I don't know. They usually keep to themselves. This is unheard of." He looked at Adaos. "Is he dead?"

Adaos studied the readings on his tablet. "No. But he will be soon if I don't surgically repair the wound in his chest."

"Do it," Dagon commanded.

Adaos summoned two medics to aid him.

Eliana motioned to the floor where the cleaning bots were vacuuming up the last of the mysterious blue substance. "How did he see and breathe under all that stuff?"

Dagon pointed to the Purveli's rib cage, which bore what appeared to be a series of parallel scars. "Purvelis can live on land *or* in the sea." Taking her uninjured arm, he drew her back as Adaos and the other medics began to repair the damage done to the Purveli.

She rose onto her toes and tried to peer around them. "Are those gills?"

"Yes. When on land, Purvelis use lungs like ours to take in oxygen from the air. In the sea, they extract oxygen from the water with their gills."

Adaos grunted. "This one's gills may not be salvageable. Whatever metals are contained within the blue liquid have damaged them severely. If I'm not able to repair his lung, he'll die."

Eliana shot Dagon an uneasy look. "But his lung can be repaired, right? I mean, with your advanced medical knowledge, you guys can fix just about anything."

Adaos shrugged. "Were it just the stab wound, I would say yes. But the blue liquid has seeped into the damaged lung and is complicating matters."

Dagon could practically see her anxiety levels rise. "What is it?" Did she think he would blame her if the Purveli died before they could extract information from him? "I know you didn't intend to kill him, Eliana."

"I know. And I appreciate that you aren't angry about that."

"Had you not stopped him, he would have continued to detonate bombs, injuring many more men and crippling the ship."

"I know. But..."

"What?"

She shook her head. Her brow furrowed as she lowered her heels to the floor and shifted from side to side in a familiar display of disquietude. "I've killed a lot of men over the years, Dagon. A lot of *vampires*. But each and every one of them was either psychotic or well on his way to *becoming* psychotic and was preying upon innocent men, women, and children. When I confronted them, I knew killing them would save countless lives because I *knew* they were bad guys who would only get worse if I didn't." She motioned to the Purveli. "But what if he *isn't* a bad guy?"

"He bears the scent of a Gathendien and collaborated with our enemies," he reminded her. "The same enemies we fear now have your friend. He injured my men with explosives meant to impede our navigational capabilities. And his people have rejected all invitations to join the Aldebarian Alliance."

She drew in a deep breath and slowly exhaled it. Her agitated movements ceased. "Yeah. That does look pretty bad."

"My men would not be standing guard if it did not."

"Okay." She watched the activity centered around the operating table. "But you've got this… Right, Adaos? You aren't going to let a measly thing like weird, snotty blue gunk keep you from showing off your brilliance and saving the Purveli's life, are you?"

The chief medical officer issued a sound that Dagon couldn't decide was a laugh or a snort. "Yes, Eliana. I've got this."

Dagon reluctantly left Eliana to linger in the infirmary while he headed to the bridge.

Barus frowned when he entered. "CC said the intruder is Purveli."

"Yes."

Confusion clouded his second-in-command's features. "How many explosives did he intend to detonate?"

"Efren found more than enough in the bag the man carried to take out every thruster on this ship and then some."

"Leaving us unable to maneuver if attacked."

"Yes." Dagon turned to his navigations officer. "Galen, keep an eye out for both Gathendien *and* Purveli ships. Bring in extra eyes to scan at maximum magnification." If any ships lingered beyond *Ranasura*'s radar range, just waiting for it to grind to halt, he wanted to know.

"Yes, Commander." Galen turned back to his station and began to speak softly, summoning all assistant navigators to the bridge.

Barus shook his head. "Why would the Purvelis work with the

Gathendiens? They know the atrocities those *grunarks* have committed."

"That's a question I intend to put to our prisoner if he survives. One of many."

The door to the bridge opened, allowing Chief Engineer Cobus to enter.

Dagon nodded at him. "Cobus, what can you report?"

"Seven men injured. None fatally." He shook his head. "Considering the size of the explosions, I'm surprised no one was killed."

Dagon had only gotten a brief glimpse of the damage as he and the others had chased down the intruder, but he had to agree. "Were the thrusters themselves damaged?"

"No." Cobus's tone reflected bafflement. "Only the systems used to operate them."

"How long will repairs take?"

The older man scratched his chin, leaving soot marks. "Eight hours."

Barus frowned. "We'd be able to detect any ship that was only hours away from us and could make the repairs and be ready to fight before they could reach us. Why not disable the thrusters themselves and delay us longer?"

Dagon pondered possible explanations. "Either they've acquired new radar-dampening technology that is enabling them to elude detection or they failed to take into consideration the possibility that we would catch the Purveli before he damaged all the thruster controls and simply planned to take the ship from us while inflicting as little damage as possible. A ship incapable of motion would be far less useful to them."

Barus swore.

"But," Dagon continued, "will the Gathendiens proceed with whatever attack they planned if they see our ship is still mobile and—by all outward appearances—unharmed?" Losing two thrusters merely slowed them down a little. They were still racing toward K-54973 as quickly as possible, hoping they would find Ava there.

His men had thus far dredged up little information on the planet. Its distance from its sun indicated that the estimated temperatures it endured could sustain life. The appearance of both landmasses and oceans suggested it held an atmosphere that could support the same. Beyond that…

They really had no idea what to expect. Their long-distance scans detected no ships, space stations, or satellites orbiting the planet. But that didn't mean it lacked settlements or civilizations. Nor did it mean any beings living on the planet lacked the ability to navigate in space. They could have sent a ship to investigate the pod and taken Ava back to their planet.

"Even if the Purveli had disabled all our thrusters," he mused, "we would retain weapons capability and still have the fighters, so there would be a battle."

It didn't make sense. The Gathendiens were thieves. They didn't destroy the things they wished to take. They didn't bomb planets and decimate the infrastructure of the civilizations inhabiting them to make way for themselves. They instead found ways to eliminate the inhabitants *without* battles and simply waited until all the sentient inhabitants were dead before moving in and taking possession of the prize.

Barus shook his head. "Why would they even engage us? We're a Segonian battleship in good standing with the Aldebarian Alliance."

Dagon swore. "They know Eliana's on board."

Barus shot him a look. "What?"

"They must know Eliana's on board. Or at least they *suspect* she's on board. There's no other explanation." The Gathendiens wouldn't risk conflict with a Segonian battleship—a conflict that would cost them lives and fighter craft despite the *Ranasura*'s presumably damaged maneuvering capabilities—if they weren't certain it held a prize they dearly wished to claim.

"Commander Dagon."

He looked up as Adaos's voice carried through the speaker. "Yes?"

"The Purveli is conscious."

Spinning on his heel, Dagon strode from the bridge.

Eliana studied the Purveli with fascination. Of all the aliens she had encountered since leaving Earth, he was the most… well… *alien* in appearance.

His features resembled those of a human. Or a Lasaran, a Segonian, or a Yona. If their planets shared similar atmospheres, she supposed it shouldn't surprise her that the sentient humanoid life forms upon them were similar, too.

Despite the dark circles beneath his eyes and his gaunt cheeks, the Purveli was handsome. His silver hair darkened to black as it dried. His brows and the stubble on his sunken cheeks did as well. Though his torso bore gills, there wasn't anything fishlike about his face. He didn't have big bulging eyes or a huge gaping mouth. Nor did she see any fins on the rest of his body.

His arms and legs bore a similar musculature to humans, but he was built almost like a marathon runner—so thin she could see the ribs beneath his gills. His fingernails and toenails were trimmed short. A few looked as though they had been cut *too* short, leaving raw pink patches. The brief glimpse she had gotten of his groin area before Adaos covered him with a sheet had yielded no surprises beyond hair similar to that on his head that started out a silvery color and had begun to darken to black. Like humans, he had one penis and two testicles, so his people must procreate the same ways humans did. No egg laying or whatever.

She had to give Adaos credit for possessing an abundance of patience. She peppered him with questions the entire time he and his assistants operated on the alien. Once the Purveli was in stable condition, the other medics retreated to check on the patients in the back rooms while Adaos studied globs of the blue goo and tiny flesh samples he had taken from the intruder. He now muttered to himself as he peered at a screen that depicted what she guessed was an illuminated and greatly magnified view of cells like one might see through a microscope.

She returned her attention to the Purveli's face. According to Adaos, the very normal-looking nose and mouth the alien bore could easily switch from taking in air and guiding it to his lungs to taking in water and sending it through his gills.

So cool. What would it be like to be able to stay underwater indefinitely without an oxygen tank? Eliana loved to swim. So did

Ava. It was something the two had bonded over while they'd gotten to know each other on the *Kandovar*. Ava had envied Eliana's ability to hold her breath for extraordinary lengths of time and had loved hearing her accounts of puzzling playful dolphins and seals by remaining underwater far longer than the creatures were accustomed to seeing humans last.

From a distance, the Purveli's flesh looked very similar to hers, though it bore a silvery tone and a subtle sheen like the kind oil left on water that formed rainbow streaks in certain lighting. Upon closer inspection, she could see a faint pattern that indicated he was instead covered in something similar to scales.

Scales that were marred by multiple scars.

Eliana moved nearer, curiosity luring her like a magnet. "Can I touch him?" she asked softly.

Adaos frowned without looking away from whatever he was studying several feet away. "Why would you want to?"

"To see what his scales feel like."

Sighing, he glanced over, confirmed the restraints they had placed around the Purveli's wrists and ankles remained secure, then nodded. "Go ahead."

She glanced at Maarev, Liden, and Efren.

Maarev arched a brow.

The other two grinned, amused by her fascination.

Eliana touched a finger to the Purveli's arm near the bend of his elbow. He might have scales like a fish, but he wasn't slimy at all. And the scales were soft like skin.

She drew her finger up his biceps toward his shoulder, going against the grain, so to speak, to see if it would feel different.

Nope. Still soft.

She traced a path back down his arm, skipping the leatherlike restraint to touch his hand. It was much larger than hers, almost as big as Dagon's. She nudged it to the side a bit so she could study his palm.

Paler than the back, it was gouged in several places and crisscrossed by scars.

"Defensive wounds," she murmured. Keeping her touch light, she gently parted two of his fingers and found a flexible webbing between them that stretched almost to the first knuckle.

"Careful," Maarev warned softly.

Eliana nodded but remained unconcerned. If the Purveli awoke and tried to grab her, she could easily escape his hold.

Releasing his fingers, she leaned down and tried to peek beneath the restraint at his wrist. There wasn't much give to it, but she managed to part the leatherlike cuff from his skin enough to spy a few marks on his flesh, some old, some new. Marks that had *not* been caused by the restraints that now bound him since he had not yet struggled against them.

A sick feeling settled in her stomach.

She straightened. Her gaze strayed to the Purveli's exposed chest. After remedying as much of the damage to the intruder's lung as he could, Adaos had coated the closed incision with a clear gel that solidified into a rubbery substance and adhered to the patient's skin without aid. Eliana compared the look of the puncture wound her blade had left behind to the scars that decorated other areas of the Purveli's flesh.

Though the other scars were longer than the one she'd left with her dagger, they were thin enough to have been neatly carved by a laser scalpel.

Something brushed her fingers.

Jumping, she looked down.

Webbed digits stretched toward hers. The wrist she had just studied pulled against the restraint, the muscles in the forearm above it flexing.

When her gaze followed a path up those straining muscles to the Purveli's face, she gasped.

The male was awake and stared at her with bright silver eyes.

Adaos spoke behind her. "Commander Dagon. The Purveli is conscious."

He was conscious all right. And his eyes didn't stray from Eliana's face as he continued to reach for her.

She heard his heartbeat pick up until it pounded in his damaged chest. But for some reason, she didn't think the fear she read in his silver eyes was spawned by guilt.

Letting instinct guide her, she covered his hand with hers.

The Purveli instantly clasped it.

Maarev, Liden, and Efren took quick steps forward, voicing

objections that blended together as they all spoke at once.

She held up a hand to silence them and kept her gaze locked on the Purveli's.

"Earthling," he croaked, his voice deep and hoarse. Moisture filled his eyes, and he grimaced in pain.

"Yes," she replied in English. When he didn't seem to understand, she switched to Segonian, doubly glad now that she had swiftly learned the language. She thought the chances of him having a translator that would allow him to understand English were slim. "I'm an Earthling."

He gave the warriors a wary glance, then met her gaze. "Where?"

"You're on the Segonian ship you tried to sabotage." The warriors did *not* like her revealing that, but she doubted it was news to the Purveli. Those silver eyes gleamed with intelligence. "Have you seen others like me?"

Dagon strode into the infirmary. He took in his men's alert posture, then focused his attention on Eliana.

The Purveli's clasp tightened.

Dagon's expression darkened. "Step away from him, Eliana."

She met his stormy gaze as he moved to stand on the other side of the bed. "He won't hurt me."

"You don't know that."

"Yes, I do. And you do, too. You've seen how strong I am. He's restrained and weak from his injuries. He *can't* hurt me."

"Won't hurt you," the Purveli promised her hoarsely.

Dagon glared down at him. "Now that you're in our custody, you won't. But you can't deny that was your intention when you boarded my ship."

She stared at Dagon. "What?"

He didn't look away from the Purveli. "Disabling the thrusters was part of a plot you hoped would end with your capturing Eliana for the Gathendiens, was it not?"

Shit. Really? She studied the Purveli.

"How long?" he wheezed.

Dagon arched a brow. "How long have I known?"

The Purveli glanced at the restraints on his wrists, then looked at Dagon. He tried to speak again but ended up growling in frustration and pain.

Eliana frowned. "Do Purveli people not speak the same way we do?" Did his throat hurt because he didn't normally use it to communicate?

Adaos answered as he moved to stand beside her. "They do. But he's suffered a great deal of damage from swallowing and inhaling what you refer to as the blue goo. The metals and toxins it utilized to block our scans also burned his flesh."

Burned it how? "Like a chemical burn?"

"Yes."

Had the Purveli known it would harm him when he'd donned the blue suit? "Can't you do anything to alleviate it and make it easier for him to communicate?" She needed to learn whatever he might know about Ava.

Dagon and Adaos visually consulted each other.

"What?" she asked as the moment stretched.

"You gave him *nahalae*?" Dagon asked.

"Yes," Adaos responded.

She looked back and forth between them. "What's *nahalae*?"

Dagon studied the intruder. "The Purveli are telepathic. The ability enables them to communicate with one another while underwater. But a drug derived from the *nahalae* plant robs them of that ability."

So all the Purveli could do now was try to force sound out through a damaged throat? "Can you reverse it? I mean, is there something you can give him to restore his telepathy so we can question him?" When both men were slow to respond, she shook her head. "What? What am I missing?"

A muscle in Dagon's cheek twitched as he sent the alien a dark look. "There *is* such a drug, but using it would be unwise. The Purveli can wield their telepathy like a weapon."

Surprise coursed through her. "They can?" She knew quite a few telepathic Immortal Guardians on Earth. And the only way she had seen any of them use their gift like a weapon was by snooping uninvited into other people's thoughts and exposing their secrets.

Releasing the Purveli's hand, she took a couple of steps back. "How?"

"They can emit a sound in your head that deafens you and

causes so much pain you collapse," Dagon told her, his face grim. "If they continue to emit the sound, the damage will be permanent."

Shit.

"They can also use *senshi* to increase the pressure inside your skull until your eyes, ears, and nose bleed and you either lose consciousness or die."

The telepaths on Earth sure as hell couldn't do that.

Well… maybe Seth could. The eldest Immortal Guardian was so powerful that there was very little he *couldn't* do.

"What's a *senshi*?" she asked. The earpiece she wore failed to find an English equivalent, and she hadn't encountered that word in her studies.

Adaos spoke. "It's a pulse of sound they use to locate each other in the darkest waters."

Like echolocation? Only deadly to others apparently. "If that's true," she said slowly, "then why didn't he emit a *senshi* as soon as he realized we'd located him in the walls?"

Adaos motioned to the blue image on the screen behind her. "The blue liquid he breathed and ingested in the suit contained *nahalae*."

That didn't make sense. "Why would he impede his own telepathic abilities?"

Dagon met her gaze. "The *nahalae* also blocks others with telepathic abilities from reading *his* thoughts. If he believed Lasarans were on board, he would've wanted to keep them from reading his thoughts and intent."

Or if he and the Gathendiens had already figured out that Eliana and her friends were not your average humans and suspected some of *them* were telepathic…

"I didn't know how long it would take the *nahalae* he ingested in the suit to wear off," Adaos said, "and did not wish to endanger the crew. So I administered some myself."

The crew. Not *some* of the crew or some of his medical staff, but *the crew.*

As in the whole damned ship.

She looked at Dagon. "Can he do that? Can one Purveli emit a *senshi* that's capable of harming everyone aboard the *Ranasura*?"

"Yes. It's why the Purveli believe they don't need allies."

Well, there was no way in hell she would let the Purveli use that crap on Dagon and the others.

Moving so quickly she blurred, Eliana drew her spare dagger and lunged over the Purveli, positioning the tip of the blade over one eye, her face mere inches from his.

Dagon and the others started. Someone gasped.

The Purveli jerked in surprise and emitted a grunt of pain as his eyes widened and focused on the blade.

"Don't look at the blade," she ordered, her voice cold and deadly. "Look at *me*."

The room went still.

Eliana caught and held the Purveli's gaze. "I'm fast," she warned him softly. "Faster than you can imagine. I'm strong, too." She glanced down at his chest, then met his eyes once more. "I'm the one who punched through the wall and stabbed you." She lowered the blade an inch, bringing it close enough that his lashes brushed it when he blinked. "I'm the one who stopped you. And I'll stop you again if you even *try* to harm us with *senshi* or any other *bura* in your telepathic arsenal. You don't know me and you may not fear me, but you should. You do *not* want to make an enemy of me. These men are my friends. I care about them. If you so much as give them a mild headache, I will inflict pain upon you like you have never experienced before." Again she glanced at his torso, then met his eyes. "And the scars you already bear will be nothing in comparison to the ones I'll give you… *if* I let you live."

One of the warriors whispered a curse, his tone full of admiration.

But Eliana continued to study the Purveli to gauge his reaction.

What she saw in his eyes was not at all what she expected.

Those silver orbs that held her stare didn't fill with fear or resentment, defiance, or even weary capitulation.

They filled with hope.

CHAPTER 15

THE ANTIDOTE ADAOS administered to the Purveli would take several minutes to work. Until then…

Dagon caught Eliana's gaze and jerked his head toward the doorway.

Without a word, she sheathed her dagger and left the infirmary.

Following on her heels, he closed the door behind them.

The security team stood straighter.

"Dismissed," Dagon said and watched them file away.

"Thank you," Eliana said as soon as they disappeared from view.

"For what?"

"For ordering Adaos to give him the antidote."

He shrugged. "We need information. That's the only way we'll get it until his throat heals."

She nodded. "And I meant what I said in there. I won't let him hurt you or the others."

She said it with such endearing earnestness that he wanted to draw her into a hug.

Instead, he arched a brow. "Because you care about us?"

A flush crept into her cheeks as she smiled. "Yes, I care about you. How could I not? You're all so damn appealing." She glanced at the closed door, then sent him a wink as she whispered, "But you're my favorite."

Leaning down until his lips nearly touched her ear, he whispered back, "You're my favorite, too." He pressed his lips to the soft skin of her neck. "And I plan to prove it again tonight." When he straightened, she stared up at him with brown eyes that acquired an amber glow. His pulse leaped when she slid her tongue across her lower lip as though she could already taste his kiss.

He shook his head. "So damn appealing."

"Awwww." Smiling, she patted his chest. "You used an Earth curse word to describe me. That's so sweet."

He laughed. "Appealing and odd," he qualified.

She wrinkled her nose. "Yeah. I was hoping it would take you longer to figure that last part out. Now quit distracting me with your sexy self. I need to tell you something."

According to his translator, *sexy* meant alluring or physically attractive.

Pleasure raced through him.

Then she stepped closer, her pretty face sobering, and tilted her head back to look up at him. "I don't think the intruder is who you think he is."

"He's a Purveli."

"I know. But I don't think he's working with the Gathendiens. Did you see the scars on his body?"

"I admit I paid them little notice." Many soldiers had scars. Some even wore them like badges of honor. And Dagon had been tense the whole time he'd been in Med Bay, ready to pounce if the Purveli said anything even remotely threatening to Eliana.

"Well, they aren't the kind one receives in battle. The fact that I heal quickly doesn't mean I don't scar. My scars just fade really fast. And his scars don't look like mine. They don't look like they resulted from battle."

"Battles on Earth are fought differently than those in space."

"I know. But I've seen the scars some of your guys carry from old blaster wounds and the like, and the Purveli's scars didn't look like that either."

He frowned. "Did they look recent?"

"Yes. And his wrists are raw beneath the restraints."

"He hasn't been conscious long enough to damage his wrists."

"Exactly."

He considered it.

"There's something else," she added with apparent reluctance.

"What?"

"When I did my thing with the dagger and threatened him, he didn't seem angry or resentful or stupidly determined or any of the things my enemies usually throw at me when I do stuff like that. He seemed..."

"What?" he asked when she trailed off.

She shrugged. "Hopeful."

He glanced at the wall behind her as though he could peer through it and study the restrained man on the other side.

"Are the Purveli good manipulators?" she asked. "I mean, could it all have been a ruse to confuse me because I don't know anything about his people?"

"No one knows much about his people. They keep to themselves and discourage others from visiting their planet."

"Then he *could* be working with the Gathendiens and just be trying to throw me off?"

Dagon slowly shook his head. "The scars and marks you mentioned indicate otherwise."

"Do any of his people ever go rogue? Could he be a criminal on the run who is palling around with the Gathendiens while he hides out and... I don't know... escapes prosecution or something?"

"I have encountered very few Purveli away from their homeworld, so I don't think it likely." He supposed they shouldn't ignore the possibility though. Being an escaped prisoner could plausibly explain the marks on the Purveli's wrists. It could also account for the Gathendiens not worrying about poisoning him with the blue suit. Gathendiens would suffer no qualms over poisoning a criminal who had already been issued a death sentence.

It could *not*, however, explain the hope Eliana had discerned in his eyes.

"I hate to ask this," she said with a hint of a grimace, "but could your people or the Lasarans or whoever maybe have been too pushy while trying to bring the Purvelis into the Aldebarian Alliance? Could they have inadvertently driven the Purvelis to work with the Gathendiens instead?"

That he could answer with certainty. "No. The Alliance never uses force to recruit new members. And the only nation the Gathendiens seem to have an accord with are the Akseli, whom they sometimes hire to do their dark bidding like the mercenaries on your Earth."

"Are the Akseli members of the Alliance?"

"No. They were expelled when their government shifted toward tyranny."

"So you don't think there's any chance the Gathendiens would try to form a pact with the Purvelis?"

"No. If the Gathendiens were interested in the Purvelis, their interest would lie not in working with them to make war with us but in obtaining the resources their planet offers."

She frowned. "Like a trade partnership?"

"Gathendiens don't form trade partnerships. Since the Lasarans have made it widely known that Gathendiens came to them in peace, then tried to exterminate them, the Gathendiens don't even *try* to negotiate trade deals. They use biological warfare instead to quietly conquer."

"I really hate those bastards."

"Many do."

"Do you think they might be trying to do that to the Purvelis?"

"It's possible. By opting not to join the Aldebarian Alliance, the Purvelis have left themselves vulnerable."

She nodded. "One thing I've seen again and again in my long life is that allies are indispensable. Bullies are far less likely to attack you if they know a shitload of your friends will back you up and help you kick their asses."

He smiled. "A universal truth, it would seem."

"So..." She frowned. "The Purveli's scars... Do you think they were experimenting on him, trying to come up with a deadly virus to unleash on his planet?"

"It's possible."

"Then why the *srul* would he be here helping them? Can they do mind control stuff and—I don't know—have put a chip in his head that compels him to do their bidding or something?"

"No. As far as we know, such is only possible with cyborgs."

"Okay—first, cyborgs are real? That is *so* awesome! I'm totally going to hound you with questions about that later. And second, then why the *drek* is he helping them? He could have sought you out as soon as he boarded the *Ranasura* and asked for help. Instead, he set off freaking bombs until we stopped him."

Until *she* stopped him.

Eliana blinked suddenly, a look of surprise washing across her face. "Oh. Wow. Yeah, that blue goo really *did* mess up his voice, because it is a *lot* smoother in my head."

Dagon stiffened. "He's speaking to you telepathically?"

She shrugged. "Sort of. He just said one word: *Earthling*."

Dagon spun on his heel and entered the infirmary.

Adaos stood beside the Purveli, studying a data tablet. Maarev, Liden, and Efren remained where he'd left them, hands on their weapons.

Stopping beside the operating table, Dagon glared down at the Purveli. "You speak to all of us or you speak to none of us."

The Purveli looked at Eliana as she joined him.

She nodded at Dagon. "What *he* said. He's in charge."

I am Ziv'ri. How long have I been unconscious?

"I ask the questions," Dagon informed him. "You answer them. Are you working with the Gathendiens?"

The Purveli's jaw clenched. *Not willingly.*

Dagon arched a brow. "I see no explosive collar around your neck. No stunner. And my chief medical officer's scans have found none hidden beneath your skin."

There is a tracker in one of my insisas.

Eliana's eyes widened. She looked up at Dagon. "The translator in my ear doesn't translate thoughts, so I'm going by what I've learned of your language thus far. Am I remembering the definition of that correctly? Is *insisa* the Segonian word for testicle?"

"Yes." Dagon glanced at Adaos.

The medic shook his head. "My scans detected no foreign objects in his body."

The exterior is an organic substance that enables it to elude your scans.

Adaos snorted. "Such does not exist."

When the Gathendiens inserted it, I heard them say they purchased it from a source near Promeii 7.

Dagon cast the man's groin a doubtful look.

The same source sold them the suit I wore that prevented you from detecting my presence.

That gave him pause. Because before today he would have insisted no such suit existed.

He shared a long look with Adaos.

Eliana cleared her throat. "Unless he can control his pupillary reactions and his heart rate, I think he's telling the truth." She looked at Dagon, then at his men. "And unless your *insisas* are less sensitive than those of Earth males, I really don't think that's an area he would invite you to investigate and slice open on a lark. Do you?"

No. Just the idea of someone taking a laser scalpel to Dagon's *insisas* made him repress a shudder and fight the urge to shield them with his hands.

He turned to Adaos. "Do it."

Adaos drew a hover tray covered with a neat array of tools closer to the operating table. "Should I administer a pain blocker?"

Dagon met the Purveli's eyes. "If explosives or stunners are not compelling you to aid the Gathendiens, then what is?"

The Purveli swallowed. *They have my brother. They'll kill him if I don't cooperate.*

Dagon saw no visual hint that he lied, so he opted to take him at his word. For now. "Administer a pain blocker." When Adaos reached for the auto-injector, Dagon looked down at Eliana. "Turn away."

"Gladly." She gave the patient her back.

A moment later, the Purveli's gaze settled upon Eliana. *I expected no less, Earthling.*

Dagon scowled. "No less than what?"

She peeked up at him. "I could feel him in my head, so I told him that whatever Adaos finds in his balls had better be what he said it is. Because if it's an explosive or something else that harms you and the others, I would do what I threatened to do: kill him slowly and painfully."

Maarev snorted. "If it's an explosive, make sure you come up with another explanation for our deaths. I'd hate to have it said that I was slain by another man's *insisas*."

Eliana laughed. "You guys really remind me of my brethren sometimes."

Dagon watched as Adaos exposed the man's genitals.

"Which one?" Adaos asked.

The left, the Purveli said, his hands curling into fists. He jumped when Adaos sprayed a pain deadener on it. *My left,* he growled, *not yours.*

A choked sound escaped Eliana.

Dagon grimaced when Adaos cut into the man's *insisa.*

Maarev, Liden, and Efren all shifted uncomfortably.

Adaos removed what appeared to be a small fleshy tumor and held it up. "This is it?"

Yes.

The medic set the tracker on the tray, then turned back to the Purveli and reached for another tool.

Ziv'ri's whole body tensed.

Eliana pivoted to face him and threw up her stabilized arm to block her view of his groin. "I won't. He isn't."

Dagon scowled and took a menacing step toward the intruder. "I said you speak to *all* of us or you speak to *none* of us."

Eliana rested her uninjured hand on his arm, stopping him from advancing another step. "He's nervous, Dagon," she said softly. "He's totally at our mercy, and Adaos is hovering over his boys with surgical tools. He's worried Adaos might use the opportunity to castrate him as payback for the injuries he caused and asked me not to let him do it."

Adaos's face displayed the same horror and disgust Dagon felt at the notion. Lips tight, the medic snapped, "You've been spending too much time with the Gathendiens."

Not by choice, Ziv'ri countered.

Adaos sealed the incision, drew the sheet back up to the Purveli's waist, then moved to destroy the tracker.

Dagon held up a hand. "Wait." He looked at the Purveli. "What was the plan?"

I was told to blow up your thrusters.

"You didn't. You blew up the controls for them."

I am aware. I knew it would be faster and easier for you to repair the controls than it would be to replace the thrusters. And I assumed you were more likely to have what you need to repair the controls than to have that many spare thrusters on hand.

"Why blow them up at all? Why not make your presence known and seek my aid if you aren't acting with them of your free will?"

I had to make it appear real. The explosives emit a signal when the timer is activated that ceases upon detonation. The Gathendiens would know if I didn't set them and told me that every moment I hesitated would bring my brother greater pain.

"So you injured my men and brought *them* pain."

Even Dagon could read the regret that filled those silver eyes.

Ziv'ri's throat worked in a swallow. *Did any perish?*

"No."

I tried to place and time the explosives so they would injure as few of your men as possible. Had I placed them nearer the thrusters and detonated them earlier in the day, more would have suffered.

Far more. An explosion close enough to a thruster's housing might've ignited the energy cell that powered it.

Please. I need to know how much time has passed since I detonated the second bomb. My brother…

"Almost one Alliance hour."

Pain rippled across the Purveli's gaunt features.

"We found your bag."

He stared disconsolately up at the ceiling.

"There were enough explosives in it to disable every thruster on this ship."

That isn't all it contains, he said, his telepathic voice almost a monotone. *Tell your men to tread carefully.*

Dagon scowled. "What else is in it?"

Half the devices were explosives. Half were aerosol canisters rigged to burst when remotely activated.

Eliana exchanged a troubled look with Dagon.

While placing the explosives, I was supposed to make short detours to position the aerosol canisters in each of the ventilation system's primary intakes, Ziv'ri continued without prompting.

"Did you?" Dagon asked.

No. While you and your men were distracted by the fires and trying to hunt down the source of the explosions, I was also supposed to seek out the Earthling, capture her, provide her with the mask in my bag, then remotely activate the aerosol canisters.

Dagon curled his hands into fists. "What's in the canisters?"

Ziv'ri closed his eyes. *Tengonis.*

Every male present, including Dagon, swore.

Eliana eyed them all with concern. "What's *tengonis*?"

Adaos answered grimly. "A swift-acting poison. One inhalation incapacitates you and leaves you no time to even reach for a mask. Further inhalations kill you. Painfully."

Dagon struggled to tamp down the fury that filled him. "If you detonated all the canisters at once, the ventilation fans would have distributed the *tengonis* throughout the ship, taking out every soldier and crew member within minutes."

Ziv'ri nodded. *Once you were all down, I was to activate a beacon that would alert the Gathendiens that both the ship and the Earthling were theirs for the taking.*

"Commander Dagon," Joral suddenly said in his ear.

Dagon was so deep in thought he nearly jumped. He tapped the earpiece. "Yes?"

"Only half of the devices in the bag are explosives. The other half are aerosol canisters linked to a device that would allow someone to detonate them from a safe distance." Joral's experience as a weapons designer extended to explosives. "The canisters aren't labeled, but we found a mask beneath them, so I doubt we want to risk exposure."

"It's *tengonis*," Dagon informed him.

"*Drek!* I'm glad none of us accidentally triggered it."

"As am I. If the Gathendiens suspect we foiled their plan, they may try to trigger them remotely, so store them safely."

"Yes, Commander. I will do so now."

"Wow." Eliana addressed Ziv'ri. "If the Gathendiens thought you could accomplish all that alone, you must be a real badass."

The Purveli offered no response.

Dagon crossed his arms over his chest. "What did they promise you in return for infiltrating my ship?"

They said they would let my brother and me go.

"And you believed them?"

No. They proved they are exactly what you and the rest of the Aldebarian Alliance have claimed. I know they cannot be trusted. I merely hoped to buy my brother time, to ease his suffering... At last he met Dagon's gaze. *And to find someone who could help us. Someone capable of defeating them.* He looked at Eliana. *Someone who was fast enough and strong enough to keep the Gathendiens from slaying my brother and Ava at the first signs of an attack.*

Her breath caught. "Then they do have Ava?"

Yes.

"She's alive?" Eliana pressed.

She was when I left.

Heavy silence fell.

Dagon motioned to the Purveli's form. "Did the Gathendiens give you those scars?"

Yes.

"Are they doing to your brother what they did to you?"

If he still lives, yes. Ava, too.

Eliana took a step forward, her expression darkening. "They're torturing them? Both of them?"

I call it torturing. They call it experimenting.

She looked up at Dagon, her features tight with anger. "I know I've said this before. But I *hate*. Those *fucking*. Gathendiens."

He did, too. Dagon looked at Maarev. "Take one of the explosives Lanaar found, place it in an ejection tube with refuse and old ship parts engineering doesn't need, jettison it, then detonate it."

Maarev strode from the infirmary.

Ziv'ri met and held Dagon's gaze. *Thank you.*

He nodded and started to leave but halted when hesitant words tinged with desperation filled his head.

Will you help them?

He turned back to the Purveli.

Ziv'ri's pale gray eyes bore into his. *Will you rescue them?*

"That's yet to be decided." He would reveal no plans to the Purveli.

If you do, Ziv'ri advised, *you should dose all your men with* galaris.

"Why *galaris*?" As far as he knew, the herb was only used to reduce inflammation.

Few are aware, but galaris *can dramatically reduce the impact of a* senshi.

Dagon glanced at Adaos.

His friend frowned and shook his head. "I have encountered no mention of this in my studies."

Turning back to the Purveli, Dagon arched a brow. "If such is true and you are not—as you've claimed—our enemy, then why should we fear you harming us with a *senshi*?"

It isn't me you should fear. It is my brother.

"You think he will attack us? Have the Gathendiens broken him and won him to their side?"

No. If the Gathendiens suspect duplicity, they will attempt to use him as a weapon.

Dagon frowned, suspicion rising. "Can't you contact him telepathically and tell him to resist, that we are coming to rescue him and Ava?"

Ziv'ri shook his head. *I can and will try, but it may not matter.*

"Why?"

Face grim, Ziv'ri looked at Eliana. *Because they will use Ava to force his compliance.*

Her lips parted. "What?"

If they torture her in front of him, he will do anything *and kill* anyone *to stop it. If that means taking down every man on this ship with a* senshi…

Eliana turned wide eyes brimming with emotion up to Dagon's.

Resting a hand on her back, he frowned at Ziv'ri. "Why hasn't he already used a *senshi* to bring down the Gathendiens? Why haven't you both? Would that not have ended the torture and secured your freedom?"

Ziv'ri started to shake his head halfway through the first question. *The Gathendiens have dosed themselves with* galaris. *It is how we learned it could prevent a* senshi *from inflicting lethal damage. It will still be painful, but not cripplingly so. Our early attempts to free ourselves with* senshi *did not succeed and sparked vicious beatings that took us close to death.*

When they brought Ava on board and began… experimenting on her, we tried again, targeting the guards who opened our cells. We were both willing to risk our lives if it would help Ava secure her freedom. But our efforts failed. And this time… He swallowed hard. *Instead of torturing us, they made us watch as they tortured her.* His silver eyes glistened with moisture. *I thought it would drive my brother mad.* He shook his head. *We have not attempted to escape since.* He turned his gaze upon

Eliana, then sucked in a surprised breath.

Dagon glanced down at her.

Eliana's pretty brown eyes glowed bright amber with fury as she stared at the Purveli. Her small hands curled into fists. The knuckles on her undamaged hand whitened. A crack sounded, startlingly loud in the quiet infirmary, as the stabilizer on her injured hand shattered, the pieces falling to the floor with a clatter.

Dagon rested a hand on her lower back and spoke softly to Adaos. "Dose him with *nahalae,* then see if you can confirm the efficacy of the *galaris*."

"Yes, Commander."

Curling his arm around Eliana's waist, he guided her stiff form out of the infirmary.

As soon as the door closed behind them, Eliana shook off Dagon's hold and began to pace back and forth with swift strides. Fury pounded through her, compounded by a helplessness that only made her angrier.

"They're torturing her, Dagon," she growled.

"I know," he acknowledged softly.

She shook her head as she clenched and unclenched her teeth. "Ava isn't like me. She isn't a warrior. She doesn't have preternatural strength. She isn't used to pain, to being stabbed or cut or suffering broken bones. She's lived a sheltered life." Even more so than most mortals who managed to escape the violence that pervaded society.

Ava's parents had been *gifted ones,* too. They had known how dangerous it would be for Ava's telepathic abilities to become known, how she would be hunted by those who sought to use her for their own gain or study her like a lab rat. So until she was old enough to understand she shouldn't respond to other people's thoughts, just what they spoke aloud, Ava had lived a very isolated life. And like most telepaths, she had continued to isolate herself as an adult so she wouldn't constantly be bombarded by other people's thoughts when they were awake or their dreams when they slept.

Eliana shook her head as she stared up at Dagon. "Ava is sweet and kind and—" Her breath hiccupped on a sob as tears welled in her eyes. Swallowing hard, she forced herself to stop her restless movements. "They're torturing her, Dagon. They're hurting her. And we don't even know how long they've had her."

Closing the distance between them, he drew her into a tight embrace. "We'll get her back, *milessia*," he vowed, cupping the back of her head and stroking her hair. "We'll rescue Ava. Then we'll deliver the punishment the Gathendiens deserve."

Wrapping her arms around him, she burrowed closer and squeezed him tightly enough to cut off his breath. "Yes, we will. An eye for an eye."

He rested his chin atop her head, his big warm body such a comfort to her. "What?"

"Some religious scriptures on Earth call for an eye-for-an-eye justice," she murmured. "If a man blinds another man, then *he* should be blinded. If a man breaks another man's arm, then *his* arm should be broken. If a man kills another man, then *he* should be killed." Grim determination suffused her as she leaned back and looked up at him. "They inflicted pain upon Ava. And Ziv'ri. And his brother. So *I* will inflict pain upon them."

He loosened his hold and cupped her face, his thumbs sweeping away some of the moisture that trailed down her cheeks. No condemnation marred his gaze, nor did he appear to consider her tears evidence of weakness. "We all will, Eliana. We will all ensure the Gathendiens experience the same pain they administered. Justice will be served."

Emotion threatened to swamp her. She was so damn grateful to have Dagon in her life now, to have found him against such astounding odds. Reaching up, she curled a hand around the nape of his neck and drew him down to claim his lips in a hard kiss that conveyed gratitude, determination, and caring all at once.

Fire raced through her body as he wrapped his arms around her and drew her up onto her toes, locking her form to his.

She broke the kiss on a gasp. "So we're in this together?"

"We're in this together," he confirmed, leaving no doubt of his commitment.

She kissed him again, her heart pounding with burgeoning love for him. "When we confront the Gathendiens, you aren't going to insist that you and the guys go in—guns blazing—while I remain behind, are you?"

"*Drek* no."

She studied him intently. "Really?"

He nodded. "After seeing the strength you displayed earlier and the skills you exhibited while training with my men, not to mention the amazing speed you revealed while leaping up to the escape pod's hatch…" His lips quirked up. "I'm not at all reluctant to admit you're our greatest asset, Eliana. Unless you object to us using you as a weapon the way the Gathendiens may try to use Ziv'ri's brother…"

"*Srul* no, I don't object," she declared, thrilled that he valued her skills. "Point me in the right direction, and I'll wreak bloody havoc. Just promise me you'll get Ava to safety."

"I will do everything I can to bring her to safety, Eliana. You have my word."

The infirmary door slid up.

Maarev poked his head out. He glanced up and down the hallway, inspected the walls, then focused on the two of them, still standing in each other's arms. He arched a brow. "Just thought I'd check to see if Eliana was out here punching more holes in the walls. We have a wager going."

Eliana offered him a wry smile. "No. Dagon calmed me down."

A twinkle of amusement entered the warrior's eyes as he stepped out. "So I see. With a hug apparently."

Liden joined them in the hallway. A boyish grin lit his rugged features as he held out his arms. "Need any more calming down?"

She laughed… even as a low growl of irritation rumbled up from Dagon's throat. "No, thank you." Reluctantly stepping back, she took Dagon's hand and twined her fingers through his. "We have a saying on Earth: go big or go home." She tossed Dagon—the tallest man present—a wink. "I'm going big."

CHAPTER 16

A TRILLING BEEP jerked Eliana awake.

"Good morning, Commander," CC announced in placid tones. "It is time to rise. First meal begins in twenty minutes."

Eliana sighed. "Even cool alien alarm clocks are annoying," she grumbled, wanting nothing more than to fall back into blissful sleep.

The warm body spooned up behind her shifted. A yawn tickled the hair on the back of her neck as Dagon's muscled arms tightened around her.

"I concur. Does this mean we've actually found some alien tech you *don't* want?" His voice was deeper and gravelly from sleep.

She smiled. "Nope. I still want one."

He chuckled, snuggling closer, seeming as reluctant to rise and start the day as she.

Eliana would love to say they were both worn out because they had spent several hours making love. But they had instead stayed up most of the night discussing Ziv'ri, Ava, the Gathendiens, and what the hell they should do now.

At Dagon's direction, more explosives had been periodically jettisoned into space and detonated, leaving trails of debris she thought believable when he showed her. Galen had reduced their speed with each explosion. And Janek had sent out a fake distress call he rigged to only reach ships within radar range so it wouldn't unduly alarm other Alliance members.

Or attract pirates to their location and complicate things further.

Eliana wasn't even sure what radar range *was* out here.

Dagon had eventually left Barus in charge long enough for the two of them to take a nap. Eliana had been surprised when Dagon led her to his cabin but relieved, too. Beset by worries for Ava, she hadn't wanted to sleep alone and probably wouldn't have slept at all if he hadn't drawn her down with him and curled his big body around hers.

Both had slept in their clothes, wanting to be ready for anything. And though she'd felt the hard length of his erection pressing against her—as it did right now—he had merely held her close, offering the comfort she'd needed more than anything else.

Eliana closed her eyes and drew his arms tighter around her.

She was falling in love with him.

How could she not? She enjoyed every minute she spent with Dagon. He was smart, strong, and honorable to his core. He made her laugh and loved to tease her. He admired her strength and skills as a warrior. He had never once treated her like a little girl who should run along and play while the big boys took care of business. On the contrary, he seemed more than willing to fight by her side and considered her an equal despite the differences in their gender, race, and rank. Maybe even *more* than an equal.

She smiled, remembering him describing her as their greatest asset or weapon. So many men back home would cut off their left nut before admitting a woman was stronger or smarter or more powerful than they. But Dagon actually seemed to *like* that about her. He respected her. He trusted her. And made her feel all warm and fuzzy inside.

Mentally, she shook her head at herself.

Yeah, she was totally falling for him. She had no idea what that would mean in the greater scheme of things. She was supposed to go to Lasara, watch over the *gifted ones* while they settled in, and ensure they weren't mistreated or welcomed with hostility. But the attack on the *Kandovar* had blown that all to hell. The only *gifted one* who had made it to Lasara, thus far, was Lisa. And as Prince Taelon's wife and the mother of the only child born into the Lasaran royal family in the past fifty years, Lisa wouldn't need any Immortal Guardians to watch over her. She would live in the palace and have all the protection afforded the sovereign family.

Dagon sighed and slid one hand up to cup her breast, scattering her thoughts. "There is a long list of things I'd love to do right now, beginning with peeling off all your clothes."

Her heartbeat sped up when he gave her breast a squeeze. Lust rocketed through her, heating her blood when he ground his hard cock against her bottom.

"Sounds good to me." She bit back a moan when his lips found the sensitive skin just beneath her ear and sent a sensual shiver through her.

"But...," he said, the solitary word heavy with reluctance.

She sighed. "I know. We have Gathendien ass to kick."

He laughed.

"Commander Dagon," CC said suddenly in her congenial voice, "you have one incoming communication."

Muttering curses, he pressed a kiss to Eliana's shoulder, then rolled out of bed.

Eliana grinned as she sat up.

His hair was adorably rumpled and his expression cranky as he crossed to the palm panel on the wall by the door... until he glanced back. Then he returned her smile and pressed a finger to the pad. "Yes?"

"It's Adaos. I've finished compiling the medical data on Ziv'ri and would like to discuss it with you."

Dagon shared a look with Eliana. Had he caught the somber tone, too? "Would you like to join us for first meal?"

"Us?" Adaos asked. And Eliana could practically see him raising an eyebrow.

Since Dagon looked as though he wasn't sure she wanted anyone else to know about their intimate relationship, she smiled. "You better not have lied about people not thinking less of me if I sleep with Dagon, Adaos."

A chuckle carried over the line. "If anything, they'll thank you for improving his mood."

She laughed.

Dagon shook his head. "We'll meet you in the mess hall."

Eliana rose. Glancing down, she grimaced at her rumpled state. "Can we stop by my room on the way? I could use a quick shower and a change of clothes."

He crossed to a wall and touched it. A rectangular portion popped out and slid to one side, revealing a closet that contained mostly black uniforms, boots, and armor. "Let me grab a fresh uniform. Then we can shower together in your quarters." He slid a neat pile of clothing off a shelf, then retrieved his boots and stacked them on top of it.

She glanced pointedly at his pants, which failed to conceal the fact that he was hard. "*Just* a shower?"

His face lighting with a grin, he closed the distance between them and leaned down to press a kiss to her lips. "Actually," he confessed, his voice husky with desire, "I was hoping we could sneak in a *chasa*."

Eliana claimed another kiss, humming her approval when he looped an arm around her and drew her up against him, his clothes and boots squashed between them. When at last he drew back, she could see her glowing eyes reflected in his.

"I sure hope *chasa* is the Segonian word for a quickie," she said breathlessly.

He grinned.

Eliana tried but could not suppress a smile as she and Dagon headed for the mess hall. Since Adaos had not labeled their meeting urgent, Dagon had escorted her to her quarters, stripped her bare, followed her into the cleansing unit, and indulged in a fervent *chasa*, which she had been happy to discover was indeed the equivalent of an Earth quickie.

Very happy.

Damn, that man is talented… both in *bed* and *out of it*, she thought with an inward chuckle.

She offered two servicemen a jaunty wave, then glanced at Dagon from the corner of her eye.

His lips curled up in a smile similar to hers. The scowl that had darkened his brow earlier had vanished. He looked languid and relaxed. Happy.

She liked to see him happy.

He must have felt her gaze because he looked down at her and arched a brow.

"You look very pleased with yourself."

He grinned. "I am."

She winked playfully. "I am, too." Glancing around, she lowered her voice. "*Chasa* is my new favorite word. Any other titillating Segonian terms you'd like to teach me? Or demonstrate?"

Leaning down, he whispered in her ear. "I'll make a list."

"*Srul* yes, you will."

He laughed.

Heads turned as they entered the cafeteria. Soldiers and crewmen occupied almost every chair, enjoying first meal before they began their shifts.

Eliana waved. "Hi, guys!"

"Eliana!" they called cheerfully, delighting her as always.

Still smiling, Dagon shook his head.

No one waited in line at the counter, thanks to Dagon and Eliana's tardy entry.

"Morning, Kusgan," she trilled when the elder Segonian stepped up to the counter.

Kusgan greeted her with a wide smile. "And how are you today, *ni'má*?"

"Hungry," she declared. "What do you have for me? Something spicy, I hope?"

"Indeed." When Kusgan turned his attention to Dagon, his eyes sparkled with amusement as though he had guessed just how and with whom she had worked up an appetite. "And for you, Commander?"

"The usual."

His lips twitched. "A larger portion perhaps?"

Dagon laughed. "I would appreciate that, yes."

Heat crept up her neck to her cheeks. As Kusgan turned away and headed into the kitchen, she leaned closer to Dagon and whispered, "Am I blushing? Because I feel like he's guessed why I'm so hungry and you're all smiles this morning."

He regarded her cheeks with a grin. "Yes, you're blushing."

Groaning, she brought her hands up to cover her face. "Curse my pale skin," she grumbled. "It won't let me hide *anything*."

"Would it make you feel better if *I* blushed?"

She peeked up at him through her fingers. And as she watched, his cheeks flushed a vivid pink, demonstrating anew his ability to change his coloring at will.

Laughing in delight, she dropped her hands. "Yes!" Then she poked him in the chest as the heat in her own cheeks faded. "I dare you to walk around like that all day."

Grinning, he abandoned the pink camouflage and let his face return to its natural color. "If I did, the men would get no work done because they'd all be too busy wondering what the *srul* you did in bed that left me blushing for hours afterward."

Eyes widening, she laughed. "You're right. Don't do it."

Kusgan returned, proffering two trays heaped with food.

Eliana drew in a deep breath as she took hers. "Ooooh. That smells delicious. And spicy. What is it?"

"Legreraa."

Dagon shook his head as he took the other tray. "We'll be needing another pitcher of *naga* juice."

"Yes, Commander." Kusgan fetched two glasses and the pitcher.

Eliana followed Dagon as he wended through the crowded tables, the two of them responding to countless greetings along the way.

Adaos waited at the opposite end of the mess hall, just outside the entrance to a private dining room she'd never noticed before. Nodding to them both, he stepped aside while they entered, then joined them and closed the door.

The three of them settled at a long, gleaming table carved from a fascinating wood that was almost white with black grain and burls that reminded her of a zebra's stripes.

Dagon motioned to the data pad that rested beside Adaos's tray. "You said you have the results of Ziv'ri's med scans?"

"I do." Adaos pushed his half-eaten meal aside and activated his tablet.

Eliana's stomach growled. When Adaos sent her a look of amusement, she narrowed her eyes. "Don't say it."

The chief medical officer wisely remained silent as she dug into her meal.

Dagon did the same when his stomach rumbled even louder.

Shaking his head, Adaos tapped the tablet's screen several times. Then a three-dimensional image of Ziv'ri rose up and hovered above the tablet. The Purveli was bare save for a strip of white that circled his hips and concealed his groin.

Eliana motioned to the strip, her eyes already starting to water from the scrumptious *legreraa*. "Is that for me?"

"No," Adaos mumbled, "it's for me." He consumed a quick bite from his tray. "I have no interest in staring at another man's *insisas* while I eat."

Laughing, she reached for the *naga* juice.

When Adaos drew his finger across the tablet's surface, the Purveli's image became translucent, allowing them to see his organs, muscles, and the bones beneath. Multiple white patches littered the image as though someone had plucked some pebbles and blades of grass and tossed them into it.

Eliana pointed her fork-like utensil at the hologram. "What are those white things?"

"Scars," Adaos said.

She frowned. They marred every organ and many of Ziv'ri's muscles and bones. And the pattern of scarring suggested it had not resulted from injury or battle.

Adaos pointed to several white marks on one of the Purveli's arms, then in his hand. "These indicate his bones were broken. This one and these in his fingers were broken more than once."

Dagon's chewing slowed as he stared.

Eliana set down her glass. "What are the black marks?" There were a lot of those, too.

Adaos's expression grew grimmer. "Places where tissue has been removed."

"*Drek,*" Dagon murmured. "He spoke the truth. The Gathendiens tortured him."

"Yes."

Eliana nodded toward the hologram. "His lungs and rib cage area are different, but other than that his organs and systems look very similar to that of Earthlings." She pointed to a larger dark splotch. "What happened there? That's where one of our kidneys would be. Did they remove his or did he only have one to begin with?"

"They removed one of his."

Her appetite shriveling, she sat back and abandoned her meal. "Why would they do that?"

Adaos consulted his tablet. "Based on the immune response the scans showed and the information Ziv'ri gave me, I assume they wished to see if one of the viruses they injected him with had damaged the organ."

Dagon's face darkened with anger. "Then they're creating a bioweapon to unleash on Purvel."

Just as they had done on Lasara and on Earth.

"Yes." Adaos met his eyes. "With your permission, I will begin growing him a replacement."

"Do it."

Dumbfounded, Eliana looked back and forth between them. "You can do that? If one of your organs is damaged or fails, you can just grow a new one?"

"Yes," both answered.

She thought of all the men, women, and children back home who were on waiting lists for organ transplants and wished Earth had such technology.

Grim silence encapsulated them as they stared at the hologram.

After a long moment, Eliana spoke. "If they're searching for a virus that will kill his people, why did they do so much damage to his wrists and hands?"

Adaos sighed. "I can only surmise." He motioned to the Purveli's fingers. "They likely broke these as part of the torture intended to force either his or his brother's cooperation." Then he pointed to the wrist and metacarpals. "These injuries I believe he may have inadvertently inflicted himself while trying to escape restraints. There are more on his ankles."

"*Drekking* Gathendiens," Dagon growled. His appetite apparently vanishing as well, he leaned back in his chair. "I believe Ziv'ri can be trusted and may prove useful to us as we devise a strategy for defeating the Gathendiens and rescuing Ava and his brother."

"Or," Adaos said slowly, "he may be so desperate to save his brother that he would lead us like fattened *braemon* to the slaughter."

Though she wanted to protest, she couldn't deny the possibility.

Dagon crossed his arms over his chest. "He could have destroyed the thrusters and taken many lives."

"Yes. He could have. Or he could have done exactly what he did instead to win our trust and throw us off if we caught him."

"You wouldn't be growing him a new organ if you believed that."

Adaos sighed. "No. But the fact that I am doesn't mean I lack doubts. I'm a healer. Repairing damaged bodies is what I do."

Dagon looked at Eliana. "What do you think?"

Tilting her head to one side, she stared at the hologram and reviewed everything they'd learned since the Purveli boarded the ship. "I'm certain the hope I saw in his eyes when I threatened him was genuine." After another moment's contemplation, she issued a decisive nod. "Yes. I agree with Dagon. I think we can trust him. We should bring Ziv'ri into the loop. I can monitor his pulse and pupils and look for other tells that might indicate he's deceiving us."

"Commander Dagon." Galen's voice sounded faintly before Dagon could say yea or nay.

She glanced at him.

He tapped his earpiece. "Yes?"

"I've detected the presence of a ship. Its current trajectory indicates it is on an intercept course, heading toward us."

"I'll be there shortly."

Eliana straightened. "Do you think it's the Gathendiens?"

Dagon rose. "Yes. They must have fallen for our ruse." He looked at Adaos. "Galen said a ship is headed our way."

All three grabbed their trays and headed for the door.

Dagon stood at the head of a long oval table in a conference room he and his men had unofficially deemed the *Ranasura*'s war room. The table could easily seat twenty people and had been carved from the wood from a *yexoa* tree. White with black grain and burls, the gleaming surface included inlaid computer screens that stretched down the center of the table. All currently lit up, displaying diagrams and scrolling feeds in Segonian.

Above the table, a transparent, three-dimensional map of the stars hovered, displaying the *Ranasura*'s current position as well as that of the approaching Gathendien ship and a nearby solar system.

Beside him, Eliana studied the small system. "It reminds me of Earth's except it has fewer planets with more moons and the elliptical orbits of the planets are vertical."

Dagon didn't realize until then that he had never examined her solar system and made a mental note to familiarize himself with it later.

Some of the displays—both in the table, above it, and gracing the walls—mirrored those at Janek's, Galen's, and Rahmik's stations on the bridge. All three men now sat at the table, monitoring them from the war room so they would be on hand to answer any questions that might arise.

Barus was present, too, as were Maarev, Liden, Efren, Cobus, Joral, and Anat, all of whom Dagon considered trusted advisors.

Ziv'ri sat across from Janek. Adaos had found him some loose-fitting pants and a pair of boots, but the Purveli's chest remained bare so the medic could keep an eye on his wound. Though Ziv'ri had swiftly accepted Dagon's invitation to join them, he seemed to be on shaky ground. Just the simple task of walking here had left his breathing labored and his skin coated with a sheen of sweat.

"Something is wrong," Ziv'ri murmured as he stared at the map. "They shouldn't be coming yet."

"We've been detonating the explosives at irregular intervals," Dagon informed him, "to trick them into believing you're still loose on the ship, doing their bidding." He motioned to Galen. "And we've reduced our speed each time to simulate the loss of another thruster."

"But you haven't detonated *all* the explosives," Ziv'ri countered, "have you?"

"No."

"And you haven't activated the beacon?"

"No."

Ziv'ri shook his head with apparent perturbation. "The plan was to wait until everyone except the Earthling was either incapacitated or killed by the *tengonis*."

Janek spoke up. "Perhaps they picked up the distress call we sent out and decided to change their plans."

Barus nodded. "They would want to reach us before any allies do."

Eliana frowned as she studied the Gathendien ship.

Dagon had seen many such ships in past battles. Half the size of the *Ranasura*, it was as ugly as the Gathendiens' nature. Whereas the *Ranasura* was smooth and sleek, the Gathendien ship was clunky and disjointed, like something pieced together from discarded parts that were a sort of putrid yellow.

Clunky or not, however, a ship like that one had destroyed the *Kandovar*.

"Could they have grown impatient?" she asked.

"Doubtful," Dagon said. "Most of the worlds the Gathendiens have conquered were procured through patience."

"Right," she muttered. "Their MO is to pick a planet, bioengineer a virus to kill off any humanoid life forms that might challenge them, release it, then sit back and wait until the species dies out, the lousy bastards."

Precisely. They had released such a virus on the Lasarans, whose life spans could reach a thousand years. And they had released another virus on Earth thousands of years ago and had only recently checked to ensure it had succeeded. Neither action indicated a lack of forbearance.

"Whatever their reasons for opting to move up their schedule," Dagon declared, "we need to prepare to meet them. Rahmik, would you bring up the schematics of a Gathendien S-27 battle cruiser?"

Rahmik tapped on the console the tabletop provided.

The map of the stars shifted to one side, allowing room for a translucent, three-dimensional representation of the Gathendien ship to appear. Segonian words hovered throughout the image, identifying key areas. Hangar bays. Air locks. Escape pods, of which there were far fewer than on Lasaran and Segonian ships. Lifts. Ladder wells. The bridge. The mess hall. A med bay. Several sizable labs.

Dagon looked at Ziv'ri and motioned to the hologram. "What

can you tell us?"

The Purveli leaned forward, resting his elbows on the table's shiny surface as he studied the schematic. "Can you render the text in Alliance Common?"

Efren typed and swiped.

Ziv'ri's hands flattened on the table as he stared. "It's a bit difficult to orient myself. I saw little of the ship until they shoved me into the Lasaran escape pod and ejected it," he murmured.

Dagon and Barus shared a look. Barus had wished to exclude the Purveli from the meeting but had bowed to Dagon's wishes.

After a moment, Ziv'ri pointed. "The Lasaran escape pod was held in this hangar. We passed these rooms here on the way there from where I was being held. All of them appeared to be soldiers' barracks."

"Do you know how many soldiers are on the ship?" Dagon asked.

"No," he said with regret. "I mostly dealt with scientists and guards until they took me to the hangar bay. If I'd had a better view of one of the rooms and knew how many beds were in each, I could estimate it, but…"

He couldn't, so they had no idea what kind of numbers they would be facing.

"Ava saw more of the ship than we did," Ziv'ri murmured, "and shared as much as she could with us telepathically."

Dagon frowned. "You said the Gathendiens dosed you with *nahalae* to keep you from communicating with each other nonverbally."

"They did. All our communications with Ava were instigated by her."

Eliana glanced up at Dagon. "Ava is telepathic. Even if Ziv'ri and his brother couldn't actively send thoughts to her, she could delve into their minds, listen in, and hear their thoughts as long as they were in close enough proximity."

Ziv'ri nodded. "But the Gathendiens didn't know that, so they didn't dose her." He pointed to another room. "Jak'ri and I were held in containment cells here. The Gathendiens *experimented* on us," he said with a curl of his lip, "in the primary lab here. They had secondary and tertiary facilities here and here. There could be more, but these were the only ones I saw. Jak'ri and I were almost always taken to the primary lab. Ava was held in a containment cell over here. I think they usually took her to the tertiary lab, because we often only saw her when…" He faltered.

Eliana's lips tightened. "When they tortured her in front of you?"

Ziv'ri's hands curled into tight fists. "Yes." Bitterness hardened his features. "They're very good at inflicting pain."

She curled her hands into fists, too. "Which just makes me want to annihilate the Gathendiens even more."

Dagon touched a hand to her lower back and gave it a soothing stroke.

"If it had stayed just the two of us," Ziv'ri said, his silver eyes meeting Dagon's, "I would not have detonated a single bomb once I gained access to your ship. Jak'ri and I made a pact. If one of us had to die in order to end the Gathendiens' research and warn our people…" He shrugged, then winced and touched his chest. "We thought it worth the sacrifice. But once they captured Ava, everything changed. They stopped punishing *us* when we didn't cooperate and started punishing *her*. We couldn't…" Sighing, he dragged a hand down over his face, then shook his head helplessly. "We couldn't cause her more suffering than she was already enduring."

So they had put themselves and their people in jeopardy in an effort to protect Ava.

Ziv'ri met Eliana's gaze. "The only time they ever mentioned killing us was when they put me in that suit and gave me their instructions. They vowed to bring my brother more pain every time I hesitated to detonate one of the explosives within the accepted time frame. And if I failed in the mission they gave me, they said they would kill him." He swallowed hard. "Our presence… our compliance… provides Ava with some measure of protection. If they lose me and kill my brother, she'll have no one."

"You're wrong," Eliana told him, her voice as hard as steel. "She has me. And the men you see around you. So does your brother." She glanced at the Segonians. "What I don't understand is why the Gathendiens changed their plans and what exactly they think they can accomplish by attacking you. This ship is almost twice the size of theirs, and you're all superlative warriors. There's no way they can win if they pick a fight with you. The bombs Ziv'ri carted along with him only damaged the thrusters—at least that's what they'll assume—not the e-cannons and other weapons. And your fighters are all intact."

"Yes," Dagon said. "But they know we can't fire on them without risking Ava's life."

"How do they even know we're aware that they have her?"

Ziv'ri leaned back in his chair. "Perhaps they guessed I've disobeyed their orders. Or perhaps they think I've been captured. Either possibility might have led to my informing you of Ava's presence on their ship."

She returned her attention to Dagon. "You're searching for my friends as a favor for the Lasaran government, right?"

"Yes."

"Would the Lasarans expect you to sacrifice your ship and your entire crew in an attempt to save just one Earthling? Would your government?"

"No," he admitted.

"Won't the Gathendiens draw the same conclusion?"

"If they're wise," Maarev muttered.

"Then I ask again, why are they barreling toward us now—in plain sight, I might add—instead of waiting a little longer to see if Ziv'ri activates the beacon? What made the most patient freaking aliens in the galaxy suddenly lose their composure, say *drek this, we can't wait any longer,* and speed toward a fight they'll most likely lose?"

Silence fell.

It was a valid question.

Ziv'ri glanced around. "Could someone have inadvertently activated the beacon?"

Joral stiffened, his craggy features darkening with a scowl. "No, we didn't activate the beacon. We know how to handle explosives and delicate tech."

Beside him, Cobus nodded.

Ziv'ri held up a hand. "I meant no disrespect. I am simply baffled and concerned by the Gathendiens' actions and sought an explanation for them."

Some of the anger left Joral's expression as he issued a curt nod.

Janek suddenly frowned at his screen and touched his ear. He looked up at Dagon. "We're being hailed by the Gathendien ship."

Eliana followed Dagon, Barus, and Janek to the bridge. Galen, Rahmik, Efren, and Maarev brought up the rear, leaving the others behind with Ziv'ri.

"Eliana," Dagon said, "I want you to remain out of sight while I speak with them."

"Okay." She was actually both surprised and pleased that she would be allowed on the bridge at all. Relaxing the rules on an average day was one thing. Relaxing them when facing a possible attack was another.

Minutes later, Dagon planted his feet shoulder-width apart beside the commander's chair and crossed his arms over his chest as he stared at the screen that descended in front of the crystal window. Eliana stood off to the side beside Janek, fighting dual urges to hover and to nibble her thumbnail.

Dagon nodded to the communications officer.

A Gathendien appeared on the screen in giant proportions.

Eliana's eyes widened. Her jaw dropped. But she *did* manage to keep from gasping or swearing.

Like Dagon, the male stood in front of what she assumed was the commander's chair on his ship's bridge. At a glance, he bore a similar physique to humans and Segonians. He had two arms and two legs, one head devoid of hair. There were, however, some eye-catching differences. Like his tail. She couldn't see all of it because it was behind him. But it appeared to be as thick as his muscled thighs where it began and tapered down to a point after… five feet? Maybe six? When it twitched on the floor behind him, she glimpsed several bracelet-like spiked silver bands that adorned it.

Eliana knew how strong a dog's tail could be. A tail as long and thick as this guy's would carry a hell of a lot of strength.

She wished he would turn around for a second. She wasn't sure how it worked with the tail, but the Gathendien wore brown pants that resembled leather. Sheathed weapons adorned his hips, both blades and blasters. His exposed chest and abs were a golden yellowish color and reminded her of the rubbery muscle suits skinny actors wore sometimes when they played superheroes. They looked hard, like armor. His broad shoulders looked even harder. The thick, green reptilian skin that covered them resembled the hide on an alligator's back and looked equally difficult to penetrate.

The same ridged green skin coated his arms, fading into a smoother golden yellow on their undersides. His fingers were longer than a human's and ended in creepy dark claws. His feet were encased in boots, so she couldn't see them.

His bald head was green and bore similar armor-like ridges that smoothed out around his features, acquiring the same yellowish hue she saw on his belly. The sides of his head were as round as the top and lacked any kind of ear flaps, showing only small holes that she surmised allowed him to hear.

His eyes seemed to radiate fury beneath his lowered, hairless brows. "Commander Dagon of the *Ranasura*," he growled.

Eliana couldn't decide whether he lingered over the *s* sound or if she'd imagined it because he was so lizard-like.

Dagon arched a brow. "You've heard of me?" he responded, his tone pure arrogance. "I'm flattered. Who the *srul* are you?"

She grinned.

The Gathendien's expression darkened. "I am Commander Striornuk of the *Cebaun*. You have something I want."

Dagon nodded. "I'm sure I do. I've seen your ship."

Eliana laughed silently.

Commander Striornuk growled. "We have reason to believe a Purveli male who escaped us is aboard your ship."

Dagon arched a brow. "Do you mean the Purveli male you sent to sabotage my ship? I'm afraid you can't have him back. We've sentenced him to death."

"You slew him?"

"Not yet. We wanted to make him suffer a little longer for the damage he did and the harm he inflicted upon my men."

"We did not send him to you," the Gathendien claimed. "He escaped us. And he stole a bag full of munitions when he did."

"Even if I believed that were true, it suggests he was not with you of his own accord."

Commander Striornuk grunted. "Of course he wasn't with us of his own accord. We have entered into an agreement with the Purveli government. We provide them with the tech they desire, and they give us every male criminal on their planet who has been sentenced to death."

Dagon arched a brow. "So you can experiment on them?"

"So we will have workers capable of building underwater settlements on planets we've claimed that possess abundant resources but little land. Since Purvelis can breathe underwater, they don't require costly equipment or breaks to refill air tanks. And as our slaves, they receive no pay." He shrugged. "As far as food is concerned, they eat what they catch. So our only expenses are the guards who monitor them and the building materials."

That actually sounded like something those bastards would do.

Have a planet that requires the construction of underwater cities? No problem. Just enslave some Purvelis and get the work done in half the time at a fraction of the cost.

Eliana glanced at Dagon, whose expression remained impassive.

"I've heard of no such agreement," he commented.

The Gathendien sneered. "The Purveli government wishes to keep it confidential. They think some members of the Aldebarian Alliance may not approve."

Dagon shook his head. "I still find it hard to believe. If the Purvelis desired tech, they could obtain it from any member of the Alliance and avoid tainting themselves with your ilk."

If green-and-yellow alligator skin could turn red with anger, Eliana suspected Striornuk's would have. He looked ready to explode at the insult.

"The Purvelis wish to remain exclusive. They have no interest in being part of your *drekking* Alliance or having to obey the rules put forth by every mewling member race. They don't want to change their currency or alter the laws of their homeworld. They don't want to participate in your childish war games."

"I rather like the war games," Dagon murmured.

"They've no desire to be yet another Alliance sycophant and have to answer the many demands of the other members. The Purvelis just want to be left alone," Striornuk snapped, "something we agreed to do."

"I think it more likely you wish to conquer their planet."

"Why conquer Purvel when its inhabitants will enable us to colonize countless others?"

Dagon tilted his head to one side. "A valid point." He moved to the commander's chair and sprawled in it, one leg bent, the other straight as if he were bored. "I admit I've never been fond of the Purvelis." His lip curled. "They think they're too good to join the Alliance… expect us to court them like a suitor wooing royalty… want us to supplicate ourselves in an attempt to gain their precious favor."

If Eliana didn't know Dagon, she would swear he spoke the truth. Every word and expression broadcast disgruntlement.

"Sir," Efren said, a one-word admonition.

Dagon shot him a glare. "Silence!"

Commander Striornuk watched Dagon carefully.

Fascinated, Eliana did, too.

"Handing the Purveli over to you *would* save me some annoyance," Dagon mused. "If I don't, I'll either face repercussions for killing him and making it further unlikely the Purvelis will join the Alliance. Or I'll have to keep the *grunark* alive and in reasonably good condition until I hand him over to the Alliance."

Maarev glanced at the screen, then scowled and stepped into view. "That *drekker* killed sixty-two of our men!" he protested. "And many more were injured in the explosions. He deserves to die!"

Dagon raised a hand as if to say *Okay, okay, calm down*. "He would suffer more if we let him live and handed him over to the Gathendiens, would he not?"

Appearing mollified, Maarev backed out of view.

A long moment passed. Then Dagon tilted his head to one side. "What will I get in return if I hand him over to you? I doubt there is anything on your ship that I want."

The light of victory briefly illuminated Commander Striornuk's features. "Supplies you'll need to repair the damage on the *Ranasura*. A tow to the nearest spaceport that can make repairs if you require it. And for your future dealings with the Purvelis… a goodly supply of *galaris*."

"What the *srul* is *galaris*?"

"An herb capable of protecting you from a Purveli's *senshi*."

Dagon raised his brows. "*Is* there such an herb?"

The smile that slithered across Striornuk's face nearly made Eliana shiver. "We wouldn't be able to enslave Purvelis without it."

Dagon's face darkened. "Half the men the Purveli slew on my ship were taken out by a *senshi* after we cut him out of his protective suit."

A sly smile touched the Gathendien's thin lips. "The Purveli government's representatives enlightened us about the benefits of *galaris*. They knew our agreement would be void if the slaves they provided killed any of us with a *senshi*."

Eliana didn't know how the Gathendiens learned about the *galaris* but was pretty sure the Purvelis hadn't told them. How stupid would it be to give potential enemies a method with which they could render you powerless?

Dagon remained silent a long moment, then nodded. "I've a task I must complete for the Alliance and need to restore full functionality to my ship so I can be done with it. We were supposed to go on leave a month ago," he muttered. Then his tone shifted from disgruntlement to crisp command. "I'll have engineering compile a list of the supplies we need, then send it over. If you can provide us with enough of it, we'll have an accord." He made a cutting motion with his hand.

The screen went dark, then retracted.

"Wow," Eliana said, motioning to the disappearing screen. "He's good."

Dagon nodded. "I didn't expect him to come up with such a plausible explanation for Ziv'ri's presence on his ship." He rose. "Although I suppose it shouldn't surprise me. The Gathendiens did, after all, manage to convince the Lasarans they were worthy allies."

She strode toward him. "You're good, too, by the way." She smiled at Maarev and Efren. "So are you. Did you guys study acting when you were younger or something? Because if I didn't know you, I would've totally believed you."

"No performing lessons." Maarev winked. "But I love to gamble."

Dagon offered her a wry smile. "And years of serving in the

military, meeting with ambassadors, and dealing with foreign military commanders has taught me much."

Barus smiled. "As has talking your way out of bar fights and other dicey entanglements when you were younger."

"I bet," Eliana said with a smile as she stopped beside Dagon. "Commander Sneersucker seemed pretty ecstatic when you didn't ask about Ava." Masculine chuckles filled the bridge at her nickname for the lizard-like commander. "I think you succeeded in tricking him into believing you don't know they have her."

"Good."

"When he suggested making a trade, I half expected him to ask you to throw me in with Ziv'ri and hand over us both. Clearly he knows I'm here."

Dagon shrugged. "I believe his intent is to catch us off guard when we allow him to dock with us. Thanks to Maarev, he thinks we're down sixty-two men, with countless others incapacitated."

Maarev bowed like an actor at the end of a show.

Eliana grinned.

"And," Dagon added, "he thinks the *Ranasura*'s thrusters have been severely damaged."

Maarev grunted. "Wouldn't take much to overwhelm the remaining soldiers and seize the ship."

Eliana rolled her eyes. "As if anyone could overwhelm you guys."

Grins broke out all around.

Dagon rested a hand on her shoulder. "But *they* don't know that."

Maarev winked. "I say we let them dock, then hurl Eliana at them and let her kill them all while the rest of us sit back, relax, and eat what's left of the *jarumi* nuggets."

She laughed. "No way, buddy. Those *jarumi* nuggets are *mine*."

The big warrior chuckled. "I notice you didn't object to the killing part."

"Because *jarumi* nuggets mean more to me than Gathendiens."

Chuckling, Dagon curled an arm around her and turned toward the door. "Let's go see if we can devise a plan that *won't* deprive Eliana of her favorite treat."

CHAPTER 17

ELIANA STARED AT the air lock and fought the urge to fidget. Patience had never been her strong suit. And having to wait while the damn Gathendiens lined their ship up and attached a docking tube to one of the *Ranasura*'s air locks was driving her crazy.

"What's taking so long?" she blurted.

"Once the docking tube attaches, it must decompress," Dagon murmured beside her.

Though the Gathendiens could have sent a shuttle over, Dagon had instead directed the *Cebaun* to dock with them. Strategically, Eliana thought it a smart move. Instead of entering the *Ranasura* in a shuttle equipped with heavy weaponry, Gathendien soldiers would have to enter through a narrow hatch that limited them to two at a time with whatever weapons they could carry.

She glanced around. Maarev and a dozen other soldiers fanned out behind them. All wore combat armor. A few dozen more clustered together out of sight of the hatch's window.

Dagon looked at those men. "Helmets up," he commanded.

Each man in the larger group donned a helmet, then touched the side of it. A clear window slid down in front, forming a bubble that covered their faces. Hisses sounded as the visors locked with the rest of the helmet.

Dagon met Eliana's gaze. "You, too. We know the Gathendiens aren't going to execute a fair trade. We don't know why they changed their tactics, but they *are* still hunting you." He touched her back. "I don't want you to be harmed by *tengonis* or any other gasses they may deploy."

"Okay," she replied somberly. "Though I don't think any gas they hurl at me could be more noxious than Maarev's after he eats *mamitwa*."

The men all laughed.

Eliana glanced down. The black, lightly armored uniform Joral had provided her with was only a little bit looser and bulkier than the clothing she normally wore. Though it wouldn't change color and make her blend in with her surroundings the way it would for a Segonian, he had assured her that it *would* offer her protection if the Gathendiens tried to gas her or if all this went sideways and landed her out in space again. That protection, however, would be more fleeting than the Lasaran space suit had provided.

It also would not stand up to blasterfire for long.

Dagon and his soldiers, on the other hand, wore full suits of what he called exo-armor.

Eliana had to admit as she surveyed the men around her that their armor made them look even more badass than usual. Sleek and shiny like some kind of titanium alloy, it repelled stunners and blasters and a hell of a lot of other weaponry and firepower. It also increased their strength, enabled them to jump higher and farther, and would provide them with oxygen if the ship lost atmosphere. The helmet, only the front half of which was clear, boasted tiny cameras that let them see everything in front of *and* behind them. It also provided infrared vision, night vision, and helmet lights in case the first two failed. The rest of the armor provided all manner of blades and blasters and other weaponry ready to pop out of this limb or that with a flick of the wrist.

Eliana thought it very cool but could easily see herself accidentally shooting someone while reaching up to scratch an itch if she wore such armor.

The larger group of soldiers flickered, then faded out of view, blending into the background like chameleons. Apparently the exo-armor—including the helmet—was infused with the same nanochromatophores their uniforms were and reacted to that special chemical in their skin, allowing them to camouflage themselves at will without dropping their drawers.

Dagon had wanted to provide Eliana with exo-armor, but nothing on the ship fit her. When he had suggested she at least try to don the smallest exo-armor they could find, she had nixed the notion, knowing it would swallow her.

She wanted nothing that might slow her down or make her movements awkward. Not when the lives of Ava and Ziv'ri's brother were at stake.

"Eliana?" Dagon said.

"Yes?"

"Helmet up."

"Oh. Right." She pressed the button he pointed to on her uniform shirt. A clear bubble sprang up from the collar at the nape of her neck and swept forward to enclose her head, hissing as it sealed in front. Unlike the men's, which were clear in front and that titanium-like metal in back, her helmet was clear all the way around. And, she was relieved to see, it didn't fog up when she exhaled, so her vision wouldn't be obscured.

"If this goes badly," Dagon said, "and you find yourself thrust into open space, we'll come for you." He pointed to his triceps. "Our armor contains micro rockets we can use to navigate to you and retrieve you. Our boots do, too."

"Your armor has rockets?" she repeated.

He nodded.

She opened her mouth to reply.

"That's so cool," the men around her chorused, beating her to the punch. "I want one."

She laughed. "I say that a *lot*, don't I?"

"Yes," Dagon said, his smile a trifle tense as he drew his hand up her back and rested it on her shoulder.

Reaching up, she covered his gauntleted fingers with her gloved ones. "Don't worry. I can hold my breath a long time." She moved a few steps away and drew two katanas from the sheaths on her back. "And I can repel blasterfire with these."

Judging by their expressions, none of the men believed that.

"I'm also as strong as you are with your fancy exo-armor. Remember, I was holding back when I fought Maarev, Efren, and Liden."

"That was holding back?" one of the men muttered.

Grinning, she moved to stand beside the camouflaged soldiers who remained out of view of the hatch.

A clunk sounded.

All levity fled as her pulse picked up.

"Remember the plan," Dagon intoned.

She nodded. "I haul ass to reach Ava and Jak'ri, then protect them while you and the others annihilate the Gathendiens." She hated to miss out on so much of the action but knew that if she didn't get to Ava and Jak'ri first, the Gathendiens would either slay them or use them as leverage.

"Take no unnecessary risks, Eliana."

"I'll do what I have to do," she replied, earning a curse.

Boots clomped in the air lock tube. A moment later, the light pouring through the hatch's window dimmed.

"CC," Dagon ordered, "open Air Lock Hatch 3."

"Opening Air Lock Hatch 3, Commander," CC replied.

Another thunk sounded. The round metal hatch swung open.

Eliana sprang forward. Moving so fast that anyone watching would only see a faint blur of motion and feel a breeze, she zipped over to the hatch.

A dozen of the lizard-like aliens waited inside the tube, their softer bellies covered with armor. And each one was already raising a weapon to fire at Dagon.

Fury consuming her, she plowed through the Gathendiens in the docking tube, blades slicing armor and rough green hide as she went. Shouts arose in a foreign language. Heavy bodies fell to the floor behind her. Then she dove through the hatch on the other side of the tube and into a hangar bay on the Gathendien ship.

Dozens of reptilian soldiers awaited.

Light flashed as they fired e-blasters in response to their comrades' cries.

Eliana swung her swords—infused with that wondrous metal *mlathnon*—like a high-speed propeller. Stymied by her speed, unable to see her clearly, most of the lizard-men lacked the time to aim properly and just fired blindly at chest level. But she repelled every shot.

Having expected a standard battle, the Gathendien soldiers shouted with alarm as their men began to fall. Some dove for cover as e-blasts ricocheted off her blades and were flung to the side and—when she was lucky—back toward them. A satisfying number of them jerked and toppled to the floor as scorched holes appeared in their armor.

"Ha!" Maarev crowed over the comm in her collar. "I won the wager! She killed everyone in the docking tube."

She grinned.

"Drek!" Efren blurted. "She *can* repel blasterfire with those swords."

Eliana wanted to linger and help the guys cut down every heinous enemy, but she needed to reach Ava and Jak'ri before the bastards in there realized they were under attack and tried to kill them. So she raced for the closed door that led to the rest of the ship, trusting Dagon and the guys to take out whoever was left.

"Grenade, Eliana," Dagon warned, his voice coming over the comm seconds before an e-grenade sailed past her shoulder.

It detonated as it hit the door.

Flames and sparks and hot air rushed toward her but didn't slow her at all as the grenade blasted a substantial hole in the door.

"Thanks, babe," she called as she dove through it.

A throat cleared. "Did she just call our commander *babe*?"

"Shut up," Dagon retorted.

She laughed. "Would you like me to call him sugarboo instead?"

"*Srul* yes," Maarev responded as snickers carried over the comm.

"Just be careful and keep your comm line open, Eliana," Dagon ordered.

Keeping her comm line open shouldn't be a problem because she had no idea how to close it, but she offered a distracted "Will do."

The Gathendien ship housed a *lot* of soldiers, she swiftly discovered. Far more than she had expected considering its smaller size. Big, lizard-like, partly armored bodies poured into the corridors as she powered forward, racing toward the place Ziv'ri believed she would find Ava.

Her swords flashed, a little more awkward in the tighter confines of the hallway but no less deadly. Shouts and cries of pain sounded behind her like car alarms.

She never slowed despite her concern that Dagon and his men might be outnumbered.

Only seconds passed before she plowed into the tertiary lab… and found it and the adjoining holding cells empty.

Swearing, she sheathed her swords, drew daggers, and sped to the secondary lab next.

It, too, was empty, as were the adjoining holding cells.

Anxiety rising, she raced toward the primary lab. She had checked the others first because Ziv'ri believed those were the most likely places she would find Ava. But they must have moved her to the same holding area as Jak'ri.

Blasterfire burned holes in the walls around her as she bulldozed her way through hulking bodies like a defensive lineman doing his damnedest to reach the quarterback. Her blades flashed. Blood sprayed. A couple of the Gathendiens around her jolted, then dropped to the ground as their own men fired upon them while trying to hit the barely discernible blur of her form.

Eliana let none of it slow her.

Bursting into the primary lab, she skidded to a halt.

Light flashed. What looked and felt like fire slammed into her shoulder. Though the lightweight armor kept it from burning her, it didn't lighten the blow at all.

Swearing, she stumbled backward.

Half a dozen Gathendiens charged her from inside the lab.

Guards for the prisoners perhaps?

Lacking the time to look around, she roared her rage and launched herself at them. Light streaked past. Eliana ducked and swung, cutting one man down, then another. Explosions sounded. When blood sprayed her helmet and obscured her view, she hastily lowered it. As soon as she did, smoke invaded her nose along with the scent of something suspiciously similar to isopropyl alcohol mixed with stagnant swamp water.

Hoping she wouldn't hit her head on the ceiling, Eliana jumped up, somersaulted over the guards, and landed behind them. Her daggers found homes in the thick hides of two of the guards before they could finish turning around and raise their blasters.

Yanking her blades free from the thicker, greener flesh of their backs proved harder than it would from a vampire's back, costing her precious time.

Another blaster fired. Ducking the scalding-hot energy that shot past her ear, she rid her next attacker of his weapon with a roundhouse kick, then punched him.

Bone cracked and crimson blood spurted as he stumbled backward, bellowing in pain.

The last guard lunged forward and swung. Eliana did, too, dragging her blade across his soft throat. While he sank to his knees, she turned and took out the last man with a final swipe. Heart pounding, breath coming fast, she glanced around as he hit the floor with a thud.

Two Gathendiens across the room stood frozen in place, regarding her with wide eyes. Three operating tables equipped with manacles lay bare. A vast array of high-tech medical machinery and tools adorned every wall and countertop.

She cast the neighboring holding cells a frantic look.

All were empty. No Ava. No Jak'ri.

Alarms blared. Shouting, blasterfire, and explosions carried to her from other parts of the ship. But no one rushed in to combat her. All those she'd passed in the corridors had been hurrying toward the hangar bay.

Sheathing her daggers, she once more drew her swords.

The shorter of the two Gathendien scientists lunged for a button on a nearby counter.

Eliana beat him to it and growled a warning.

He stumbled backward and huddled next to the other one while the second scientist glared at her defiantly.

"You do *not* want to *drek* with me right now," she warned them in Segonian. "Where's Ava?"

The shorter one—who was about five feet eight inches tall—anxiously looked up at his comrade. That one, who stood a foot or so taller than Eliana, clamped his thin lips together in a mutinous line.

She brandished her swords and took a threatening step forward. "Where is Ava?" she shouted. "Where's the Earthling?"

The shorter one wrung his clawed hands.

The taller one spat something in Gathendien that her little earbud translator refused to translate, which it usually only did when it didn't know the translation or if whatever word spoken was an expletive or something equally crude.

Sheathing a sword, she zipped forward in a blur and snapped the taller Gathendien's neck.

The short one gaped as his colleague fell, lifeless, to the floor.

Eliana gripped the short one's shirt just beneath his chin. Hoisting him off the ground, she shoved him none too gently against the tall cabinet behind him. "Where is she?" she bellowed.

The scientist gripped her wrist and kicked his feet. When his claws pricked the skin of her forearm, she shifted her hold to his throat and cut off his air.

His eyes widened.

"Keep your claws to yourself and answer me. Where is she?"

A heavy tail hit her in the back like a freaking cudgel, knocking the breath from her.

"Damn it!" She'd forgotten about their tails. Fortunately his didn't bear those spiked metal rings. Though she stumbled, Eliana maintained her grip on the Gathendien's throat.

The tail struck again, then wrapped around one of her legs and tried to yank her off her feet.

Had she not braced herself and were she not stronger than the average human, it would've succeeded.

Growling, she let go.

The Gathendien's eyes widened as he dropped to the floor and fell to one knee.

Before he could regain his feet, Eliana yanked her leg free and drove the blade of her katana down through his thick tail… and the floor beneath it.

The scientist shrieked in pain and crumpled to the deck.

"I told you not to *drek* with me," she snarled and palmed a dagger.

"Eliana?" Dagon called, concern in his voice, the sounds of battle carrying over the comm.

"Ava isn't here," she told him, panic rising and speeding her words. "I checked all three labs. She isn't in any of them *or* in the holding cells. Jak'ri isn't either. And this bastard isn't cooperating."

"What bastard?"

"One of the scientists."

Spittle flew from the scientist's lips as he bit out some slur and wrapped both hands around the grip of her sword. Several hard tugs failed to move it. After only two or three tries, he gave up and gripped his tail again, moaning in agony.

"I'm going to leave him here for you to question later. I need to go search the rest of the ship."

"Wait until I can join you. I'm heading your way now."

Shaking her head, she exchanged her dagger for shoto swords. "No time. If they think they're losing the battle—"

"They are."

"—then they may be trying to abscond with her. I'll meet you somewhere in the middle."

Without waiting for his response, Eliana raised her helmet and tore out of the lab.

Dagon swore as he pressed forward down the corridor. The hangar bay behind him was secure, all enemies either sorely injured or dead. But this ship housed a *srul* of a lot of Gathendien soldiers, and his armor's camouflage had been marred in enough places that he was only partially invisible to his opponents now.

As he advanced, he picked off one Gathendien after another with his osdulium rifle. Efren and Liden fired their O-rifles beside him. More men behind them watched their backs.

"Maarev, report," Dagon ordered as they approached an intersection.

"We encountered a sizable contingent in the secondary hangar," his friend said as blasterfire, grunts, shouts, and cries of pain carried over the comm.

"Do you need additional troops?"

"No. We'll finish this soon and secure it."

Dagon glanced at the translucent map that lit up the right side of his helmet's visor. A red dot moved in quick starts and stops, indicating Eliana's location. Every time the dot stopped, grunts and a litany of Earth curse words carried to his ears. Then sound would stop and the dot would dash along a little farther.

She was on the other side of the ship. Too far away for him to reach her quickly if large numbers should overwhelm her or if her lightweight armor sustained enough damage to render it unable to afford her protection from blasterfire.

Dagon held up a hand to stop his men's forward progress. Fallen Gathendiens littered their path. But he suspected more lurked in the corridor that bisected this one.

Releasing his O-rifle, he let it dangle from the strap that crossed his chest while he retrieved a Bex-7 from the pouch magnetically attached to one thigh. The round weapon was about the size of his palm and vibrated as soon as he activated it. A green circle lit up its surface, revealing a tiny command screen. A few taps, and Dagon nodded to Liden.

Liden swiftly programmed his Bex-7. Then the two of them tossed both into the air.

The small stun grenades hovered a moment. Then each darted around a corner of the intersection and disappeared in opposite directions.

Warning shouts betrayed lurking Gathendiens. Then bright light poured from the hallways.

Dagon squinted and readied his rifle.

The light dimmed.

Bodies thudded to the floor.

Silently signaling his men, he moved forward. At the intersection, he swung right while Liden swung left. Two men accompanied Dagon. Two accompanied Liden. The rest remained in the intersection to keep an eye on the corridor and cover their backs.

At a glance, Dagon counted eight Gathendiens down on this side. "Keep an eye out for the Earthling and the Purveli," he reminded his men softly. "They weren't in the labs." And they were the only reason he had used a Bex-7 stunner instead of an e-grenade. He didn't want to inadvertently kill the very people he sought to rescue.

Blasterfire erupted in the primary corridor.

"More coming to meet us," Efren muttered behind him.

Just as Dagon started to turn back the way he had come, three Gathendiens lumbered around the far corner. Dagon fired his O-rifle in short, sharp bursts.

Liden did the same.

A hand grabbed Dagon's ankle and yanked.

Swearing, he stumbled but kept his feet beneath him. A Gathendien who had escaped being stunned (probably by ducking behind one of his fellow soldiers) clambered to his feet.

Still firing his rifle at the end of the corridor, Dagon straightened his free arm and flicked his wrist. The armor protecting it elongated into a chain that slipped down through his fingers. A heavy metal ball formed on the end, sharp spikes rising on its surface. Seconds later, Dagon swung.

The flail caught the Gathendien in the chest, its spikes long enough to penetrate armor and pierce flesh. The Gathendien roared in fury and pain. Dagon tugged on the chain. Light flared from the spiked ball, delivering an incapacitating jolt of energy.

The Gathendien's voice cut off midshout. His body jerked and stiffened. Dagon used the reprieve to aim better at the enemies at the end of the hallway.

With Liden's help, they eliminated all of them.

Keeping his rifle at the ready, Dagon released the chain. The light dimmed. The spikes retreated into the ball. Then the Gathendien's eyes rolled back in his head as he sank to the floor, unconscious.

A twitch of Dagon's wrist retracted the flail into his vambrace. After confirming all his opponents were down and that Ava and Jak'ri were not among them, Dagon rejoined the others at the intersection. "Any signs of the prisoners?"

Efren shook his head. "All Gathendien."

Nodding, Dagon led his men farther into the ship, taking out enemies along the way, determined to reach Eliana as quickly as he could while eliminating Gathendien foes. The number of soldiers they continued to encounter stunned him. Was this the ship that had destroyed the *Kandovar*? Were the Gathendiens preparing to launch an all-out war with the Lasarans? Or was whatever research the scientists conducted aboard the *Cebaun* so important that the Gathendiens wished to guard it heavily to prevent it from ending up in Alliance hands?

"Commander Dagon," a voice said over the comm. "Kewan reporting. We've secured the bridge."

"Excellent. See if you can locate Ava and Jak'ri. Eliana said they weren't in the labs."

"Yes, sir."

No one knew alien tech like the young technology officer. If any record of the two prisoners existed—anything that might indicate where they were now, if they were alive or dead, what experiments had been performed on them—Kewan would find it.

The red dot indicating Eliana's position grew closer. It also stopped more and more often as she came up against Gathendiens who were either running from Dagon's men, seeking to protect the labs, or trying to abandon ship. With both hangars secured, the Gathendiens' only means of escape were the few pods the ship boasted.

Dagon quickened his pace. The longer it took him to find Eliana, the more fear for her safety grew. All it would take was one lucky shot with a blaster...

Every group of Gathendiens he encountered infuriated him more as urgency drove him onward at a fast clip. He wanted to break into a run but couldn't risk his men's safety by acting rashly.

Kewan swore suddenly.

"Report, Kewan," Dagon ordered as he fired at two more Gathendiens and swung his flail at a third.

"I haven't found the prisoners yet, but I've located Eliana," he said, his voice tight with tension. "She's injured. And she's about to— *Drek!*"

Eliana heard Kewan yammering on about something to Dagon but didn't digest his words quickly enough. She had searched this whole side of the ship and still hadn't found Ava. They must be moving her, trying to get away with her, or—

She raced around the next corner. Her eyes widened.

A dozen huge Gathendiens faced her.

"Oh shit."

The three in front fired their weapons, which looked big enough to take out a freaking fighter craft. *Sheesh!* Was it even safe to fire those on a ship?

Still racing forward, she dropped low and slid toward them feet-first like a baseball player. Bright blasts shot past above her, so close she could feel the heat before her boots slammed into those of two of the Gathendiens, sweeping them off their feet. Caught in a tangle of limbs, she dodged tails while she swung her shoto swords at anyone she could reach.

"Eliana?" Dagon called over the comm.

A Gathendien kicked her in the side as she scrambled to her feet. "Oomph! Little busy," she gritted and ducked a tail sporting shiny spikes. She thought it unlikely that these soldiers were hovering near the escape pods without reason. So either they were helping some of their men abscond with the prisoners or they intended to leave themselves.

Well, not on *her* watch.

"Efren, Liden, with me," Dagon ordered grimly over the comm.

In recent years, vampires had outnumbered Eliana many times. But few of them had been trained soldiers and none of them had borne skin that was difficult to penetrate with a blade. Or had a tail that could strike like a battering ram, yank her off her feet, or impale her.

With Eliana in their middle, the Gathendiens couldn't fire their weapons without shooting each other. They must not feel threatened enough by the tiny human in their midst to risk it, because they all holstered their blasters and drew blades.

Triumph filled her. *That* she was comfortable with.

That was how most of the vampires back home had attacked her.

Fighting with every ounce of her superior speed, Eliana got in multiple slashes for every one of theirs, spinning and kicking, disarming some, stabbing others. One Gathendien fell. Then a second. And a third.

A tail slammed into her hip, the spikes wrapped around it puncturing her suit and piercing her flesh. Swearing, she spun, swung, and sliced with all her might. The Gathendien who had landed the strike howled and stumbled backward, minus his tail. But the damn spikes stayed embedded in her flesh, the heavy tail tugging on it every time she moved.

She had to duck half a dozen more slashes and get in a couple of her own before she could yank the spikes out. A Gathendien tackled her, taking her to the floor amid the still forms of those she had defeated. That thick skin must weigh more, because he was heavy as hell. Grunting as the big bastard tried to squash her, she worked her legs up between them, planted both feet in his gut, and shoved hard.

The Gathendien's eyes widened as he flew up, hit the ceiling, and burst right through it onto the next level.

Apparently the ceilings on this ship weren't metal like those on the *Ranasura*.

While the other soldiers gaped up at the hole, Eliana flipped up onto her feet and swung. Two more fell beneath her blades before the Gathendiens regrouped and renewed their assault. When another tail caught her across the back, she whirled around, intending to sever it.

Blasterfire abruptly lit up the corridor, so much it nearly blinded her.

The hulking lizard-men around her jerked as scorch marks and holes appeared in their armor and on their tough skin.

Eliana turned to face the new threat and swung her swords protectively in front of her.

The blasterfire stopped.

Every Gathendien toppled to the floor.

Not one shot hit Eliana.

She lowered her swords.

Odd splotches of red and black hovered in the air several yards away. Then Dagon, Efren, and Liden flickered into view. Several more men appeared behind them, their shiny armor now peppered with scorch marks and blood splatter the camouflage couldn't hide.

Damn, they looked good.

She grinned and tapped the button that made her helmet recede back into her collar. "Excellent timing."

Dagon shook his head as he raised the visor on his helmet. "I told you to wait for me."

Pain burned through her hip like fire as she stepped over the Gathendiens. More simmered in her back. "My way was more fun."

Several of the men chuckled.

Dagon didn't. He frowned as he watched her limp toward him.

"Besides..." She motioned to the fallen aliens. "I think these guys were heading for the escape pods. And there was no way in hell I was going to let them leave." A wave of dizziness swept over her. Sheathing her shoto swords, she drew her last katana and unobtrusively placed the tip on the ground to help her maintain her balance.

She hadn't lost much blood in the skirmishes. As far as she knew, she had only incurred the hip wound, the blow to the back, and a few cuts from Gathendien blades she hadn't been able to evade. Why did she feel so light-headed?

Dagon closed the distance between them, the furrow in his brow deepening. "You're injured."

She shrugged, not wanting him to worry. "I've had worse." At least this battle hadn't left her with broken bones. "But I might try to talk Joral into making me some of your fancy exo-armor for future battles." Hopefully it wouldn't restrict her movements or hinder her exceptional speed too much.

"He's already working on it." Dagon cupped one side of her face in a cold, gauntleted hand.

"He is?" She smiled, excited by the prospect. Now if there were only a way Joral could make her armor camouflage her the way it did Segonians, she would be unstoppable.

Her whole body abruptly flushed with heat. Beneath her lightweight armor, her skin broke out in a cold sweat. Nausea rose.

She staggered. "Oh crap."

Alarm flaring in his features, Dagon gripped her upper arms to steady her. "Eliana?"

"Something's..." Her tongue felt thick. Her words...

Was she slurring her words?

"Something's wrong," she managed to work past numb lips. Her knees buckled.

Dagon caught her up against him. "Eliana?"

She tried to speak, but couldn't.

"Medic!" Dagon shouted as darkness crashed down upon her.

CHAPTER 18

DAGON DREW HIS thumb across the soft skin on the back of Eliana's hand. Sprawled in the chair Adaos had provided, he fought a smile as he watched her fidget. Whenever Dagon had needed wounds treated, he had found the beds in Med Bay to be annoyingly cramped. But Eliana made this one look large and roomy. Her small form made barely a ripple in the covers.

Or it *would* if she didn't move around so much. His little Earthling did *not* like being idle.

Nor did she like Adaos *coddling* her as she called it.

"I'm not coddling you," Adaos murmured as he passed his hand scanner over her.

Expression darkening, Eliana batted the scanner away. "Yes, you are. I'm fine. I don't need your scans to tell me that."

Adaos arched a brow. "Well, I do. And I'm chief medical officer, so you have to do whatever I say."

Eliana turned to Dagon. "Can't you order him to give it a rest and sign me out already? I've been here for two days."

Adaos spoke before Dagon could. "In Med Bay, my orders supersede Dagon's unless it's a security issue."

"That's *Commander* Dagon to you, mister high and mighty," Eliana countered. "And this *is* a security issue."

Again Adaos arched a brow, just to annoy Eliana, Dagon suspected. "Oh? And why is that?"

"Because if you don't let me out of this bed soon, I'm going to grab some of your fancy stabilizer goo and *secure* your ass to a chair."

Dagon barked out a laugh.

She squinted her eyes at him. "You aren't helping."

"Yes," Adaos agreed, his expression surly despite the amusement that sparkled in his eyes. "You aren't helping, Commander Dagon. Your Earthling is the worse patient I've ever had." He motioned to the bed. "Can't you climb in there and fornicate with her or something? *Anything* to occupy her mouth so I can have a little peace? I will happily pull the curtains to give you two some privacy."

Assuming a thoughtful look, Dagon eyed Eliana and the bed.

Her mouth fell open. "You aren't actually considering it, are you?" Leaning closer, she whispered an appalled, "They would *hear* us!"

Grinning, he stole a kiss. "And they would all envy me my good fortune."

She laughed, all crankiness evaporating, then turned back to Adaos. "I'm a terrible patient."

His lips turned up in a faint smile as he passed his hand scanner over her once more. "No need to point out the obvious."

"I'm sorry. I'm just worried about Ava."

"And embarrassed about fainting?" he asked innocently.

She grimaced. "I did *not* faint. I lost consciousness."

He shrugged. "Either way, I'm sure exhibiting such weakness distressed you."

"Weakness!" she bleated. "Weakness, my ass! I was *poisoned*, in case you've forgotten."

"I *haven't* forgotten," he intoned, "which is why you aren't leaving that bed until I say you can."

Her brows drew down in a frown as she looked at Dagon. "I walked right into that one, didn't I?"

"Yes, you did." He drew the back of her hand to his lips for a kiss. "Let him run his tests, *milessia*. You scared the *srul* out of us."

She really had. After collapsing in his arms, Eliana had been completely unresponsive. And when he and Adaos had removed her armor, her skin had been cold and damp. A quick scan had revealed *bosregi* in her system. Apparently some of the Gathendiens had dipped the tips of their spikes in the deadly poison before fastening them to their tails. Their blades, too. Since

Dagon and his fellow Segonians had never encountered such tactics before, Med Bay's stock did not include an antidote.

Eliana's body had valiantly fought the poison. But dark striations originating in her hip wound had spent hours stretching farther and farther across her pale skin. And her viral count had dropped alarmingly low.

Dagon knew well what would happen if the bioengineered virus that infected her was destroyed. Fear for her had *vuan* near brought him to his knees. But he was commander of the *Ranasura*. And as such he had carried out his duties, issuing orders and interrogating the prisoners while Eliana lay unconscious in Med Bay. Panic had burned inside him every minute he was away from her, urging him to return to her side. Fortunately, several transfusions of her own blood—drawn by Adaos days earlier while it was heavily pervaded with the virus so he might study it—had enabled her to win the battle and awaken.

She sent Dagon a penitent look now and offered a soft, "I'm sorry." The full-body scanning wand descended from the ceiling and passed over her. "I'm not used to being sick. Poisons on Earth don't affect me. And I hate that I missed the rest of the battle and didn't get to watch you interrogate the Gathendien prisoners. You're hot when you're all menacing and deadly."

He smiled, having known her long enough to understand that she wasn't referring to temperature when she said *hot*. "I'm glad you think so."

"I don't *think* so. I *know* so." She gave him a long, leering once-over, then sighed. "And I *am* embarrassed about fainting."

"You were poisoned."

"So?"

"Would it make you feel better if—instead of fainting—we said you..." He thought for a moment. "...gallantly ceded the battlefield to the rest of us so we could have fun, too?"

Adaos snorted a laugh.

Eliana smiled. "Yes. I like it." She sent him a mischievous look through her lashes, then waggled her eyebrows. "Almost enough to let you climb in here and fornicate with me."

Relieved to see both her health and good humor restored, Dagon shook his head. "Damn, that's tempting."

"Awwww." She gave him an affectionate smile. "You used an Earth curse word again. I'm rubbing off on you."

"Speaking of rubbing," Adaos muttered.

Laughing, she motioned to the wand that currently lit up her legs. "Do you think if we did something scandalous enough, it would break Adaos's scanner?"

"Perhaps," Dagon murmured thoughtfully. "Want to give it a try?"

"All right, all right," Adaos said before Eliana could respond. "Enough. Get out. Both of you. I'm done."

Her face lit up. "Really?"

"Yes." Adaos studied his data pad. "All traces of the poison are gone. And you should know that I purged every reference to the poison from our records. After studying its effect on you, I've concluded that—in large enough doses—it could successfully eradicate the virus in your body and thus be weaponized to eradicate your kind."

"Crap. Do you think the Gathendiens know that?"

"No. They would have already used it on Earth if they did. And in most alien species, *bosregi* poisoning—though it induces illness—is rarely fatal. The bioengineered virus that infects you merely made you unusually susceptible."

That was scary. "But you said I'm okay now, right?"

"Yes. Your viral count is back to what it should be. You are officially as healthy as a *munia*."

"I don't know what a *munia* is, but it better be *drekking* healthy."

Dagon rose. "It is. It's also extremely hard to kill."

"As am I," she quipped. "Let's hurry up and go before Adaos changes his mind."

After throwing back the covers, Eliana slid out of bed and landed barefoot on the floor. The healing garments she wore dwarfed her so much that she had to hastily grab the waist of the pants to keep them from falling down. The sleeves of the shirt dangled past her fingertips.

Sighing, she looked up at him with a long-suffering expression. "You guys are freaking huge."

He laughed, so relieved to see her well that he couldn't stop smiling.

"You didn't by any chance bring me a change of clothes, did you?"

"I did."

Smiling, she gave him a hug. "Thank you."

Her pants dropped to her ankles.

Dagon bit back a laugh. Adaos didn't even try to stifle his.

Fortunately, the shirt was so large on her that it covered her to her knees.

Without releasing Dagon, Eliana said, "Please tell me this shirt isn't like the hospital gowns on Earth that gape in the back and show your bare ass."

He grinned. "It isn't. If it were, I would be pummeling Adaos right now."

"I'm a medic!" Adaos protested. "I see bare asses all the time."

Releasing Dagon, Eliana turned to Adaos. "I don't know if that's something you want to brag about."

"Being a medic?"

"No. Seeing bare asses all the time." Before Adaos could respond, she looked up at Dagon. "Now where are those clothes?"

A few minutes later, they exited Med Bay… and stopped short. Both sides of the hallway were lined with soldiers and other crew members. All straightened as soon as Dagon and Eliana appeared.

"Eliana!" they cheered happily.

Dagon glanced down.

Eliana's pretty face lit with delight as she flashed them a smile. "Hi, guys." She glanced up and down the hallway. His men stretched as far as they could see. "What's all this?"

Brohko stepped forward, his hands clasped behind his back. "We were worried about you and wanted to visit you, but Adaos wouldn't allow us to enter Med Bay."

"Awwww. Thanks, guys. That means a lot to me."

"We also thought to bring you gifts to cheer you during your recovery since that is a custom we've observed in many cultures."

Her eyebrows rose with surprise. "Really? That's so sweet."

Chest puffing out with pride, Brohko brought his hands out from behind his back and held out his gift.

Eliana stared at the big bag of *jarumi* nuggets he proffered, then grinned. "I love it! It's perfect! Thank you." As she took the bag from him, the other men all extended the gifts they had brought her as well.

Every single one of them held large bags of *jarumi* nuggets.

She laughed and looked up at Dagon. "I think my secret snack obsession isn't such a secret." Turning back to the men, she sent them all smiles. "This is awesome, guys. Thank you!"

Her stomach growled.

Everyone laughed.

Her cheeks flushed. "I can't help it. Adaos wouldn't let me eat anything fun while I was recovering."

Dozens of males immediately commiserated with her, each trying to outdo the other while detailing the disappointing meals the med bay staff had served them in the past.

Amused, Dagon shook his head and cut them off. "All right. It's time for last meal. Brohko, why don't you oversee delivering Eliana's gifts to her quarters while I have Kusgan serve her something more palatable than Med Bay's fare?"

The young warrior grinned. "Yes, Commander!" He and a few others started hastily collecting the bags. Dagon suspected that once they stacked them in her quarters, there would barely be enough room for Eliana to move around.

When Brohko held his hand out to Eliana, she shook her head and clutched the bag he'd given her to her chest. "I'm keeping this one with me."

Chuckling, Dagon wrapped his arm around her and guided her toward the mess hall.

She reached out and snagged another bag. "This one, too. Just in case Kusgan hasn't fired up the grill yet."

Drek, he loved her.

Everyone else on the *Ranasura* did, too, judging by the pleasure they exhibited at seeing her up and about again.

Kusgan heaped Eliana's plate even higher than Dagon's with her favorite *vestuna*, earning another growl from her stomach.

Once more, the two of them seated themselves by a holowindow, which displayed a beach scene this evening with a breeze that carried the scent of the sea. So many men stopped by their table that Dagon had little opportunity to speak with Eliana himself until she had nearly finished her meal.

"Okay," she said, eyes tearing up from the spicy dish as she reached for her glass of *naga* juice, "fill me in. You said Ava and Jak'ri escaped."

"Yes." He had told her little more than that because Adaos had wanted to keep her stress levels down while she recuperated.

"How?"

"When we took the ship, Maarev noticed some of the Gathendien fighter craft were missing."

She frowned. "We didn't see any leave the *Cebaun* as it approached us."

"Because they had already left. When we interrogated the captured Gathendiens, two admitted that Ava and Jak'ri escaped several days ago. It's why the Gathendiens abandoned their original plan and sped toward us instead of waiting to see if Ziv'ri would accomplish his mission. They had lost the only Earth woman they had managed to capture and didn't want to risk losing another if Ziv'ri failed."

"Did they say how the *srul* they even knew I was on board the *Ranasura*?"

Anger filled him. "Someone has been feeding them information and updating them on the search for survivors of the *Kandovar*." He and the other commanders who had been conscripted to search for survivors had all assumed the Gathendiens had found some way to bypass the Lasarans' security measures and steal the information. But they apparently didn't have to. Someone else already had and was selling them information.

"Who?"

He shook his head. "They didn't know. Commander Striornuk dealt with the informant directly and could have told us, but he was slain in the battle. As far as we can tell, no one else on the *Cebaun* was privy to that information. Kewan was able to access the *Cebaun*'s systems and transferred all communications records to Janek and Rahmik. They're scouring them now and hopefully will discover who the *srul* has been sending Striornuk tips."

She frowned. "Did the Gathendiens say where Ava and Jak'ri went?"

"Only that they left in an escape pod and three fighters gave chase."

She swore.

Reaching across the table, he took one of her hands. "Rahmik was able to determine the direction the escape pod took. He and Galen both believe they are headed for the planet we intended to search before the *Cebaun* distracted us."

"And we're—"

"On our way to K-54973 now."

"How quickly can we reach it?"

"We'll reach it in two days. Until then, we're monitoring comms and scouring radar, hoping to pick up a transmission from them."

Her brow furrowed. "Or transmissions from the fighters chasing them?"

"Yes." He wished he had better news to give her.

She fell silent for a long moment, worry painting her pretty features. Covering their clasped hands, she turned them so his was on top and traced the veins on the back of it. "How fast are Gathendien escape pods? Can they outfly a fighter craft?"

He had wished to know the same thing and had consulted both Cobus and Anat. "Gathendien escape pods *are* faster than most other escape pods. Gathendiens have a lot of enemies they have to outrun, so they equip their pods with greater speed. But the fighters are faster."

She bit her lip.

"If sufficient time elapsed between Ava and Jak'ri's escape and the fighters embarking upon their pursuit, then the two still could have reached the planet first in the pod."

"What if the fighters immediately gave chase?"

He shook his head. "It's difficult to say. The fighter pilots haven't contacted the *Cebaun* since their departure."

"You don't think they would destroy the escape pod, do you? In retribution if they know the *Cebaun* lost the battle?"

"Considering how much they want to get their hands on an Earthling? No."

"What are their options then? I still don't know enough about how things work out here. Can fighters dock with escape pods?"

"No. And fighters aren't equipped with acquisition beams they can lock onto the pod. I think the only option that leaves them is to follow the escape pod to the planet and attempt to recapture Ava and Jak'ri there."

"What then? If they don't know how the battle on the *Cebaun* ended, would they return to the ship?" She frowned. "Wait. Where *is* their ship? What did you do with it?"

"It's too large to fit in any of our hangars, and towing it would slow us down. So we disabled it, locked it down so only members of the Alliance can enter it, and tagged it for retrieval. The only way Gathendiens can regain access to it is if they cut their way in. Should any try, we left a few traps for them. And Kewan patched us in to the *Cebaun*'s system, so we'll know if anyone attempts to use the controls. He's also scouring their records for any mention of other Gathendien ships capturing Earthlings."

"Has he found anything yet?"

"No."

"What about the Gathendiens *you* captured?"

"I reported directly to my sovereign and her military advisors. When I did, she ordered me to put all the Gathendiens in cryo so they can face judgment by Aldebarian Alliance courts when we return home."

"That's really a thing? You can freeze people and wake them up again?"

He blinked. "Yes. You can't do that on Earth?" Preparations for such were minimal and well known throughout the Alliance. The earliest Segonian space explorers had used cryo sleep to prevent aging while traveling to distant systems before advancements in speed and technology like the *qhov'rum* dramatically reduced travel time.

"No," she said. "Anyone who freezes on Earth dies."

"Hmm." He tried to keep his expression neutral but feared he did a poor job of hiding his shock. Earth was further behind than he'd thought.

Fortunately, she took no offense. Rather, she seemed amused by his astonishment. "Your sovereign is a woman?" she asked, changing the subject.

"Yes." He drew her small hand to his lips and kissed her palm. "I asked her permission to continue searching for your friends, Eliana, and she granted it. If they're out here, we'll find them."

"Thank you."

It had actually been far easier than he'd thought to obtain clearance to continue the search. Thus far, Dagon and the Akseli pirate Janwar were the only ones who had succeeded in rescuing any of the Earthlings. The fact that Dagon had reduced the Gathendiens' numbers during his search for Ava had helped his case, of course. The Segonian sovereign was a former soldier who appreciated a good fight and also understood the importance of maintaining strong ties with allies. To that end, she not only wished to support the Lasarans, she also seemed quite intrigued by Seth, Eliana's commanding officer, who had spoken to the leaders of each Aldebarian Alliance nation via the holocomm system Prince Taelon had given him, making him another potential ally.

"And thank you for coming to me in Med Bay as soon as I regained consciousness," Eliana said softly.

It had been a long *drekking* wait for that. Dagon had resented every duty that had kept him from her side, but there had been much he needed to address.

"I was worried about you," he admitted. "I know you're difficult to kill. But if you had received a larger dose of the poison, and if Adaos hadn't had a goodly supply of your blood on hand..."

She grimaced. "I might've died. I realize that. I think that's why I've been so cranky." Her shoulders lifted in a sheepish shrug. "I haven't come that close to dying in a *very* long time."

How many times *had* she come close to dying?

"Well," she added with a little wrinkle of her nose, "except for nearly blowing up with the *Kandovar*. Before *that*, I hadn't come close to dying in a long time."

So... more than twice? Three times? Four? Ten?

He hated to think about it but couldn't seem to stop now.

"And even when the *Kandovar* blew up," she said slowly, the hesitance that entered her voice sharpening his attention, "I think the idea of floating out in the great nothingness of space—alone in such a foreign environment—scared me more than the concept of dying."

Dagon found that both unsettling and worrisome.

Soldiers knew that every time they dove into battle they courted death. But that didn't mean they didn't fear it. He'd had to discharge a few soldiers in the past when it became apparent that their mortality meant nothing to them. Since they'd held no fear of death, they had repeatedly taken unnecessary risks that had put their lives *and* those of their unit in danger.

If Eliana didn't fear death…

"But on the Gathendien ship," she continued, disrupting his thoughts, "when the poison started to affect me and I could feel that something was really wrong… I was afraid." She looked ashamed as she confessed it. "I still am whenever I think about it. And I don't really know how to handle that."

"Why didn't you fear death before?" Even battle-hardened soldiers feared death.

She squeezed his hand. "Because I had nothing to lose."

For a long moment, he didn't breathe. "And now?"

"Now I have you." Her lips turned up in a half smile. "Or at least, I'd like to." She glanced around the empty mess hall. "I know this isn't the appropriate time or place to say this, but…" Her brown eyes met his. "I've never felt like this before, Dagon."

His heart began to pound. Because he had never felt like this before either. As if he'd found some part of himself that had been missing all these years. A part that he hadn't even realized *had* been missing.

"I'm falling in love with you," she said, an amber glow lighting her brown irises. "And I'd like to see where this might go. Dying would kinda ruin that."

He stared at her. "You're falling in love with me?"

"Yes." She didn't hesitate. Didn't make light of it. Just answered him with one straightforward, can't-possibly-be-misinterpreted word. And how he appreciated that. "But there are some things I should tell you—"

He held up a hand. "In my quarters." She was right. This *wasn't* the time or place. He needed to be alone with her in the true sense of the word in a place where he could drag her into his arms if he was so inclined.

And he was definitely so inclined.

She blinked in surprise. "Okay."

Dagon rose, stacked their trays, then piled their empty dishes atop them.

Eliana reached for the two bags of *jarumi* nuggets she hadn't had time to eat. "Can I bring these with me?"

He grinned. "Yes."

It took far longer to reach his quarters than Dagon had hoped. Every man they passed in the corridors stopped to chat with Eliana and tell her how glad he was to see her well again. Dagon was practically growling with impatience by the time he finally pressed his palm to the access panel. The door slid up.

"Eliana!" someone called from down the hallway.

"No," Dagon blurted. Shoving her forward, he ducked inside.

The door dropped down.

He sighed with relief.

Turning to face him, she laughed. "I like your guys, Dagon, but—"

He cupped her face and lowered his lips to hers.

She gasped, allowing him to slip his tongue inside to stroke and tease hers. A hum of approval escaped her as she wrapped her arms around his waist and pressed closer.

Lowering his arms, Dagon banded them around her and lifted her onto her toes so he could ravage her lovely mouth without having to bend so much. When he finally drew back enough to peer down at her, her eyes bore a bright amber glow and her lips were puffy and kiss-swollen.

"Have I told you how much I love your mouth?" she murmured, the husky tenor of her voice stroking him like fingers.

He let a cocky smile lift one corner his lips. "Several times." After his tongue had driven her to multiple orgasms.

She laughed. "So I have."

Though desire thrummed through him, Dagon couldn't resist pulling her into a tight hug and resting his chin atop her head. "You really did scare the *srul* out of me," he whispered.

She hugged him tight. "I'm sorry."

He shook his head. "You weren't at fault. And I made sure those who were paid for it with their lives."

A moment passed, making him wonder if perhaps now hadn't been a good time to remind her of that.

She cleared her throat. "Is it weird that that turns me on?"

He chuckled. "No. We're both soldiers." He pressed a kiss to her soft black hair. "What would *you* have done if they had poisoned *me*?"

Loosening her hold, she leaned back enough to send him a chagrined look. "Honestly?" She wrinkled her nose. "I probably would've lost it and killed everyone who wasn't wearing Segonian armor."

Because she was falling in love with him.

Drek, that aroused him.

Lifting her, he urged her to wrap her legs around his waist. As soon as she complied, he turned and pressed her back against the door. His lips found hers once more, hungry and fierce.

Eliana didn't object. Instead, she curled her arms around his neck and adjusted her position until she could grind her core against his erection.

Dagon moaned and thrust against her.

Again she gasped and lifted her lips from his. "This door won't open, right?"

If he hadn't been so desperate to get her clothes off, he would've laughed at the sudden mental image of the two of them tumbling into the hallway, preferably with no clothes on. "Right."

This time *she* claimed *his* lips, her taste both sweet and spicy as she used her tongue to tease and torment.

Dagon slid a hand up to cup her breast.

"Wait," she protested.

He bit back a curse when she drew back again.

"There are some things I want to tell you."

He shook his head. "Tell me after. I need to be inside you. I need to feel you against me. I came too close to losing you."

Expression softening, she nodded. "After." She patted his shoulders. "Put me down."

Though every impulse balked at the request, he backed away from the door. Unlocking her legs from around his waist, she slid down his front until her toes touched the deck. He groaned, *really* wanting to take her against the door. Right now. Or as soon as he could get their clothes off.

He barely completed the thought before she blurred. He felt a hard tug and heard a rip. Then Eliana stilled.

Dagon glanced down… and gaped. She had torn off all his clothes. Everything except his boots. He met her gaze, saw the familiar glint of amusement in her luminescent eyes, and grinned big.

She winked. "Take your boots off, babe, and lower the bed."

"*Srul* yes." He bent to yank off a boot. "Lower bed!" His big bed descended behind him. Dagon backed toward it as he tugged off the other boot but kept his eyes on Eliana, who remained by the door.

Smiling, she blurred. The sound of rending cloth again filled the room. Then she stilled.

Clothing fluttered to the floor, leaving her entirely naked, even bereft of shoes.

The backs of Dagon's thighs hit the side of his mattress. He stopped… and just drank in the sight of her. Not a single wound marred her beautiful body. Every inch of pale flesh was perfect, not even hinting at the punctures and gashes she'd suffered. The terrifying dark striations the poison had painted her hip with had vanished. Her long, midnight hair tumbled down her back in a thick curtain. Her full breasts with their tight pink tips begged to be touched and sucked and pinched.

"*Drek*, I love you," he uttered hoarsely.

The light in her eyes flashed brighter. "Dagon?"

"Yes?"

"Catch." She crossed the room in a single leap and tumbled him back onto the bed.

No more words passed their lips. Nor did laughter. They were both too desperate for each other.

Dagon rolled her beneath him and settled himself between her thighs. He palmed one of her full breasts and teased the stiff peak as he plundered her mouth.

Eliana reached down between them, curled her fingers around his cock, and guided him to her entrance, already slick and warm. Her movements grew almost frantic as she locked her legs around his waist and dug her heels into his ass, urging him to take her.

Vowing to go slower next time, Dagon thrust deep. He groaned. She was so tight. So good. Her warm sheath squeezed him, ratcheting up his need. He didn't hold back. Pounding into her. Knowing she could take it. Knowing this was how she wanted it. Hard and fast. Slaying all worries. Banishing all thoughts of pain and death. Leaving only lust. And love.

He stroked her lovely breasts, altering the angle of his thrusts so he'd hit the most sensitive part of her.

"Dagon," she moaned. "I need you. So much. Yes. Right there." Planting her feet on the mattress, she arched up to meet him, again and again, her hands shifting to his ass and clamping down.

His breath shortened as he fought to hold back his release. He pinched the sensitive peak of her breast, thrust deep, and ground against her.

Throwing her head back, she cried out in ecstasy. Her warm walls clamped down around his cock, squeezing and releasing until his own orgasm rushed up. Shouting her name, he poured his heat into her.

Heart slamming against his ribs, Dagon braced his elbows on the bed and burrowed his arms beneath her to hold her close. He could feel the rapid beat of her heart beneath the breasts pressed to his chest. His own heart matched it as he lowered his head to the pillow beside hers. His breath fanned her hair as she slid her arms around him and squeezed him tight.

Pressing a kiss to her slender neck, he rolled them to their sides and locked her against him, never wanting to let her go.

CHAPTER 19

ELIANA SAT CROSS-LEGGED on the bed, one of Dagon's big short-sleeved shirts covering her down to her thighs.

Dagon lay on his back beside her, his big, muscled body relaxed and gloriously naked. His hands clasped behind his head, he watched her with a smile rife with affection while she ate her way to the bottom of a bag of *jarumi* nuggets.

Her appetite always seemed to amuse him, and the awesome bout of lovemaking they'd enjoyed had left him happy and content.

She liked seeing him happy and content.

Eliana didn't want to say or do anything to wipe the slight smile from his face. But she needed to know. "Did you mean it?" she asked quietly.

A moment passed as he mentally replayed the few words they'd spoken since secluding themselves in his quarters. "That I love you?"

She nodded.

"Yes. I meant it."

The backs of her eyes began to burn. Ducking her head, she stuffed another crunchy nugget in her mouth and hoped he'd think the moisture in her eyes resulted from the spicy snack.

She should've known better.

Dagon sat up, the motion bringing him close. Crooking a finger beneath her chin, he gently raised it and forced her to meet his eyes. "That distresses you?" he asked softly.

She shook her head and swallowed past the lump in her throat. "Just the opposite," she whispered. She had waited so long for this, to find someone she loved who could love her back. She was almost afraid to believe it.

Dagon pressed a sweet kiss to her lips. Stroking a finger down her cheek, he collected a bead of moisture. "Then why the tears?"

"You don't think it's too fast, us falling in love?"

He shrugged. "It happens that way sometimes. My father swears he fell in love with my mother the moment he accidentally bumped into her and knocked her down." He smiled. "My mother said it took her a little longer."

"How long?" she couldn't resist asking.

"A couple of weeks." He tucked a stray lock of hair behind her ear. "Like us." His smile turned wry. "Or like you. I've been falling for you ever since I first heard your voice."

"No, you haven't."

"Yes, I have." He arched a brow. "Would you like proof?"

Curiosity drove her to nod.

He winked, then leaned over and tapped the screen of the personal data tablet he kept on the shelf beside the bed. "Play 'Eliana.'"

Seconds later her own voice floated from the tablet's speakers, crooning her favorite song, "At Last." Her eyes widened as she stared at him.

"You've sung me to sleep almost every night for weeks," Dagon confessed, his expression tender.

The knowledge sent a little flutter through her tummy. "That's less an indication that you love me and more an indication that you have poor taste in music."

He laughed. "I have excellent taste in music. You have a lovely voice." He pointed at her. "And that right there is one of the reasons I love you. You make me laugh." He shrugged, still smiling. "I'm happy whenever I'm with you, Eliana. I've been content for years. But I haven't truly been happy. Not like this. I've never found someone who could make even the most mundane routine fun. I enjoy talking with you. Teasing you. I even enjoy just sitting quietly with you on the bridge."

She bit her lip, every confession filling her with elation.

"Still don't believe me?" He shook his head, a smile flirting with his lips. "Ask CC what *milessia* means."

For once, she didn't look up when she addressed the computer, choosing instead to keep her eyes locked with Dagon's. "CC, what does *milessia* mean?"

"*Milessia* is a Segonian term of endearment," CC reported pleasantly. "According to my data banks, the closest Earth English translation is *my love*."

Eliana's heart threatened to break through her rib cage. "But there's so much you don't know about me," she told him softly.

"What I don't know doesn't worry me, Eliana, because I've yet to find anything I don't love about you. I love your courage, your ferocity, your skills as a warrior... even though sometimes you scare the *srul* out of me. I love your intelligence, your sense of humor, the kindness you display toward others."

But would that be enough?

He cupped her cheek. "Tell me what's inspiring the spark of fear I see in your eyes."

He really did know her well. "I'm old," she told him miserably.

He clamped his lips together. To keep from laughing? "How old?"

"Almost four hundred years old."

His eyes widened.

She winced. But after a moment, she realized he didn't look weirded out by their age difference, just surprised by it.

"Are you like the Lasarans then?" he asked. "Do you age very slowly?"

She'd forgotten until then that Prince Taelon's parents were her age, or thereabouts, but their hair had only just begun to gray at the temples. "No. I don't age at all."

His expression still exhibited no signs of an impending freak-out. "Because of the virus?"

"Yes."

"Cool," he replied with a smile, borrowing her word.

Cool? How was that cool? "But you *do* age," she whispered. And unlike her immortal brethren who had found love in the past decade, she couldn't transform Dagon so he could spend the rest of eternity with her. They had no idea what the virus would do to him, if he would eventually suffer brain damage like ordinary humans that would drive him insane, or if he would react more like a *gifted one*. Or if the virus would prove fatal and kill him.

His smile softened, turned tender. "Is that what worries you? That I'll age and you won't?"

"I assumed it would worry *you*." And yes, it did worry her. She had *finally*—after centuries of living—fallen in love. She had finally found *the one*.

She didn't want to lose him to old age.

He shook his head. "If we became lifemates, I would seek the Sectas' aid."

Her pulse quickened at the mention of them becoming lifemates. What a beautiful dream that would be. "I don't know what that means."

"There have been instances in the past in which Segonians have bound themselves to Lasarans. Segonians usually live around one hundred and fifty years. Lasarans live far longer. Hundreds of years longer, in fact. So those couples sought the aid of the Sectas, who extended the Segonians' lives to match that of their Lasaran lifemates."

Her heart began to beat faster. "They can do that? They can extend someone's life span… indefinitely?"

"Yes. They only do it for lifemates and keep the identities of those they aid confidential to discourage individuals who seek longevity for less noble purposes. Though the Sectas have sometimes been mislabeled cold and clinical because they mire themselves in science, their society highly values love."

So if she and Dagon became lifemates, she wouldn't have to lose him to old age. They could be together forever, just as they would if he were a *gifted one* who could be transformed.

She wanted to jump up and down as hope rose, but she shoved it aside until she could gauge his response to her next revelation. "But I can't have children."

He continued to stroke her cheek with his thumb, his look sobering. "You're certain?"

She started to nod, but hesitated. "Well… no female Immortal Guardian has ever gotten pregnant. We can sense when we ovulate and avoid… um… sexual activity that can lead to pregnancy during our fertile period because we don't know what the virus would do to an infant. Or a fetus." Which was another reason she had been shocked to discover that Immortal Guardian Marcus Grayden had fathered a child with Ami. She'd thought the couple had adopted Adira. But something in Ami's extraordinary Lasaran physiology had prevented Marcus from infecting either her or their child with the virus. "It's why I told Adaos he could study me. When he was explaining Segonian courtship rituals, I asked him if not being able to have children would be a deal breaker."

"It wouldn't," Dagon said softly. "It isn't."

She stared at him, wanting desperately to believe him. "Really?"

"Not for me." Leaning forward, he brushed his lips against hers in a kiss so tender it brought tears to her eyes. "Not if I could have you in my life."

Throwing her arms around his neck, she squeezed the stuffing out of him. "I know it's early to talk about things like this. We've only known each other a couple of weeks."

"We've actually known each other a month longer than that," he reminded her, sliding his big hands up and down her back in soothing strokes.

She supposed they had. Loosening her hold, she peered up at him. "Adaos said there may be a way to prevent transmission of the virus from mother to child in the womb."

He nodded as though such didn't surprise him. "Perhaps while he's researching that, Adaos can also tell us if any difficulties may arise from combining Segonian and Earthling DNA." His entire form changed color, blending so perfectly into the light bedding and the wall behind him that he appeared to vanish. Then his color transmogrified again to a brown several shades darker than his natural bronze. The texture of his skin changed, too, assuming the look and feel of rough tree bark. "You *do* hail from a distant solar system, after all, and there are notable differences between our species."

She blinked. "I didn't even think of that."

His camouflage faded, surrendering to his normal coloring and texture. "I did. And I meant what I said, Eliana. I love you. We may not have had a lengthy courtship, but in the brief time we've spent together, you have completely enraptured me and shown me what life could be like with you by my side." He pressed a sweet kiss to her lips. "I want that."

"I want that, too." More than anything.

He shook his head, rubbing noses with her. "You don't have to say that if you need more time."

"I'm nearly four hundred years old, Dagon. I know what I want." Happy to prove it, she rose to her knees. Slinging a leg across his, she straddled his lap and scooted closer until not an inch separated their bodies. "And I want *you*."

His eyes darkened with desire as he dipped his head and took her lips in a passionate exploration that sent fire licking through her veins. "*This* is all that matters, Eliana," he whispered, his voice deepening as he rested his hands on her hips. "Just you and me. Together. We'll figure out everything else as we go."

She nodded. "Okay. I really love you, Dagon."

"I love you, too." He nipped her lower lip. "Are you still hungry?"

"Only for you."

"*Srul* yes," he growled and fell back against the pillows with her.

Eliana paced the bridge as she stared through the large window. Wispy white clouds failed to obscure the view of a lovely planet. K-54973 bore an atmosphere similar to Earth's but was a lot larger and had less landmass. Roughly two-thirds of Earth was water. On this planet, the ratio was more like four-fifths. There *were* several continents sprinkled about. Lovely, majestic mountains of a dark grayish-purple color rose from some in the northern hemisphere, the higher elevations adorned with a heavy coat of snow. Most of the continents in the southern hemisphere were swathed in thick forests, their enormous trees rising so tall some pierced the clouds.

The *Ranasura* had been flying grid patterns over one continent after another for two weeks now and hadn't caught a single glimpse of a downed escape pod. Nor had they found any evidence of civilization, advanced or otherwise.

Eliana didn't know why she had thought she'd hear a quick *Yep, there they are* or *Nope, no sign of them* the moment they arrived. It wasn't as though the advanced technology the *Ranasura* boasted could miraculously make it a smaller planet that would only take a few minutes to search.

But not knowing if the escape pod had even made it this far gnawed at her. Dagon thought it a good sign that they had encountered no debris fields or wreckage on the way here that might've indicated the Gathendiens had done the unexpected and destroyed the pod. If the pod had made it to the planet though, then where the hell was it?

For what seemed like the millionth time, she wondered if it had crashed. She had no idea how hard it was to land one of those things. What if the damn pod had just plummeted to the ground like a freaking meteor? What if Ava and Jak'ri had died in the crash? What if they hadn't and were injured somewhere, desperately needing medical attention? They had already been tortured for unspecified lengths of time on the *Cebaun*. Could they survive more wounds added to those the Gathendiens had delivered?

Eliana glanced over at Ziv'ri. The Purveli had healed well under Adaos's care and now occupied a seat at an unmanned assistant navigator's station.

Ziv'ri looked as frustrated and disheartened as she felt.

"Nothing," Rahmik murmured.

"Mark it," Dagon ordered. "Maarev, report."

"No signs of the pod, Commander."

One by one, other pilots reported the same.

"Return to the *Ranasura*."

"Yes, sir," all chorused.

Every time the *Ranasura* reached another continent, a squadron of those sleek, sexy fighter craft shot out from their hangar and sped away to cover more ground. Though the planet did not appear to support humanoid life forms, it did provide a home for a smorgasbord of animals that prevented Rahmik from simply looking for heat signatures that might lead them to Ava. Each infrared search he performed revealed both land and ocean that teemed with life of all sizes.

As if on cue, a flock of birds that must have twelve-foot wingspans descended from the clouds and flew alongside the ship, casting it curious looks. One of the birds kept pace just outside the windshield as it peered in at them. It was beautiful. Its long beak, legs, and belly were jet-black. The feathers on its head were a stunningly bright turquoise that seemed almost to glow in comparison and formed a topknot similar to that of a cardinal. The blue segued into brilliant yellow and red on its back and wings while vibrant purple coated its chest.

Most striking of all, its tail—longer than that of a peacock—flowed behind it in a river of plumage that seemed to showcase every color of the rainbow.

The lovely creatures scattered as two of the Segonian fighter craft returned.

More fighters followed.

"Wait," someone said over the comm.

"Report, Anat," Dagon ordered.

"I saw something," the pilot said. "Changing heading now."

A long pause ensued, chipping away at Eliana's nerves. *Please. Please. Please.*

"Looks like something crashed through the trees here, but the canopy is so dense..." Another interminable minute passed.

"Escape pod located," Anat announced triumphantly and rattled off coordinates. "It looks like it's taken some damage."

"From a crash or from blasters and e-cannons?" Dagon asked.

"Hard to tell. The foliage is obscuring my view too much. I can't even see the whole pod, just enough to recognize it for what it is."

"Any signs of Ava or Jak'ri?"

"No, sir."

Dagon looked at Rahmik. "Has the rest of the squadron returned?"

"Yes, sir."

"Good. Galen, take us to the coordinates Anat sent. If the escape pod is there, the Gathendiens likely are, too, so stay vigilant."

"Always, sir."

"Rahmik, man every primary and secondary weapons station."

"Yes, Commander." Turning back to his console, he began to speak softly, summoning men to the bridge.

Dagon turned to Barus. "Assemble a team. We're losing light, and I want to see if we can find Ava and Jak'ri before the sun sets."

He nodded. "Will you be leading them?"

"Yes."

"I will, too," Eliana blurted. "I mean, I won't be leading them, but I want to go." Worried that Dagon might object, she turned to him and tapped her nose. "If Ava and Jak'ri aren't in the pod and I'm the first one on the scene, I should be able to track them." Maybe. If it hadn't rained since they had wandered off. "If your men land and scout the area first, I'll lose their scent."

He issued a curt nod. "Let's go arm up."

The two of them dropped by Eliana's quarters first so she could swiftly don the lightweight armor Joral had delivered shortly after her recovery. She couldn't tell if it was the same armor she had worn on the *Cebaun* or a new suit. But if it was the former, Joral's team had done a fantastic job repairing it. She saw no tears or scratches or blemishes of any kind.

All business now, Dagon helped her strap on her blades and the T-23 blaster he insisted she carry. Then they headed to his quarters. Eliana paced while he donned his suit of exo-armor. Tossing his helmet on the bed, he reached out and touched the wall. Not a button or a lever. Just a spot on the wall that looked no different from the rest.

A chime sounded. Then a panel slid back and revealed a wall of weapons not unlike the one Eliana had drooled over in Joral's workspace.

Her jaw dropped. "Has that been there all along?"

"Yes." He reached for an O-rifle and looped the strap over one shoulder.

"Why do you keep all those beauties hidden? If they were mine, I would leave them out in the open where I could gaze dreamily at them until I fell asleep."

He grinned as he retrieved two bags the size of large pants pockets and touched them to his thighs. Thunks sounded as magnets inside the bags fastened the pockets in place. He winked. "Maybe I want you to gaze dreamily at me instead."

"I already do that, sexy," she said, returning his smile. "What's in those?"

He patted the pockets. "Bex-7s in this one. Z-12s in this one."

She stared at him blankly.

"Bex-7s are stun grenades. Z-12s are e-grenades like the one you caught while observing Quoba, Tarok, and Brohko's training simulation. You don't want to be near either one of those when they go off."

"Good to know."

A knock sounded on the door. Dagon closed his private armory before he answered it.

Ziv'ri faced them out in the hallway. The Purveli stood straighter, his broad shoulders back now that his wounds had healed. He also bore a grimly determined expression. "I would like to accompany you to the planet's surface," he announced, then added, "if you would permit it." When Dagon hesitated, Ziv'ri continued earnestly, "My greatest hope is that Jak'ri and Ava both survived the landing or the crash and are simply awaiting our arrival. But if Ava *didn't* survive and Jak'ri sought shelter in the sea, I can find him."

Eliana hadn't thought of that. There was a *lot* of water down there. If they didn't find Jak'ri—or his remains (she cringed a little inside at that notion)—in the pod or elsewhere on the continent, Eliana wasn't sure how much time Dagon and his men would be willing to devote to searching the vast oceans, particularly since Jak'ri could have been recaptured by the Gathendiens and no longer even be on the planet.

Ziv'ri's gaze met and held hers. "And if Jak'ri didn't survive and Ava *did*, I owe it to my brother to help you find and protect her."

"Why?" she asked.

"Because I believe he has feelings for her."

That was unexpected. His earlier words about his brother being a danger to them and the Gathendiens using Ava as a weapon to force his compliance resurfaced.

If they torture her in front of him, he will do anything *and kill* anyone *to stop it. If that means taking every man on this ship down with a* senshi…

Eliana had thought it more of an act of chivalry or a desire to protect the more fragile female in their midst. She hadn't realized it might stem from a deeper attachment Jak'ri had formed with her.

How exactly had that happened while both were prisoners and being tortured?

And how had it happened so fast?

She glanced at Dagon and realized the latter wasn't much of a mystery. Hadn't she fallen hard for Dagon in a short period of time? And he had admitted he'd started falling for her the first time they spoke.

"Can you sense them?" she asked Ziv'ri. "Either one of them?" She didn't think her telepathic brethren could automatically sense the presence of another who shared their gift, but things might work differently for a Purveli.

"No. Chief Medical Officer Adaos has been injecting me with *nahalae*. But the latest dose should wear off soon. Once it does, the only thing that will impede me is distance."

Dagon shook his head. "You'll remain on the ship. If we don't find Ava and Jak'ri on land, I'll have a shuttle bring you down to search the ocean."

Ziv'ri dared to take a step inside the cabin. "I am not your enemy, Commander Dagon. If anything, I am in your debt. You and your people saved my life and are affording me the only opportunity I have of finding my brother. I will not harm your men."

"Unless your brother is being held by the Gathendiens and they threaten to kill him if you don't?" Dagon asked.

Eliana had been ready to have Ziv'ri join them, sympathizing with his plight, until Dagon posed that question.

The Purveli shook his head. "I can't issue a *senshi* until the *nahalae* wears off."

Dagon's expression didn't change. "You just said the *nahalae* would wear off while we're down on the planet."

"Even then, I couldn't do it without endangering Ava," Ziv'ri said. "My brother would never forgive me for that, nor would I forgive myself."

"And if your brother lives and Ava is dead?"

Eliana felt like someone had poured acid into her stomach.

Ziv'ri looked as disturbed as she felt at the suggestion. "If you distrust me, then dose your men and Eliana with both *nahalae* and *galaris* before we depart for the planet. Your medic can assure you that neither one prompts adverse side effects." His features creased in a faint grimace. "And though advising you of this makes me feel disloyal, I suggest you do that even if I *don't* accompany you."

So his brother couldn't harm them?

Dagon eyed him for a long, uncomfortable moment. "Have you completed any combat training?"

"Yes. Few outside our planet have attempted to attack my people, but our civilization is not without strife. We do occasionally war against each other."

Was it weird that Eliana felt a little relieved that Earth wasn't the only planet that still did that crap? Because both Lasara and Segonia were peaceful planets that lacked such conflict.

Dagon issued a curt nod. "Then you may accompany us, but you will remain unarmed. And if you decide to seek your freedom and run, we will leave you to whatever fate you meet here."

"Understood."

"Let's go."

The shuttle that carried Dagon, Eliana, Ziv'ri and fifteen soldiers down to the planet wasn't nearly as fancy as the royal transport that had conveyed the Earth women up to the *Kandovar*. That one had belonged to Prince Taelon, had been intended to ferry royalty to and from planets, and had shown it with plush carpeting, swanky sofas, a kitchen, bathroom, med bay, and even a bedroom. This one merely had a control room she mentally called a cockpit, rows of benches for the soldiers to sit on, a bare deck beneath their feet, and cargo space in back for whatever supplies they decided to bring along.

Dagon piloted the shuttle himself while Tugev occupied the copilot's seat. Eliana sat on the first bench behind them, squeezed between Maarev and Liden.

The latter kept smiling down at her.

She shook her head. "You're really starting to freak me out, Liden." When that merely broadened his grin, she looked up at Maarev and jerked her head in Liden's direction. "Seriously, what's up with this guy?"

Maarev sent his friend a smirk. "Probably just enjoying your company. Women don't usually let him get that close."

"Yes, they do," Liden protested indignantly.

"No, they don't."

"That big-breasted woman on Promeii 7 didn't mind me getting close to her."

Maarev snorted. "That wasn't a woman. That was a man."

"No, it wasn't."

"It may as well have been. Her shoulders were broader than yours."

Eliana smiled, reminded of the razzing Immortal Guardians and their Seconds often engaged in.

"Who cares how broad her shoulders were?" Liden quipped, his good humor restored. "Her breasts were a handful and her mouth—"

"Nope." Eliana threw up a hand. "I don't want to hear details."

Both men chuckled.

The view through the front windshield distracted her as they descended below the clouds.

Verdant forests stretched beneath them, some of the trees taller than the highest skyscrapers back home. Dagon flew down until the tips nearly brushed the belly of the shuttle. Most of the arboreal giants were green with some dark purple, almost black foliage mixed in here and there.

The shuttle slowed, then halted, hovering soundlessly near a hole the escape pod had punched through the canopy. Eliana leaned forward and peered down through it. The leaves of the trees that bracketed the gap reminded her of those on the elephant ear plants Nick's next-door neighbor Kayla had planted in her yard, except these were larger. Each frond had to be at least ten feet long and six and a half feet wide. Below them… far, *far* below them… the pale exterior of an escape pod slumped in the shadows. Not much of it was visible, but what she saw was dented and scorched.

Were Ava and Jak'ri in there? Were they hale and hearty and eager to be rescued and fed something other than nutrition bars? Were they trapped inside, unable to open the dented door? Did they hunker down in the tight confines to stay safe from whatever roamed the forest?

Were they even still alive?

Eliana kept her gaze fastened on what she could see of the pod. If Ava and Jak'ri lingered outside it, they didn't step into view or react to the shuttle hovering high above them. Not that the shuttle made any noise or stirred up any wind that might attract their attention. Even the sleek black fighter jets, she had discovered much to her amazement, moved soundlessly without blasting everything around them with wind or backwash.

"Heading in," Dagon murmured.

The shuttle lowered through the gap. The escape pod had broken a lot of branches on the way down, clearing a path of sorts for them. The light dimmed as they sank beneath the forest's thick canopy.

Eliana released a little sigh of relief. Dagon had assured her that the helmet that could spring out of her light armor's collar would protect her from sun exposure. But she couldn't track Ava's scent while wearing it and had dreaded seeing the other men's reactions if she had to venture into direct sunlight. What would they think when her skin began to swiftly pinken with a burn, then blistered and worse?

She had only suffered "worse" once and had no desire to do so again but *would* if it would help her find Ava.

Movement in the tree limbs drew her anxious gaze.

Furry animals leaped from branch to branch, their big eyes following the shuttle's descent. They were about the size of a large house cat and looked like a cross between a kangaroo and a lemur as they jumped or swung from tree to tree. Black and white stripes adorned their backs and long tails. A furry black mane framed triangular faces dominated by big brown eyes. They hooted back and forth to each other, the sounds so loud they carried easily into the shuttle.

"Awwwww. They're so cute," she said.

"I want one," the men behind her said in unison.

She laughed, knowing her fascination with everything alien amused them. "What do you think, Dagon? Can we take a couple back with us?"

"If we did," he said, deadpan, "they'd probably eat all your *jarumi* nuggets."

"Then they shall remain where they are," she promptly retorted.

The men chuckled.

Alas, the distraction the adorable animals provided was a short one. All her concerns returned with a vengeance as Dagon landed the shuttle near the escape pod with nary a bump or a shudder.

Please let them be okay, she wished fervently as she unlatched her harness. Rising, she grabbed her katanas, slipped her arms through straps attached to the scabbards, and settled them against her back.

Time to find Ava and Jak'ri.

CHAPTER 20

DAGON LOOPED THE strap of his bag over his head and one shoulder so it hung down his back, then grabbed his O-rifle.

Tugev slid into the pilot's seat he'd vacated, ready to lift off at a moment's notice, and immediately began to monitor the foreign environment.

Dagon had seen nothing in the shuttle's scans of the surrounding area that would indicate Gathendiens were in the area. But their scanners hadn't picked up Ziv'ri's presence on the *Ranasura* either, so he would rule nothing out.

"How's the atmosphere?" Maarev asked.

"Breathable," Dagon said. Even so, he and the other men lowered their helmet visors. He glanced down at Eliana. "But if I tell you to raise your helmet, do it immediately."

"Okay." She took a step toward the hatch.

Dagon grabbed her shoulder. "We go together, or you don't go at all." He knew she wanted to be the first one off the shuttle so he and his men wouldn't bury whatever scent she might catch of her friend, but there was a limit to how much he would allow her to risk.

The second "okay" she issued was more reluctant than the first, but she issued it nevertheless.

Dagon positioned himself to one side of the closed hatch with Eliana just behind him.

The rest of his men divided themselves into two groups. Half lined up behind Eliana. The other half—led by Maarev—lined up on the other side of the hatch. All had their rifles in hand, ready to fire. Ziv'ri brought up the rear.

"Any movement, Tugev?"

"No, Commander."

Dagon pressed a palm to the reader. The hatch opened. A ramp extended outward, then angled down until the far edge came to rest in the soft detritus that coated the forest floor. Hoots from the animals Eliana thought so cute floated down around them as the creatures swung in the trees above them and drew closer to observe the newcomers.

At least he hoped they merely intended to observe them. Even small animals on foreign planets could prove deadly in unexpected ways.

Rifle at the ready, his finger near the trigger, Dagon started down the ramp.

Eliana followed, issuing a faint grunt of annoyance when he wouldn't let her advance and walk beside him. Dagon didn't react. He would rather anger her than lose her. And if Gathendiens lay in wait for them, his exo-armor would shield her from blasts far better than the lightweight armor she wore.

Because the thick canopy above blocked much of the sun, the vegetation that sparsely inhabited the forest floor was neither tall enough nor thick enough to conceal an enemy. The tree trunks, on the other hand, were massive columns resulting from centuries of unchecked growth that made both the shuttle and the escape pod seem small. Each trunk could easily hide multiple enemy combatants.

At the base of the ramp, Dagon stopped. It surprised him a bit when Eliana did, too. But she was a warrior and must know that surrendering to one's impatience could lead to surrendering one's life.

Both remained still while he listened, watched, and waited. Translucent words and numbers scrolled down one side of his visor, confirming Tugev's determination that no enemies lurked nearby. In the skies far above them, Anat hovered in his fighter, ready to blast any Gathendien craft that might appear.

The rest of Dagon's men exited the shuttle. Most took up stances on the ramp. But a couple jumped down and circled around to guard the back.

At last, Dagon stepped aside so Eliana could join him but again stayed her before she could pass. Lowering his rifle, he let it hang down his front on its sling and drew his bag around to delve into it.

Silently she drew the katanas she loved so much and surveyed their surroundings with a piercing gaze while he retrieved a *ziyil* and the data tablet linked to it. Tossing the ball into the air, Dagon used the controls on the tablet to guide the *ziyil* into the partially open door of the escape pod's hatch. Light burst forth from within. Then the ball returned and hovered in the air before them.

Eliana's shoulders straightened and a muscle in her jaw leaped as she braced herself for whatever it would reveal.

Dagon tapped the screen. A three-dimensional holographic image appeared in the air above the globe.

Her breath rushed out.

Though the interior of the pod was cluttered, no bodies sprawled on the floor or in any of the four seats it boasted.

"It's empty," she whispered.

"Almost," he qualified. "The *ziyil* picked up a heat signature there." He pointed to a red splotch in one corner. "But it's too small to be Ava or Jak'ri."

"Maybe it's one of Eliana's future pets," Maarev murmured, looking up at the striped mammals that watched them curiously from the trees.

Dagon gave Eliana a nod.

Though every step she took away from him made his nerves jangle, he remained at the base of the ramp so he wouldn't muddy whatever trail remained with his scent or boot prints.

Eliana studied the ground carefully, pausing here and there before she continued on to the Gathendien escape pod. Scored and scorched in places, it had come to rest on its side with the hatch's opening a few hands higher than the top of her head. Once she stood beneath it, Eliana stared up at it. A few seconds later, the door swung wide open with a creak.

Dagon's men immediately crouched and aimed their weapons. When nothing burst forth from inside, Dagon concluded Eliana had merely exercised the telekinesis she'd mentioned.

Bending her knees, she leaped nimbly up into the entrance as if guided there by a hoverboard and disappeared from view.

For a long moment, no sound emerged. Dagon had seen firsthand how silently Eliana could move and wondered if she were creeping around in there or standing still and letting her senses explore.

Then a rustling noise reached his ears. He glanced toward the pod's hatch.

Rapid scuttling preceded the appearance of three small, fuzzy rodents. Upon spotting the soldiers outside, they leaped into the air and flung their paws wide. Flaps of skin stretched from the front paws to those in back, allowing them to catch the breeze and take flight. As soon as they reached the trunk of the closest tree, they skittered up it and out of sight.

Dagon lowered his gaze and studied the area again.

The rodents must have been the life form the *ziyil* detected.

Eliana appeared in the hatch's entrance and jumped to the ground, landing with practiced ease. "Ava and Jak'ri were definitely in there, but their scent was almost buried beneath that of Gathendiens and the little squirrel things that just scampered out of it. The Gathendien scent was the strongest, so they've definitely been here."

"And may still be on the planet," Dagon finished.

She nodded, face grim. "There was blood. Old, not fresh. And not enough to indicate someone had bled out. I also found some discarded bandages, so at least one of them—Ava or Jak'ri—is injured." She circled the area, studying the ground. A few times she knelt and drew a long breath in through her nose.

Though Dagon remained where he was, he too studied the ground. Crushed leaves and disrupted dirt revealed multiple boot prints.

"Damn, those Gathendiens stink," she muttered.

He could smell nothing in his helmet, thanks to the air filtration it provided. "How many, do you think?"

She shook her head. "I can't say for sure because the boot prints crisscross each other. But a lot. Maybe twice as many men as we have with us."

He'd drawn a similar conclusion. "Did they recapture Ava and

Jak'ri here?"

"I don't think so. The Gathendiens' tracks seem to radiate out from here in all directions as if they weren't sure where to begin their search." Her brow furrowed as she studied the ground. "I can't find any of Ava's prints. I don't know if they're buried beneath the others or if maybe she was carried away."

Dagon glanced at his men and jerked his head. "Spread out. See what you can find." Joining Eliana, he helped her scour the ground and vegetation for clues.

Frustration filled her pretty features. "All I smell this way are the Gathendiens."

And all he saw were large boot prints and the snakelike tracks their tails left.

Long minutes passed.

"Commander Dagon." Liden spoke softly over the helmet's comm. "I found something. Two *veks* east of the pod."

Eliana glanced up at him, hope and dread warring in her brown eyes.

He touched her shoulder. "This way." After leading her back to the escape pod, he circled around it and headed east.

Liden waited in the distance, his silver armor standing out starkly against the foliage.

As soon as Dagon and Eliana joined him, Liden squatted down and drew back the lacy leaves of a low-growing plant.

Eliana's breath caught.

There in the dried mud and decaying leaves lay the outline of a small bare foot. A larger print—that of a man Dagon's size—rested beside it.

The land behind the pod sloped down, forming a shallow basin that must hold rainwater whenever it managed to seep through the canopy, because the ground here was not as dry as that he had searched earlier and held more clearly discernible footprints.

"She's limping," Eliana murmured.

Dagon agreed. It appeared Jak'ri was helping her along.

Eliana sheathed her swords and knelt. Leaning close to nearby plants, she again drew in a deep breath and held it. A moment later she nodded. "I have her scent. Jak'ri's, too." Rising, she moved as though she intended to take off after them.

"Wait," he murmured.

She complied, shifting from foot to foot while he issued orders to his squad.

A third of his men would accompany Dagon and Eliana. A third would remain with the shuttle. And a third would track the Gathendiens.

Four of his soldiers joined them, accompanied by Ziv'ri.

As soon as Dagon nodded to her, Eliana palmed two daggers and took off. She made almost no sound as she strode forward, her pace swift. Her head tilted downward, her gaze focused on the ground. Dagon remained close to her and kept a sharp eye out for signs of danger she might miss while concentrating on the tracks.

She halted suddenly, then backtracked.

Dagon and the others stayed out of her way as she walked in a slow circle.

The ground here was flatter, drier. He could find no discernible tracks.

She walked several paces in a northeasterly direction and sniffed, walked toward the southeast and sniffed. Nodding, she took off again, heading east-southeast. The ground began to slope up sharply, rapidly approaching a climb. After a few more stops and starts, the sound of running water reached them.

Dagon motioned for the group to tighten up. Quietly they crept forward. Plant life on the forest floor thickened, providing cover behind which Gathendiens or dangerous wildlife might lurk. Rocks and boulders topped with orange and green moss appeared. Birds twittered. Hoots filled the air above them as some of Eliana's furry friends swung past, then dropped to the ground and hopped forward. Dagon thought he spotted some of those little rodents that had camped out in the escape pod before they ducked out of sight.

Easing forward, he peered through the brush. A wide stream bounced and burbled its way over a rocky bed. No large predators currently drank from it, only the little hooting mammals. A couple of birds bathed in the shallows.

He stepped into the open, Eliana only a breath away.

When no Gathendiens leaped out at them, she lowered her gaze to the ground once more. Dagon stood guard while she searched, her movements becoming stiffer with frustration.

"I can't find any tracks, and I've lost their scent," she growled in a whisper.

Dagon nodded to his men.

All spread out to see what they could find while Ziv'ri remained with Dagon and Eliana.

"This would be a whole lot easier," she grumbled, "if we could just call their names."

Alas, the Gathendiens' possible presence precluded that.

She looked up at Ziv'ri. "What about you? Has the *nahalae* started to wear off yet? Are you able to get anything?"

He glanced around, brow furrowing. His lips tightened as he closed his eyes. After a long moment, he loosed a huff of impatience and opened them. "The effects of the *nahalae* are weakening, but I'm not sensing anything."

"Here," Liden murmured over the comm channel.

Dagon used the map on his visor to locate him, then led Eliana and Ziv'ri across the stream and through the brush on the other side.

The land here became even rockier. Liden waved them over and jerked his head in the direction of some boulders. "There's a cave." He pointed to a crevice between two rocks that didn't look wide enough for a man to fit through, then motioned to the ground where a small footprint lay atop a larger one.

Dagon activated the lights on his helmet but could not see far into the crevice, which seemed to wend to the right. He tried to squeeze into it but couldn't even fit when he turned sideways. He swore. "I'll have to remove my armor." Even then, he wasn't confident he could make it.

"No, you won't," Eliana said. "I'll go."

He wanted to balk at the notion but thought her small enough to navigate it. "Take a flashlight."

"I don't need it. I have excellent night vision."

"Some of the native wildlife probably does as well. I doubt a Gathendien could fit through there, but predators and serpents can. If they're nocturnal, blinding them with the flashlight will buy you time to either kill them or flee."

She sent him a rueful smile and took the flashlight he fished out of his bag. "Thank you. I'm not used to having to worry about that kind of thing. The only predators I faced on a regular basis on Earth were vampires." She started to duck between the large rocks, then paused and turned back to him. The corners of her lips tilted up in the first faint smile he'd seen since they left the *Ranasura*. "Mind if I cop a feel, handsome?"

He smiled back, familiar with the Earth phrase. "*Srul* no."

Sliding closer to him, she rested a palm on the side of his waist, then slid it down his armor and delved into the bag on one of his thighs. When she stepped back, she held a Bex-7 stun grenade. She winked. "Just in case."

In the next instant, she was gone, slipping through the crack. Dagon and Liden faced the cave entrance, rifles at the ready while Ziv'ri paced and the other men watched their backs.

Minutes passed.

Ziv'ri caught Dagon's eye. "Got another flashlight?"

Dagon fished a second light from his bag.

Ziv'ri took it and turned it on. Swiveling to the side, he wedged himself into the crevice. The Purveli wore no armor, not even the lightweight armor Eliana had donned. And his long stay with the Gathendiens had left him lean enough to squeeze through and disappear from sight.

Liden shot Dagon a look. "You sure you trust him at Eliana's back?"

"No," he answered honestly. "But I trust Eliana to be able to kick his ass if he tries anything nefarious."

More minutes passed. Quiet fell, broken only by birdsong as the hooting mammals Eliana thought so cute grew bored and wandered off.

A pebble rolled out of the crevice and leaves rustled as Eliana shimmied out of it. A streak of dirt traveled horizontally across her breasts, another across her bottom, revealing how tight a squeeze it had been. A cobweb dusted her left side from her hair to her biceps.

Dagon reached out and thumped a bright yellow-and-white arachnid perched on her shoulder, sending it flying.

She glanced down, then grimaced. "Do you see any more?" She turned in a slow circle as Ziv'ri emerged behind her.

Dagon swiped at the webs. "No."

"Good."

Many more dirt streaks marred Ziv'ri's borrowed clothing, attesting—along with the grimace on his face and the scrapes on his arms—to how hard it had been for him to follow her despite his weight loss.

She motioned to the hidden cave. "They aren't here, but they were. It's slow going getting in there, but it opens up once you do."

Dagon finished sweeping the cobwebs off her. "They were both in there?"

She nodded. "There's no way any of the Gathendiens I've seen could get in there. I doubt you could either, Dagon. It's a good place to hunker down and wait for reinforcements. There's even a water source nearby. I don't know why they didn't stay."

Ziv'ri caught Dagon's eye. "The Gathendiens brought *sedapas* with them."

He swore. "You're sure?"

"Yes. I found their prints and spoor in the cave."

Eliana looked back and forth between them. "What are *sedapas*?"

Dagon's translator could find no Earth English equivalent. "They're spiked lizards that are nearly as long as you are tall. They scent things through their tongues and have an excellent sense of smell. They also have poisonous saliva and three rows of teeth that rend and tear flesh easily. The Gathendiens use them for hunting."

She blinked. "Of course they do. Because Ava and Jak'ri's situation wasn't already bad enough without poisonous alien hunting lizards chasing them."

Dagon rested a gauntleted hand on her lower back and gave her a sympathetic pat. "Let's see if we can pick up their trail again."

It ended up not being as difficult as he'd thought it would be. Ava and Jak'ri must have been in more of a hurry when they left. If Jak'ri had seen or heard the *sedapas*, he wouldn't have wanted to wait around.

Dagon and the others picked up their pace as the tracks became easier to follow. Down the hillside the trail took them until Eliana slowed with a grimace and a look of dread eclipsed her features.

"What is it?"

She brought the back of a hand to her nose. "Something dead."

He touched the side of his helmet. As soon as his visor lifted, he grimaced.

Something or someone had definitely died.

He lowered his visor. The exo-armor's air filtration system swiftly eliminated the carrion odor.

Eliana turned suddenly and stared into the foliage ahead. "Someone's coming," she whispered at the same time red dots appeared on his helmet's display, identifying several heat signatures approaching them.

Dagon and his men raised their weapons.

Eliana slid a hand down to the hilt of the dagger lashed to her thigh, then relaxed. "It's Maarev."

Dagon shared a look with Liden. Maarev had been tracking the Gathendiens who ransacked the escape pod. If the Gathendiens' tracks had led him here, then Ava and Jak'ri might have found themselves trapped between two contingents.

They continued forward until they met Maarev and his team.

Maarev jerked a thumb over his shoulder. "The Gathendiens we tracked stayed together until about four *veks* that way, then split up. Half the tracks continued west, the other half led us here."

Dagon glanced around. Numerous sticks and twigs were broken, clods of dirt had been kicked up, and blood speckled the ground.

"They put up a hell of a fight," Eliana murmured, studying the scene.

In truth, Dagon could not determine who had emerged the victor. He spied at least four places where blood had pooled beneath a body and seeped into the dirt. Insects crawled all over it, scavenging what they could. Clouds of more hovered over a shrub that had one boot sticking out of it. A quick look confirmed a Gathendien corpse lay behind it. A couple of dead *sedapas* lay not far away.

"What the hell are those?" Eliana asked, her face scrunching up in disgust as she stared at them. "Or what *were* they?" With her superior sense of smell, the gag-inducing odor must be unbearable.

"*Sedapas*," he told her.

"They look like spiky Komodo dragons with two tails."

At least she had something on Earth to liken them to.

A couple of places indicated that large bodies had been dragged away. Each trail led them to Gathendien corpses that had been gutted and mutilated.

Again Eliana grimaced. "Are Gathendiens cannibals?"

"No." He motioned to a large paw print. "Looks like predators feasted upon them."

She placed her booted foot beside the paw print and stared. Two of her feet could easily fit inside one print. "*Large* predators."

"Yes." He glanced around. "Let's keep moving in case they decide to return for another meal."

This time Dagon found the tracks that led them away from the carnage.

"I'm feeling cautiously optimistic," Eliana murmured, her eyes on the trail as they headed toward the coast. Every once in a while they caught glimpses of prints left by bare feet, almost buried beneath those left by boots.

"I am as well," he said.

Ava and Jak'ri had survived the escape pod crashing or being shot down. They had found shelter. They even appeared to have survived whatever confrontation had taken place in that bloody clearing. He didn't think it out of the realm of possibility that they might still be breathing and thwarting any Gathendiens that might remain on the planet.

Red warnings flashed on Dagon's visor. He held up a hand.

Eliana raised her eyebrows.

"Multiple heat signatures up ahead," he whispered. "None of them belong to my men."

Eyes narrowing, she looked in the direction they were traveling. When she reached over her shoulders to clasp the hilt of a katana, he stayed her hand.

Dagon looked at his men, issued several hand signals, and received nods all around. Drawing a tablet-sized board from his bag, he snapped off one corner and dropped the larger piece. It instantly expanded into a hoverboard just long and wide enough for a man to stand on with his feet braced a shoulder's width apart.

His men all did the same.

Eliana's eyes widened.

Dagon stepped onto the hoverboard and held out his hand. She eagerly took it and stepped up onto the board too. Positioning her small feet between his, she wrapped an arm around his waist.

"Hold on tight," he murmured.

She nodded.

The entire team silently rose high into the trees, then eased forward with Dagon and Eliana in the lead. Dappled sunlight shone ahead where the forest ended. Voices reached his ears shortly before he slowed to a halt. Shielded by blanket-sized leaves, he and the others peered down at the figures below. Fourteen Gathendien soldiers occupied a brief meadow that stretched between the forest's edge and a jagged cliff. Some of the soldiers skinned a couple of large mammals they had killed, preparing to roast them over a campfire. A few slept in the shade where a tarp offered dubious protection from the elements. Those would likely keep watch while the others rested tonight. A few more sat around a fire just beginning to blaze.

But three of the Gathendiens stood close to the cliff's edge, conversing while they stared over the side where thick ropes disappeared.

The drop to the water below was a long one. From this angle, Dagon couldn't see what snared their attention.

They're looking for Jak'ri and Ava.

He started when Ziv'ri spoke in his head. Some of his men did, too.

Eliana didn't. Perhaps her previous experience with telepaths made it feel less invasive or disconcerting.

Dagon glanced over his shoulder.

Ziv'ri stood on a hoverboard beside Maarev's. The *nahalae* must have worn off, enabling him to utilize his telepathy.

Maarev held up two controllers, silently letting Dagon know he controlled both his and the Purveli's hoverboards.

Good. Such would prevent Ziv'ri from making impulsive actions that might endanger the rest of them.

Ava and Jak'ri are still alive? Eliana asked.

Dagon blinked. Was Ziv'ri a strong enough telepath that he could broadcast mental conversations he had with people?

If so, how strong a *senshi* could such a mind create?

I don't know, Ziv'ri answered. *The Gathendiens tracked them here a few days ago. The trail ended at the cliff's edge, but no bodies lay at the base of the cliff, so the Gathendiens believe Ava and Jak'ri sought safety in the sea.*

Eliana bit her lip. *Ava might be a strong swimmer, but she can't hold her breath for days.*

Dagon caught the Purveli's eye. *Ziv'ri, can you let her hear me?*

Yes.

He gave Eliana's waist a light squeeze. *They could have swum parallel to the coast and returned to the forest once they left their pursuers' sight.*

She nodded, indicating she'd heard him.

But Ziv'ri shook his head. *Based on what I'm seeing in the Gathendiens' minds, this cliff is impossible to climb without hoverboards or other gear and stretches as far as they can see in both directions.*

Dagon watched one of the lizard-men at the cliff's edge kneel and reach down. A gloved hand clasped his. Then the Gathendien helped one of his fellow soldiers clamber up over the edge.

That one sprawled on his back a moment, then rose and shuffled toward the campfire, his leathery armor wet, every movement radiating fatigue.

Two more soggy reptilian males followed.

There seems to be some disagreement among them, Ziv'ri murmured. *Half of them believe their former prisoners died in the fall from the cliff and merely hope to recover the bodies so the Gathendien emperor won't have them executed for failing to keep the prisoners in custody. Most of the rest believe Jak'ri still lives and Ava is dead, her body likely consumed by some of the ocean's larger aquatic creatures, which have slain two Gathendiens thus far.*

And the rest? Eliana asked.

One of them thinks they both still live. He pointed to a small island so far away Dagon could barely glimpse it. *They searched that island and found nothing. But he speculates there might be caves beneath it that can only be accessed through the ocean.*

Eliana met Dagon's gaze, her brown eyes flaring with hope.

Are you a strong swimmer? he asked her.

Very strong, she replied instantly. *And I can hold my breath for a long time. I mean, a looooooooooong time.*

He nodded, then sent Ziv'ri a speculative look.

If they're down there, the Purveli said, *I'll find them.* He glanced at Eliana, then back at Dagon. *And I can protect her from any aquatic predators we may encounter.*

Dagon returned his attention to Eliana. *We'll handle the Gathendiens while you two search.*

Okay. She looked down at the Gathendiens. Then her lips turned up in a mischievous smile. *You want me to divert their attention and freak them out a little on my way so they won't see you coming?*

He grinned. *Do what you do best,* milessia.

She hugged him as well as she could while he was encased in armor. *I would so kiss you right now if you weren't wearing a helmet.*

He raised his visor.

As soon as he did, Eliana rose up on her tiptoes and planted a scorching-hot, thought-scattering, lust-inducing kiss on his lips. *Lower me to the ground, babe, so I can wreak some bloody havoc.*

Drek, he loved her.

He and the others retreated, letting the forest swallow them once more before they descended to the forest floor.

As soon as he released her, Eliana started to unfasten her armor.

Dagon stared. *What are you doing?*

I'll swim faster with fewer clothes and no boots on.

She would also be completely vulnerable to the Gathendiens' blasterfire and whatever beasts the ocean might throw at her once she dove in.

Hold my katanas for a minute.

Dagon took her weapons, silently reminding himself that she was—in her words—*very* hard to kill. But it did little to assuage his fear for her. Once she hit the water, he would have no way of knowing what happened to her. She said she could hold her breath for a long time, but how long was that? Minutes? Hours? How long was *too* long? How would he know if she was just holding her breath longer than he thought she could or if something had gone terribly wrong? They didn't know what lay beneath the surface. She had never mentioned engaging in battle underwater. What if—?

I will keep you apprised, Ziv'ri said.

Dagon glanced at him and found the Purveli peeling off his clothing, too.

And I will protect her with my life, the male vowed.

That thought would comfort Dagon more if he knew Ziv'ri better and if the male were in good health.

Ziv'ri stripped down to his underwear, which consisted of the stretchy, formfitting shorts that were standard issue in the Segonian military. Though he had gained some weight during the two weeks they'd scoured the planet, his ribs were still prominent beneath the lean muscle that remained.

Beside Ziv'ri, Maarev looked past Dagon. His eyes widened.

Dagon swung around and nearly broke the silence with an obscenity. Eliana had stripped down to her underwear as well, which consisted of a lacy garment she called a bra and tiny matching panties. Both were black and stood out starkly against her pale skin.

Soooo much pale skin.

His gaze traveled down over her full breasts, narrow waist, and lightly muscled abdomen to her shapely legs and tiny bare feet.

And his wasn't the only gaze that feasted upon her.

He shot his men a glare.

She glanced at Ziv'ri and tapped her temple, then looked up at Dagon. *Can I stow my other weapons in your bag?* she asked, all business, oblivious to the men's regard.

Nodding, he turned his back so she could tuck her smaller blades inside.

Once she finished, she looped her arms through the straps attached to her katana sheaths and let them settle against her back. Then she tucked her smallest dagger into one of the narrow straps of her panties at her hip. She looked up. *Everyone ready?*

The others swiftly focused their eyes on her face and nodded.

Maarev, she asked, *can you use the hoverboard thingy to help Ziv'ri keep up with me?*

Maarev looked at Dagon.

He nodded.

Yes.

Ziv'ri stepped back onto the hoverboard.

Eliana met the Purveli's silver eyes. *I'll see you in the water.*

Ziv'ri nodded. *See you in the water.*

She looked up at Dagon. *And I'll be careful.*

Before lowering his visor, he bent and gave her another quick kiss.

You be careful, too, she entreated.

I will. Give us a fifty count to get into position.

Okay. Stepping back, she drew her katanas and flashed them all a grin. *Who's ready to kick some Gathendien ass?*

We are!

Her eyes flashed with amber light as she backed away, swung her katanas in a flourish, then gave them a cocky salute.

As one, the men rose on their hoverboards and zipped forward to surround the Gathendiens' makeshift camp, this time in full camouflage. Dagon issued several hand signals, then settled in to wait.

"*Woooooooooooo-hoooooooooo!*" Eliana bellowed suddenly somewhere down below as if she were playing on a hoverboard and having the time of her life.

He tensed.

The Gathendiens did, too. Leaping to their feet, they looked around wildly.

Loud rustling erupted in the forest. Knowing how silently Eliana could tread, he wondered with some amusement if she were racing through it with her katanas held straight out to the sides, because it sounded as though some large beast careened toward the coast.

Three *sedapas* that had been sunning themselves on rocks turned to the forest and snarled, baring rows of jagged teeth.

The Gathendiens reached for their weapons… too late.

A small form shot from the foliage in a blur. Blood sprayed from bare necks and bellies as Eliana charged through them.

Once again, Dagon marveled at her speed. If he hadn't anticipated her appearance, he wouldn't have known what the *srul* was happening.

Several Gathendiens staggered backward while the rest blurted cries of alarm. Two dropped to their knees, blood pouring down their chests.

Then Eliana hit the edge of the cliff and jumped.

Dagon's heart nearly stopped beating as she took off like a missile, sailing far… far… *far* across the ocean. *Drekking* amazing!

"Come and get me, boys!" she taunted as her momentum finally slowed long enough for them all to spy her… and the obscene Segonian hand gesture she turned to direct at the Gathendiens before she laughed, drew her arms over her head, and pierced the blue water with a graceful dive that sparked almost no splash.

Ziv'ri zipped past Dagon and shot out over the ocean on his hoverboard.

The Gathendiens who weren't injured grabbed their weapons and raced to the edge of the cliff.

Dagon and his team moved in and started firing before the Gathendiens could shoot the Purveli. They remained on the hoverboards long enough to dispatch the *sedapas,* then leaped off so the boards wouldn't give away their positions.

The Gathendiens swung around, not one of them wearing the infrared goggles that would clue them in to their attackers' positions. And the battle began in earnest.

The last thing Dagon saw as blasters and rifles fired was Ziv'ri executing a dive as graceful as Eliana's and disappearing into the ocean.

CHAPTER 21

ELIANA CUT THROUGH the cool, blue water like a torpedo. The salt it bore stung her eyes, but the water was so clear she could see for miles.

The sand far below her was a dark purplish gray. In startling contrast, coral bloomed like a flower garden, boasting every color of the rainbow as crustaceans scavenged and a fascinating array of fish—large and small—zigzagged through it like cars on freeways.

With powerful strokes, she arrowed toward the island in the distance.

Movement in the periphery of her vision drew her attention.

She glanced over.

Something that looked like a dolphin with the markings of a killer whale and a narwhal horn swam beside her. Another joined it. And another. Then more appeared on her other side until half a dozen bracketed her.

She eyed them warily, never slowing. Those horns looked like they could do a lot of damage… and likely would if they decided she'd make a tasty treat. She had no experience at all fighting underwater.

Fortunately, they didn't seem inclined to harm her. Rather, they watched her curiously as they kept pace.

She smiled, elation filling her. How long had it been since she had swum with dolphins and seals and some of the other wonderful sea creatures back on Earth? Perhaps sensing the pleasure she took in their presence, her sleek companions cavorted playfully, swimming circles around her, darting forward to show off their speed, then falling back to meander beside her.

The lovelies on her left suddenly veered away, leaving a gap between her and them.

A new form appeared at her elbow. Ziv'ri, cutting through the water as swiftly as Eliana and matching her preternatural speed, his dark hair now silver.

Wow. He was *fast* in the water. That bit of webbing between his fingers and toes must really make a difference.

He issued her a brief nod. *I see you've made some friends.*

She grinned. *Yes. Are you getting anything from Jak'ri yet?*

No. We may still be too far away.

The dolphin-like creatures resumed their play, apparently deeming Ziv'ri a friend.

What about a senshi? she asked. *If he's at that island, would he hear it from here and respond so we could at least know we're going in the right direction?*

If he's in the water near the island, he'll hear it.

Would it hurt these guys? She glanced at their swimming partners.

No. They've bounced several mild ones off me since I joined you, trying to communicate with me.

Then go ahead and do the senshi *thing.*

Would you like to surface while I do it? Water mutes the effects, but it may still prove uncomfortable for you. And any senshi *I emit underwater won't extend above it.*

Okay. I need to take a breath anyway. And we should be beyond shooting distance of the cliff now.

He smiled. *I think you were beyond shooting distance before you even hit the water.*

Smiling, Eliana angled upward. Though she wanted to burst onto the surface and drag in a great gulp of air, she slowed to nearly a standstill, then gently poked her head above the water so as not to draw attention.

Half a dozen of her new aquatic friends burst out of the water around her, leaping high and splashing as they emitted squeaky calls.

Sputtering, she wiped her eyes and smiled wryly. So much for not attracting attention.

She swiveled to face the cliff, surprised to see bright flashes of light. She'd thought the battle would be over by now. The Gathendiens must really be putting up a fight.

Either that or reinforcements had arrived.

As she drew in several deep breaths, she tried to distinguish Dagon's form from the others, but the Segonian soldiers were all camouflaged and the dolphin things kept splashing her.

Jak'ri didn't respond to my senshi.

She frowned. *If Ava's with him, they may not be in the water.*

Such was my thought. Are you ready to resume?

Yes.

She filled her lungs with a deep breath, then dipped beneath the surface and dove down to join Ziv'ri.

She wasn't certain how much time passed before she noticed shadowy forms swimming toward them from the island. *Company's coming,* she warned, uncertain how sharp Ziv'ri's vision might be.

I see them.

Maybe they heard your senshi *and are coming to investigate.*

Maybe.

But it ended up being more of the playful dolphin-like creatures.

They were here! Ziv'ri suddenly exclaimed in her head.

What?

Jak'ri and Ava. They were here. I can see them in the creature's minds – the ones swimming toward us. They followed Jak'ri and Ava to the island the way these are following us.

Excitement and hope lent Eliana's strokes greater speed. Soon even their aquatic friends couldn't keep up as she and Ziv'ri powered forward. The island loomed closer. The ocean floor began to slope up toward the beach.

Ziv'ri? an unfamiliar male voice said in her head.

Eliana nearly sucked in a mouthful of water she was so startled.

Yes! Ziv'ri exclaimed. *I'm coming, Jak'ri. Where are you?*

Silence followed.

Eliana glanced over at Ziv'ri and saw him nod. Perhaps Jak'ri had switched to a more private mental channel.

Ziv'ri slowed and looked at Eliana. *He showed me the way. You'll need to take another breath before we enter the caverns.*

Okay. She surfaced and drew several deep breaths into her burning lungs.

Afterward, she let Ziv'ri take the lead.

He swam around to a dark tunnel that appeared to be made of lava rock. Perhaps this island used to be volcanically active and this and the other tunnels that branched off it were extinct lava tubes.

Ziv'ri proved he did indeed have excellent vision, for he had no difficulty navigating the many dark twists and turns. Light appeared at the end of the tunnel they currently navigated. Then the walls around them opened up into a large subterranean lake. The water in here was as clear as that which they had just left. Long, towering strands of something that resembled kelp stretched up from the bottom, the sand at their base black as night rather than purplish gray.

Eliana kept pace with Ziv'ri as he swam for the opposite side, careful not to get tangled in the marine plants.

The water grew shallower.

Splashes disturbed the surface as two legs ending in bare feet invaded the waters ahead.

Eliana broke the surface the same time Ziv'ri did and looked around. The lake took up half a cavern the size of a football field. Some kind of bioluminescent ore bisected the black rock that formed the high ceiling and walls with deep veins that emitted blue light bright enough for her to see clearly without the enhanced night vision immortality granted her. Pink moss coated some of the stalagmites, stalactites, and rocks near the water's edge, emitting dim light of its own, increasing visibility even more.

A man wearing ragged pants and nothing else who closely resembled Ziv'ri waded forward and yanked Ziv'ri into a tight hug. "I thought you dead," he uttered, his voice hoarse with emotion… or perhaps with illness. He looked about as bad as Ziv'ri had when they'd pried him out of that blue suit. "They said they killed you, and I could no longer sense you. Ava couldn't either."

Ziv'ri hugged his brother. "They lied."

A body slammed into Eliana, knocking her backward while she was distracted by the men. Her feet slipped on some of that pink moss, and down she went. Water closed over her head. Then arms locked around her and swiftly helped her find her footing.

She came up sputtering.

"Sorry!" a familiar voice cried. "I'm sorry, Eliana. I'm just so happy to see you."

"Ava." Eliana stared at her friend but had only enough time to note tousled hair and a gash on her friend's forehead before Ava threw her arms around her and squeezed the heck out of her. Eliana hugged her back, tears pricking the backs of her eyes.

She'd survived. Ava had survived!

Ava released a pained grunt.

Jak'ri released his brother and stretched a hand toward them, his brow furrowing. "Careful. She's injured."

Alarmed, Eliana immediately released Ava and stepped back to assess her.

"I'm okay," Ava said. Then her sweet smile faltered as she staggered.

Emitting a cry, Eliana reached for her.

But Ava turned to Jak'ri and reached for *him*.

He quickly grasped her hands and pulled her closer, looping an arm around her waist.

"Oh crap," she muttered. "I'm *not* okay. I'm think I'm gonna…" Her eyes rolled back as her knees buckled.

Jak'ri caught her and lifted her into his arms, strong despite his apparent fragility.

"Ava?" Eliana called.

"She's unconscious," Jak'ri stated, expression grim as he carried her out of the water and over to an area they had made into a camp of sorts. Kneeling, he carefully laid her on a bed of those massive leaves that reminded Eliana of elephant ears.

"What's wrong with her?" she asked. "What happened?"

"The Gathendiens happened."

Eliana knelt beside him and examined Ava's still form. Her skin was a sickly shade of pale. A pair of undershorts somewhat similar to those Dagon wore beneath his uniform covered her pelvis and the tops of her thighs. But they sagged loosely, revealing hipbones made more prominent from the days or weeks she had been tortured. Or perhaps from not finding adequate sustenance here on the planet. Bandages that must have once been white but now bore pink and gray streaks wrapped around and around her breasts and shoulders, forming something similar to a sports bra. More bandages—stained with red splotches—adorned her arms, one thigh, and her midriff, adhered there by a clear rubbery substance.

"I managed to grab one of the Gathendiens' med kits when we escaped," Jak'ri said. "I tended her wounds as well as I could. And she seemed to improve for a time." Resting a hand on her forehead, he tenderly brushed her hair back. "But she was injured again when more Gathendiens attacked us and has weakened since we came here." He nodded at the cave that surrounded them.

Eliana looked up at Ziv'ri. "Go to Dagon. The fighting should be over by the time you reach him. Tell him Ava needs immediate medical attention and see if they can land the shuttle on the island."

Nodding, Ziv'ri sent his brother a look, then turned and dove into the water.

Jak'ri rose and moved away.

Eliana rested her hand where Jak'ri's had been, smoothing a thumb across Ava's forehead. Her friend felt a little warm but wasn't raging with fever. "Ava?"

"She's been tired and sluggish for a few days now." Returning, Jak'ri knelt on the other side of Ava. One large hand now held something that resembled a hollowed-out coconut with a rind similar to an orange. The other held a ragged piece of cloth the same color as his pants. He dipped the rag into the water in his makeshift bowl, squeezed out the excess, then draped it across Ava's forehead.

"I'm Eliana." She extended her hand.

He clasped her arm. "I'm Jak'ri. Ava has mentioned you often. She said you were the one who enabled her to escape the *Kandovar* before it was destroyed, that you put her in the escape pod."

"Yes." She took Ava's hand. "I'm sorry it took me so long to find her." She mustered a faint smile. "To find *both* of you. But I was lost myself for a while."

He nodded. "She feared you hadn't survived."

"I nearly didn't."

"What of the others?" He resumed stroking Ava's hair. "The other women from Earth? Ava has been very worried about them."

Eliana swallowed the lump that rose in her throat. "So far only one other has been found. She's safe on Lasara. We're still searching for the rest."

Silence fell between them, not awkward, just chock-full of concern for the pale woman who lay between them.

After some time, Jak'ri glanced over her shoulder.

Splashing sounded.

As Eliana turned, Ziv'ri strode out of the water.

"The transport was already hovering above the island when I left the caverns," he said.

A large form encased in exo-armor rose up behind him, water sluicing off it and obscuring the wearer's face. The helmet's visor slid up.

"Dagon." Rising, Eliana hurried past Ziv'ri and threw herself into Dagon's arms.

He hugged her tight. "You're all right?"

She nodded. "You?"

"I'm well. Ziv'ri said Ava requires medical attention."

Again she nodded, her throat tight. "She's injured and lost consciousness right after we arrived."

He patted her back as more exo-armor-clad forms exited the water behind him. "The *Ranasura* arrived just as the battle ended. It's positioned above the island now."

One of the armor-clad warriors behind him raised his helmet's visor.

Relief rushed through her. "Adaos."

"Dagon said you require a medic."

"Ava does. She's right over there." She pointed to where Jak'ri stood protectively beside Ava's pallet.

Adaos strode past her, issuing orders as he moved to tend his new patient.

Jak'ri stuck close to Ava, refusing to relinquish her hand as Adaos passed his precious handheld scanner over her.

When Adaos didn't appear unduly alarmed by Ava's condition, more of the tension that knotted Eliana's shoulders and back eased.

"We found her," Dagon murmured, his voice a reassuring rumble.

Eliana nodded and hugged him tighter, wishing they weren't separated by his armor.

As though he wished the same, he released her long enough to remove his helmet and set it aside, then drew her into his arms once more. He pressed a kiss to her wet hair, then rested his chin atop her head. "We'll take good care of her, *milessia.*"

She knew they would. "Thank you."

Eliana grinned as she watched Ava's eyes well with tears. "I warned you it was spicy."

Ava nodded as she swiftly chewed the mouthful of *vestuna*, then lunged for her glass of *naga* juice.

Eliana and Dagon sat side by side at their favorite table in the mess hall while Ava sat across from them, wedged between Jak'ri and Ziv'ri. Both Purveli males were endearingly protective of her. But only Jak'ri gazed at her as if she were his entire world.

After downing several quick gulps, Ava set her glass down. "Wow," she wheezed. "You weren't kidding."

"Nope. But it's good, right?"

Sniffling, she scooped up more. "Delicious."

Jak'ri cast her a dubious look. Ava smiled at him as she chewed.

A long moment passed, during which Eliana suspected they were conversing telepathically.

Amusement filled Jak'ri's silver eyes. Then he winked and bumped his arm against her shoulder.

Eliana didn't know much about the Purveli male, but he clearly adored Ava. He hadn't left her side longer than it took to use the lav while she recovered in Med Bay. Though her physical wounds were gone now, Eliana suspected it would take the psychological wounds instilled in Ava by her captors longer to heal. Her friend now suffered nightmares every time she slept. When she had admitted she dreaded closing her eyes, Eliana had asked Adaos to give Ava a private recovery room so Jak'ri could climb into bed with her and hold her when the nightmares struck. And it had helped. A lot.

Ava loved him. She had made that plain when she rejected Dagon's plans to have the Purveli brothers bunk together and provide her with her own quarters down the hall from Eliana.

Eliana supposed the love Ava and Jak'ri shared shouldn't surprise her. The two had been through a lot together. Eliana hadn't been through nearly as much. Yet she'd fallen hard for Dagon.

So hard that she had pretty much moved into his cabin.

Ziv'ri had opted to join the Segonian soldiers in their barracks. Both he and Jak'ri were fervently petitioning the ruler of Purvel to rethink his refusal to join the Aldebarian Alliance and foster ties with the people who had rescued them. Since the Gathendiens had managed to snatch the brothers straight from their planet, Eliana thought it wise.

Ava covered her mouth and laughed, then gave Jak'ri's shoulder a playful shove. His teeth flashed in a grin. So did Ziv'ri's.

It was good to see them so happy.

Ava met Eliana's gaze. Her smile twisted into one of chagrin. "Sorry about that. For a long time, the only way we could communicate was telepathically. It sort of became a habit."

Eliana waved away the apology. "No worries. I'm used to being around telepaths."

"Commander Dagon."

Eliana glanced at Dagon when Janek's voice floated over his earpiece.

"Yes?"

"You have an incoming communication designated urgent."

Dagon set his utensil down. "I'm on my way."

"The communication is for Eliana as well."

She set her fork-like utensil down. "Maybe the Lasarans have news."

"Who is the communication from?" Dagon asked as they rose.

"Janwar."

Eliana's eyebrows shot up. "The Akseli pirate?"

Dagon nodded. "We're on our way."

Ava stared up at them with wide eyes. "There are pirates in space?"

Eliana reached for her tray. "Apparently."

Ava stopped her. "Don't worry about your trays. If you don't come back before we leave, we'll bus them for you."

"Thank you."

Eliana and Dagon spoke little as they headed to his office. Once there, Dagon motioned for her to sit in the chair behind his desk.

"Nope. You're the commander. You should sit in it."

"Then let me bring in another chair for you."

She smiled. "No need. I'm fine standing, Dagon. Unless you don't want me to loom over you."

He chuckled as he took his seat. She wasn't sure what he found so amusing until she circled the desk, stood beside him, and realized his face was still a little higher than hers.

"I'm not sure that constitutes looming," he said with a wink.

She laughed and combed her fingers through his hair. "You're so tall."

Grinning, he looped an arm around her waist and stole a kiss. "You're so small."

The affection in his gaze filled her with such a warm, fuzzy feeling that she had to snag another kiss.

"Encrypted communication coming through now, sir," Janek announced through some speaker she couldn't see.

Sighing, Dagon released her and straightened in his chair.

What appeared to be a clear sheet of glass about the size of a large iMac hovered vertically a few inches above the desk. It flickered with light suddenly. Then a figure appeared on it.

She gaped.

The man sprawled in a commander's chair much like Dagon's on the bridge of his ship. Like so many of the men she'd encountered out here in space, he appeared to be quite tall and had a slender, athletic build like an Olympic swimmer. His skin was tan with a distinct reddish hue, as were his eyes. She blinked, uncertain which she found more arresting—the reddish-brown eyes or the long, thick black lashes that framed them.

His jet-black hair was drawn back from his face in cornrows. The rest fell down his back and over his shoulders in waves intermingled with tight braids, some of which were decorated with beads. A closely cropped mustache and beard coupled with a loose shirt and tight breeches lent him a definite piratical look.

Holy shit, she thought with some amazement. *It's Jack Sparrow.*

Dagon greeted the Akseli pirate with a neutral expression. "Janwar."

"Commander Dagon." He smiled when his eyes lit upon Eliana. "I see you've found another Earthling. Lisa will be pleased to hear it."

Dagon arched a brow. "Do you mean *Princess* Lisa? I heard you conveyed her and Prince Taelon safely to Lasara."

Janwar grinned. "I did indeed, along with their baby girl. And I can tell you that Lisa prefers to be addressed by her first name. She is not at all comfortable with being treated like royalty."

Eliana smiled, remembering Lisa's expression each time a Lasaran bowed to her. "She really isn't."

"I suppose you're wondering why I'm contacting you," Janwar drawled.

Dagon's lips turned up slightly. "I admit I'm curious."

Some of the levity left the pirate's expression. "As you know, the Lasarans are concerned about the security of their communication system. They believe some messages regarding the Earthlings might have been intercepted."

"They told you that?" Dagon asked cautiously.

Janwar smiled. "Prince Taelon and I have developed a friendship of sorts over the past several years, one that was strengthened when I discovered where he could find his sister."

Dagon stared. "You're the one who learned she'd traveled to Earth?"

"Yes."

"How did you manage that? Even the Lasaran military's intelligence division failed to locate her."

Janwar shrugged. "Sometimes I misappropriate goods, other times it's information. I'm a pirate. It's what I do."

Eliana grinned. "I like this guy."

Janwar sent her a smile, then continued. "The Lasarans have upgraded their comm systems and are using the strongest encryption their technology offers, which should prevent whoever has been rifling through their communications from continuing to do so."

"Gathendiens are doing it," Eliana muttered disparagingly. "Or rather they're paying someone else to do it."

Janwar nodded, amusement again brightening his handsome features. "I see you share my low opinion of them."

"Hell yes. The only good Gathendien is a dead Gathendien."

He laughed. "I agree. The Lasaran's encryption *should* prevent the Gathendiens or their mysterious tech-savvy helper from viewing new messages. But to be doubly certain... particularly sensitive communications are now being funneled through me. Or, more specifically, through my ship."

Dagon frowned. "How does that make the communications more secure?"

Janwar arched a brow, his smile oozing arrogance. "No one can break my encryption, Commander. My ship boasts the most advanced technology in the known universe."

"More advanced than the Sectas'?" Dagon challenged.

"Most assuredly," the pirate responded, a certainty rather than an empty boast.

"Interesting," Dagon muttered.

"I have one such communication for you and the lovely Earthling Eliana," Janwar said, straightening in his chair. "The communication will carry to you live. And just to be clear, I am *only* conveying it, stripped of any hint of its origin and sufficiently encrypted to prevent other eyes from viewing it. I also will refrain from listening to it or observing it myself."

Considering the man was a pirate, Eliana wasn't sure how much faith they should put in that promise.

Janwar nodded to someone she couldn't see.

The screen flashed white, then displayed the face and shoulders of a man in a different location. A very handsome man with wavy black hair that fell to his shoulders and rows of towering bookshelves behind him.

Eliana released a cry of surprise.

Dagon's head snapped around as he looked at her with concern.

"Seth," she breathed.

As soon as Seth's brown eyes—so dark they were almost black—alighted upon her, they flashed with bright golden light. "Eliana."

Tears blurred her vision and spilled down her cheeks as she moved in front of Dagon, dropped onto his lap, and leaned toward the image as if she could dive in and yank Seth into a bear hug. "I can't believe it's you."

His Adam's apple rose and fell with a swallow. "You're all right? They said..."

"I'm all right." She sniffled, so damned happy to see him her breath hitched with a sob.

One of Dagon's arms slid around her waist and delivered a comforting hug.

She smiled. "Actually I'm *better* than all right. We found Ava."

Seth nodded. "Taelon and Lisa told us and sent us a copy of her medical file through that Janwar fellow, detailing her physical recovery. How is she otherwise?"

"She's well, considering everything she's been through. Jak'ri said she has nightmares about her captivity, but she's doing okay. She's powering through it."

His glowing gaze sharpened. "Jak'ri? He's the alien male who escaped with her?"

"Yes. He's been through hell, too. But they're a couple now and draw comfort from each other. He's really nice and clearly adores her. And Ava loves him."

Seth arched a brow. "And you? It hasn't escaped my notice that you're perched upon a man's lap."

Laughing, she leaned to one side so he could see Dagon better. "Seth, this is Dagon, commander of the *Ranasura*. Dagon, this is Seth, leader of the Immortal Guardians."

Dagon offered Seth an affable nod. "Good to meet you, sir."

Seth studied him. "You're the one who continued to look for Eliana long after everyone else assumed she was dead."

"Yes, sir."

"Thank you. I owe you a great debt."

Dagon shook his head with a smile. "Not at all. Eliana told me she could survive until we found her, and I wanted to believe her."

Looping an arm around his neck, she kissed his cheek. "He's been a real sweetheart, Seth. Particularly since I shoved a blaster into his ribs and threatened to kill him the first time we met face-to-face."

Seth's lips twitched. "Not the best way to foster positive Earth-Segonia relations, I'm thinking."

She laughed. "I had to go into stasis to conserve oxygen until he could reach me, and I suffered temporary memory loss. When I woke up on the ship, I thought I was being held in a mercenary compound."

Seth winced. "How many Segonians did you kill?"

Dagon snorted a laugh and muttered, "He knows you well."

Eliana swatted him on the shoulder. "None. I just… rendered two men unconscious. Or rather I rendered one unconscious and made Dagon knock out the other."

"And are *they* being sweethearts about it?" Seth asked.

She laughed. "They've been very good sports, yes."

"If you're to know the truth of it, sir," Dagon interjected, "most of my crew is enamored of her."

He smiled. "I don't doubt it."

"Hey, Seth?" Eliana said. "I was thinking. There actually *is* something you could do for us… if you truly feel you owe Dagon a debt."

Amusement entered the Immortal Guardian leader's features. "Oh? And what might that be?"

"The Segonians do this weird thing where they equip their military ships either with all-female or all-male crews. So Ava and I are breaking the code, so to speak."

"You're the only women on board the *Ranasura*?"

"Yes. And I want to keep searching for Mia, Dani, and the others. Do you think maybe you could charm the Segonian monarch into letting Ava and me remain with Dagon and his crew? Rumor has it she was very impressed with you."

A pretty woman who was nearly six feet tall leaned into view beside Seth, her long brown hair falling like a curtain behind her. "Who said what now?"

Eliana laughed and waved at Seth's wife. "Hi, Leah."

She smiled. "Hi, Eliana. I'm so glad you and Ava are okay. We've been worried sick about you."

"Don't be. We're fine now. And we're determined to find the others."

"Good." Leah crossed her arms over her chest and squinted her eyes. "Now what's this about some Segonian woman flirting with Seth?"

Dagon tried but failed to stifle another laugh.

Eliana smiled. "I didn't say she *flirted* with him. I said she was impressed with him."

Leah winked at her husband. "I don't blame her. He's pretty damn impressive."

Seth's teeth flashed in a grin as he looped an arm around Leah. "Would you like me to speak to the Segonian sovereign? She seemed quite reasonable when I spoke with her before. I don't think asking her to allow you and Ava to remain on board the *Ranasura* until you locate some of the others will be a problem. She was very sympathetic to our plight."

"Actually..." Eliana glanced at Dagon and bit her lip.

Dagon tightened his arm around her and addressed Seth. "Actually, we were hoping for a more permanent arrangement, sir. I know Eliana was supposed to make Lasara her new home. But I've come to love her and would very much like her to become my lifemate."

Leah gasped and touched the fingers of one hand to her lips as she stared at them with wide eyes that sparkled with budding happiness.

But Seth's face remained impassive as he studied the two of them. "You love him, Eliana?"

"Yes," she answered exuberantly. "*So* much. I don't want to leave him, but I also don't want him to have to abandon his military career to be with me."

Dagon gave her another squeeze. "I may be able to obtain a position as liaison between the Lasaran royal family and the Segonian military so I could accompany you to Lasara."

She wrinkled her nose. "Babe, you know you wouldn't be happy with a desk job. And Lasarans are so strict about the whole no-touching thing. If we lived there, I wouldn't be able to grope you or grab your ass in public."

Seth barked out a laugh. "I see you *do* love him."

Leah grinned. "And I can see why you'd hate to give up the ass grabbing."

Eliana laughed. When Leah had come into Seth's life, she had shocked the hell out of the Immortal Guardians by grabbing their immensely powerful, very intimidating, and often taciturn leader's ass in their presence.

"I've also come to love Dagon's crew," Eliana added. "The guys remind me a lot of my brethren back home. They're so much fun to be around. We razz each other all the time. And nothing I do shocks them the way it would the Lasarans."

"Well," Dagon tossed in, "you stripping down to your bra and panties before racing into battle shocked them a little."

Seth and Leah regarded her with wide eyes. "You did what?" they asked in unison.

Eliana laughed. "There was a reason for it. Trust me."

Seth smoothed his features into a thoughtful expression. "Hmm. Perhaps I can convince the Segonian monarch that the *Ranasura* would benefit from having an ambassador to Earth as a permanent member of the crew. Does Ava wish to remain aboard the *Ranasura* as well?"

"I'm pretty sure she's hoping we'll eventually drop her off on Purvel so she can marry Jak'ri."

"This Jak'ri isn't Segonian?"

"No. He's Purveli." Leaning forward, she whispered, "He has both lungs and gills, his fingers and toes are webbed, and he can stay underwater indefinitely. His hair even changes color when it's wet. It's *so* cool."

Leah gaped.

Seth's only comment was another "Hmm."

Eliana bit her lip. "Do you think the Lasarans will be angry?" They might not object to Eliana and the other immortals residing elsewhere. But the *gifted ones* from Earth were supposed to see if they could find mates among the Lasaran males so they could help repopulate the planet.

"No," he responded instantly. "King Dasheon and Queen Adiransia are distraught over failing to transport you all to Lasara safely. If anything, they will help smooth things over with the Segonian monarch and whoever presides over Purvel."

She relaxed. "That would be great. Thank you."

A man with skin as dark as midnight strolled over to stand beside Seth. Long, pencil-thin dreadlocks covered the top and one side of his head, disappearing over his shoulder and falling to his hips. The hair on the other side of his head was shorn close to the skin in a fade with an elaborate design shaved into it.

More tears welled in Eliana's eyes at the sight of Seth's second-in-command, who had long been another father figure to her. "Hi, David. It's so good to see you. I miss you so much."

David's brown eyes flashed amber as a smile full of affection tilted his lips. "Eliana," he said, his deep voice tinged with an Egyptian accent. "You gave us quite a scare. It's good to see you happy and well." He arched a brow. "Though I can't say I approve of the ass grabbing."

She emitted a sound that was half-laugh, half-sob and combed her fingers through Dagon's hair. "That's okay. As long as Dagon approves of it…"

David, Seth, and Dagon all laughed.

Then more of her adoptive family crowded in around Seth, David, and Leah.

"Max!" she cried when she saw her Second, the only human in the mix.

He grinned big. "Sounds like you're having a hell of a lot of fun out there. Racing into battle in your underwear? Really?"

She laughed.

Then her former hunting partner Nick appeared, his wife Kayla at his side. "Seriously?" he said, his eyes wide with exasperation. "You get transferred to another freaking planet and don't tell me? What the hell, Eliana? I thought you were just going back to New York!"

"It was supposed to be kept hush-hush," she responded on a laugh.

Still more beloved faces found their way onto the screen. Eliana laughed and cried, missing them all desperately. Then Ava and Jak'ri joined her and Dagon, and Eliana laughed some more at the looks of astonishment the Purveli male generated. Fortunately, he was a good sport about it.

When the call ended and Eliana and Dagon were once more alone in his office, she cupped his strong jaw in her hands, so happy she couldn't stop smiling. "You really want me to be your lifemate?" she asked softly.

"I do."

She pressed a tender kiss to his lips. "So do I."

"I love you, Eliana."

"I love you, too."

He claimed her lips in a longer, deeper kiss that swiftly heated her blood while his hands roamed her back. "What do you say we engage in some of that groping and ass grabbing you mentioned earlier?"

She laughed. "Absolutely."

FROM THE AUTHOR

Thank you for reading ***The Segonian***. I hope you enjoyed Eliana and Dagon's story. I had so much fun writing it. If you missed the first book in the Aldebarian Alliance series and would like to see more of Prince Taelon and Lisa… *and* get a bigger glimpse of Janwar and his pirate crew, as well as Seth and the Immortal Guardians, you can find their adventurous story in ***The Lasaran***.

If you liked Eliana and are curious to see what her life was like before she embarked upon her space adventure, you can find her hunting with her partner Nick and causing mischief in ***Broken Dawn***, a stand-alone novel in my Immortal Guardians series.

And if you're curious about my Immortal Guardians family and would like to know more about Prince Taelon's sister, Amiriska, you can witness Ami's early months on Earth in ***Darkness Dawns*** (Immortal Guardians: Book 1) and watch her come into her own as a warrior and fall in love with Marcus in ***Night Reigns*** (Immortal Guardians: Book 2). You can even see what Marcus's life was like (before he became an Immortal Guardian) as a young squire in Medieval England in ***A Sorceress of His Own*** and ***Rendezvous with Yesterday***.

It might also interest you to know that my Immortal Guardian males, as well as those in The Gifted Ones series—much like the Segonians—absolutely adore strong women and love to laugh and tease.

Thank you again for reading ***The Segonian***. If you enjoyed it, please consider rating or reviewing it at an online retailer of your choice. I appreciate your support so much and am always thrilled when I see that one of my stories made a fellow booklover happy.

Dianne Duvall
www.DianneDuvall.com

ABOUT THE AUTHOR

Dianne Duvall is the *New York Times* and *USA Today* Bestselling Author of the acclaimed **Immortal Guardians** paranormal romance series, the exciting new **Aldebarian Alliance** sci-fi romance series, and **The Gifted Ones** medieval and time-travel romance series. She is known for writing stories full of action that will keep you flipping pages well past your bedtime, strong heroes who adore strong heroines, lovable secondary characters, swoon-worthy romance, and humor that readers frequently complain makes them laugh out loud at inappropriate moments. *The Lasaran* (Aldebarian Alliance Book 1) hit #1 on Audible's Movers & Shakers Bestseller list. Audible chose her Immortal Guardians audiobook *Awaken the Darkness*, as one of the Top 5 Best Paranormal Romances of 2018. Reviewers have called Dianne's books "fast-paced and humorous" (Publishers Weekly), "utterly addictive" (RT Book Reviews), "extraordinary" (Long and Short Reviews), and "wonderfully imaginative" (The Romance Reviews). Her audiobooks have been awarded AudioFile Earphones Awards for Excellence. One was nominated for a prestigious Audie Award. And her books have twice been nominated for RT Reviewers' Choice Awards.

Dianne loves all things creative. When she isn't writing, Dianne is active in the independent film industry and has even appeared on-screen, crawling out of a moonlit grave and wielding a machete like some of the psychotic vampires she creates in her books.

For the latest news on upcoming releases, contests, and more, please visit www.DianneDuvall.com. You can also connect with Dianne online:

Website: www.DianneDuvall.com
DianneDuvall Books Group:
www.facebook.com/groups/128617511148830/
Blog: www.dianneduvall.blogspot.com
Instagram: www.instagram.com/dianne.duvall
Facebook: www.facebook.com/DianneDuvallAuthor
Twitter: www.twitter.com/DianneDuvall
BookBub: www.bookbub.com/authors/dianne-duvall
Pinterest: www.pinterest.com/dianneduvall
YouTube: http://bit.ly/DianneDuvall_YouTube

Printed in Great Britain
by Amazon